The
Tempest

Peter Cawdron

thinkingscifi.wordpress.com

Imprint: Independently published

ISBN: 9798361326501 — Paperback

ISBN: 9798361326617— Hardback

To the teachers that shaped my curiosity and imagination at Penrose High School in Auckland, New Zealand during the 80s (now known as One Tree Hill High School)

A human being is a spatially
and temporally limited piece of the whole,
what we call the 'Universe.'
He experiences himself and
his feelings as separate from the rest,
[but that's] an optical illusion of his consciousness.

—Albert Einstein

Act I

The Tempest

Sewage

"You should program a bot to do this," Emma says, holding a spotlight within the darkened hull of the *Sycorax*. Her voice echoes. Shadows stretch out below her, being cast by the aluminum grating beneath her feet.

Marc hangs from the walkway beneath her. He's working with a wrench. All of his tools have straps attached to them, not only so they won't fall, but in case they're ever used outside the spacecraft, they won't float away.

"It's too complex," Marc replies. For him, this isn't a chore so much as a passion. "I've got to be sure I'm retrieving viable material and not sludge."

"I meant to hold the light," she says, "not take samples, although a synth could do that too!"

"Where's the fun in that?" he asks.

Emma shifts her weight. The angle of the light changes. Shadows dance across the holding tanks extending the length of the interstellar spacecraft.

Marc is dangling easily fifty meters below her on a climbing rope. The shaft beneath him extends another fifty meters again, leading down to the engines at the rear of the *Sycorax*. As the craft is under power, generating a warp bubble to maintain a relativistic speed, there's a sense of artificial gravity. They're not accelerating—not in the traditional sense of the word—but it feels like it.

Even though the *Sycorax* is cruising at 60% of the speed of light, the illusion of gravity is closer to what's felt on Mars than on Earth. If Marc fell, the impact would be fatal, but his harness is secure. Even so, a slight slip on the rope causes his heart to race. To him, it feels good to be alive and in the moment. It beats the dull monotony of their normal flight routines.

Six hexagonal storage tanks surround him, recycling sewage. Out beyond them, fuel tanks wrap around the hull, placing him and Emma in the center of the bullseye. The shaft is barely wide enough for him to descend on the rope. Maintenance was somewhat of an afterthought. Basic monitoring indicators were included, but access to the tanks while in flight wasn't considered important. Warp drives get more attention than sewage.

Life on the *Sycorax* is boring. Eighteen thousand colonists lie in stasis tubes awaiting the end of their journey in another star system. The crew of ten has been divided into five teams of two. Each team has been assigned an 18-month rotation, which equates to six years in stasis followed by a year and a half on duty. Then it's a case of rinse and repeat until they arrive in orbit around *New Haven* in roughly fifty years. This is Marc's third duty on the watch. Each time he wakes from cryo-sleep, the stars look the same. It's as though the *Sycorax* is stationary rather than plowing through the Milky Way at an ungodly speed.

"And you're sure this is a problem?" Emma asks, sounding annoyed. "You're not just inventing work because you're bored?"

"It's a *potential* problem," Marc replies, twisting around on his rope as he looks up at her.

Each of the crew has a specialist role extending beyond their general training. For Marc, it's effluent treatment and bio-regeneration. It's not glamorous, but it got him a berth on the *Sycorax*. Even in cryo-stasis, eighteen thousand people produce a helluva lot of excrement. Who knew there would be interstellar career opportunities in piss and shit?

He says, "The bacterial load has to be finely balanced. We've got to make sure we're cultivating the right microbes in the right proportions or we could get fecal blooms that throw out the whole mix."

"All I hear is *blah, blah, blah,*" Emma replies, shaking her head over the railing. She pokes her tongue at him, teasing him with mock indifference.

"I'm serious," Marc says, extracting another sample from an access port. He's taking samples every ten meters so he can better understand the microbial population density at various depths within the tank. Tiny monitoring LEDs have been strung out on each of the tanks like Christmas tree lights running the length of the hold. They glow with a soft green, a pale yellow or a deep red to indicate temperature variations due to the bacterial load within the tanks. There's only one red light near the top of the primary effluent tank but it's due to a faulty sensor. Most of the LEDs are green.

"It's not a problem," Emma says.

"It could be."

"When?"

"In four months. In four years."

"And you don't want to be dragged out of stasis to fix a leak, huh?"

"It's a lot easier to fix now," he says. "Before it becomes a problem."

"Ah," she says, wagging a finger at him. "So I was right. It's *not* a problem."

"I'm being proactive."

"Whatever!"

Emma is less than impressed by his diligence.

Marc's not sure why she wants to get back to the bridge. It's not like they do anything beyond watching fluctuations in the warp bubble as their compacted region of spacetime soars through wisps of interstellar hydrogen. Seeing the odd fragment of dust light up as it vaporizes in the outer shell of the bubble is oddly satisfying, but it only happens a couple of times a day. Grains of sand will glow like fireflies for a few seconds. And just like bugs hitting a windshield, they'll go splat and then peel away to one side, being dragged along by the electromagnetic current within the warp bubble. As beautiful as they are, they're doomed to fade and disappear into obscurity.

Although it may be slight, there is a danger of extra-solar comets and stray asteroids colliding with the warp bubble surrounding the *Sycorax*. The craft's long-range sensors will detect anything larger than a basketball at a distance of several light hours, giving them plenty of time to maneuver. On an interstellar spacecraft, there's always p—l—e—n—t—y of time. Time is the one resource they're never lacking. Adjustments in the warp bubble can be executed by the flight computer in milliseconds. Even if the duty crew did nothing at all, the onboard navigation system would kick into effect at a distance of one light minute—that's eighteen million kilometers to avoid a garden-variety rock. At that range, a course correction of 0.001 degrees will translate into hundreds of kilometers separating them as they sail past.

Small collisions, though, are spectacular. Anything the size of a baseball will smear around the bubble and glow like molten gold for a few seconds. Emma calls them angel poop. She saw one a few months ago. Marc was in the bathroom at the time. He got to see the replay from the logs, but it wasn't the same.

"Hurry up," Emma says from the walkway above him. She's getting impatient. "There's a rogue on the radar. I wanna see that baby. It's the only interesting thing out here for a dozen light-years."

Marc lowers himself to the next access port. The rope twists, causing him to spin. He kicks with his legs, pushing against one of the tanks and resisting the torque.

Bubbles of spacetime aren't always entirely predictable. Fluctuations in the warp field cause irregular acceleration on their bodies. It's only by a few centimeters per second, but it's unnerving. And it can come at an angle, causing him to slip or stagger when moving around the cockpit. If they're passing through a gas cloud, walking around inside the *Sycorax* is like tiptoeing down a driveway covered in black ice.

The *Sycorax* is a deep space hauler. She's designed to maximize profits not comfort. As the passengers are popsicles, there's no need for luxury. The corridors within the *Sycorax* are narrow tubes barely wide enough to crawl through. On those rare occasions when the ship is not under power and experiencing weightlessness, the passages are easy enough for someone to pull themselves through. While under warp, they're like crawling through tunnels at a kids' playground. The only thing that's missing is the ball pit.

Technically, the same laws of physics apply inside and outside the warp bubble, but it doesn't always seem that way. The *Sycorax* is soaring along several orders of magnitude faster than what its engines can achieve in regular space. Warp bubbles are the cheat code of the universe, but nothing can break the speed of light. Given time, spacecraft can get close, with the record being 86% relative to nearby stars, but nothing can travel faster than light itself.

As he dangles there, Marc thinks about how bonkers/crazy it is to be racing between stars. Emma might be bored. Marc's not. He might not understand astronavigation, but he appreciates how astonishing it is for a bunch of hairless apes from the third boulder in orbit around Sol to be plowing through spacetime at speeds his ancestors could never imagine. For them, light was divine. Light brought life. The ancient tribes that dotted the African savannah could have never dreamed of a spacecraft like the *Sycorax*. Or perhaps they did. Perhaps, instead of dreaming of it in a single night, they dreamed across generations.

The Greek poet Homer wrote of Bellerophon, who caught Pegasus and rode the winged horse into the sun-drenched sky. A thousand years later, the French philosopher Voltaire wrote of Micromégas sailing to Earth from the star Sirius, gliding on a sunbeam. In an age where the moons of Jupiter were hazy blobs seen darkly through a looking glass, Voltaire could not have known about life on the fourth planet in orbit around Sirius—and yet he dreamed of it and wrote about it regardless. Oh, the Sirians turned out to be microbes rather than ten-mile-high giants, but they are very much alive, just as he suspected. Then came the 20th century and a bazillion books, films and TV shows about the exploration of space. Flash Gordon, Forbidden Planet, Star Trek and Star Wars all captured the imagination of the public—and yet the nature of light was still misunderstood. Traveling at the speed of light was akin to riding on a magic carpet. A flash of stars would streak by these fictional spacecraft, racing behind them in a blur as they jumped into hyperspace. In mere seconds, these tiny plastic models hung from fishing wire in front of cloth-covered green screens would fly from one imaginary planet to the next.

Marc knows better.

Light isn't magic, but it is far simpler than it seems. Light is energy. It's a form of radiation. Light radiates *from* matter. Far from being arbitrary or the equivalent of a freeway speed sign, the speed of light isn't a limit as such. It's simply the rate at which energy flows unimpeded through spacetime. If something could go faster than light then light would go that fast as there's nothing holding it back. Matter has a pesky little attribute known as mass which resists change. Light *is* energy, whereas mass *requires* energy to move—it's a subtle but important distinction. Light has an advantage over mass. It's already as energetic as it could possibly be. Having grown up in Hawaii, Marc likens the motion of the *Sycorax* to surfing a wave. He can surf a wave off Launiupoko, but he can't surf from his wave to another one in front of him for one simple reason: it's the wave that carries him on.

The exotic matter drive on the *Sycorax* compresses and stretches spacetime, but there's only so far it can go on the mass/energy seesaw. Light isn't special, it's just more obvious than other forms of radiation. Spacetime is malleable like plasticine—it can be molded and stretched but not broken.

The *Sycorax* is a marvel of modern engineering. It's been designed around the concept of mass symmetry. To keep the warp bubble stable, the spacecraft's mass is evenly distributed. The tanks around Marc balance the sewage, water treatment, nutrient reclamation and protein harvesting for the colonists in suspended animation, constantly cycling from one tank to another. The fuel tanks are evenly spaced further out around the bio-farm. Rather than drawing from one tank and then another, the engines draw from all twelve fuel tanks evenly. If an effluent tank gets clogged and too much mass accumulates within it, the warp bubble will shift, flexing and changing its shape accordingly. Balancing the tanks is important, or so he keeps telling Emma.

Emma sighs as Marc fiddles with another collection kit.

Emma is a flight engineer. She doesn't like it when Marc calls her a grease monkey. She may not appreciate it, but the sludge circulating in these tubes recycles nutrients with 99.997% efficiency. With the nearest Costco over a bazillion kilometers away, it's a case of, "*Recycle or die.*"

Although technically they're always on duty while out of cryo, there's a lot of downtime on the *Sycorax*. Sometimes, during their artificial evenings, they'll sit around drinking some of Marc's illicit home-brewed beer, debating the pros and cons of galactic colonization. Marc argues that bio-engineering is more important to the colonies than the warp drive. Emma just laughs. To her, such a concept is absurd, but Marc insists there's no point traveling to another planet if you can't live there.

"Come on," she says, urging him to hurry up collecting samples. "Our closest pass is 80 AU—in about ten minutes. I really want to see this thing!"

Marc has no interest in a rogue planet adrift in space without being in orbit around a star. Rogues are dark and cold. They're the billiard balls of the universe—the eight ball. They've been given a nudge and sent soaring through interstellar space bereft of their host star. If this rogue is an ice giant, it'll probably still light up in infrared with a gravitationally compressed, molten metallic core and lots of radioactive elements. To astrophysicists, though, anything beyond helium is a metal so there could be any old trash in the core. It won't be visible to the human eye—not at eighty times the distance of Earth to the Sun. Marc imagines a darkened Jupiter drifting aimlessly through space. Emma's not going to see much even with the powerful scopes on the *Sycorax*. 80 AU is four times the distance from Earth to Uranus.

"At best, it's a failed star—a dark star," Marc says, taking another sample from the tank. "That's all. You won't see much. Just a faint smudge on the console."

"It's better than staring at poo," Emma replies, leaning on the railing.

"Hah," Marc says, smiling as he looks up at her. He recognizes something subtle in the way their conversation is unfolding. What sounds like casual banter has a deeper meaning. Although he can't see her face beyond the glare of the light shining in his eyes, he's reasonably sure he knows what she's thinking.

"What?" she asks, looking at the clumsy grin on his face.

"Nothing."

Emma needs to go *number two*. Oh, she wants to see that rogue planet as well, but the way she's fiddling with the light suggests more than boredom. Marc's had Emma down in the hold for almost two hours. She needs to go to the bathroom, probably for *ones* and *twos*. Looking at a vat filled with excrement doesn't help—apparently.

"I'm on my way up," he says, ignoring the last couple of access ports. He's got enough samples to work with. After labeling the sample, he places it in the collection bag hanging from his belt. The tank tends to contain a smooth gradient matching known patterns. As long as there are no significant deviations in the samples he's collected, he'll be able to extrapolate and fill in the blanks. If there's a healthy curve matching the model, it'll be fine. If not, he can always come back and collect the rest.

"Oh, finally," she says.

Yeah, he thinks. She *really* needs to go. And he's been his usual oblivious self, bumbling along reading every metric except her social clues. There would have come a point where she couldn't wait any longer and would have had to say something. Marc's glad he picked up on her hints before then.

Emma is an extroverted introvert. Marc didn't think such a combination was possible, but she'll be bubbly and boisterous one moment and then immerse herself in a book for hours. She'll go from manic rabbit to deeply pondering the origins of the universe in a heartbeat. There's no romance between them. Oh, he wouldn't mind if there was. And he suspects she would like a bit of a fling, but they've still got a bunch of shifts to complete. It seems they both know how torturous those could become if their relationship went sour. Professionalism is for the best. Maybe when they get to *New Haven* something will happen between them. Emma's already joked about spending a couple of months at the resort in the *New Hawaiian Islands*. Joked. Yeah, he laughed as well, but it's not quite a joke. Perhaps once the responsibility of caring for eighteen thousand people has lifted they'll both relax.

Emma smiles as he hauls himself up the rope using a climbing ratchet. She knows he knows. She appreciates him calling it quits. It's the way she's looking at him that gives it away. Being considerate never goes unnoticed.

"Just leave the light," Marc says, hanging a few feet below the grating. He swings his tool bag up onto the walkway and clips it onto an anchor point. The collection samples are in a bag hanging from a line dangling beneath him. He hauls the bag up and clips it onto the same anchor point. Climbing up over the railing is easier if he doesn't have equipment rattling around on his harness.

"Are you sure?" she asks, followed by, "Why didn't they put lights down here? They should have put in lights. Isn't that dumb?"

"Yes," he says in answer to two of her three questions. As for why there are no lights—he figures it probably never occurred to anyone outside of the star base maintenance crew. Back there, they can run power cables in from the dock. "They should have."

Before he can say anything else, he feels a rush of nausea. His inner ear swirls. Blood rushes to his head. Something's wrong. In the blink of an eye, the starship seems to flip upside down, which, in the darkness of the hold, seems impossible.

Emma grips the handrail with white knuckles. Her legs fly out from beneath her. She leans forward to face him, wanting to say something but all that comes out is a cry of alarm.

The flashlight dies. Not only that, but all the various monitoring LEDs on the tanks fade. The hold is plunged into pitch black darkness.

Marc is thrown into the gantry above him, but that's impossible. How could he fall up? His mind tells him he's supposed to be hanging from the gantry, not lying on it. Everything is topsy turvy. His head strikes the metal grate. His body twists, colliding with the underside of the walkway. The climbing rope supporting him goes limp. In less than a second, he finds himself lying upside down on the wrong side of the gantry.

Emma screams.

The *Sycorax* is undergoing rapid deceleration. As the change in momentum comes in waves, pulsing around them in the dark, the sensation is terrifying. The dead flashlight tumbles, colliding with the tanks as it flies into the roof of the chamber. Echoes reverberate around him. Marc hears rather than sees the dead flashlight fall.

The sound of Emma screaming allows him to locate her with surprising precision in the dark. She's still holding onto the railing. He swings his legs over the edge of the gantry, falling up past her. Well, it was *up* moments ago. With the warp bubble collapsing, their inertia gives them the illusion of falling toward the ceiling. The rope goes taut. His harness holds. Her hands won't hold for much longer.

Marc reaches around Emma's waist. He loops a strap around her hips. It's not a harness as such and will hurt like hell if it pulls taut, but it'll stop her from plunging up into the underside of the suspended animation chamber on the floor above them. He clips the carabiner at the end of the strap back onto his harness. With his fingers, he can feel the strap hanging around her. If anything, it's too damn loose. In the darkness, he can sense Emma slipping as her strength gives. She grunts. The tendons in her fingers are failing. She lets go of the railing and swings in beneath him, grabbing his legs. The strap pulls tight.

"Got you," he says, reaching down and tugging at her clothing.

"Th—Thanks."

"What the hell is happening?" he asks as she swings below him—or is it above?

"Not sure," Emma says, working her way over his ankles and up his legs, wanting to get a better grip on him. "I think we've lost our warp field."

Marc's ears are ringing. His head hurts. When the warp bubble burst, his jaw caught on the underside of the walkway, jarring his teeth. His forehead struck a metal cross-member. Drips of blood form at the tip of his nose. He can't see them, but he can feel them falling away into the darkness.

"How?" he asks, reaching down and taking a good hold on the collar of her flight suit. The strapping he used to hold her is loose around her tiny frame. It's the same strap he had for his toolkit and extends about three meters. Given the way the pulses of deceleration wash over them, stretching and pulling on them, she could easily slip through. Even with her arms wrapped around his legs, Marc's not taking any chances. He clenches his fist over the thick cotton on her suit, squeezing tight.

"Dunno," Emma replies, dangling beneath him.

In the pitch-black darkness, his sense of orientation is confused. For now, down is anywhere below his feet, regardless of where they're positioned. It's that or vomit in response to his swirling inner ear.

"H—How long?" he asks.

The climbing rope shifts with the changing tension. One moment, it feels as though he's hanging there with Emma beneath him, the next it is as though he's been snagged by a great white shark and the line is stretching as the monster drags him into the depths. Her weight varies from a measly 140 pounds to that of a baby elephant wrapped around his legs, tugging at his muscles and tendons.

"A minute. Maybe two. Not long."

13

As she speaks, the tension on the climbing rope fades. Within seconds, they're drifting in weightlessness. Up and down have lost all meaning. The blood dripping from his nose pools over one nostril, making it difficult to breathe. He wipes his face with the back of his hand. For now, surface tension prevents the blood from floating away within microgravity.

Lights appear in the darkness within the heart of the *Sycorax*.

Stars flicker in and out of view.

Streaks of light cut through the night like meteors racing across the sky back on Earth. But that's not possible. There are no hatches or windows this deep within the spacecraft. Tiny flashes of light blink in and out of existence. Marc squeezes his eyes shut but the sparks still appear before him. He opens his eyes. Thin meteors streak through the maintenance area, glowing briefly before fading into the darkness.

"Not real," he mumbles, knowing that if the skin of the *Sycorax* had been punctured by micrometeorites they'd be losing their atmosphere. The pressure would drop along with the temperature. Even a slow decompression would cause his ears to feel blocked. That hasn't happened. Besides, the warp field itself would have consumed anything this small without collapsing. No, something else is happening to the spacecraft, but what?

"Marc?" Emma says, holding onto his jumpsuit as she frees herself from the strapping. She works her way up his body, moving as though she were underwater.

"Here," he replies, loosening his harness and floating next to her.

Emma's fingers reach for his face, touching lightly at his cheeks within the pitch-black interior of the sewage access shaft. Like him, she's seeking assurance within the madness. Thin beams of light dart through the darkness, but they don't illuminate anything. For a brief moment, they appear like scratches on an old-time film.

"Did you see that?" he asks.

"Yes," she says with a tremor in her voice.

"What is it?"

"Not good. Really not good. As in—very bad."

Emma gets hold of his sleeve. She pulls on him, propelling herself on.

"We've got to get to the bridge."

Marc's still fiddling with his climbing rig, releasing the carabiners and straps. His eyes are open but he can't see anything beyond the odd flash of light ripping past in the darkness.

Emma tugs at him, urging him to follow her. Both of them are floating in microgravity, making the walkway useless for anything other than handholds. Marc kicks his harness free of his legs.

"What is that?" he asks, feeling his way along the railing. He works hand over hand toward the corridor running the length of the craft.

Sparks of light race around them like comets streaking through the night. They crisscross each other in the darkness.

"Impossible," Emma mumbles.

"What is?"

"Cosmic rays. Not this deep. Not within the core of the *Sycorax*. We're shielded by all that fluid. We shouldn't be seeing anything like this."

"I don't understand," Marc says, feeling along behind her as she makes for the hatch. At the moment, the glamour of spaceflight feels distinctly like cave diving several kilometers beneath the surface of a darkened planet.

"The warp bubble should have protected us," Emma says. "Not only that, we're protected in here. We're surrounded by mass. Counting our fuel and your bio-farm, there are at least thirty meters of liquid between us and the hull on all sides."

"So?" he asks.

"At an atomic level, liquids are densely packed. Nothing should have reached us in here, but I'm seeing primary, secondary and even tertiary collisions."

"You can tell the difference?" Marc asks, reaching the curved opening of the hatch and pulling himself into the accessway leading to the bridge. Ambient light spills off the chrome fixtures, coming from the windows in the cockpit. The feeble light of distant stars provides what little illumination they have.

"Cosmic rays leave streaks," Emma says. "They're long and thin. Then there's Cherenkov radiation. It's the equivalent of a sonic boom inside your eyeball—only with light instead of sound. The particles passing through you are moving faster than the speed of light within the fluid in your eye so you see a blue flash of light."

"Well, that doesn't sound crazy at all," Marc says, using sarcasm to deflect from his sense of panic. Truth be told, he's happy to be distracted by Emma's obscure observations. He suspects it's intentional on her part. Something catastrophic just happened. From the waver in her voice, it's all she can do to hold herself together. At a guess, she's surprised they're still alive.

"Did you notice piercing white blobs? Ones that linger? They're direct hits on your retina, but they're secondary radiation, occurring *after* a cosmic ray has hit atoms in the tanks around us, scattering them like balls on a pool table."

"And the tertiary ones?" Marc asks for no other reason than to maintain the illusion of calm that comes with having something explained to him. They're fucked. They both know it. Starships don't lose power. That's just not something that happens in the 23rd century. The *Sycorax* is dead, but for now, at least, they're still alive—until they burn through whatever residual oxygen is drifting around within the cabin.

"The dimmer flashes," Emma says, reaching the bridge. "They're lower in energy. They're tertiary particles. Imagine a pool table. The white ball is a cosmic ray. It hits a bunch of balls that scatter, hitting a few more balls lying up against the cushion and so on. Before long, you've got balls flying every which way within your eyeball—and all through your body."

"Oh."

16

"Imagine a bowling ball hitting pins at the end of the lane. That big, old black ball smashes through to the pit at the back. The pins go flying, knocking each other over and—*sssss-strike!*"

"Got it."

Emma pulls herself down into the pilot's seat. Marc joins her, strapping into the navigation seat. The stars beyond the cockpit windows provide the only light around them. They're magnificent. In the midst of the chaos, they're relaxed. Marc breathes deeply, settling himself.

Emma is frantic. The controls are dead. She flips the command console up, exposing a complex wiring loom reaching into various sections of the glass. The thin plexiglass she's working with is four meters wide. It has trillions of semiconductors etched into the various laminated layers. The electronics are invisible to the naked eye. Under normal lighting conditions, the sum aggregate total of them appears as grainy lines hidden deep within the glass. Beneath the panel and its neatly bundled packets of wires, there's a set of secondary controls. Emma runs her fingers over the old-school gauges and switches. She flicks a few. Nothing happens.

"Not good."

"I'm glad you know what you're doing," Marc says, trying to sound upbeat.

"I don't," Emma replies. "But if we can't get the power back up, we're dead."

"I don't understand," Marc says. "What did we hit? There's nothing out there."

"And there's no structural damage," Emma says. "Doesn't that strike you as strange?"

"This whole damn thing strikes me as strange."

"We hit something—and yet we hit nothing at all."

"Something collapsed the warp bubble," Marc says.

"Still seeing streaks and flashes?" Emma asks.

"Yep."

"Me too."

She unscrews several wing nuts and hands them to Marc. With methodical care, she removes the panel from the secondary, backup controls.

"What are these?" Marc asks, not having seen wing nuts before. Most of the panels and seams on the *Sycorax* are sealed with welds, rivets or tiny screws.

"These are engineering genius," she says. "These are an architect back at star base saying *fuck you* to the bean counters and project management dweebs that wanted to cut corners. They all said, *You'll never need this. It's a waste of space and adds extra mass. Get rid of it. Blah, blah, blah.*"

"I don't understand," Marc says, trying to make out what Emma is doing in the starlight. She hands him a plastic panel along with several more wing nuts.

"Don't lose those."

He doesn't need to be told that, but, "Okay."

Emma says, "I need you to hold the main control panel at a forty-five-degree angle behind me."

"Ah, sure," Marc says, slipping the wing nuts into a velcro'd pocket on his flight suit. He's confused by her request but willing to help. He unbuckles himself and pushes out of his seat. The glass control pane has drifted near the ceiling so he floats over and turns it back toward Emma at an angle.

"Higher... A little more to the left... Give it a little flex. I'm hoping it's going to act like a mirror. If you can, I need a concave shape to help focus the starlight."

"Oh," he says, realizing there's a faint glow in the shadows around her. He's reflecting the ambient light back at her so she can see better.

"What are you looking for?"

"The test flight controls," she says. "They're buried under the backup system. Macmillan told me they were down here. Those wing nuts are the result of a design engineer realizing that if shit ever got so bad that we needed the original test controls, we'd have no power, no automatic releases, and no ability to undo a bunch of tiny screws. They knew if anyone dug this deep beneath the console they were in a world of pain and needed things to be as simple, easy and straightforward as possible. May *Lord Brahma* bless all the aerospace engineers!"

"Test controls?"

"Yeah, they're supposed to pull them out when the backup panel goes in, but there's nothing better than an engineer planning for every eventuality."

"What were they testing?" Marc asks.

Emma digs around beneath the console. "When they build these birds, they run them through all kinds of shock tests. It's part of the flight certification process. The test controls are a contingency in case an EMP knocks out the primary and backup systems."

"Ah," Marc says. "Which just happened."

"Maybe," Emma says. "I'm not sure what happened, but this old stuff is goddamn bulletproof."

Marc grimaces. Pain surges through the right side of his forehead, causing him to close his eyes. Streaks of light cut down from above. It's as though a meteor shower has erupted inside his skull.

"What the hell?" he says, shaking his head, trying to rid himself of the sudden onslaught of pain.

"Sweet *Vishnu*," Emma calls out, curling into a fetal position in microgravity as she cradles her head with both hands. "That hurts. That hurts so bad."

Marc screams, "Arghhhh!"

Nerve impulses force his eyes open against his will. Across the bridge, there are sparks of light, only these aren't within his eyeball. Flashes of light tear through the cabin of the starship. They're as fine as a needle and all streak in the same direction. It's as though there's a shower of molten metal tearing through the *Sycorax*. The only time Marc's seen anything even remotely similar to this is while visiting his father's workshop in the starship yard foundry on the Big Island of Hawaii. Automated machines would carry crucibles with molten metal from the furnace to the casting molds. To his young mind, they poured liquid gold. If the stream hit any moisture whatsoever, showers of molten metal would erupt across the factory floor. To him, it looked like sparklers on the 4th of July, but it was far more deadly.

"This is so not good," Emma says, turning and rummaging beneath the console with her legs drifting out behind her.

Marc presses his hands against both sides of his head, wanting to block out the pain. Somehow, he manages to respond with, "By *not good*, I take it you mean, really *fucking* bad."

"This isn't possible," she says.

"What isn't possible?" he asks.

Emma ignores him, snapping, "I need light. I need more light, goddamn it!"

Marc works through the pain and grabs the console again. He arches his back, flexing the plexiglass panel between his hands and his feet. He bumps gently against the hull. He can't get much of a bend, but it's enough to focus at least some of the starlight on Emma.

"Got it," she says.

Suddenly, a single, bright white LED turns on overhead.

"Power," he says. "We've got power!"

"We've got test-rig power," she replies, correcting him. "We're a long way from a functional spacecraft, but we should have enough to fire up the engines and get the *naraka* out of here."

Emma's of Eurasian descent and was raised in India. She curses in Hindi. From the context, Marc figures *naraka* means hell.

"Can we get back to warp?" he asks.

Emma laughs. "There's no way in *Shiva* that's happening. Not without restarting the fusion core. As it is, life-support is going to be a struggle."

"Then we work on one problem at a time," Marc says, trying to latch on to the optimism of that single LED glowing within the cockpit.

The Monster

One by one, Emma brings the basic systems on the *Sycorax* back online, starting with hibernation life support, as even the supposedly bulletproof triple-redundant backup had dropped to less than 10% of its capacity. Most of the interactive control screens are blank, but she gets navigation back up. Nothing is operating as it should. What few metrics there are all blink red.

She says, "Okay, we can't generate a warp field, but we can fire our engines."

"But?" Marc asks, suspecting there's a caveat to her point.

"But there's no sense in jumping from the frying pan into the fire. We've got to be sure about what's out there before we engage."

"I don't get it," Marc says. "What did we hit?"

"Not hit," Emma says. "Hitting. Whatever we ran into, we're still in it."

"I'm confused."

"The streaks of light," she says. "We've flown through what I guess is a dense molecular cloud of some kind—only it's in motion relative to the *Sycorax*. It's screaming across our bow."

"How is that possible? How did it get through the warp bubble?"

"I don't know," she replies. "But this is far too dense for interstellar hydrogen. I'm still trying to figure out exactly what's happening. Can you run a parsec scan? I need to know what else is out there."

"There's nothing," Marc says, flipping through control systems on the digital interface. "Nothing other than your rogue planet, but that's like 80 AU away."

"We've flown into a tempest," she says. "A storm of inbound particles."

"Particles?"

"It looks like some kind of intense stellar wind. The damn thing is as thick as fog. Far too dense. It's like we've flown through the corona of a star."

"But there are no nearby stars," Marc says.

"I know. I know," Emma replies, sounding frustrated. "But it's there and it's moving at a phenomenal speed... Sweet *Saraswati*, that stream is clocking 99% of the speed of light."

"Cosmic rays?" Marc asks, surprised.

"Too dense. Far too dense," Emma replies, flicking through a few more screens and recalibrating the sensor array. "I'm trying to isolate the source. Whatever this is, it's coming from just off our bow at an angle of maybe ten degrees."

"What could cause this?" Marc asks.

"I don't know," Emma replies. "It's like we're being sandblasted."

"B—But there's nothing out there," Marc says. "Space is empty. It's a whole lot of nothing."

"Not this time."

Emma continues working on the restored control panel. Marc flicks through various sensors. There are a lot of screens he hasn't seen before and several he only saw in passing while ignoring his induction training on Earth. Back then, if it wasn't on the exam, he didn't want to know about it.

"I'm not seeing anything," he says. What he means is, anything he understands.

"Check the logs in the hour or so leading up to the hit. We approached something out there. Our forward sensors should have flagged anomalies. Look for any unusual patterns, particularly in the high-energy range. Normally, these are filtered out as background noise."

"Not this time," Marc says.

It's another couple of minutes and several more disruptive streaks of light racing through his eyeballs before Marc finds anything relevant.

"Okay, I've been able to isolate our approach vector. We're passing through some kind of highly energetic gas flow."

Marc brings up a display, showing her the motion of a molecular cloud falling like rain in a storm.

He says, "Without the warp field, our relative motion is interplanetary rather than interstellar."

"What's our velocity measured against that nearby rogue?" Emma asks, still trying to get core systems back online.

"47,000 kilometers per hour," he replies. "Man, we're dawdling. We are not going anywhere without that bubble."

"Strap in," she says, working herself into the footwell so she can access the test flight controls. "A two-minute burn at a right angle to the direction of the storm should get us clear of the flow or at least to the outskirts of this damn thing."

Before he can tighten the straps of his harness, Emma fires the main engines using the test flight control system. Far from the smooth, gentle acceleration of an asteroid avoidance or an orbital insertion burn, this is chaotic. Fuel is being dumped into the various engine bells without being balanced by a computerized injection system. The engines surge and wane. Not only is the fuel load inconsistent, but the precision-machined parts within the twelve engines have been scoured by whatever they flew through.

Emma rides the *Sycorax* like a bull at a rodeo. She feels the acceleration, relying on that to maintain their course. She keeps their path reasonably straight by feathering the burn rates across the engines. For Marc, it's unnerving. The superstructure of the craft shakes. He can feel it vibrating through the back of his seat. He clenches, fighting against five gees of acceleration shoving his body around like a rag doll. His cheeks sag back as his head sinks into the cushion on the headrest.

"Y—You good?" Emma asks, struggling to speak. She's wedged her body against the lower part of the seat. From where she is, she can't see out of the cockpit window, not that there's anything to see. She's steering on instinct, using her own body as an accelerometer. Pain is a compass.

"G—G—Good," he replies, being unable to muster a proper sentence. Streaks of light continue to tear through his eyes. It feels as though red hot needles are being poked through his skull. They cut through skin and bone, passing through his forehead, nose and cheeks, but the angle has changed. Instead of coming from above, they're off to the side now. Blood drips from his nose. Most of it runs back into his throat. Those few drops that reach his nostrils quickly streak away, running back to his ears under the acceleration. He wants to wipe them away, but he can't move his hands. If he lets go of the armrest, he'll never get his hands back there again.

"Six gees... Seven... Eight."

It's all Marc can do not to swallow his own tongue. Anatomically, he knows it's impossible, but it swells in the back of his throat regardless, threatening to block his airway. As it is, all he can manage is shallow breaths. His ribs feel as though they're being crushed by a car. Accelerating at eight times the gravitational pull of the entire Earth is insane. During their training, they undertook g-force loading in a centrifuge as well as in jet aircraft, but that was different. It was planned. It was conducted under controlled conditions. Back then, blood pooled in his legs. Clenching his thighs allowed him to remain conscious. Here on the *Sycorax*, though, blood is pooling behind his back, which is an unnerving sensation. He's gripping the armrests of his seat, but he can feel the blood draining from his fingers and hands. Blood is accumulating in his buttocks, in his back, in his shoulders, and even at the back of his neck. His heart is struggling to pump what feels like sludge around his body.

"N—N—N—Nine."

The skin on Marc's face feels as though it's been peeled back. His lips stretch. The cabin is shaking. Panels rattle under the strain. His vision blurs. For all he knows, the *Sycorax* is breaking apart under the stress.

"And... we're clear," Emma says, shutting off the burn. Normally, the *Sycorax* throttles up and down with the purr of the engine on a Rolls Royce. This time, the engines simply die. Marc is thrown forward in his seat. If he hadn't managed to clip into his seatbelt, he'd slam into the cockpit window. The loose control panel smacks into the dash and ricochets up, twisting as it collides with the galley. Cracks run through the glass. It's all Emma can do to hold on and not be flung around the cabin.

For a moment, Marc floats there without speaking. They made it. They're safe—for now.

Emma's crying. She tries to hide her tears, brushing them quickly away, but she's hurt.

"Hey," he says, unclipping and reaching over to touch her shoulder. "It's okay. You did good."

Her eyes are bloodshot. Snot clings to the side of her cheeks. She wipes it away with the back of her hand.

"No, I didn't," she replies. "Don't you understand? This shouldn't have happened. Not on my watch."

"There was nothing you could have done."

"I shouldn't have been down there. I should have stayed on the bridge. I might have seen something. I—I could have changed course."

"No, you couldn't," Marc replies, flipping through the log files. Marc's not overly familiar with the raw data but the thousands of zeroes before him are self-explanatory. "There was no indication of anything out there in the darkness. If the nav computer picked this up, it didn't recognize it. Nothing has been flagged in here for investigation."

"I know, but..."

Like all good leaders in a crisis, Emma's rethinking her response to the emergency. She's not content but she shouldn't torture herself.

"But nothing," he says. "If you were up here, you would have taken a full dose of that crap. And what good would that have done?"

Emma lowers her eyes.

"You did what you could," he said. "You haven't made any mistakes."

Emma clenches her jaw at that comment. He's hit a nerve.

"I need to—"

"Hey," he says, taking her arm gently as she drifts nearby. "You're human, okay? We all are. You did your best. You got us out of there."

She nods.

"No regrets, okay?"

"None," she says, reluctantly. "We're stable. We're secure."

"We are," he says, squeezing her hand. "You've done well."

Emma lowers her eyes, not wanting to acknowledge that point. She pulls away and pushes off the bulkhead.

"See if you can get that nav panel back online."

"Me?" he says, joking with her. "Oh, sure. And I'll pull a rabbit out of a hat while I'm at it."

Emma isn't impressed with his lame attempt at being funny. To be fair, even he thinks his comment fell flat.

Emma examines a dead control panel over by the life-support controls. After that, she drifts toward the bathroom at the rear of the cockpit. She's discreet but the head is hardly private, being little more than an alcove beside the environmental controls. She pulls a folded sheet of plastic in front of her. It's flimsy. Emma fixes a tiny latch to hold it in place. The screen is opaque, transforming her into a grey blob twisting in a narrow space. She wiggles out of her flight suit. The sound of the vacuum pump starts as she straps herself onto the toilet.

Marc turns away. Privacy wasn't a key consideration for the

engineers who built the *Sycorax*. Life in space is awkward at the best of times. The human body isn't a machine and can't be treated like one. It needs food, water, rest and relief.

Marc stares out at the stars. After the tension of the last hour, he needs to decompress. His fingers tremble. It's an entirely human response. Reality is catching up to him. He feels overwhelmed. It's not a sign of weakness so much as exhaustion. Uncertainty eats away at his mind. Apparently, they're not going to die. For now, at least.

Some people act like robots in a crisis, pretending they're something other than human when dealing with stress, but even synths need downtime and maintenance. The enormity of all that's happened hits him hard. Somewhere behind him, people have died in their cryosleep—passengers and crew. How many? Dozens? Hundreds? Thousands? How many more will die before they restore the warp bubble for interstellar flight? *If* they restore the bubble? There's also another possibility he doesn't want to consider but must, and that's that everyone onboard may die out here in the cold dark of space. Tears well up in his eyes.

Marc doesn't mean to put on a front or any kind of pretense, but he doesn't want to cry in front of Emma. Like her, he's trying to be strong when he feels helpless. What would she think of him if he bawled like a child? Would she consider him weak or simply human? It's a question he doesn't want answered. As she returns, he reaches up and wipes the faint tears from the corner of his eyes. It seems they're not so different. Denial is an anesthetic, numbing the pain. For all their exploring, it seems he's yet to find himself.

Marc turns away from her, tapping at the barely functioning panel in front of him. He's hungry. Of course, he is. He's human. For now, he'll deny the urge. Like a good little robot, he feels he needs to focus on the task at hand. He ignores the hunger pangs and works with the handful of functions available in the safe-mode configuration of the nav system. Even without its core systems and running on less than 15% of its processing power, the AI interface within the *Sycorax* is trying to resolve hundreds of faults.

Are computers an extension of humans, or is it the other way around? Honestly, some days Marc feels it could go either way.

"Found anything?" a distinctly calmer, more relaxed Emma asks. It seems she too needed a moment alone to get composed. She drifts behind him, resting her hands on his shoulders as her head comes up next to his. Touch is human. This is just the kind of distraction he needs. He's got to stop thinking about what happened and start looking at what can be done next. If they're to survive, it's going to take some mental fortitude.

"With a bit of distance, we're getting better imaging. That storm is nigh on invisible. I'm getting slight distortions as it passes in front of distant stars but there's nothing much on the radar. Just some streaks."

"Good work," Emma says. "Bring up the flow on the main screen. I need to see what the hell we're dealing with."

"Wait," Marc says, looking at a data table from the sensors. The confusing array of numbers contains positive figures at various points, but at a certain distance, they all drop to zero. It's not that they slowly decrease but rather that they end abruptly. "This doesn't make sense."

"What doesn't make sense?"

"It stops."

"What do you mean it stops?"

"I can trace the particle flow based on its direction of motion, but I can only trace it back maybe 50 AU then it just disappears. It vanishes. Gone. Beyond there, it's like it never existed."

Emma says, "That's not possible. It can't just disappear. It's got to come from somewhere."

"This storm seems to appear out of nowhere."

"Doublecheck your data," Emma says. "Switch to another sensor to confirm your collection's valid. You need to make sure you're not seeing an electronic ghost."

Marc already did that. He asks, "How is this possible?"

"That's what you need to figure out."

Marc laughs. "Hey, I'm the sewage and bio-life-support guy, remember? I leave the crazy astronav stuff to you."

Emma says, "Throw it up on my console."

"It's as straight as an arrow," Marc says, graphing the data in three dimensions as he punches in the collaborate command. He says, "I've centered the graph on the point of origin and aligned the graph with galactic north. Our location is circled with a vector marking our relative velocity with a motion vector."

Emma squeezes her eyes shut for a moment, speaking under her breath as she says, "By the *Srimad Bhagavatam,* this cannot be."

"What?" Marc asks, confused. "What am I looking at?"

"A black hole."

"A *what?*" Marc says. He shakes his head, saying, "No, no, no, no. That's not possible. There must be some mistake. There's nothing on any of the scans."

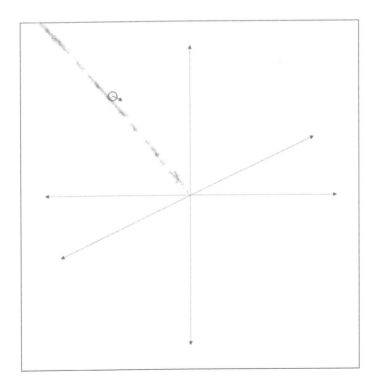

Emma says, "I know. There are no historical observations, no records on our charts, and no glow within the electromagnetic spectrum—no radiation whatsoever. There's nothing there—and yet there is!"

Marc asks, "If there's a black hole out there, shouldn't there at least be an accretion disk around it?"

"It may be too diffuse to undergo fusion," Emma says. "Can you map that rogue planet onto this spatial data set and re-plot your graph? Be sure to include historical tracking and extrapolate the ice giant's motion."

"Um. Okay, sure," Marc replies, running his fingertips over the virtual keyboard in front of him. "Oh..."

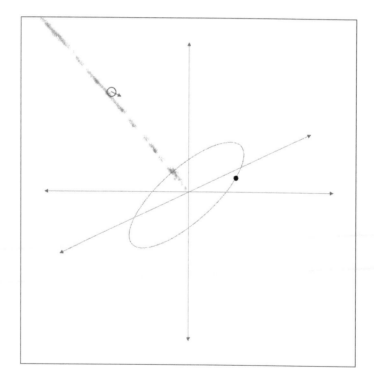

"And there it is," Emma says. "That rogue planet is orbiting the point at which the tempest begins."

Marc says, "But nothing is showing up on the scope. No star. No radiation profile. There's a faint outline in infrared, but it's barely there at all. The computer has logged that as a brown dwarf, but it estimates the distance to it as 1.8 light years, not 50 AU!"

"This wasn't accounted for in the astronav modeling," Emma replies. "No one ever thought we'd come across a quiet monster."

"I know what I'm about to say sounds silly," Marc says, "but if you're right, this is a *black black black* black hole!"

"It's dormant," Emma says. "It has to be. It seems this beast stopped feeding and fell quiet a long time ago. What's left of its accretion disk is being drawn up into the relativistic jet and pushed out along its poles."

"But why is there only one jet?" Marc asks. "If this is a relativistic jet then why isn't there another one going toward galactic south in the other direction?"

"There is," Emma says. "But you can't see it because it's moving away from us. Jets like these only light up if you're in the line of sight or the material runs into a gas cloud. Otherwise..."

"It's invisible," Marc says.

"Yep."

"That's why it's not on any of our charts," he says.

"It's been out here a long time, sitting in the dark, waiting for some damn fool to wander too close."

"How big is the black hole?"

"Big. Damn big."

"How big?"

"Well," Emma says, "if you calculate our motion since coming out of the warp bubble, I think you'll find we're being drawn in toward it, slowly accelerating into a highly elliptical orbit. If you run our current distance from the collision through the nav computer and include our last burn and the angle of gravitational perturbation, it'll give you the mass of that thing."

Marc fumbles with the interface. Even though Emma has spelled out the process, he's embarrassed to say he has no idea how to make this specific calculation work.

Emma is kind. "Pick *orbital insertion* from the side menu."

Marc looks around the screen for the data sets she wants in the calculation. Emma points, raising her eyebrows slightly, but she avoids the temptation to micromanage him. She lets out a slight hum as he skims over the vast array of data grouped before him, giving him hints as to what he should include.

"Oh, ah," he mumbles. "Got it. Wait. This can't be right."

"It's correct," she says, looking over at his screen.

"Umm, it's saying there's a gravitational presence roughly four hundred thousand times the mass of the sun." Marc scratches at the dried blood above his lip. "We're fucked, aren't we?"

"That's the technical term," Emma replies. "If we can't get that warp bubble active, the *Sycorax* is going to get awfully toasty when we swing down next to that thing."

"What do you mean?" he asks.

"It's a monster. It has consumed most of its accretion disk but it's still got a few surprises left. It's eating itself."

"And the jet?" Marc asks.

"It's all that's left of some star consumed millions of years ago. It got ripped apart as it swung too close. That jet is the bones. It's the remains of the carcass. It's the tidally disrupted remnants of a dead star—including the heavy byproducts of fusion in its core. And we flew right through the middle of it."

Marc clenches his teeth. He pulls the tendons on his neck tight as he says, "Yeah, that doesn't sound good."

Emma says, "We got hit by unusually fast particles. The warp bubble should have absorbed them, but it collapsed under the sheer onslaught. Rather than plowing into an asteroid, we got hit by a shotgun blast full of atoms, probably ions like oxygen, carbon and iron.

And there would have been hydrogen, lots and lots of fast-moving hydrogen. We were struck by whatever didn't get drawn down into that monster."

"I think we're clear of the stream," Marc says, bringing up the position of the *Sycorax* on the graph. "We're okay. We're going to be okay."

"Nope," Emma says, shaking her head. "We're not. We're falling in toward that singularity. We won't hit. The chances are we'll swing wide, but without that warp bubble, we're not getting out of here."

"But we've got time on our side, right?" Marc says. "It's a monster, but it's got to have stable orbits. Look at that rogue planet. That's good news, isn't it? It means the system has been stable for hundreds of millions, perhaps billions of years. I say we wake the rest of the crew, ride out the approach, and repair the warp drive."

"It's not that simple," Emma says. "Get too close to that monster and its magnetic field could fry us to a crisp. The tidal forces alone could tear our ship apart. If more matter falls in while we're nearby, we could get saturated with radiation."

"Not good," Marc says.

Emma jokes with him, repeating his point from earlier. "And by *not good*, I take it you mean, really *fucking* bad."

He laughs.

"Tell me about that rogue," she asks. "It's big, right?"

"About twice the size of Jupiter," Marc says. "And glowing in infrared."

"That's good."

"Why?" he asks.

"If it's got an active core with heavy metals, it's going to be throwing out a magnetic field. If we can get down there, it'll provide us shelter from the storm."

Emma works away on something in a console window. She taps at a virtual keyboard on the glass display. Rather than entering individual commands, Emma sets up a series of pre-existing routines to run in a prescribed order, complete with logic loops. She's programming a script. It seems she's trying to coax the *Sycorax* back to life.

"Find out everything you can about that ice giant," she says.

"On it."

It's another few minutes before Marc speaks again.

"There are a couple of moons. I make five, but there could be dozens of smaller ones down there."

"Good, good," she says. "How far is the ice giant from the hole?"

"Just under 20 AU," Marc replies. "If it were in our solar system, it would be orbiting at the distance of Uranus."

"Those moons are going to be cold," Emma says. "But we need raw materials. We should be able to find mineral deposits on at least one of those moons—if they're not completely buried in ice."

"One of the moons is big," Marc says, unsure how much more he should say. He doesn't want to distract her from whatever she's coding, but this seems important.

"How big?"

"Ah, it's hard to say. There's not much to go on here as the albedo is so low without a nearby star to light things up."

"Any atmosphere?"

"I'm not sure," Marc says.

"If there is, we might be able to harvest methane," Emma says. "Plot a course for that moon. Use the astronav to bring us in with the minimum number of burns. Once I've stabilized the craft, we'll wake Raddison and tell him what's happened."

"Working on it," Marc says, desperately trying to remember his nav course during basic training. It was only ever supposed to be informative. He was never actually supposed to do anything other than watch the computer do its thing. Although the crew was cross-trained in the various disciplines required to fly the *Sycorax*, no one ever actually thought these skills would be needed. Marc finds himself wishing he'd paid attention to something other than just getting a pass mark on the exam.

He says, "It's going to be tight, but with four burns we can avoid that outflow and swing into orbit at 20 AU. We can nestle right in beside that ice giant."

Emma nods.

Her lack of reply is a not-so-subtle hint. The time for talking is over. She needs to focus on restarting the fusion drive at the heart of the *Sycorax*. For the first time since he was hanging beneath the gantry, Marc doesn't have to rush anywhere or do anything. He can think rather than react. He looks out into the dark of space, wondering where the invisible monster lies. He has no idea about the orientation of their spacecraft relative to the black hole. He could be staring right at the monster and not know it. The craft has a twist in its motion. They're tumbling, but only slightly.

He looks at the path the computer has plotted, desperately hoping Emma's plan is going to work. He'd feel better if she checked his work.

Commander
Raddison

Marc is seriously regretting signing up for the interstellar colonial service. What seemed like a grand adventure has turned into a nightmare—and one from which he may not escape.

Marc grew up on the Big Island of Hawaii. He loved visiting Oahu, but it was the Big Island of Hawaii itself that felt like home. Surfing was a religion. He misses sitting out on his board, feeling the swell roll beneath him, looking for a wave to ride in to shore. There's something spiritual about getting up before dawn and carrying a long board across the sand. It's the rhythmic sound of the waves crashing on the rocks, the slight hiss of water rushing back across the beach and the call of sooty terns drifting on the breeze.

Marc was seventeen when he joined the US Interstellar Flight School. The next six years were a blur. His grades weren't that good. Somehow, he passed the entrance exam, but it seemed to be a fluke as that effort didn't help him pass any of his flight exams while in college.

Marc threw himself into his ebooks, avoided partying with the rest of his dorm, worked weekends at the local bar, woke early to study before class, and still failed most of his core subjects. *Fail* is an overly harsh term as the pass mark was 75%. To his horror, he'd hit a consistent 72% to 74% in most units. A mere 76% was cause for celebration. To Marc, it was like hitting a hole in one. A couple of his lecturers took pity on him and gave him extra credit for his papers, allowing him to make up for the deficiency, but he quickly realized he would *never* command a starship. Emma scored in the mid-eighties. Commander Raddison averaged 97%. Across forty-five modules, he averaged ninety-*fucking*-seven percent. And he was at every party. What a bastard. But deep down, Marc couldn't fault him. Raddison was three years ahead of him, but had no ego. He was never anything other than kind.

At the end of his second year, Marc took bio-cultivating as his specialist subject. The supposed transmutation of feces into food wasn't exactly a popular course, but Marc knew it gave him his best shot at getting onboard a flight. When it came to bio-engineering, he finally hit his stride, lifting his average above seventy-five. He called his results, *"the high seventies,"* whenever he spoke to his mom and dad as that sounded much better than scraping by with a mere one or two percent above the pass mark. They weren't happy about seeing their youngest son take off to explore the galaxy, but Marc had a wanderlust that couldn't be satisfied on Earth. Now, he wonders if he'll ever see Earth again.

Marc signed on for a twenty-year tour. He's got six shifts outbound to *New Haven*. That's nine years on duty out of the roughly fifty years spent in flight to get to the exoplanet. Suspended animation will halt his aging, but accounting for time dilation, almost sixty years will have passed on Earth by the time the *Sycorax* reaches *New Haven*. Unless the long-touted salvation of gene therapy ever works on something larger than a rat, everyone he knew back there will be dead long before he returns in a hundred and twenty years' time.

When it comes to spaceflight, calculating one's age is a bitch. If Marc only counts his years on duty, he'll be thirty-two when he reaches *New Haven*. If he counts actual Earth years elapsed, he'll be eighty-nine but he'll feel as though he's in his early thirties. On reaching *New Haven* the crew gets a two-year paid holiday—and he fully intends on using it to surf. The remaining nine years on his contract can be served on a return flight to Earth or by working on in-system cargo runs and mining ships, although most of those won't have any need for a bio-farm engineer. Maybe he could work as a cook—if he makes it out of this alive.

"We need Raddison," Emma says, snapping him out of his lethargy.

"Ah, yes. Right." Marc is flustered. "Ah, how do we raise him?"

Like most of the systems on the *Sycorax*, the cryo-pods are highly automated and have redundant backup power. It makes sense, as it's impossible for everyone on the crew to have the specialist skills required to manage the hibernation process themselves. Besides, the maintenance of a pod is impossible beyond star base. The *Sycorax* is carrying spare pods in case a failure arises, but no one talks about them. If a pod fails, the colonist inside will die within ten minutes, which makes the need for spares redundant. The spare pods are the lifeboats of this particular Titanic. Technically, they're needed. In reality, they're for show. They look good in the brochures.

When it comes to a change in the duty shift, the onboard computer automatically wakes the next team. Once they're up, there are three days allocated for handover, and then the previous team is off to a dreamless sleep. Years pass with a few blinks of cold eyelids.

"Ah, we lost power," Marc says, pointing at the hatch at the rear of the cockpit leading down to the hibernation chamber. "Is anyone still alive back there?"

Emma pushes herself out of her seat. Marc follows her.

"By my reckoning, we were without main circuit power for about seventeen minutes. Auxiliary was still pulling current. The oxygen feed is under mechanical pressure precisely because the pods are vulnerable without power. They wouldn't have had meds or waste fluid exchange, but they should still be under. Once the main power came back, the base life support system rebooted. The stasis routines are low-level. They don't need much beyond a spark. The backup power should have kept them humming. I hope. They should be fine."

Should—she doesn't sound convinced. It's what she wants to be true, but like Marc, doubts are creeping in.

Waking abruptly from cryo-sleep is the stuff of nightmares. It's like waking in a coffin buried six feet beneath freshly turned dirt. As part of their training, the crew had to go through an uncontrolled wake so they knew what to expect in an emergency. They were given detailed descriptions of every sensation they'd experience—and yet that made absolutely no difference whatsoever. Waking abruptly from cryo-sleep was horrific. The trainers joked about it as *hazing the new crews.* In Marc's class, no one laughed.

The lid of the casket—and there's no other way to describe a pod—sits less than an inch from the tip of the nose. To call it claustrophobic is to undersell the sheer, abject terror of waking in a dark, damp, cold, confined space. The first thing Marc felt was the pain of the IV lines going into the crook of his arm. Although he was sedated when he went under, the trainers cut the meds before waking him. It felt as though rats were gnawing at the crook of his arm. The fluid entering his veins was as cold as ice water. Regardless of everything they told him during his training session, he and everyone else— absolutely everyone else—panicked. It's a reflex survival instinct. The brain screams *fight or die!*

Even though Marc knew it was a training run, he freaked out when he woke abruptly. They told him he'd be under for no more than ten minutes but the difference between minutes, hours, days and even years is a blur in cryo-sleep. He felt as if his whole life had been truncated into oblivion. His existence meant nothing. All his memories were a lie. Like someone drowning at sea, he was terrified by the wretched horror of all that was happening to him. He felt helpless, frustrated, defeated. Flexing every muscle in his body was an exercise in futility. There was nothing he could do that would make any difference. He was dying.

The pod was so confined he couldn't even raise his hands to his chest, let alone his face. The best he could do was bang his knees and the side of his wrists against the cold plastic as he screamed. And oh how he screamed. At that moment, it felt as though he was the only person alive anywhere in the universe. And it felt as though he wouldn't be alive for long.

When they popped the lid, a rush of warm air swirled around him. Marc was supposed to wait for the hibernation tech to remove his IV line but there was no way he was lying there a moment longer. He was up and out of the pod in a heartbeat. Someone grabbed him. They were trying to stop him from tearing the IV line out of his arm. Marc didn't care. He was so jacked up that he punched the tech. Blood ran from the tech's nose as he howled in agony, clutching at his face. Afterward, Marc learned that his was an *average* response.

Somewhere near a massive black hole, two lone astronauts drift through the darkness down to the medical bay. Emma floats up beside him, holding a needleless injector.

"Nanobots," she says, seeing the distant look in his eyes. "We took significant cellular damage during the tempest. This is gonna hurt like *Mahakali* but it'll repair your fine tissue injuries."

"Do it," Marc says.

Emma holds onto the hull of the *Sycorax* to get some leverage. Marc braces, grabbing a handle by the hatch. He turns his neck sideways, giving her a clear shot. Emma pushes the injector and squeezes. At first, there's no discomfort, just a rush of cool fluid entering his body. Then the nanobots hit. For a few seconds, his head feels as though it's going to explode.

"Oh, that stings like a bitch," he mumbles, squeezing his eyes shut and gritting his teeth. The pain he feels is acute, being confined to various, unrelated parts of his head. It feels like someone just stabbed him with a set of knitting needles. It's as though several invisible steel rods passed through the top of his skull, down the side of his neck and into his chest, exiting out of his pectoral muscles. He reminds himself this is the repair process. The *needles* hit him a while ago—it's just that he never realized how bad those flashes of light were until now.

The nanobots find several other points of deep tissue damage in his buttocks, his thigh and his ankle.

"Do you want some painkillers?" Emma asks. She's not taking any. Pride gets the better of him. Emma's already at the med-console bringing up the pod rotation control, using it to resurrect the commander.

"No, I'm good." Marc rolls his ankle one way and then another, trying to shake off the ache in his bones.

"Suit yourself."

Damn, she can read him like a book. He should have said *yes,* and both of them know it, but the moment is gone. Next time, he'll be honest. Or so he'd like to think. In reality, his pride is a function of his ego—it's not going anywhere.

"Sweet *Shashti,*" she says. "This is wrong. This has got to be wrong."

"What?" Marc asks, floating up beside her. The console in front of them is peppered with dead pixels. Those that are working glitch. They shimmer, struggling to settle. The colors, though, are telling. In among the green heartbeats, there are dozens, no, hundreds—no, *thousands* of flat red lines. His heart sinks.

Marc's mind immediately reaches for alternatives to the grim reality facing them. "Sensor failures?"

"Not likely," Emma replies. "Some of them, maybe. But not all of them."

Neither of them says anything else. Several thousand colonists have died in their pods. The silence is painful. Neither of them wants to know precisely how many people have died. There will come a time for reckoning. For now, they're in survival mode. It's enough to realize the *Sycorax* has become a morgue.

The cold storage used by the crew is smaller and separate from the main hibernation unit. Six of the eight pods have red lines running through their metrics. Raddison, though, is alive. Marc desperately wants to say, "Bring him up," but telling Emma how to do her job when she's already working at the console would be equal parts annoying and redundant. As the youngest and least experienced member of the crew, he keeps his mouth shut.

Normally, resurrections unfold slowly over the course of several hours as the patient's meds are lowered and their body temperature is raised. Emma looks calm, but she has to be rattled. She's skipping a lot of the prompts displayed by the computer, rushing to wake the commander.

Marc is still trying to grasp just how fucked they are. They might have restored basic functions, but there's no reason to rejoice. The *Sycorax* is a long way from nowhere with a crippled warp drive. It'll take years for a rescue craft to reach them. Hell, it'll take years for anyone to even realize they're in need of being rescued. Emma's right about the ice giant. They need a safe harbor in the storm. Unless Raddison can work magic on the warp drive, they're going to be stuck out here for a long time.

The casket/pod rises from the floor of the hibernation chamber. Vapor drifts from the cold storage hold beneath the floor. A sliding door closes beneath the pod, but the temperature in the med-bay has already dropped twenty degrees, sending a chill through his bones.

Dozens of metrics are displayed on the lid of the pod, but they're meaningless to Marc. The bright flashing red light, though, is ominous.

Emma has her back to the pod. She's monitoring progress on the main console. With her feet looped under a rail on the floor to hold her in place in microgravity, she taps madly, entering various commands. Marc would follow each and every computer prompt to the letter, but she's selective, accepting some and sweeping others away with the brush of her hand. She works through a checklist of fifty items within a minute.

A deep thunk comes from the pod. The hatch opens. White mist drifts out from within the slick tube, dissipating in the air.

Given he's been woken in a rushed, uncontrolled manner, Marc expects Commander Raddison to spring from the pod like he did during basic training. To his surprise, the commander doesn't move. He's breathing, but he looks dead. His bloodshot eyes stare at the ceiling.

Emma drifts over to the pod. She leans over him.

"Sir, this is Lieutenant Emma Madi."

With tears forming in the corner of his eyes, he stutters. "M—

Madi?"

"Yes, sir."

"W—What happened?"

"Best I understand it, we flew through a particle storm—a relativistic jet. We've dropped out of warp. We've lost a lot of systems. At the moment, we're entering orbit around an unseen gravitational anomaly."

"B—Black hole?" he asks, but his eyes haven't moved. He hasn't blinked. He's not looking at her. He's looking past her, staring through her to the ceiling beyond. His hand twitches.

"I think so, sir. There's nothing on the charts. Nothing on the nav instruments. I've never heard of anything like this before, but it's out there. Sensors indicate the presence of a mass equal to four hundred thousand Sols. And there's a planet down there—an ice giant. At first, we thought it was a rogue. We're going to seek a safe harbor there and shelter from any magnetic storms. I—I think we might be able to mine basic resources from its moons."

"G—Good job, Emma. Well done. You're doing a good job. You've done a great job."

"Sir?"

Emma doesn't realize it yet, but Marc does—the commander's paralyzed, probably from the neck down.

Marc sails over to the med-cabinet and retrieves a nanobot pack and injector.

Commander Raddison says, "Get us in a stable orbit. Radio for help. Go into stasis to conserve power and await rescue."

"Sir, I don't understand."

She was expecting him to take charge.

Marc hands her the nanobot injector. He speaks to the commander, saying, "We're going to get you out of there, sir. We'll give you a shot of bots and you'll be right."

"No. No," he says. "You have your orders. P—Put me back

46

under."

"We have nanobots," Emma says.

Drops of blood drift from the commander's lips. "Follow your orders, lieutenant."

Again, his fingers twitch but don't move. He adds a feeble, "Please," which shouldn't be necessary from a starship commander. His jumpsuit is soaked in blood. The deep red fluid has frozen around his abdomen. Unlike regular bleeding, it's patchy, forming large blobs.

Emma looks at Marc with tears in her eyes. She goes to speak but words fail to come out. Marc taps the close command on the lid of the pod. A slight *hiss* indicates the life support routines kicking in as the pod lowers into the floor.

"W—What? What just happened?" she asks, stunned. She looks at the nanobot injector in his hand. "I don't understand. Why? Why wouldn't he try?"

"Too much damage," Marc says. "He must have known. He must have been able to sense it—to feel it in his bones. My grandfather went like this. They call it multi-organ failure. I'm sorry."

"But we have nanobots," she says.

Marc is somber in his assessment. "We could prolong his agony, but not his life."

Tears well up in her eyes. Marc's sure Emma knows he's right, but in the heartbreak of the moment, she wants to hear it from someone else. It's one thing to know nothing can be done. It's another to accept it. Death never comes easy.

In the weightlessness within the *Sycorax*, Emma's tears build up in front of her eyes, forming large blobs of clear water. It must affect her vision, but she's too distraught to notice. Her hands are shaking.

"Hey," Marc says, pushing softly off the hull and drifting over to her. He hugs her. Emma buries her head in his shoulder and sobs. He understands. She's held herself together for the sake of the crew and the colonists. To suddenly realize most of them are dead is too much. To see her commander paralyzed and dying cuts deep. Mercifully, the pod will put him back to sleep—where he'll never wake.

The two of them float there, holding each other for a moment. Life demands comfort. All they have is each other. As bad as their injuries were, they were protected by the dense fluid in the holding tanks. Marc can't help but wonder how many of those remaining green metrics in the hibernation system are slowly failing, waiting to be revived, only to die.

His heart sinks. They're all going to die out here in the bitter, cold darkness of space. Marc suspects they'll be dead long before a rescue craft can reach them in several decades' time.

Altair IV

Miranda wanders through the endless night on the icy moon known as Altair IV. Her eyes adjust to the ambient starlight. Hundreds of thousands of kilometers away, an ice giant looms over the horizon. It's barely visible in the sky but it blots out the stars as it rises into the eternal dark. Thin wisps of ammonia ice caught high in its stratosphere reflect what little light reaches the planet, suggesting rather than announcing its presence. To Miranda, the faint, white ribbons curling around the distant equator are beautiful. The differences between them are subtle, changing from one day to the next. To her, it's as though they're curtains blowing in a breeze—and they are, only that *breeze* is a cyclonic wind whirling around the ice giant at hundreds of kilometers an hour.

Miranda knows the ice giant is in orbit around a black hole, but the concept is meaningless to her. The black hole is so far away she can't hope to see even the faintest impression with her naked eye. Her father, Professor Spiro, has used his telescope to show her how the black hole warps spacetime. She remembers peering through the scope and watching as a distant star smeared itself around a tiny point in the sky. One moment, the star was burning bright, high and to the right, and the next it was low and to the left, while the other stars remained where they were. *"That's it,"* her father said when she queried him about it, *"that tiny invisible point is the black hole."* Miranda doesn't understand why her father calls it a hole. It's the remnants of a star—a dead star. It may not give off any light, but neither does her moon. Her father speaks of the black hole with a sense of reverence. She's more interested in the ice giant Altair with its dark, swirling clouds. To her, Altair is pretty.

Miranda has a satchel slung over her shoulder. She holds a bunch of flowers in her left hand. She picked them from the greenhouse before walking out into the wilderness. In the darkness, their vibrant reds and yellows appear as muted shades of grey, but her mom would love them regardless.

Miranda walks on toward the distant plateau. Crushed rock crunches beneath her boots. Behind her, each footstep lights up in pale shades of blue as alien microbes react to her presence. It takes a few minutes for their bioluminescence to fade. The glowing trail behind her extends for thirty to forty meters, revealing the path she trod.

Miranda walks beneath a jagged cliff. The vast shadow blocks easily half the star field. She takes a handful of grit from her satchel, scattering it ahead of her like a farmer sowing seeds in a field. As the tiny bits of gravel bounce across the path, bioluminescent archaea spark into life, lighting her way. These single-celled extraterrestrial organisms lack a nucleus. They're invisible to the naked eye until dislodged by a landslide or a handful of pebbles. On a planetoid without a nearby blazing star, they evolved to emit light as a warning to grazing animals that they should eat something else. They're toxic chemotrophs, feeding on the sulfur and ammonium released by geothermal vents scattered around the equator of the moon. Miranda's father has told her these particular chemical compounds stink, but she barely notices. She's grown up with them. To her, they're normal.

Rolling fields of glass grass stretch out to one side of her, reaching up to waist height. The grass on Altair IV forms in a manner similar to corals on Earth. Microbes grow at the tip of the crystalline leaves, leaving silicates that form a structure as fine as spun glass on Earth. The fields are fragile. Storms periodically ravage the grass, crushing the glass like some giant stomping across the land. The microbes, though, are hardy. They regrow these complex structures within days, reaching up for what little, precious starlight there is to feed upon.

Firefly-like insects dance above the crystalline grass, calling to each other with waves of light. They blink in and out of existence. They compete with the stars for attention—only they have a motive—to attract a mate.

In the distance, a herd of bioluminescent deer grazes on the field of glass. These elegant alien creatures float above the sea of sharp edges, being held aloft by dozens of overlapping balloons growing out of their backs like blisters. Their floatation bladders light up with the remnants of the tiny creatures they're eating. Deer nibble at the tips of the glass, consuming microbes and spitting the silicates back to the ground. Little do they know, their saliva contains the nutrients needed for the worms that host the microbial larvae that form the glass. They're feeding the next generation—a generation they'll eventually eat.

During the mating season, the stags will fight over the does for mating rights. Aerial dogfights will unfold with a rainbow of colors as various males seek to puncture their rival's gaseous bladders with their antlers. Males will seek the best approach, wanting to outflank each other before committing to a charge. Foes are vanquished rather than crippled. It's rare to see a deer lose all its buoyancy as wounded bucks will flee once they start losing altitude. For now, the deer are content to feed.

Miranda reaches the original landing site of the *Copernicus*—the interstellar craft that brought her and her father to Altair IV. The *Copernicus* departed the icy moon decades ago, but the temporary labs and containers it dropped off still dot the landscape. There's no power so they appear as little more than sharp right-angle corners in the darkness.

Miranda walks up to her mother's memorial. Rocks have been piled on top of a shallow grave. The headstone is rough and unfinished. Only one face has been polished. It catches the starlight, making the words engraved there easy to read. There's no name, no age, no date of birth or death, just a few solemn, sad words carved into the rock. It's both a testament and a promise.

I love you.

I will never forget you.

Miranda kneels in the gravel. Bioluminescent dust swirls with her motion, settling over the rocks and causing them to glow.

"Hi, Mom," she says, laying her flowers on the grave.

Miranda feels torn. Her father says it isn't healthy to talk to the dead. She disagrees. She knows her mother cannot hear her, but it doesn't matter. She's content to speak for herself, roleplaying a conversation with a mother she never really knew. It's important to remember the dead. Speaking as though they can hear is neither mad nor sad. It's honest. It's defiance—a refusal to forget.

"I'm letting my hair grow now. Yes, the angsty teen days are gone. No more crew cuts."

Why is she talking about her hair? Her mother wouldn't mind what she did with her long, flowing locks, and her dad doesn't care. On an alien moon, her hairstyle doesn't matter to anyone other than herself.

Deep down, Miranda wants to be understood. Perhaps that's why she cut her hair short in the first place, to provoke her father into seeing her with more than mere eyes. She wanted him to see her as an adult, not a child. Would her mother be any different? Or would she side with her father when arguments invariably arose? Miranda's aware that her dreamy desire for a mother full of understanding and compassion could be entirely misplaced, but she knows she's inherited her mother's traits. Miranda's seen the video logs. She has more than her mother's blonde cowlick of hair rising from her forehead before curling down beside her face. She has more than her mother's pale blue eyes and fair skin. She has her aptitude for art, her humor and her curiosity.

Miranda fusses with the rocks. She picks up a few stones that have become dislodged by an ice storm. Gently, she places them back on the grave.

"I'm eighteen. Can you believe it? Eighteen years old!"

Tears fall from her eyes. In the dry cold, they evaporate from her cheeks within a few seconds. As it is, she has to wear lip balm whenever she's outside to prevent her lips from getting chapped. Her eyes always feel dry, but it doesn't bother her. Tears, though, are unusual. Miranda never cries. Why be sad on a world where you can have anything and everything you want? Is it her mother she misses or friendship with someone other than her dad? Her father means well, but he's stuffy. What he sees as care, she finds stifling. His concern is overbearing. He's too protective. He wants to be her friend, but he can't be. It's the imbalance between them. Friends are equals.

She speaks softly. "I mean, you'd know. You'd remember. I'm sure you would. Dad didn't. I don't think he's being mean or anything. It's difficult for him to keep track of dates.

"What do Earth years mean on a moon with days that only last sixteen hours? With no sunrise or sunset to mark each day? We orbit Altair once every five of our brief days. What does that even mean in Earth days? Dad tells me we undergo a hundred and eighty-two orbits of Altair for every one revolution of that dark monster at the heart of our system. What does that make a year out here compared to a year back there? I could get Ariel to do the math for me, but I don't want to know.

"As for me? I'm like you. I can't let go of Earth. If I were back there, I'd celebrate with a party. Out here, I'd celebrate being ten years old or something dumb like that, but Ariel assures me I'm eighteen in Earth years so I guess I am."

She laughs.

"I've never seen Earth, but it's home, right? Not here. Not Altair IV."

Miranda wipes her eyes.

"You're the only one I can talk to, Mom. Ariel doesn't understand me. She's a machine—my father's machine. She's supposed to be you, I think. She means well."

The cold seeps through her clothing, chilling her bones. Miranda gets up off her knees. She stands before the grave, dusting herself off and watching as bursts of blue light settle to the ground.

"He doesn't mean to forget," she says as her fingers settle on the words engraved on the tombstone. "He remembers you in his own way. I know he does. It's just that Earth dates are meaningless to him."

The ground shakes. A deep rumble reaches her ears. Miranda doesn't care. She continues talking to a woman she doesn't remember, to a mother she never knew but feels she understands.

"Birth means different things to men and women. A mother never forgets. I know you wouldn't forget. Oh, how I wish you were still here."

In the distance, a geyser erupts from the plateau. Steam races into the sky. The boiling hot water freezes as it rises high into the eternal night. A fine white snow forms as the geyser hits the thermal boundary almost a kilometer above the surface of the moon. After rushing up in a column, it drifts sideways, creating a snow cloud in the dark sky.

Miranda blows a kiss over the grave, saying, "I love you, Momma."

She turns and walks away without looking back.

She can't.

Distant lights guide her home.

The dim outline of her footprints are still visible beneath the cliff.

Out to her right, down by the shoreline, boiling water emerges from the honeycomb of caves that riddle the mantle. As the tides ebb and flow beneath the surface of the moon, water surges, exploding out of blowholes. It crashes against the rocks, sending out a wall of white spray that quickly freezes, falling as ice crystals along the edge of the cliff. Bioluminescent microbes glow in the wake of receding waves, washing across the shore as the water drains back into the caves.

High in the sky, a flash of light catches Miranda's attention. A meteor blazes through the night, but the trajectory is wrong. Miranda's seen plenty of space rocks and dust particles burn up in the atmosphere, but this is different. There's no chemical glow. Miranda prides herself on identifying meteorites. Red indicates the presence of lithium. Green highlights copper. Potassium is pink, while calcium burns yellow. This meteor, though, is a brilliant, bright white.

As the various meteors that strike Altair IV are drawn in by the ice giant Altair itself, they tend to streak in that direction. This one, though, is moving at a right angle to the massive, dark planet and it's high, far too high. It's almost as though it missed both the moon and the ice giant, but that's not possible. It has to skim the atmosphere of something to burn up. It's then Miranda realizes she's looking at an object well beyond the reach of her tiny moon, beyond even the vast reach of Altair. She's seeing something in deep space. How and why is it lighting up? If it's well beyond Altair, the amount of energy being released must be astonishing. What could cause that?

Miranda runs.

"Father... Father," she yells, running down a tunnel set into the mountain and throwing open the heavy door to their home. She jogs up the granite staircase, following the curve carved into the mountainside. The stairs seem endless. It's the excitement coursing through her veins.

"What is it?" her father calls out in alarm. From the tone of his voice, he's expecting her to be hurt, but Miranda is beaming with excitement.

"Did you see it? Tell me you saw it."

"Saw what?" the professor asks, leaning over the railing of his fourth-floor laboratory as she comes up the stairs. The professor's home is grand, having been cut into the side of the mountain. Each of the floors is a balcony in its own right. There are no walls beyond the various storage rooms, bathrooms and bedrooms carved directly into the rock. The open-plan lounge, kitchen and dining room on the first floor are lavish, but the furniture is sparse given the size. A clear dome surrounds the home. Warm air circulates.

"The flare," Miranda says, rushing up the final flight of stairs to reach him. She's out of breath but she doesn't care.

"The flare?"

"It wasn't a comet," she says, panting for breath. "Or a meteor. It was something else."

"Okay," he says, laughing at her. He holds out his hands. "Slow down. Tell me what you saw."

"Look up there," she says, leaning forward and holding onto her knees as she draws in deep breaths. The sky, though, is dark.

"I'll take a look through the logs," he says, smiling at her contagious enthusiasm. "I'm sure it'll be in there."

"I think it's a spaceship."

"A spaceship?" the professor says, raising an eyebrow. "I doubt that. We're a long way from the space lanes."

"Look for it, Papa. Look."

"I will, I will," he says, bringing up a hologram in the middle of his laboratory on the top floor of his spacious home.

As the mansion is built into the side of a granite mountain reaching several thousand meters above the plain, the various levels are offset from each other. Even though there are only two of them living there, the house is large enough for fifteen to twenty people to live side by side in comfort. There are bedrooms along with bathrooms scattered on the various levels. Polished marble floors give way to rough-hewn walls carved out of the granite hillside by robotic diggers. A single diamond-infused glass dome spans all of the floors, allowing the starlight to drift in on every level. The dark canyon beyond the glass gives way to a broad plain and distant mountains and finally stars. The decor is modest, which makes the home seem even larger.

"There," Miranda says, pointing at the replay rushing past on the hologram.

"Interesting," the professor says. "Well, you're right. It's a spacecraft. Or it was."

"What do you mean?"

The professor uses his fingers to manipulate the hologram. He zooms in while changing the portion of the electromagnetic spectrum that's visible in the image. A false-color sphere appears, only it's a teardrop in shape, with a tail reaching out behind it like a tadpole.

"That's a warp bubble," he says, pointing. "See how it forms like a drop of water falling from a tap?"

He zooms in. The spacecraft itself is little more than an elongated smudge within the bubble. The leading edge of the sphere is red in the direction of travel, while the tail fades to blue.

"That's a warp signature, all right," he says. "It's distorting spacetime, bending light around the spacecraft, but watch what happens as I replay the logs."

With a slight twist of his wrist, the timestamp races forward. Rather than bursting, the bubble dissipates, fading to match the background. The craft contracts and slows, but it remains a blur.

"What happened?" Miranda asks.

"From what I can tell, they flew through the jet emanating from the black hole."

"Jet?" she asks, confused by the concept.

"It's like a geyser," he says. "Any matter that doesn't get drawn into that monster is sent hurling out into space along its poles. It would have shredded their spacecraft. For them, it would have been like flying through a hail storm."

Miranda asks, "Who were they? Why did they come here?"

"The outer colonies must have expanded into the Nu Phoenicis system. It was only a matter of time before they did. That would bring them near us."

"But why?" Miranda asks.

"Nu Phoenicis has a lot of similarities to Sol. Same radiation profile and age."

"Is it close?" she asks.

The professor chuckles. "In a universe spanning *billions* of light years, everything we can see is close. Oh, I think it is roughly twenty light years from here. At a guess, it's probably about fifty light years from Earth."

"They didn't see it?" she asks, surprised. "They didn't know about the monster?"

"No one knows about it," the professor says. "And it needs to stay that way."

"But they'll send a rescue ship," Miranda says.

"Maybe. Maybe not. It depends on whether they get a distress call and whether they think it's a survivable incident. Even if someone has survived up there, they're probably not going to survive for long."

"But they might want to investigate."

"It doesn't matter. It'll take years for another craft to get here. Decades."

"And by then?" she asks.

"By then, we'll be gone," the professor says. "All of us. You. Me. Ariel and even Caliban."

Miranda hesitates. Her father seems to catch her reluctance.

"It's not worth it," he says.

"Earth?" she asks, even though she knows what his response will be.

"Our future lies with the Krell and that black hole," he says.

Softly, she replies, "I'd like to see Earth."

"I know."

Now, it's his turn to measure his words. Whether he's lying or withholding the truth is impossible to tell, but Miranda is no fool. Outwardly, she smiles. Inwardly, she seeks to decipher the truth.

"Our work is important," he says, but she notes he's unable to come up with an actual reason for not letting her visit Earth. Miranda was hoping for something more from him.

"I know," she says, echoing his earlier sentiment. That doesn't mean she agrees with her father, but she keeps that thought to herself. "But..."

"They're dead," he says, tapping the console with his fingers.

"They must be."

The professor is getting impatient with his daughter. His hand lingers over the controls but he's not inputting any commands or directing the computer. It's habitual. He drums his fingers, reinforcing his point.

Miranda's not sure why her father felt he needed to emphasize their loss. She never questioned him about the spacecraft. If anything, his insistence causes doubts to linger in her mind. He seems to sense her reluctance.

"Given the amount of energy released when they flew through that tempest, if they're not dead, they're dying."

"That's sad."

"It is," he says, looking away from the hologram and out at the stars beyond the dome.

"Wait," she says. bubbling with excitement. She points. "Look, Papa. They're alive!"

"What? How could you possibly know that?" the professor asks, turning back to the hologram. There's hesitancy in his voice. It's not that he wants them dead. That can't be his motive. It's Ariel and Caliban. She knows he doesn't want anyone else to learn the secret of Altair IV.

"Look," she says. The hologram is still racing through the log retrieval at an accelerated rate. What has been just a few seconds for them would be ten to fifteen minutes for that distant spacecraft. "They're performing a burn. They're changing course."

"Hmm," he says, narrowing his eyes as he looks at the faint glow of engines at the rear of the craft. He works with his fingers, running them through the air and touching at a virtual keyboard. The controls automatically position themselves within reach of his hands as he moves around the edge of the spherical hologram. Miranda's father could activate his implants. Miranda finds them easier to work with, but he seems to prefer laying out calculations visually.

"It's a controlled burn, but they haven't reached escape velocity."

"I don't understand," she says.

"They're firing at an acute angle," he says. "To leave this system, they should be firing long. They need to climb out of the gravity well of this monster."

"But?"

"But they're dropping into it."

"Why would they do that?" she asks. "Why would they fly in toward a black hole?"

"They're not." His jaw drops. "They're coming here."

"Really?" she says, unable to hide her excitement.

"It's impossible," he says with a growl in his voice. "Futile. The damage they've suffered would be immense. It will take them months to reach us. They'll be dead before they get here. This is desperation. They won't make it to Altair."

Miranda dares to defy her father, saying, "Maybe they will."

Adrian

Marc bounces softly off a dead instrument panel at the rear of the cockpit. It's cold within the *Sycorax*. Emma has been able to revive the CO_2 scrubbers but not the heaters. Fresh air circulates around Marc, gently pushing him on.

Frost forms on the glass panels. The moisture in the air is condensing as the temperature drops below freezing.

Marc wraps his arms around his chest, keeping himself warm. He's put on two layers of shirts and trousers along with a jacket to trap body heat close to his skin but it doesn't seem to help. At some point, they're going to have to suit up to get the passive thermal insulation system in their spacesuits working for them. If he was thinking clearly, he'd climb into his sleeping bag, but he knows it'll take time to warm the material. Marc's tired. Too tired. Wriggling into a cold sleeping bag is as appealing as jumping into a lake in the dead of winter.

Marc yawns. His mind demands rest. He knows he needs to recharge his brain cells if he wants to think clearly. As it was, the two of them were almost eight hours into their shift when the *Sycorax* struck a relativistic jet streaming off the poles of that darkest of black holes. That was easily ten hours ago.

Emma's already asleep. She slipped on a second flight suit and cuddled up in the pilot's seat. Even though it's eight days until the next orbital burn, she's not going to abandon her post. For now, they're safe. Logically, they both know that. Deep down, though, they're both afraid. The laws of physics say the *Sycorax* is following a well-understood trajectory and will swing past the black hole, but it seems neither of them can shake the feeling they're about to be torn apart by a monster looming somewhere out there in the pitch-black darkness of space.

Seatbelt restraints loop over Emma's shoulders, holding her loosely in place just inches from the controls.

Marc prefers to float as he sleeps. The sensation reminds him of the ocean swell back home. He pushes off the side of the hull and drifts toward his quarters. There's no light beyond the single LED on the flight deck. A soft touch on the bulkhead allows him to float on. Shadows grow around him. He drifts into the crew deck and positions himself near the hatch.

Marc feels he needs to be ready to react if Emma suddenly yells for help—not that a poop specialist can do much with electronics. He tells himself not to worry. The ship's systems might not be fully functional, but the *Sycorax* is stable. Nothing is going to happen. He needs to sleep.

Even on the best of flights, space travel is short bursts of insane intensity followed by long periods of utter boredom. Now is the time for nothing much of anything. Marc's a biologist. He's excess baggage in an emergency. Oh, Emma humors him by having him work on the astronavigation console, but only ever under her watchful eye. Emma can work on system repairs, but even she's limited by what she can accomplish. Any radiation damage to their computer circuitry would have happened at the nanometer range, putting it well below anything they can fix with the equipment onboard the *Sycorax*. They need spares from a star base—and that's going to take decades. The best they can hope for is to stabilize the ship and drop into cryo-sleep to await rescue. Marc hooks one leg under a strap and drifts off to sleep.

He snores. With no clocks running and most of the electronics fried, there's no way to tell how long he's out, but when Marc wakes, he finds he's drifted into the hibernation bay on the lower deck. It's unsettling to wake up where Raddison died.

The sound of distant drums reaches his ears.

"What the hell?"

That there's any noise at all is alarming, shocking him into sudden, conscious awareness.

"What is going on?" he mutters. "Emma? Is that you?"

Why would it be?

There's no reply beyond the deep, resonant thump of what could be a large bongo drum. The rhythm is erratic. One, two or three beats and then a pause for a few seconds. At first, doubts linger in his thinking. Is he still dreaming? Is he imagining this? But the banging continues.

Marc turns his back on the noise. He pushes out into the shaft leading to the cockpit.

"Emma? Are you awake?"

A feeble, "*Yes,*" is offered in reply. Emma's not convincing. She floats into view at the end of the darkened corridor. Her hair is disheveled. Like a lion's mane, it sticks out at all angles in microgravity. Her darkened silhouette blots out the stars. "Is everything okay?"

"No," he says. "I need light and power in medical."

"Oh, no, no, no," she says, shaking her head. Her hair ruffles in response to that motion. She must be able to hear the thumping noise drifting down the corridor. "We've got to keep them under. You heard the commander."

"Someone's awake."

"It's not possible," she replies, but she's been through the training. She knows. If someone is awake down in the hold, they'll be panicked and in pain.

Emma stutters. "I—I divided the remaining nanobots between survivors—and I upped the meds. They're out of it. They must be. They have to be."

"If someone's awake," Marc says, "we have to let them out. We can't keep them in a coffin."

"No, we have to keep them down," she says, drifting toward him. "You know the protocol. Even if the *Sycorax* was under power, we couldn't bring them up. We don't have the capacity to support wakers.

Standard Operating Procedure says we put them back to sleep."

"The SOP is gone," Marc says. "It's over. There is nothing standard about what we're doing."

"I know. I know," Emma says, grabbing at her forehead. Like him, she's dehydrated and suffering from a headache. "But we can't bring anyone else up. Our supplies are frozen. Food, water, and waste management are all in the red. As it is, we don't have enough power to sustain ourselves. Before long, we too will have to go into stasis. It's that or we won't reach that moon alive."

"He's awake, Em. You know what that means."

"Which capsule?" she asks. "I'll see if I can increase the meds remotely."

"It won't work," Marc says. "If he's awake, he's lost his IV line. We need to bring him up."

Emma is adamant. "Then he goes straight back down. Agreed?"

"Agreed."

Emma has a handheld flashlight. She turns it on and shines it in Marc's eyes, ruining his night vision. It's deliberate. She's not happy with him. He squints, turning away, but he understands. The pressure is getting to her. Their feeble hold on reality is tenuous at best. They don't need this. It's a waste of power, a waste of meds, and a waste of their time, but someone's awake down there.

Emma uses a battery-powered screwdriver to open a console on the wall by the door. The tiny nuts are magnetized, allowing her to touch them against the metal casing to stop them from floating away. She positions the light beside her, leaving it drifting in the frigid air as she works with her tools to bring the power on within the medical bay. This will give them more light to work with than when they brought up the commander, but it'll put more of a drain on the batteries. The hibernation controls come to life followed by the main lights.

Marc hovers nearby.

"Do you mind?" she says, peering over her shoulder as he floats there, watching what she's doing by the main power console.

"Sorry. It's just I—"

"What?" she snaps.

"I just want to help. I feel useless."

"Welcome to the club."

Emma pushes off the hull. She glides through the air, flying over to the hibernation controls. Marc hangs back.

"Let's see who's making all this noise."

To his surprise, there's no change in the erratic tempo or the intensity of the beat. Whoever this is, they have no idea he and Emma have sprung into action. The hibernation capsules/coffins are hermetically sealed, insulating them not just from heat and/or atmospheric loss but even external lights and loud sounds. It's supposed to be soothing. It's not. Whoever it is that's down there, they're persistent, but isn't hope always that way? Since when has life succumbed without a fight?

"Fuck," Emma mutters.

"What?" Marc asks, drifting up beside her. He feels as though her comment is an invitation to get involved.

"It's not one of the colonists. It's Adrian."

"Adrian?" Marc replies, surprised by her concern. "But that's good. He's flight crew. He specializes in warp dynamics."

"It's not good," Emma says, rummaging through a drawer. "We need to leave him down there."

"What? No!"

"You still don't get it, do you," she says. "We're dead in the water. There's no warp field. There won't *be* a warp field. The fusion core is shot to hell."

"But we have to try."

"No, we don't," she replies. "The commander was right. Our best strategy is to send out an SOS and make for that ice giant. It'll shield us from any future radiation storms. Hell, we might even find some raw material on one of those moons. With a bit of luck, we might make it out of this cluster fuck alive."

Emma floats over by one of the medical cabinets, saying, "At the moment, the difference between a slow, lingering death and surviving is a pretty damn thin line. Regardless of what happens next, we're on our own for the best part of two decades. It's gonna be a long time until help arrives."

She pulls out an injector-less plunger and primes it with a sedative.

"What are you doing?"

"Preparing to put him back under."

"But you don't know what's possible. Adrian's an engineer. He might be able to fix stuff."

Emma fights back tears. Marc can see them welling up in the corner of her eyes, near the bridge of her nose. She wipes them with the back of her hand, saying, "It has to be this way."

"Why?" Marc says, challenging her. "I don't understand."

Emma swings around to face him, saying, "Because he outranks me. Okay?"

"You're afraid," Marc says as the hibernation pod rises from the storage rack.

"We're alive," she says. "We've got a viable strategy. I don't want to risk that."

"But he might be able to help us repair the *Sycorax*."

"Help?" she says. "I know Adrian. I've worked with him for years. I know what he's like. He'll second-guess everything. He'll revisit every step I've taken."

"Is that such a bad thing?" Marc asks.

"It wastes time. It wastes resources. Right now, we've got a narrow flight window. We've got the fuel and the opportunity to drop down into that gravity well and settle into a stable orbit around the ice giant. Down there, we've got options. We've got flexibility. We can mine the moons. We can shelter in the shadow of the ice giant out at L2. You heard the commander. We need to take this shot while we can."

"But?" Marc asks.

"But Adrian will want to drive us out toward the space lanes. He'll burn through our fuel reserves trying to escape this gravitational well. He'll be so damn confident. He'll swear he can repair the warp core. He can't."

"Maybe he can."

Emma raises an eyebrow. "And maybe Santa's gonna bring me a new fusion containment vessel for Christmas."

The thumping continues from within the pod but it's changed to three quick hits followed by three slow thumps. Adrian must know he's been heard. He wouldn't be able to hear them talking, though. If anything, they'd sound muffled and muted. He must have felt the change in orientation as the pod was raised. He's sending out an SOS, knowing someone's bringing him up.

Emma sniffs. "We get one shot, Marc. Just one. We have to make a decision and stick to it. This isn't a sim. We won't get the luxury of a do-over."

"We need help," Marc says.

"No," Emma says. "We don't. We need to take shelter and wait out the storm."

"Another set of hands, another mind, another perspective."

Emma is blunt. "I don't want to follow Adrian to my death."

"You won't."

"No offense, Marc, but while you've been scrubbing shit off the inside of holding tanks, I've been working in his team. He's not a leader. He's a greaser. And he's got an ego to rival Julius Caesar."

Marc says, "Maybe he'll see something different. Maybe there are other options, things we've missed."

"I've done the math. I've run the calcs," Emma replies. "You need to trust me on this. We can't make the space lanes. And even if we could, they're useless to us."

"Why?" Marc asks, wanting to understand her logic even though he only knows the basics of astronavigation.

"There are no straight lines in space. When it comes to interstellar travel, everything's a brachistochrone."

"A what?" he asks as she relents, giving in to him. She presses the injector against a velcro strap on the hull, leaving it there.

"A curve," Emma replies, working with the controls on the hibernation pod to bring up Adrian. "In space, the shortest route between any two points is always a curve—only you can curve in a lot of different directions and still reach the same point. Imagine a skipping rope swinging around between two people. You can take any of the paths along the rope—down below, up over the top, out in front—it doesn't matter. All the paths are equal. They all lead to the same place."

"And we're on one of those paths," Marc says.

"Were," she says as vapor drifts from the lid of the pod. "We were on one of thousands. If we go back into the space lanes, we could be stuck out there for years waiting for someone to come along. And when they do, they could be on any of those *other* paths. They could still be up to half a light-year away from us at their closest approach."

"So what difference does it make?" Marc asks as the hydraulic motors on the pod whine. "Whether we're out there or down around that ice giant?"

Emma points at the hull. He gets it. She wants him to think about what lies beyond a couple of layers of insulation and a few thin metal panels. She says, "In deep space, we have no resources beyond what we're carrying. In orbit around that ice giant, we can mine the basics: oxygen, water, carbon dioxide and methane. Down there, we stand a chance."

The pod cracks open. Light spills out from the inside.

"We need to be careful," Emma says, looking at a readout on the medical monitor. "He's jacked up. His hormone levels are all over the place. His adrenaline is off the charts."

Marc peers into the pod. He's expecting to see another crew

68

member ravaged by high-energy particles. Commander Raddison was barely able to move. Marc floats closer, ready to help Adrian out of the electronic coffin. As he approaches, the lid flies open.

Adrian springs out of the pod. As Marc is closest, Adrian launches himself at him, screaming in rage.

"I'll kill you! I'll fucking kill all of you, you assholes!"

Marc is taken by surprise. Spindly hands grab his throat. Fingers dig into his neck. He chokes, gagging as he tries to speak. The two of them soar across medical. The back of Marc's head strikes the hull.

"Adrian, please!" Emma yells, but he ignores her. His eyes are wide with anger. His pupils are dilated.

Marc grabs Adrian's hands, trying to pry them from his neck.

"Let him go!" Emma yells, grabbing the first officer and pushing him to one side.

The three astronauts roll through the air, tumbling into medical equipment.

Adrian yells, *"You left me in there to die, you bastard!"*

"No one left you," Emma says, trying to pull the two of them apart. "We got you out as soon as we knew you were awake."

Behind them, an IV line floats free from the pod. Blobs of deep red blood drift through the air like tiny planets.

Marc gets his leg up and pushes against Adrian, catching him on the edge of his hip. He shoves him away.

"Calm—the—*fuck*—down," Emma says, holding her hand between the two of them.

Adrian has bloodshot eyes. Burst capillaries beneath his skin stain his cheeks with thin red lines. His face is swollen. Dried blood has crusted around his nostrils.

Marc coughs, trying to clear his throat and breathe properly.

"Straight away," Adrian yells at her. *"You should have got me out of there as soon as I woke! Not four-*fucking-*hours later"*

"We—didn't—know," Marc says, still struggling to breathe and fighting against a bruised windpipe to speak properly. "No—power."

"What?" Adrian says, finally calming down. He looks around medical. There are dozens of screens that, ordinarily, would be pulsating with metrics. They're all black. The overhead lights are on but the only active system is the hibernation retrieval control.

"We're running cold," Emma says. "We dropped out of warp."

"Why have you brought us out of warp?" Adrian asks, turning his ire on Emma.

"Not us," Marc says. "We ran into a storm—a tempest."

"What is this nonsense?" he asks, shoving Emma to one side. Adrian thumps her, hitting her chest with both palms and sending her soaring across medical. "What the fuck is going on?"

"Stop it," Marc says.

Adrian ignores him. "What *fucking* storm? There's no such thing as a storm in space."

"Adrian, please," Emma says. "You need to listen to us."

"Listen to you?" Adrian says. "You're a goddamn Q4 on the night watch. What the hell have you done to the *Sycorax*?"

"There's been an accident," Marc says. "You, the ship, the commander, the colonists. You've been exposed to near-lethal doses of radiation. It's—It's crippled our controls. It's affecting your thinking."

"Where is the commander?"

"He's dead."

"Who's in charge?"

Emma raises her hand.

"Not anymore." Adrian sticks his head out into the darkened corridor. The lack of power seems to convince him things are bad. He pushes off, leaving them and heading for the bridge.

Emma and Marc follow along behind him. A single glowing LED provides the only form of illumination on the command deck. One navigation panel is active along with the backup flight controls. Lights blink on the redundant testbed controls.

70

Adrian says, "We need to deploy a distress buoy with a backup of the flight recorder on auto-broadcast."

"I've already deployed one," Emma replies.

"Then deploy another."

"They have to be manually—"

Adrian snaps at her, "I don't want excuses. I want you to do your *goddamn* job!"

"Yes, sir," Emma says, lowering her head.

He looks at the navigation screen. "Why have we deviated from our original course?"

Emma says, "Commander Raddison, sir. He said we should take shelter around a nearby ice giant while we wait for rescue."

"No," Adrian says. "We need to stay in the space lanes. That's where they'll be looking for us."

"No one's going to be looking for us," Emma says. "Not for years to come."

"Bullshit!"

"Don't you want to know?" Marc asks, interrupting the argument. He's still rubbing his sore neck.

"Know what?" Adrian replies.

"What happened?"

Adrian looks confused. "You lost power. You lost the core."

"No, sir," he replies. "That's a symptom, not the cause. The *Sycorax* passed through a plasma stream. We were peppered with high-energy ions. It was a tempest! It was like flying through a particle beam—flying through hundreds of particle beams all at once."

"Never have I heard of such a ridiculous notion," Adrian says. "Not in thirty years of service. There's no such thing as a tempest. I want to see a full log of events leading up to the power outage."

Emma says, "I haven't been able to get the main computer online. We've got partial—"

"*I want those goddamn logs!*" Adrian yells at her.

Marc blurts out, "There's a black hole!"

"A what?" Adrian says, turning to face him. "That's absurd. There are no black holes within a hundred parsecs of this run. We've never observed anything even remotely like that in this region. No gamma-ray bursts. No gravitational wave fluctuations. No accretion disk. No relativistic jets."

"There is, sir," Emma says, supporting Marc. "We flew through its jet."

"Stop lying to me," Adrian says, gritting his teeth and growling at her. "You're only making this worse for yourselves. I don't know what went wrong or what the hell you did, but I *will* get to the bottom of it. And you will face a full tribunal for endangering this flight. For now, we need to get the *Sycorax* back on course."

Adrian turns his back on Marc. He shouts at Emma. "Where's that *goddamn* distress beacon? I want it prepped now!"

Marc reaches around from behind Adrian, grabbing his head and yanking it to one side. He pushes the injector with the sedative against the man's jugular, saying, "I'm sorry, sir."

Adrian wrestles to get free, but as they're both floating in weightlessness, Marc has the advantage. He wraps his legs around the officer's waist, holding himself on the man's back as he empties the plunger into Adrian's neck.

"This is mutiny," Adrian says. His words become less pronounced and more slurred the longer he talks. "You'll fry for this. By god, I'll make sure you fry!"

Emma is as white as a ghost.

Long Haul

As the hibernation pod disappears into the floor of the medical bay, Marc says, "I'm fucked, ain't I?"

Emma is calm. "You did the right thing."

"But he's right. They'll burn me alive for this."

"It's our word against his," Emma says. "There are no logs from the cockpit. No audio or video evidence. The black box is in emergency mode. It's only recording flight metrics at the moment."

Marc clenches his teeth. What's done is done. There's no going back. He's committed now. He only hopes Emma's right.

"Hey, look on the bright side," she says.

"There's a bright side?" he asks, surprised by the notion.

"Sure. You have to live long enough for them to kill you."

"Not funny."

"Relax," she says. "We'll truncate the story. We'll tell them our version of what happened. He was jacked up when he woke and he assaulted you. We had no choice. We had to sedate him. We had to put him back under. It's the truth—kind of."

Marc nods.

"Hell," Emma says. "That was an intramuscular sedative. It's supposed to be a gentle descent administered through the shoulder muscle. You pumped that junk right into his carotid artery. From there, it went straight to his brain. He's so doped up right now that I doubt he'll remember anything when he wakes." She laughs, adding, "He probably won't even remember his own name."

Marc's not convinced. "I hope you're right."

Emma taps on a touchscreen interface.

"What are you doing?" he asks.

"I'm bringing up two of the crew pods. We're going to have to clean them out."

"Clean them?"

"We need to go under," Emma says.

"Hang on," Marc says, realizing what she means. *Clean,* in this context, is a euphemism for disposing of bodies.

"We'll flush them out an airlock," she says, seeing the look of horror on his face.

"I love how you think that somehow makes it better," he says. "These are our crew mates, our friends."

"And they're dead," she replies. "There's nothing more we can do for them."

"Can't we leave them down there?" he asks. "I mean, we could bring a couple of spare pods online."

"Spares?" she asks, looking at him as though he's joking. "There are no spares."

"But—"

"That's just what they say in the brochures. In reality, we're always two pods short as there are supposed to be two of the crew awake at any one time."

Marc says, "You want me to go into a dead man's pod?"

"It's just a pod," she says.

A casket rises from the floor—there's no other way Marc can think of it. Vapor slips from beneath its lid as the hydraulics kick into action.

Marc points. "I—I can't go in one of those things, not after someone died in there."

"We have to," Emma says. "We have no choice. We don't have enough consumables to survive the five months until we reach that ice giant."

"And what if the autopilot fails?" he asks as the lid of the metallic coffin opens.

"Then we'll never know," she says. "We'll simply go to sleep and we won't wake."

"Jesus!" he says. "Do you know how fucked up that is?"

"I know. By all that *Chandra* sees, I know, but we're out of options. Every breath we take, every amp we use, every moment we waste up here is one less we'll have in orbit down there."

Marc asks, "What about the fuel reserves on the scouts?"

"No. If we use them, we're dead in the water. We need to conserve our resources. I have no idea what we'll find on those moons, but if we can harvest oxygen and snag some ice, we stand a fighting chance. If we can find some methane, we'll be able to run the turbo pump on the main engine and charge the batteries. It'll be a waste of propellant, but it'll keep us alive. If we're lucky, we may even be able to extract residual energy from the fusion core. There won't be enough for warp, but it'll keep us warm. As it is, our internal reserves aren't going to last much longer. If I shut down everything other than nav and hibernation, I can stretch the batteries to about eight months, but that's it."

"And we can't stay awake?" Marc says.

"If both of us are awake, we last two months. With one of us, we last three. The only way we're reaching that ice giant is if we *both* go under."

"Fuck, fuck, fuck," Marc says, holding onto a handle on the bulkhead.

"If it's any consolation, Adrian would have run us out of consumables in about three weeks. As it is, we'll only have enough fuel for a handful of recon flights in a scout."

Marc mumbles, "We're shooting craps in Vegas."

"Yep."

Emma opens the lid of the pod. Deep red blood has soaked into the white cloth lining on the inside of the casket. Ensign Philippa Davis looks peaceful enough. Her eyes are shut. She has a neutral expression on her face. At the very least, she didn't feel any pain. Her body, though, is a mess. Thousands of pinpricks of blood stain her tunic. Each one is as fine as the point of a needle. Her waist is soaked. Frost has formed on her trousers. Although her clothing is intact, thick, stringy blood vessels have ruptured from her stomach. In the weightless environment, they've slipped from beneath the waistband of her top. At first glance, it looks as though she's been hit from behind by a blaster.

Marc fights his gag reflex.

Emma detaches the IV port from the dead woman's arm and releases the straps holding her in place. "I'm so sorry, Philippa."

For a moment, the two astronauts drift there motionless, offering hollow silence to the heartbreaking loss before them.

Marc grabs a sheet from the examination table in medical and hands one end to Emma. Together, they wrap the body. In weightlessness, it should be easy but it's not. Sir Isaac Newton was right: Every action results in an equal and opposite reaction, and that makes working with another body mass awkward. In the cold, rigor mortis is slow to set in. The limp body twists and turns, reacting to their motion. Despite their best efforts, the sheet floats around the body rather than clinging to it.

"No one thought of body bags, huh?" Marc says.

"No one was supposed to die," Emma replies. She uses a length of cord to keep the sheet from drifting away from Philippa's face. The thin cotton sticks to the coagulated blood around the woman's waist. A dark red patch appears on the stark white fabric.

As they move the body around, the sheet drifts away from Philippa's feet. Marc doesn't care about seeing her legs. It's her face that's haunting. She's wearing pants and slippers. Only a thin sliver of skin is visible around her ankles. It's her eyes that terrify him. It's an unspoken horror—one neither of them will give voice to. Were it not for

Marc's pedantic desire to keep the bio-tanks in equilibrium, this would be them. This could still be them at some point in the near future. Their nav controls are flakey. If the calculation on the outward stream is wrong and they fly back through the tempest, their internal organs will be shredded by high-energy particles tearing through the *Sycorax* once again.

"Who's next?" Emma asks. It's only then Marc realizes there's a choice to be made. Seven of the eight crew pods have flat red lines next to them, indicating the loss of life. Raddison died shortly after they returned him to cold storage. Adrian's alive, but for how long?

Emma looks at Marc with hollow eyes. She wants him to choose the next person. That gets him to pause. He's curious about her choice. Philippa wasn't a random selection. In the back of his mind, he recalls seeing Emma and Philippa in the space dock before departure. They were friends. He's not sure, but he thinks Emma may have tried to alter the roster to share shifts with Philippa. But they're both navigators. There was no way Raddison would put them together. The company likes to match flight crew with non-essential workers like him. The idea is there's a better mix of skills and it avoids groupthink.

Damn it, they were close. Marc remembers seeing the two women staggering between bars in the artificial gravity of the torus. He was coming back from dinner and they were propping each other up, laughing as they wandered the thoroughfare with its market stalls. He's not sure whether they even noticed him. It was the night before launch and cryo-sleep is an amazing cure for a hangover. Several years in suspended animation tends to negate alcohol-soaked brain cells.

Marc swallows. She can't pick the next body. She won't. She's looking for him to make the call. This isn't a trash run. It's about respect. She wants him to pick someone meaningful to him.

"Anders," he says.

Emma nods and taps at the controls. The empty pod recedes and the chassis rotates, selecting the next pod.

"He was always cheerful," Marc says, knowing he doesn't need to justify his choice. Like her, he wants to give meaning to their grim task.

77

"Never had a bad word to say about anyone."

Emma nods. They could pick people at random, but this is a chance to give dignity to the dead.

Although neither of them wants to admit it, their chances of rescue are slim. Even if a craft is dispatched to find them—and that's a big if, as the flight metrics included in the distress call will suggest they're a lost cause—finding a cold craft is nigh on impossible. The rescue team will be looking for an eccentric orbit profile, not a neat, tidy orbit in resonance with a bunch of moons around an ice giant. If they're spotted at all, they'll look more like an asteroid than an interstellar spacecraft. And if their beacon fails, they'll be ignored.

If the *Sycorax* runs out of power during the intervening years they'll die quietly in their sleep. The chances are they'll drift aimlessly for eons. Down around that ice giant, their orbit will eventually decay. They'll either burn up in the clouds of the ice giant or impact one of the moons. And if that happens before a rescue craft arrives, there will be nothing left to find. The *Sycorax* will go down as *missing-presumed-destroyed*. At the very least, Anders and Philippa will be committed to the deep by people who knew them. It's poor consolation, but it's better than what awaits the passengers and the rest of the crew—including Marc and Emma.

Marc readies himself with another sheet.

The next pod opens. Like Philippa, Ander's has been peppered by heavy ions. Tiny red dots line his clothing. They form patterns reminiscent of density waves. At some points, they're closer and more intense. Near his groin, they're spread out. As they descend his legs, the waves appear closer together again. Apart from those tiny dots on his white clothing, he looks as though he's asleep. Emma disconnects his IV line and releases his waist strap.

"Sorry, my friend," Marc says. This time, Marc's positioned by the head. Emma takes the man's legs. Gently, they roll the body in the sheet and secure it with a strap.

The main airlock is on the next floor of the spacecraft. The two astronauts escort the bodies one at a time, positioning them within the chamber. Normally, the air within the lock is evacuated before the outer hatch opens but there's an emergency release allowing the lock to open at 20% residual pressure. The intent is to allow for rapid egress in an emergency. Far from being flushed into space, loose items will simply drift out of the hatch. Although the standard operating procedure is to have a tether in place, even something as simple as a handhold would suffice to keep a living astronaut anchored during the decompression. For these poor souls, it will be a slow, steady jaunt into the deep.

"Do you want to say something?" Marc asks as Emma stares through the glass on the inner hatch.

"You say something," she says.

Marc takes a deep breath, exhaling slowly. He thinks carefully about his words.

"Life," he says, resting his hand on the cold glass window. "Our lives are a rounding error within the cosmos. Not only are our lives far too short, our bodies are made from off-cuts. Regardless of whether we're thinking about galaxies, stars, planets or asteroids, our bodies are a tiny scrap of minerals, fluids and metals clumping together for a short while. Our bodies are comprised of such a small amount of mass it's easy to round the amount down to zero—and yet here we are! We might seem insignificant compared to the might of a black hole or the raging furnace of a star, but we're not. We're the masters of this chaos—even if only for a fleeting moment."

He hangs his head.

Emma hits the emergency release. The outer door opens. A light smattering of dust and tiny bits of cotton swirl through the thin air, being drawn out of the cracks between the panels. The two bodies bump gently against each other as they float out of the airlock and into the darkness.

Marc says, "We commit you to the deep. Your lives may have ended, but every atom will continue on into the future."

Emma rests her hand on his shoulder. In microgravity, it's a gentle touch. She wipes away her tears and turns from the window. With a light touch on the hull, she drifts back down toward medical.

Marc waits. He watches as the bodies drift into the pitch-black of interstellar space. He waits until the white sheets have faded into the endless night. Only then does he shut the outer hatch. As the polished metal dome closes over the star field, he realizes that, if the two of them die out here, there won't be anyone to say any words over their lifeless bodies.

Contact

"I don't like this," Marc says as he swings around in front of the cryogenic pod, ready to lower himself into the chamber. "I really don't like this at all."

"I know," Emma says. "But there's no other way."

In a weightless environment, he has to position his body inside the casket so his feet don't drift away. Marc's hands are trembling. Straps float loosely within the pod, being anchored to the mattress behind him. He grabs hold of them and cinches the buckle around his waist, ensuring it's tight. With a tug on the strap, his body is pulled hard against the rear of the pod. Marc's hair brushes against the headrest. He tries to slow his breathing but he can't. Bloodstains line the inside of the lid. Emma tried to wipe them away but the blood has smeared, making the congealed, deep red color appear brighter than it otherwise would be.

"Promise me," Marc says as Emma prepares the IV line. "You're going to get me out of here."

"I promise," she says, although they both know it's not a promise she can guarantee she'll keep. Regardless, those few words help settle his mind.

Marc takes slow, deep breaths. He breathes in through his nose and out through his pursed lips. Emma fusses with the equipment. Marc doesn't want to know what she's doing. He keeps his eyes forward.

Immediately across from him, there's an environment detection unit. It's directly above the pod. That's his point of focus. He can't look at Emma or the bloodstained coffin lining. It's all he can do to stare at the rivets holding the tiny atmospheric probe in place beneath a small grate. Although the obvious threat is smoke, it's been designed to detect any imbalance in the air, including a build-up of noxious gases like carbon dioxide. Marc concentrates on the collection unit, knowing someone dedicated their entire career to understanding how gases circulate in the weightless, closed confines of a spacecraft like the *Sycorax*. The design and even the placement of probes like these are the results of decades of research. Although he never knew them, everyone involved was committed to his survival.

Thinking about the build process of the interstellar spacecraft helps calm his nerves. Nothing is haphazard. Everything's designed to preserve life—including the cryo-pods. He and Emma might think of them as glorified coffins, but to the architects and engineers that worked on the design, they're marvels of bio-science.

A sharp pain bites at the crook of his arm. Emma applied some numbing cream when he first climbed in, but the IV line still hurts. This is what he hates most of all—feeling the tubes going into his veins. Cold fluids seep into his arm. He squeezes his hands into a ball.

"Easy," Emma says.

Still, he can't look at her.

"I'm right here," she says. "I'm not going to leave you."

"Bring me back, okay?"

"I will. I promise. I swear, I will."

Marc blinks. His arm feels heavy, which is an unusual sensation in the weightlessness of deep space. The right side of his neck goes numb. He clenches. He's not supposed to fight the process, but he can't help himself. It's the realization that these could be his last conscious moments. He's being lowered into an induced coma from which he may never wake. Fuck.

Fuck. Fuck! *Fuck!*

Through gritted teeth, he says, "I really hate this sh—"

"Oh, thank *Vishnu*," Emma says, cutting him off mid-sentence. Tears well up in her eyes. She leans into the pod and wraps her arms around his shoulders. Her face brushes against his cold cheek. She's warm. She buries her head into his neck. Her arms are trembling. "I—I thought... For a moment, I thought I'd..."

"What?" Marc says, slurring his speech. His lips are numb.

"I thought I'd lost you."

He blinks rapidly, feeling confused. She leans back and sniffs, rubbing her nose with the back of her hand. His vision is narrow, being blurred on the edges, but he can see her dark brown eyes with clarity. There's something different about her. It's her hair. She had it loose before, which in microgravity caused the thin strands to fan out in all directions around her head like a halo. Now, though, she's pulled it back into a ponytail. When did she do that?

"But it's okay," she says, trying not to cry. "You're okay."

"I don't understand," he says as she reaches around his waist and releases the belt holding him in the pod. His body floats free.

"Five months," she says, smiling at him. "We made it! We're here!"

"F—Five? Wait. What? How?" he says, feeling as though his lips are made from rubber. With a limp hand, he points over his shoulder at the lining of the pod behind him, saying, "No. I was just going under. I wasn't under yet."

She laughs. "You were under for four months, twenty-eight days, seven hours and seventeen minutes."

Emma reaches in and helps him out of the pod.

He stumbles through his words. "W—We're here?"

"We're here. We're alive! The burns unfolded perfectly. I was woken by the auxiliary computer within four hours of arriving in the system. The *Sycorax* is currently in orbit around the ice giant with a perigee of eighty thousand kilometers and an apogee of just over a hundred thousand. We're slightly off the plane of her moons, but we're here!"

"Damn," he says, spilling forward out of the cryo-pod. "I—can't—feel."

"Your legs?" she asks.

"Anything," he replies.

She rolls up his sleeve and pushes an injector into his forearm, saying, "Relax. It'll take time for this blocker to kick in."

Marc looks down at the crook of his arm. Emma's already bandaged the wound left by the IV line. His muscles feel stiff but he finds he can push through the lethargy.

"We're... here," he says, feeling a sense of euphoria even though *here* is meaningless. They're nowhere of note. They're nowhere safe. The *Sycorax* is orbiting an ice giant swirling around within the gravity well of a black hole that's hundreds of thousands of times more massive than the Sun. As he blinks, they're burning through their resources with no chance of resupply for the best part of two decades. If they can't mine basic minerals, they're dead. They've lost half of the colonists and almost all the crew, and yet somehow, Marc feels a sense of relief.

Emma powers down the controls within the medical bay, plunging the floor into darkness. Her silhouette drifts into the corridor. Marc follows. Although his legs are numb, he only needs his arms to pull himself along.

Marc's not sure what he's expecting but it isn't the behemoth beyond the cockpit windows. The ice giant is as dark as the Coalsack Nebula. There's no hint of light around the edge of the giant, not like there would be when circling around behind Saturn or Jupiter. The shadow of the massive planet hides most of the star field. Lightning crackles tens of thousands of kilometers below them, lighting up the cloudbanks with brilliant flashes of neon blue and white. An aurora glows over what he assumes is the north pole of the planet, forming a faint green halo that flickers on the edge of his vision.

The dark world is divided into bands of clouds moving at different speeds. Most of the clouds are black, but occasionally white streams billow into view like cream being stirred into coffee. The sheer amount of lightning is astonishing. Jagged bolts tear through the tall cumulus clouds rising from the murky depths. To be visible at this distance, the clouds would have to be hundreds of kilometers high and stretch for thousands of kilometers as they wind their way around the planet. The energy being released with each crackle of light is on par with the detonation of thermonuclear weapons.

"Wow!"

"She's something, ain't she," Emma says.

"Haunting," Marc replies.

"It seems we've made a pact with the devil."

"How so?" he asks.

"Well, we're sheltered here, but only just. Most of the radiation coming off that black hole will be deflected by the ice giant's magnetic field, but this giant's got her own lethal zone. There are belts of radiation half a million clicks out that could fry us to a crisp. It's good luck rather than good management that we avoided them."

Marc says, "Here's hoping our luck holds."

"How do you feel?" Emma asks, offering him a drink pouch.

"Like shit," he says.

"Me too."

Marc pushes back the clip on the straw. He sucks the contents out of the plastic bag. Ice cold orange juice bites at the cracks in his lips, stinging the inside of his mouth, but it's sweet. A sugar hit is welcome, although he'd prefer caffeine.

Emma floats over to the pilot's seat and straps herself in. It's symbolic. She hasn't tightened the straps. If anything, Marc suspects she's trying to embolden herself. With Commander Raddison dead and First Officer Adrian Kozlov in deep sleep and the rest of the crew dead, she's in charge—she's *got* to take charge. Feelings follow convictions. She may not feel like a leader, but she has no choice. Marc's determined to do whatever he can to support her. He drifts over to the navigation console next to her and pulls himself down into the seat.

"What's the plan?"

"We've got a safe harbor," Emma says. "I've sent an update to star base so they'll know we're down here—eventually. I've deployed a navigation buoy to act as a beacon. Now, we have to hunker down and survive. Without that fusion reactor online, we need fuel. Lots of fuel. The scouts have atmospheric reclamation units. If any of these moons hold an atmosphere, we might be able to harvest trace amounts of methane. The odds are, though, we're going to have to mine it from subsurface deposits."

"How much do we need?"

"For the next twenty years? I don't know. All of it?" She turns to him, asking, "Can you bring up the specs on these moons?"

"Sure," he says, not because he can but because he's supposed to be able to perform rudimentary tasks like this. For Emma, this request is a case of delegating so she can think strategically. For him, it's guesswork with a control panel he largely skipped in training.

Marc taps at the smart glass. Thankfully, the controls are intuitive. When he inevitably runs into a dead end, he checks a few of the menus at the top of the screen. It takes what feels like an inordinately long time for him to skim through the various interfaces looking for anything of interest, but Emma doesn't seem to mind. She's content to let him plug away at his screen while she checks system metrics on her console. Even she's slow. Marc sneaks a glance at her workstation. On a couple of occasions, she stares blindly at an almost blank screen. It seems he's not the only one struggling with the enormity of surviving on a crippled spacecraft for twenty years before help arrives. If anyone ever comes for them, it'll be a miracle.

Almost an hour later, Marc says, "There are thirty-four moons in this system."

"Thirty-four," she replies, surprised. He suspects she's equally as surprised by him finally speaking aloud as by the number. For a while there, it seemed as though neither of them would ever speak again. It's the insular proposition of being marooned in space, waiting to die. If just *one* critical system fails—for whatever reason—they could be dead within minutes. Oh, they could make for the scouts and drag things out a little, but those spacecraft are designed for transit hops, not as long-term living quarters, certainly not for years.

He says, "Most of the moons are on highly elliptical orbits, but a few of those in close have more regular orbits."

"Orbital resonance?" she asks.

"Umm," he says, madly flicking through screens. He saw that term on one of the menus. If only he could find it again.

"I'm going to assume: yes," Emma says, reaching out and touching him on the shoulder. There's a look of sympathy in her eyes. "This system has been stable for billions of years. The moons must be in resonance at this point."

"What does that even mean?" he asks, not wanting to sound dumb but taking no pride in his ignorance.

"It's like a kid on a swing," she says. "There's a natural harmony to their motion—a rhythm. There's only one point at which the kid can lean back and swing further forward."

"Ah," he says. To Marc, there's a big difference between a kid at the local park, playing on a swing, and a bunch of moons orbiting a planet, but okay.

"The mutual, gravitational attraction of these moons will cause them to tug and pull on each other," Emma says. "And that will keep them in predictable orbits. It'll cause things like tidal warming."

"And that's good?"

"It's good for us," she says. "It'll mean any ice moons are going to have an ocean beneath their crust and that'll ensure volatiles rotate in cycles and get carried to the surface."

Marc stares at her with a blank look on his face.

Emma simplifies her point. "It'll make mining easier."

"Cool."

"Cold," she says, toying with him. "Dial up the infrared sensor on the scanner. Let's see if any of these moons have subsurface oceans."

Marc knows how to do that. He makes a show of quickly punching in the correct menu commands.

"Hey, look at this one," he says. "The fourth moon."

"Oh, that's good," Emma says. "See those stripes beneath the ice? That's heat coming from an active ocean. And look at how smooth the northern hemisphere is—that can only mean one thing."

"It's a snowball," Marc says, guessing.

"In the very literal sense," she says. "See all these craters in the south? They're absent in the north. That means there's fresh snow in the north. And that means all those nice volatiles like frozen methane are being brought to the surface through geysers and chasms."

"And this rocky region," Marc says, pointing at a spot near the equator. "Look at how it lights up in infrared."

"Huh," Emma says. "It's above freezing. Not by much, but if there's a decent atmosphere down there, we might find liquid water."

"That's good right?"

"It's unexpected," she says, reaching over in front of him and tapping at a few menus. She could have done all this in a matter of seconds instead of leaving him floundering around but it was good learning for him. Marc watches as her fingers tap at various controls. She brings up a histogram showing the heat distribution around the moon.

"That's crazy."

"What's crazy?" he asks.

"Look at the thermal extremes on that moon. The poles are almost three hundred degrees below while the equator is right around zero. In some places, it's a little above. That's one helluva temperature gradient. It's got to cause all kinds of weird atmospheric patterns and stresses on the crust. And that moon's big."

"How big?"

Somewhat naively, Marc looks out the window, hoping to see the moon and make an ill-informed estimate, but it's too dark to see with the naked eye. Emma releases her straps so she can lean over and continue flicking through screens on his console.

"Will you look at that?"

"What?" he asks.

"That fourth moon is somewhere between the size of Titan and Mars."

"That's a damn big moon!"

"Yeah. And she's holding a decent atmosphere. Damn, if we can find liquid water on or near the surface, that's huge."

"Why?" Marc asks.

"Because water is a solvent. If there's water, there are lots of other chemicals just waiting to be extracted. And that mountain range along the equator is geologically active. Let's light her up with radar imaging and see if we can peek below the ice."

Emma reaches in front of him and taps at his screen. Marc watches silently as her eyes dart between his screen and hers as she multitasks.

Emma mumbles, "Getting some good spectroscopy." From the focus on her face, Marc gets the idea she's talking herself through the results.

After a few more minutes, she says, "Well, there's definitely methane locked in the ice near the poles! And not more than a few meters beneath the surface."

"That's great news," he says.

"Yeah," she says, smiling for the first time since the disaster. "I'm also getting readings for nitrogen and oxygen in the air. The pressure's low. Barely 450 mbar."

"But we could breathe it?" Marc asks, surprised by the possibility.

"Maybe. Probably not," Emma says. "It would be like standing on Everest. Perhaps somewhere near base camp. You could breathe the air, but probably not for long. Besides, there could be trace gases down there that reach toxic levels."

"But this is good, right?" Marc says, getting ahead of himself. "We could set up a camp down there. If we can establish a pressurized base, we could ferry survivors to the surface."

"Hold on there, cowboy," Emma says. "We don't have any industrial 3D printers and there are only two of us. Let's walk before we run, okay? If we can mine some methane we can kickstart the turbo-pumps and buy ourselves some time up here. For me, that's a win. Let's just—"

"What's that blinking light?" Marc asks, cutting her off. He points at an LED on the far side of Emma's flight controls.

"No way."

"What?"

Emma says, "It's an active radio contact. Someone's trying to talk to us in real-time on the Ka-band."

"But that's impossible," Marc says. "There's no one out here."

"There's no one within twenty light-years of us," Emma replies.

Marc holds his hands out wide. "So someone's calling us? Are you going to answer?"

"Um, ah. Yes."

Emma flicks a toggle switch on the emergency flight control console and a voice cuts in mid-sentence. The signal is weak. The automatic booster circuit makes the voice sound electronic, as though it were spoken by a robot rather than a human. The message, though, is clear.

"—no landing. Altair IV is under quarantine."

Quarantine

"What the hell?" Emma says, flicking a few more antiquated switches left over from the shakeout test flights. She turns to Marc saying, "Trace that signal!"

"On it!"

Marc has no idea how to trace a radio signal. What does that even mean? It's not like a piece of yarn the cat's playing with that leads back to the kitchen. Or is it? He flicks through menu options, looking for something useful.

Emma slips on a wireless headpiece and positions the microphone next to her mouth. A green light on the tip of the mic indicates she's transmitting.

"Altair IV, this is the *Sycorax*. We are a colony ship outbound from the Westminster Star Base to New Haven. Come in. Over."

"Sycorax, this is the Altair IV research station. Attempt no landing. Repeat. Attempt no landing. Altair IV is under quarantine."

Emma speaks slowly, enunciating her words with care. "Altair IV. The *Sycorax* is crippled. We have lost warp function. Our fusion drive is down. We have sustained mass casualties. We are in need of assistance. Over."

"Sycorax. Altair IV is unable to provide assistance. Attempt no landing. Altair IV is under strict quarantine. No physical contact is possible."

Emma pushes a button on the console and the LED on her mic

switches to red. She turns to Marc, saying, "What an asshole!"

She breathes deeply, steeling herself, and then hits transmit again, saying, "Negative, Altair IV. This is an SOS. The *Sycorax* is declaring a class one emergency. In accordance with the Interstellar Convention on Celestial Safety, the *Sycorax* requests immediate assistance to prevent the loss of life and vessel. Mayday. Mayday. *M'aidez. M'aidez.* We are in distress and unable to continue."

There's silence for a few seconds.

"*Sycorax. Understood and acknowledged. The Sycorax is in distress but Altair IV is unable to provide assistance. No landing is possible. In-orbit resupply is not possible. Altair IV recommends the Sycorax explores Altair VII for raw materials. Over.*"

Emma grits her teeth.

"I don't get it," Marc says. "How did he even know we were up here?"

Emma turns off her mic, saying, "Our radar burst must have pinged a radio telescope or something. He's probably been monitoring us for a while, wondering what we were up to. Once we started mapping that moon, he realized we were serious about going down there."

"So what are we going to do?"

Emma is frustrated. She slaps her hand on the control panel, saying, "I don't get it. Sure, we can mine another moon, but he's right there! We thought we were alone, but we're not. Methane and oxygen would be nice, but what we really need is working electronics. If he's out here on his own, he's got to have spare parts—a lot of spares in case of an emergency."

"Like this," Marc says.

Emma hits transmit again, pleading with him. "Altair IV. We need your help!"

"*Negative, Sycorax,*" the man replies. Emma mocks him on the other end of the radio. The red light on the tip of her microphone reveals she's no longer transmitting. She speaks in perfect unison with him, saying, "*Attempt no landing. Altair IV is under quarantine.*"

Reluctantly, she concedes, switching to transmit and saying, "Copy that." She sighs, adding, "*Sycorax* will conduct mining operations on one of the other moons. Over."

"*Altair IV. Over and out.*"

Emma says. "*Sycorax* out."

She turns back to Marc, asking, "Did you find him?"

"Oh yeah." Marc points at a high-resolution image of the fourth moon. "Right here. In that temperate region near the equator. He's nestled into the side of the mountains."

"Nice," she says, nodding.

Oh, what Marc would give to be able to read her mind. He knows her well enough to realize there's no way in hell she's honoring some nebulous concept of a quarantine when the *Sycorax* is dying. He wants to know what she's thinking. There are no known exploration craft or settlements within at least fifteen to twenty light years of them. How the hell is there one here? Who is this guy? Where did he come from? Who else is down there? What is so damn bad that the entire moon needs to be under quarantine? And what the hell is he doing here in the first place? Why is he orbiting an ice giant that's trapped inside the gravitational well of a goddamn black hole? How did he even find this place?

"So what now?" he asks. "We check out some of those other moons?"

"Hell, no," Emma says. "He's lying."

"He's lying? About the quarantine?"

"I can't see how a quarantined base on the equator prevents us from mining methane near the poles. Can you? No, leaving a crippled craft in orbit around an ice giant is a big *fuck you!*"

Marc raises an eyebrow. Even when she's under pressure, Emma tends to use Hindi terms from her childhood in Hyderabad, India. He can count the number of times she's used western profanity on one hand.

"What are we going to do?"

Emma unlocks her seat restraints. "Well, we're not staying up here."

"You're going down there?" Marc asks, raising his eyebrows.

"We," Emma replies, grinning. "Not me."

"Ah, shouldn't one of us stay with the *Sycorax*?"

"Technically, yes. But two of us can get through twice the work on the surface. And, as it is, we need to deploy atmospheric concentrators, robotic miners and a portable refiner. That's a lot of work for one person."

"But what if something goes wrong up here?" he asks.

Without hesitation, Emma says, "Everyone dies."

There's silence between them for a moment. When Marc doesn't speak, Emma says, "Regardless of whether we're here or down there, if the main power bus fails or the battery cells fuse, we're going to lose everyone. The best thing we can do is uplift our energy reserves as soon as possible. Then we can start running redundant systems. If we can replenish our fuel reserves from that moon, we stand a fighting chance up here. If we can talk him out of some spare circuit boards, we might even get the core back up and running."

"But the quarantine?"

"You didn't buy that crap, did you? I mean, seriously. We have spacesuits. What's getting through them? I'll tell you what: *nothing*. And the airlock on the scout has an atmospheric decontamination unit. Nah, he's lying."

Marc's confused. "Why would he lie?"

"That," she says, waving her finger at him. "That's the question. That's what I want to find out. We've got three hours before we swing back around near Altair IV again. That's enough time to prep a scout."

Emma heads into the darkened corridor. She has a handheld light to ward off the shadows. Marc follows her, pushing off the hull and drifting along a few meters behind her. Black screens and idle workstations line the route.

"We can be there and back in about six to eight hours," Emma says as he trails along in her wake. "And with a full load of fuel."

"Ah-huh," is all he can say in response.

"And maybe, just maybe, we can convince him to give us a server rack to cannibalize for electronic parts."

One of the criticisms Marc had from his trainers back in the spaceflight academy was that he was a follower rather than a leader. At the time, it annoyed the *fuck* out of him. Why is following such a bad trait? If everyone's leading then no one's going anywhere as everyone's going in different directions. To him, clashes between cadet leaders always seemed to amount to arrogance rather than substance. Marc wanted no part of their pissing contests, but somehow it was his attitude the trainers found problematic. Somewhat ironically, his temperament excluded him from a leadership role. His contention was that those who didn't want to lead were actually better suited to leading others because they weren't driven by ego, but his instructors disagreed. Now, though, he's gaining a glimpse into what they struggled to describe to him back then: Emma's leading with conviction. He's following along behind her, but is it blind obedience? He thinks not. To him, it's measured.

Marc doesn't agree with Emma's decision to leave the *Sycorax* without anyone conscious at the helm. He wants to debate the idea with her but he won't. To be fair, she probably wouldn't dismiss his concerns out of hand. She's reasonable rather than prideful, but he already knows the outcome of any discussion: *there are no other viable options!* For him, this is the leadership conundrum. No one has a crystal ball. Confident leaders make decisions as though they can see the future when they can't. They're guessing. Emma's guessing. It's an educated guess, but a guess nonetheless. There are a million things that could go wrong down there. But she's right. There are a million things that could go wrong up here. The difference is what they stand to gain by going down to that moon. Up here, things can only get worse. Nothing is going to get better of its own accord. As much as he might dislike her approach, she's correct. This is their best option.

Drifting along in silence, it seems both of them are preoccupied with a future neither can predict. If they knew what was about to unfold they could make good decisions. For now, there are just decisions. They're neither good nor bad—yet.

Marc hopes Emma's right. That she's decisive is beyond question. His personal default is to fall on the side of inaction and lean on the status quo, but he's aware that's a blind spot in his thinking. He'd like to think his instructors were wrong about him being passive. They said he had a propensity to blindly follow the most dominant personality. He thinks that's bullshit. Right now, he's following someone he trusts, someone he believes is competent. Regardless of what happens next, he'll do everything he can to help her succeed. He'll support Emma as the ranking officer—even though he anesthetized the last, highest-ranking officer. If the two of them get stuck on that moon, everyone up here dies. But what difference would staying here make? If critical systems fail, they'll all die anyway. At least down there, he can help improve the odds.

"Are you okay?" Emma asks as they drift into the mechanical bay above the engines.

"Fine."

Through the grates in the ceiling of engineering, Marc can see the recycling tanks where this nightmare began. From where he is now, the bio-tanks appear as little more than long shadows above them, but he's glad the two of them were in there when this whole mess unfolded. If anything, it puts lie to the notion that he's always a follower. *Emma followed him in there!* He told her he needed to check the tanks and, like a good leader, she listened and followed when it was appropriate. And he was right. In between looking for moons, he checked the analysis of those samples registered before the storm hit. The number four tank was experiencing a fecal bloom when they sailed through that tempest. He has no idea how those microbes fared, but with roughly half of the passengers dying, they won't get fed nearly as much.

Emma senses he's distracted. "Are you sure?"

"I'm all good," Marc says, knowing she's giving him an opening to voice any concerns he may have. "Let's do this."

Marc's not following so much as kickstarting himself into action. If they're to survive, it's going to take some grit. Keeping the nav lights on in the cockpit isn't going to sustain the surviving colonists for years to come.

The air within mechanical is frigid. Vapor forms with each breath. As Emma has on each of the other decks, she opens an access panel and manually powers up the bay. Lights flicker overhead. While she's doing that, Marc drifts between the three scouts, checking their readiness.

The scouts are mounted on the outside of the interstellar spacecraft, being evenly spaced around the hull above the engines. The outer hatch on each scout acts as an internal entry point on the *Sycorax*. To the untrained eye, it looks like there's a short corridor leading to each of the shuttlecraft, but the corridor isn't part of the *Sycorax* itself. Once they're ready to depart, a metal panel on the bulkhead will slide into place and the hatch on the scout will close from the inside.

Marc says, "Two has full tanks and 80% charge. One and three are both lower but their preflight checks are all in the green."

"Two it is then," Emma says, still working with settings in the mechanical bay. Marc notices her checking the warp core panel.

"Bad, huh?"

"We're not going anywhere without a new fusion drive."

Marc loads up the cargo hold on the scout with equipment. Working with heavy items in a weightless environment is something he loves. Although there's no weight as such, the crates of equipment still have mass, though, which means they take effort to move. The difference is once they're in motion they can be guided on their journey through the bay with a deft touch. Stopping them takes as much muscle as getting them started.

Marc plants his feet under a rail to get some leverage on a crate that, on Earth, would weigh in at over three hundred pounds. In space, it's weightless but still awkward to work with. He lines up a path across mechanical and through the airlock on the scout. With a shove, it's on its way. He then pushes off the hull and glides next to it, drifting slowly in front of the crate. He beats it to the inner hatch. Once on the other side, it's a case of anchoring his feet and using his hands to act as a cushion, absorbing the crate's momentum and bringing it to a halt. It's work, but it sure is fun.

It takes an hour to fill the hold with equipment originally destined for the colony. During that time, Emma barely moves. Marc is quiet, giving her the opportunity to concentrate as she reviews flight logs and looks at the monitoring data for the engines on the *Sycorax*, the warp core and the fusion drive.

"Can you do preflight on the scout?" she asks as he finishes stowing the equipment.

"Sure," he says. Flying scouts is something Marc loves. Out of all the training sessions he went through, racing around in a scout was his favorite. As the scouts are lifeboats, everyone on the crew had to be rated for orbital flight as well as atmospheric flight. The scout has wings that deploy from within the hull. It handles like a brick, but it does get some lift, making it fun to fly even if only for short hops.

He starts going through the checklist on the main screen within the scout. Emma's just outside the airlock, still in engineering. He catches a glimpse of her checking out the configuration of the other two scouts. Does she doubt his assessment? She's looking at their flight controls. Rather than get offended, he finishes and gets bored. Before long, Marc finds himself up against the windows on the scout waiting for her to come onboard. He looks out at the stars.

"What are you looking for?" Emma asks, finally coming up beside him as he stares out of the cockpit on the scout.

"A monster."

"The black hole?" she asks.

He nods.

Emma drifts over next to him. She leans forward, looking at the star field along with the imposing shadow of the gaseous ice giant they're orbiting. Altair is off to their right. If it picked up a little more starlight, it would probably look like a cross between Jupiter and Neptune.

"Out there," she says, pointing. In the low light, Marc can see a smattering of stars as tiny pinpricks of white but they're all well beyond the reach of this rogue system. "It's tiny. Well, it's massive in terms of gravity, but at this distance, it's impossible to spot."

"Can't we see it?" Marc asks. "I thought we'd see it distort the stars behind it."

"With a telescope, you could see that," Emma replies. "But not with the naked eye."

"So it's a ghost."

"Kind of," Emma says, pulling herself down into the cockpit seat. "A really dense ghost distorting spacetime around it. I mean, it's astonishing when you think about it. Black holes are small but their gravitational reach is massive."

Marc straps himself into the copilot's seat.

"Do you think we'll ever understand it?" he asks.

"Black holes?"

"Gravity," he says.

Emma says, "Yeah, it's crazy, huh? It's insane to think there's a star or a black hole or an ice giant out there, hundreds of thousands or even millions of miles away from us, and yet it can reach through the empty void of space and grab us."

Marc laughs. "Now it really does sound like a ghost."

Act II

The Island

Strangers

Miranda is distracted. She mumbles to herself, "They're coming."

If her father hears her, he doesn't respond.

Somehow, she feels the presence of the strangers long before their spacecraft has entered the atmosphere. She's not sure why, but her heart races. Sitting in the basement workshop opposite her father, she feels her pulse flutter in her neck. Sweat breaks out on her brow. Her hands feel clammy. She flexes her fingers beneath the desk.

"Is everything okay?"

Her father may speak those words, but he doesn't mean them. He's too focused on the interface with the crystalline access port rising from the workshop floor. Miranda doesn't understand much about the alien technology scattered around the basement. All she knows is her father is obsessed with it. He barely looks up from the dense bundle of wires he's working with. He's tracing a fault in the human interface. Flashes of light flicker on the other side of a pod as a robotic assistant welds a panel in place. The mismatch of technologies is apparent. Anything human has wires and circuit boards and panels while the alien machine shimmers like jewelry under the lights. Only the upper portion of the alien tech is visible, with most of it being buried. It seems to rise out of the ground like an iceberg. In the far corner of the basement, a few lone crystal stalagmites have pierced the floor. These are new, having risen only in the past few days. To Miranda, the alien machine seems alive.

Seeing he's distracted, she says, "I might just—umm."

"Sure," he says, peering through the binocular lens of a scanning electron microscope on a nearby workbench. He's examining a router point. "Can you hand me the interferometer? These fiber optic links haven't been calibrated in over a decade."

Her father reaches back behind himself with an outstretched hand. Miranda picks up a clunky device with a rubberized handle and slips it into his palm.

"Thanks."

She backs away, stepping lightly on the concrete floor within the mechanical workshop. At no point does she turn her back on her father. It's silly, but she's anxious. She feels as though she has to keep this secret from him or he'll get angry.

Miranda takes the stairs back to the first floor. A vast dome encases her home. It's set on a mountainside, providing a view of the canyon that meanders to a broad open plain.

"Do you need something?" a woman's voice asks from the living room. Beyond the dome, out above the surface of the moon, the stars glisten like diamonds.

Ariel floats several feet above the polished granite floor. Normally, she remains invisible. That she's materialized is unusual. She too must feel the change coming. For Miranda, it's like static in the air as a storm rolls in.

"My father needs help," she says to the ethereal, ghostly woman.

Ariel drifts toward the stairs. She's capable of taking any form she wishes and often assumes the avatar of a slim woman in her twenties. She seems troubled. Her shape shimmers and changes. She takes her most rudimentary form. Miranda's only ever seen her like this once before.

A glowing ball of plasma floats through the air, soaring past Miranda, lighting up her facial features. There's no radiant heat, but the surface of this mini-star is a raging furnace. Currents swirl across the golden globe, forming convective cells that merge and fade, being consumed by more cells welling up from beneath. To her, they appear like the stippled surface of an orange or perhaps a basketball, only they're constantly on the move, changing their shape and position. Often, they clump together for a few seconds, forming basic geometric shapes like the rough outline of a pentagram or a hexagon. Blink and they're gone. Ariel is a spherical kaleidoscope of seemingly random interactions that mirror each other.

How Ariel speaks is beyond Miranda. Her ability to synthesize basic items like food out of thin air is almost magical. *"Krell science,"* that's what her father calls it, but Miranda's never quite sure. Is Ariel alive? Her father describes her as a sentinel, an alien robot, but Miranda's not so sure. After all these years, she's afraid to ask Ariel herself. Personally, she prefers it when Ariel is incorporeal.

Miranda stands at the top of the stairs watching as the ghostly ball of plasma floats down to the basement, lighting up the cracks and rocks in the unfinished walls. The glow fades as Ariel drifts into the vast subterranean mechanical bay.

Miranda turns and runs out the front door of her home. She sprints down along the tunnel out onto the rocky ground, leaving the protective glass dome behind her.

Gravel crunches beneath her boots. Her eyes struggle to adjust to the darkness. A mist has formed over the ground, hiding sharp rocks from sight, but Miranda knows where each one lies. She's played here since she was a child. She follows a path toward the distant plateau. It winds along the edge of the rocks above the honeycomb of caves leading to the subterranean ocean of Altair IV.

Beneath the cliff, waves crash on fallen boulders as the tide surges within the canyon. Once she reaches the plateau, the night creatures appear. The fog clears. Sparkles of blue light glow at the tips of the glass grass growing out of the plain. Iridescent blue fireflies drift over the fields, blinking in and out of existence once more. If only life itself was cyclical like that, but no, she has only one life in which to shine. And Miranda wants to shine brightly.

Now she's clear of the mountain, she turns and looks back. She can't explain why, but she knows someone's coming for them—for her. Off to one side, out above the ridge, a stream of light cuts through the night. A fiery yellow streak blazes through the thin, high-altitude clouds, causing them to part. Miranda watches in awe as the spacecraft turns back towards her instead of rushing out over the plateau and into the distance.

She mumbles, "They know we're here."

The spaceship is still little more than a speck of light high in the sky but Miranda can already distinguish between its glowing heat shield and the sporadic kick of its engines as it fights to shed its orbital speed.

The craft undergoes a series of turns as it loses altitude. A sonic boom rattles her bones, causing her to wince and shrink. In unison, the fireflies disappear. Darkness descends for the best part of a mile. It takes another minute or so before the glow of alien flora and fauna returns to the moon. Once again, these mute animals flicker in the darkness.

Miranda continues on to the plateau. She watches as the spacecraft circles out wide. It has deployed glide wings, allowing it to bank as it comes in. Tiny lights on the wingtips reveal the breadth of the craft. As it approaches, a set of brilliant landing lights come on, bathing the rocks in a blinding white light.

The craft pitches up at the last moment, exposing its underbelly and flaring its wings as its engines fire, slowing it. Landing gear extends beneath the fuselage like the talons of an eagle. Large pads unfold into mechanical feet. Miranda can see the crew in the cockpit. They're busy. They're looking at their controls rather than the surface of the moon, trusting in their instruments more than their eyes.

A cloud of dust is kicked up as the spacecraft lands in between the old huts used by the original science team from the *Copernicus* decades ago. Miranda shelters from the artificial storm, crouching behind a boulder.

Like a deep-sea submersible, floodlights surround the craft on all sides, lighting up the landing zone. A ramp lowers from an airlock beneath the cockpit but the hatch remains closed.

"You knew," a voice says from beside her.

"Ariel?" Miranda says, replying to the darkness. The fiery ball of plasma consuming itself has been replaced by a tiny speck of dust no larger than one of the fireflies. Like the creatures that inhabit this moon, it glows in a soft, neon blue, drifting beside Miranda's shoulder. For a moment, Ariel is Tinker Bell.

"How did you know?" Ariel asks her.

"I don't know. I just did."

Miranda was there on the top floor laboratory within the dome when her father spoke to the crew of the *Sycorax*. She could hear the frustration in the woman's voice on the other end of the radio call. Her father was stern. He's used to getting his way. He thinks he can huff and bluff and bully and command anyone and everything to bow to his will, but Miranda could hear the defiance in the woman's final few words. As she signed off, it was apparent she was going to ignore him. And why wouldn't she? Why would she listen to Miranda's father? If she's telling the truth and her spacecraft is in trouble, she'd be desperate—and desperation demands defiance when obedience would be cowardice. From that moment on, Miranda has been watching and waiting.

White steam hisses from around the hatch at the top of the ramp. The airlock opens, revealing two astronauts in spacesuits. They walk slowly down the incline. Even though the gravity on Altair IV is gentle compared to Earth's oppressive one gee, they watch their footing. Big, clumsy boots step off onto the gravel.

"What is this place?" the woman asks, looking around. She walks out in front of the spacecraft. The spotlights on the side of her helmet ripple over the abandoned huts.

"Looks derelict," the man says, walking over and using his gloved hand to push aside a torn curtain in a broken window. He peers into the abandoned lab, looking through the cracks in the shattered glass. "But there's someone down here, right?"

"I guess," the woman says. She pauses. "I don't like the look of this."

Miranda listens from behind a boulder. She peers around the jagged edge, watching the astronauts from the darkness out on the fringe of the spotlights. She's never seen astronauts before. They look tiny inside the curved glass domes of their helmets. Their suits are big and bulky. Multiple layers of fabric wrap around their arms, shoulders and legs. Their boots are three sizes too big and their gloves make their fingers look swollen. Their arms are bloated. They have computers wrapped around their forearms. Miranda's clothing is simple by comparison. She's wearing a jumpsuit designed by Ariel. The phase-change material is as thick as her thumb, trapping warm air next to her body and insulating her from the cold. She has gloves and boots, but they're nowhere near as cumbersome as the astronauts in their suits. The breeze chills her cheeks, but she's used to the cold.

"This stuff is old," the woman says, resting her gloved hand on the side of a rundown laboratory and examining a broken control panel. "This place was abandoned a long time ago."

The man replies, "Doesn't inspire confidence, huh?"

The two astronauts are talking to each other through microphones in their helmets. To Miranda, their voices sound muffled. The wind, though, has died down, allowing her to pick up on their conversation. The two astronauts turn away from her. As they examine a doorway leading into one of the habitats, their voices become indistinct. It's only when they face her again that she can hear them.

"What the hell happened here?" the man says, turning to face the woman. If his eyes were adjusted to the light, he'd probably be able to see Miranda crouching by the boulder, but he misses her entirely.

The inside of the lab looks as though it has been ransacked. Chairs lie on their sides. Broken glass litters the floor. The structure is little more than a shipping container raised up on steel legs. A set of stairs leads to the open door.

"Are you seeing what I'm seeing?" the man asks.

"What are you seeing?" the woman asks as the man leans

forward, pushing the door open further. The lights on his helmet sweep across the floor. Broken computer displays, test tubes and microscopes lie scattered on the linoleum.

Miranda is fascinated by their discussion. They see the same things she's seen since childhood, but they see them in an entirely different light. For her, these labs were somewhere to explore and play, even though her father told her not to. She wondered about the scientists that worked here, but she simply accepted they were gone without asking why. Now she finds herself intrigued by their absence. Like the astronauts, she wants to know what happened to them. Oh, she knows the broad strokes about the *Copernicus* crashing on the northern slopes, but who were they? Why did they come here? Why did they leave? Why was it only her family stayed behind? Were it not for that decision, like them, she would be dead. She's interested to see the labs in a new light, through the eyes of these explorers.

The man says, "A complete lack of biocontrols. Where are the entryway decontamination showers? Why aren't there HVAC HEPA filtration systems attached to each of these huts? Why don't these dwellings have double-glazed windows with hermetic seals? These labs should have been protected with an isolated positive-pressure purified air supply to keep contaminants out."

"It's like they didn't care," the woman says.

"It's a serious oversight for a scientific mission."

The woman turns away, looking out across the spiky sea of glass grass beyond the landing site, saying, "Well, they are dead."

"Not all of them," the man says. "We spoke to someone down here. Someone's alive."

The woman holds up her wrist in front of her. With her other, gloved hand, she taps at a series of controls. A metal crate mounted on treads comes rolling down the ramp.

"Setting up the methane extractors," she says.

"I'm going to look around," the man says.

"Don't stray from line of sight."

"Copy that."

The man moves with a gentle lope, working his way down the slope leading away from the landing zone. Even though he's in low gravity, his suit makes his motion awkward. He bunnyhops, scuffing the ground with his boots. Clouds of microbes spring to life, glowing around his legs as they slowly settle back to the rocks. The lights on his helmet blot out the subtle effect, but he seems to notice something. He comes to a halt and fiddles with the controls on his wrist.

Miranda watches as he stands near her mother's grave.

From out of the darkness, Ariel says, "You should tell your father."

"No," Miranda whispers in sharp reply.

"He needs to know."

"You shouldn't have followed me out here."

"What are you going to do?" Ariel asks.

"What you always do," Miranda says. "Watch."

With that, Ariel falls silent.

The astronaut turns off his lights. As he's out on the fringe of the spotlights cast by the spacecraft, he appears as little more than a silhouette. The other astronaut seems to recognize the change in an instant. She reacts with horror, speaking as though something has gone horribly wrong.

"Marc? MARC!"

"I'm here," he replies.

"Where?"

She turns, scanning the area. Panicked, the woman rushes forward, but unlike Miranda, she's not accustomed to moving around in low gravity. She fails to lean forward, probably because it feels unnatural. Running on Altair IV is akin to a controlled fall. Whereas in one gee, runners lean forward at an angle of about 10 degrees, on Altair IV it's closer to 45 degrees. It's the only way to get any traction.

"Marc," Miranda whispers from behind the rock, repeating his name to herself. She instinctively wants to learn all she can about him.

Miranda wants to get closer to Marc. She crouches in what amounts to a sprinter's starting position at the Olympics. Instead of pushing up and off the blocks, she pushes long and low, scrambling over to another boulder. Miranda needs to remain near him if she wants to hear their conversation.

To the uninitiated, scooting around on Altair IV is unnerving. The other astronaut is also moving out of the spotlights, but she's clumsy. She pushes off the ground instead of along it. Although she's scrambling to make headway, she doesn't travel very far. Instead, she floats in midair with her feet swinging, searching for the rocks below her. Slowly, she settles only to push off again as she tries to rush on.

"I hate this moon," the woman says. The harder she tries, the slower she goes. The low gravity conspires to thwart her efforts, leaving her bouncing on the tip of her boots.

"Come on, Emma," Marc says. "This was your idea."

Miranda comes up behind the cluster of rocks near her mother's grave.

"Emma," she whispers, fascinated by the names of these interlopers on her icy world. She's close. She's so close to Marc that she could reach out and touch the backpack on his bulky suit. She's tempted to just for fun, just to see if she can get away with it without him noticing. Her fingers twitch, urging her on.

"Turn on your lights," Emma says.

"No," he replies. "Turn yours off."

"What?" she asks, but she does as he suggests.

"Look!"

Marc leans forward, dropping awkwardly down onto a thick, padded knee. He scoops up a handful of gravel. It's difficult for him to stand. He almost topples over, but he turns to Emma, showing her the grit and stones held in his thick gloves.

"I don't get it," she says, hidden safely behind her glass visor.

"Watch," he replies, turning his wrist over and scattering the dirt

111

in front of him. Tiny flecks of light fall from his fingers like glitter.

"What is that?"

"Life," he says. "This moon has some kind of bioluminescent microbial life. It springs into action when disturbed."

He kicks his boots, scuffing them against the rocks and ice. Pebbles scatter. At the point where the debris lands, the soil lights up in blue specks.

Emma laughs. She repeats his uncontrolled experiment, giggling as tens of thousands of bioluminescent microbes packed within a tiny patch of soil respond to her stimulus. Life glistens around her, just outside the reach of the spotlights on the spacecraft.

"This is wonderful," she says, smiling within her bulky helmet. "What a delight!"

"I know, right? Who would have thought life could arise in a system dominated by a goddamn black hole!"

"How is this possible?" Emma asks. "I mean, there's no star. Surely, you need a star to provide energy."

Marc says, "All life requires energy, but here on Altair IV, it's not coming from sunlight. Perhaps it's tapping into the tidal friction warming the subsurface oceans. Or maybe these are chemotrophs or radiotrophs. I'm not sure, but they're alive. I need to take samples back to the *Sycorax*. I really want to examine these things under a microscope."

Emma says, "Well, this explains why they set up a research station."

"But why did they abandon it?" Marc asks.

"Dunno."

"And why haven't we heard about this place?"

"Dunno."

"And what about the quarantine?"

Emma shakes her head, asking, "And where did everyone go?"

Marc turns to a pile of large rocks lying before a headstone, saying, "Look. Not everyone made it out of here alive."

Emma notices the bouquet of flowers lying on the loose gravel beside the grave. The exhaust from their spacecraft blew them off the rocks. It takes her considerable effort to grab them, but she persists, crouching as she reaches down to pick them up.

Marc brushes his hand against the headstone. He mumbles, reading the words carved into the rock.

I love you.

I will never forget you.

"Someone died here," he says.

"And yet someone's alive down here," Emma says, placing the flowers back on the grave. She lays the bouquet with a sense of reverence and respect. She ensures the stems point toward the foot of the grave while the flowers brush up lightly against the tombstone.

Miranda steps out from behind a nearby boulder. As the astronauts are facing the grave, they have their backs to her. She speaks with a loud, clear voice.

"She was my mother."

The two astronauts spin around to face Miranda. Emma looks like she's seen a ghost. She lights into the air as she jumps in fright. It takes her almost a second to drift back to the rocky surface of the moon. Marc crouches slightly with his arms in front of him, wanting to keep Miranda at bay. He shuffles backward.

"W—Who are you?" Emma asks.

"Why aren't you wearing protective gear?" Marc asks.

"They won't hurt you," Miranda says, gesturing with her long spindly arms. She points at the sea of glass grass and a million glowing tips fading in the distance. It's only now the astronauts have had time for their eyes to adjust to the darkness that they can see the faint specks of light stretching over the field.

Fireflies flash as they dance through the air. A couple of floating deer munch on the sharp tips of the glass over by a rocky outcrop. They're not more than fifty yards away, being held aloft by dozens of overlapping blisters forming flotation bladders on their backs. To the human eye, it's a hideous deformation. To evolution, it's efficient and effective.

Emma keeps her distance from Miranda.

Marc steps closer, asking, "What's your name? Where did you come from?"

"I'm Miranda. My name means *marvelous, wonderful, wonderous.* And I didn't come from anywhere. This is my home. Those are my flowers."

"No, no, no," he says. He's in shock. He mumbles to himself rather than talking to either Miranda or Emma. "This is an active zeno-biosphere. She should be dead."

"I'm fine," Miranda says, trying to put his mind at ease.

"You don't understand," Marc replies. "Regardless of how benign or compatible this ecosystem may be, even the slightest deviation at a cellular level could cause all kinds of complications and unintended toxicity."

Emma ignores Marc's comment, asking Miranda, "And you live here?"

Miranda nods.

Marc is still mumbling to himself. "Hell, even on Earth there are plenty of lethal environments, like algae blooms in rivers."

Miranda holds out her hand as a firefly drifts past, blinking in and out of the darkness. The tiny insect lands on her outstretched fingers.

"They're cute," she says.

Marc points at it, saying, "On Earth, cute is often lethal. The blue-ringed octopus is cute. It's pretty. It's the size of a toy in a Happy Meal. And its bite is painless. Its toxin doesn't even hurt, but it'll kill you within minutes."

Miranda laughs. "What kind of meal is happy?"

"You're missing the point," Marc says, but Miranda is undeterred in her enthusiasm.

"Welcome to Altair IV," she says.

"Your father," Emma says from behind her sealed visor. "Is he the one that spoke to us over the radio?"

"Yes."

Marc is worried. "He said this moon was under quarantine. Why?"

Miranda looks at the lightning rippling through the clouds beyond the spacecraft. She speaks with a sense of urgency, saying, "Because of Caliban."

Caliban

"What happened to your mother?" Emma asks, looking down at the grave.

To Miranda the answer is obvious. "She died."

Even within the confines of her helmet, Emma's concern for Miranda is apparent. It's the way her head tilts, the tenderness in her eyes, the soft tone of her voice.

"I know. I'm sorry. Can you tell us what happened here? Can you tell me what happened to your mother? What happened to the rest of the crew?"

"You shouldn't have come here," Miranda says. "Caliban won't be happy."

"Caliban did this?" Emma asks, pointing toward the decimated labs.

Miranda nods.

"The storm?" Marc asks, following Miranda's gaze out over the hills. Were it not for the lightning crackling within the clouds, the astronauts would have no idea how close the storm was or how large it has become. In the darkness, it's imposing.

"We should go," Miranda says. "You should turn off your lights."

"Where is your father?" Marc asks.

"I'll take you to him," Miranda replies. "But you must turn off your lights. All of them."

Marc and Emma look at each other.

"Do you believe her?" he asks.

"It doesn't matter what I believe," Emma replies. "That storm is about to hit."

"And?"

"Do as she says. Kill the lights on the scout. I'll power down the methane extractors. The last thing we need is an electrical strike frying the circuits."

"Understood," Marc says, bounding over the rough terrain. He hops along, kicking up dust in front of him.

He's slow.

Miranda runs alongside him.

"Lean into your stride," she says. "Stay low. Don't bounce. You'll go faster."

"Thanks," he says, but he still seems unsure of himself. It seems he's far too conscious of falling, but what is running other than a controlled fall where you constantly catch yourself? To Miranda, running is tumbling forward while never hitting the ground.

Miranda says, "Trust me. Long strides. Lunges."

To his credit, Marc takes her advice. He copies her stride. Regardless of his thick suit material and bulky backpack, his pace doubles as he leans into his run.

"Nice," he says, waving as she peels away, leaving him to rush up the ramp and into the airlock on the spaceship.

Marc stands at the top of the ramp, tapping his thick gloved fingers at a control panel on the outside of the ship. As the storm is approaching, he yells within his suit. Miranda only catches some of his words.

"—remote access enabled—power down—wake cycle on—"

The wind whips across the plain, making it difficult to hear anything beyond the howl of the storm. Dust curls around the legs of the spacecraft and through the huts. Out beyond the spotlights, the storm is descending on the hills, hiding them from sight.

A tiny speck of light glows beside Miranda's shoulder, but it's not a firefly.

"We need to go," Ariel says. "Now!"

"You go," Miranda says, standing beside one of the methane extractors. "I'm not leaving them."

"You should."

Emma moves between the extractors, powering them down. Like Marc, even though she has a radio, she's yelling to be heard above the thunder rumbling through the air.

"—cycle—confirmed. Wake on remote access enabled. I'm gonna—"

Six crates were offloaded on robotic treads. They unfolded into miniature factories with inflatable bladders to hold the captured gas. The flat side panels that lay on the ground now fold back up, protecting the equipment from the storm.

Ariel speaks to Miranda. "You must go. I can't protect all of you out here."

"They don't know the way," Miranda replies. "They could get lost in the storm."

"Who are you talking to?" Emma asks as she turns one of the devices off. The tiny LED lights on the control panel fade as the components retract.

Miranda ignores her, saying, "We need to hurry."

"To where?"

"My home," she replies, pointing along the narrow stretch of land leading from the plateau to the mountains. The track passes under a cliff. Waves crash on the rocks roughly a hundred meters below the ledge. Spray hangs in the air, slowly settling into the honeycomb of caves that wind their way beneath the crust of the planet.

The lights on the scout die. Marc appears back at the top of the ramp. He drops over the side, falling to the rocks not more than ten meters from the two of them. In the light gravity, he lands gracefully. Both of the astronauts have activated the lights on the side of their helmets.

"You need to turn those off," Miranda says, leading them toward the hillside.

Neither of them hesitates. Marc, though, grumbles. "I don't like this."

Miranda says, "Once your eyes adjust to the dark, you'll be fine."

Sleet comes down in waves, washing over them. Miranda takes Emma's gloved hand, while Marc rests his hand on Emma's backpack, following along behind her.

The wind drives hard across the field. Shards of glass break off the grass. The needle-like splinters are picked up by the storm. They're driven across the plateau like hail. As the storm is coming from behind them and slightly to one side, Marc takes the brunt of the debris. Glass embeds itself in his backpack. Tiny bits tear through the cloth on his arms and legs, but it's only the outer layer that's breached. Thin lines streak along the side of his helmet, scratching the surface of his visor.

Miranda screams at the storm, yelling, "*Cali—bannnn!*"

Thunder rumbles through the air. Lightning crashes around them, striking the edge of the cliff in fury. Boulders are dislodged. In slow motion, they tumble down, striking the path around them.

Miranda calls over the raging tempest, "Ariel, I need you!"

In response, an eerie yellow glow forms in the air, but it's only on the windward side of Miranda.

"Wait," Emma says, slowing her pace and dragging Miranda to a halt. "What is this?"

Hundreds of glass shards vaporize not more than ten feet away from them. The tiny flecks soar through the air toward them like daggers only to come to a halt. The yellow glow in the air forms a boundary between them and the storm—a shield. At that point, the shards are transformed into molten glass. Droplets fall to the ground, forming a dark slag in the cold.

"A forcefield?" Marc says, reaching out with his hand. "How is this possible?"

He's on the verge of touching the shimmering haze when Miranda says, "Don't. Come. We need to be quick. She can't hold him off for long."

"Who?" Emma asks. "Who can't hold him off for long?"

"Ariel."

Miranda rushes forward. The yellow glow follows her. The two astronauts struggle to keep up. They rush to remain within the shelter provided by the forcefield. It's only visible when fragments of glass strike its surface, but it's not a bubble. It doesn't extend entirely around them. Bits of glass caught in the updraft swirl before Marc and Emma, but these fragments are harmless. Without the momentum imparted by the storm, they tumble like snowflakes.

"This way," Miranda says, urging them to hurry along the narrow path.

It's dark. Emma trips on a rock. She falls forward. In the low gravity, her motion is slower than it would be on Earth. She holds out her gloved hands. On Altair IV, she's able to perform what equates to a pushup and bounce back off the ground. Marc grabs her pack to steady her. White vapor leaks from a tear on her backpack.

"You're venting oxygen," he says.

"How much further?" Emma asks as Miranda grabs her gloved hand, urging her on.

"Just up there."

In rapid succession, two lightning strikes pound the ground beside them, hitting just beyond the flickering forcefield. The flashes are blinding, destroying not only their night vision but their ability to resolve any shapes for a few seconds. All Miranda can see is the glowing remnants of the lightning bolts impressed on her retina.

The crack of thunder is deafening, rattling her bones. All three of them cower. It's clear the bolts were intended for them and, were it not for Ariel, they would have found their mark. The smell of ionized air lashes Miranda's nostrils. It's hot and heavy in stark contrast to the cold.

Miranda yells at the storm, *"Caliban, stop this madness!"*

Ahead, her father beckons from a doorway carved into the granite. Above him, a dome stretches over four floors of a home built into the mountainside.

"Quick," she says, pushing them ahead of her into the entrance tunnel beneath the dome.

Λlien Biosphere

The two astronauts stumble down the tunnel away from the storm.

"Are you okay?" Marc asks Emma.

"Yeah, fine. I think."

Hundreds of tiny bits of glass have embedded themselves in his suit. The inner layer has held, but the thick outer material on his left side looks as though it's been dragged down the road behind a truck. There are scuff marks and bits of insulation torn from his arm, but his suit pressure holds.

"What about you?" Marc asks Miranda.

"I'm okay," Miranda replies. She dusts some snow from her shoulders and shakes her arms, but her clothing is intact. Marc looks at the damage to his gloves. Her bare hands should be bloody and torn but they're not.

Emma also notices. Both of them are surprised to see the teenage girl is unscathed given the pounding their suits took.

"If it wasn't for that forcefield..." Emma says.

"You can remove your spacesuits," an elderly man says, cutting her off.

They're standing in a dimly lit entrance carved into the mountain. Rocks litter the ground. In the middle of the walkway, the rocks have been crushed as fine as gemstones and rolled flat. A gentle slope leads up into a subterranean basement, but the door is partially closed. There are stairs, leading up to the dome. Lights have been drilled into the rock wall, giving the illusion of warmth. A waft of vapor rises as the man speaks, betraying the cold inside the mountain.

"You're quite safe in here, I assure you," he says.

Marc looks at Emma. There's no way in hell he's removing his helmet. Emma, though, powers down her suit, tapping at the controls on her wristpad.

"What are you doing?" he asks, taking her by the shoulders. "We don't know what kind of microbial contaminants are present on this moon."

"But we do know, don't we," Emma says, looking across at the man and his daughter.

The man nods.

Miranda says, "There is nothing here that will hurt you."

"Other than that?" Emma says, pulling away from Marc. She points at the entrance to the tunnel. Hail lashes the opening. The wind rushes past, whipping by at hurricane speeds. Lightning continues to strike the plateau. In the distance, the dark silhouette of their spacecraft looks menacing. Emma reaches up and releases the locking ring on her collar.

"No," Marc says, seeing her hands set on either side of her visor, ready to twist and remove her helmet.

"I have no choice," she says. "I'm losing internal pressure."

To make her point more vivid, she swats at the side of her backpack with a gloved hand. Emma's unable to reach the loose flap of material waving around as her suit vents a fine mist into the air. Beneath the layers of insulation, a tiny hole reaches through the fiberglass casing on the backpack.

Marc says, "I might be able to—"

"It's okay," Emma says with a sense of confidence Marc cannot muster.

"No, it's not."

Marc may have been disinterested during his flight training, but his astrobiology background has prepared him for this moment. He understands this is more dangerous than juggling sticks of dynamite.

Life is aggressive. It's like a point guard in the NBA Playoffs, constantly hassling for an advantage. Species have to be aggressive to survive. It's a case of, "*Go compete or go extinct.*" Ever since the first cell divided on Earth in some primordial soup four billion years ago, the race has been on. At a microbial level, cannibalizing anything that gets in your way is a fair strategy. Throw exotic alien biomes into the mix and the competition for microbial dominance is unavoidable. Why would life on this moon be the exception? It wouldn't. The only way life could adapt to such a harsh, cold, dark, energy-poor environment is through aggressive competition. Survival of the fittest means life for those species that can exploit a niche.

Their eyes meet. The look of desperation in Emma's dark pupils tells him more than words ever could. Like him, her mind has raced through the possibilities and arrived at this as the only viable conclusion.

Marc wants to stop her, but he can't. Oh, he could try to overpower her, but what would that accomplish? He could insist they buddy-breathe, but that would only exhaust both of their supplies. A suit patch won't work. It's her backpack that's leaking, not the inflated suit bladder supporting her body. Although it was the flying glass that bothered him most in the storm, he felt the sting of tiny stones being flung up and hitting his suit trousers. Emma must have been struck by a sharp fragment hurled around in the storm like a bullet. Without dismantling her backpack, it's impossible to know whether it struck a pipe, a valve, the tank regulator or the filtration unit. Regardless, a cloth patch is useless on anything other than their cloth suits.

With nothing more to say, Emma removes her helmet. She exhales slowly and sniffs at the air.

"What can you smell?" Marc asks from behind the safety of his visor.

"Well, my nose isn't as good as yours, but I'm guessing ozone

125

from all that lightning. The air is thin. I feel as though I need to hyperventilate just to breathe... Ah, there's ammonia. And rotten eggs. What smells like rotten eggs?"

"Hydrogen sulfide," he says, although he's looking at the readout on his wristpad computer rather than guessing in response. It's analyzing the atmosphere based on local sampling. "I'm seeing trace amounts of methane, carbon dioxide, nitrous oxide. Stuff like that. But this filter won't detect viral particles or airborne microbes."

Emma hoists her helmet on her hip. She rests her left arm over the top of it and offers her right hand to the old man in a gesture of friendship.

"Lieutenant Emma Madi of the *Sycorax* colony transport out of Westminster Star Base."

"Professor Antonio Spiro," the old man says, shaking her hand and smiling. "And you've already met my daughter, Miranda."

"I don't like this," Marc says. He looks around, but not at anything specific. He's trying to take in the enormity of all that has transpired. "We're in the middle of an active alien biosphere."

"I've been here for almost twenty years," the professor says with warmth, charm and a smile. "Our two biospheres coexist without competition."

"I don't buy it," Marc says. "Evolution allows species to adapt in an astonishing variety of ways. This biome has evolved over *billions* of years. You've been here for twenty. That's hardly comparable. This place might need thirty years to cannibalize your cells. For that matter, it may have only needed ten and you haven't noticed yet."

The professor says, "You're quite the alarmist."

"Quite the rationalist," Marc replies. He turns to Emma, saying, "We need to get you back to the scout."

"You want to go back out there?" Miranda asks, pointing at the storm.

As if in response to her question, the gale increases in its intensity. Rocks fall over the mouth of the cave. It's not a landslide. The entrance is still open, but if any of those rocks had struck Marc, they would have crushed his helmet.

The professor asks a bitter question. "How long will your oxygen last?"

Emma is subdued.

Marc looks at his wristpad computer, saying, "Another four hours."

"You won't make it forty feet out there," the professor says. "Storms like this can rage for days."

"I—I can't," Marc says, addressing Emma. "I can't take this off. It goes against everything I've been taught."

"You don't have a choice," she says.

The professor says, "Our two biomes compete for similar primary resources, but tend to ignore each other. I've detected trace bacterial loads beyond our home, but never in large microbial colonies. And I've never encountered intrusions into our residence."

Marc asks him, "And you've tested for contamination within human subjects? You've looked for analogs of deep-tissue viral reservoirs? You've checked your spinal fluid? You've examined either side of the blood-brain barrier?"

"I have," the professor replies, triumphant.

Marc's not sure how much he believes the professor. The old man rattled off a simplistic answer to complex questions with a little too much glee, but he's right about one thing. Marc won't last long in his suit. Reluctantly, Marc concedes. If he makes a run for the scout, he'll be blown off the edge of the cliff or struck by lightning—and that's if his suit isn't torn to shreds first. As much as he wants to hold out until the last breath of air leaves his oxygen tank, all he's doing is delaying the inevitable. Against his better judgment, he taps at his controls.

"There's no cellular compatibility," the professor says. "Life here uses entirely different chemical pathways."

Emma says, "But you told us this moon was under quarantine?"

"From Caliban."

"Who or what is Caliban?"

As the two of them talk, Marc powers down his life support system. He equalizes the pressure and removes his helmet.

The professor says, "Caliban is a planetary defense structure put in place by the Krell."

"Woah, there," Marc says, holding his helmet by his side. "You're talking about extraterrestrial *intelligence*?"

The professor nods.

Emma says, "Hang on. In over five thousand surveyed worlds, and after detecting microbial life on, what? Less than one percent of terrestrial analogs? We've never found anything more complex than a cockroach, let alone sapien-level intelligence."

"Until we found Altair," the professor says.

Emma points at the storm swirling before them in the darkness beyond the entrance to the tunnel. "Wait. You mean the ice giant, right? Not here. Not on this moon."

"That's correct, lieutenant."

Emma spins around. She turns her back on the professor. With her one free arm, she raises her gloved hand and presses it against the side of her forehead as though she were trying to clear a migraine. She speaks softly with Marc.

"This is wrong. Something here is horribly wrong."

"Oh, I know," Marc says. He addresses the professor, speaking slowly and measuring his words with care. "This is First Contact. If you've discovered an intelligent extraterrestrial species, why is this the first we've heard about it? Why isn't this all over the news back at star base?"

"You shouldn't have come down here," the professor says, refusing to answer his question.

Marc turns to Miranda. "What's going on here?"

"I... My father..."

"Miranda was born here," the professor says. "This is the only life she's ever known."

"Why haven't you told anyone about your discovery?" Emma asks.

Marc focuses intently on the professor, looking for any hesitation in his response or eye movements that might reveal a lie.

"The Krell are millions of years more advanced than us," the professor says as though that plain statement of fact were an explanation in its own right. He seems relaxed. He's not bothered by the discussion.

"So?" Emma says.

The professor laughs, responding with, "To them, we're chimps. We've barely made it out of the trees."

Emma does not look impressed.

"Come," he says. "Let me show you my laboratory and we'll talk about the Krell."

He gestures for them to follow him.

"A million years isn't a reason," Marc says, walking up beside him.

"Oh, but it is," the professor replies, chuckling. "You have no idea what you've done by coming here."

"But you're here," Emma says, walking on the other side of him. "Where's your ship? Where's the rest of your crew?"

"They're dead," the professor says with cold, clinical precision. "The *Copernicus* crashed. Caliban brought it down roughly two hundred kilometers northwest of here as it attempted to leave the moon."

They walk past the stairs and past the partially open door leading to a brightly-lit basement. Marc and Emma both peer through the gap as they walk on. Inside, large semi-transparent crystals rise from the floor. Machines surround them, monitoring them.

"Ah," Marc says, pointing at the door and wanting to see more, but the professor ignores him. He leads them to an elevator. To Marc, the whole place is like something out of an old James Bond film. What little he saw of the basement was reminiscent of a supervillain's secret lair.

"What's in there?" Emma asks, turning back toward the basement as they step into the elevator.

"Krell technology," the professor says, offhandedly.

The elevator rises. Roughhewn rock slides past just beyond the smooth, curved glass as they pass from inside the mountain to the home outside. The elevator clears the rock wall. They emerge within a dome stretching over the mountainside, providing them with a rain-soaked view across the darkened valley. Several floors pass quickly beneath them. The lighting is dim and tinged with red. The furniture is sparse. Polished concrete floors form a semicircle ending with a sweeping balcony on each level. As the vast building is set on the slope of the mountain, each balcony is set back slightly from the previous one, allowing an atrium to form within the dome. The effect is such that it's possible to stand on any balcony and see the whole structure.

The storm rages beyond the dome. Rain lashes the smooth, glassy surface, fighting to get in. Lightning ripples through the clouds.

Marc tries to ignore the distractions around him and focus on the central issue. He says, "Even if these guys are a million years more advanced, why does that matter?"

Emma reinforces his point, saying, "A million isn't going to cut it as an explanation. You're going to have to do better than that."

"A million years is beyond human comprehension," the professor says, stepping out on the top floor of his home. "You might think you know what it means, but you don't."

"Try me," Emma says, walking into the professor's laboratory. Marc's known her long enough to know when she's barely able to contain her rage. It's not unbridled anger she's bottling up. Emma's not like that. She's not someone that flies into a fit of swear words. No, she's focused.

Krell Science

Emma paces to the far side of the lab. He knows what she's doing. This place is familiar to the professor and his daughter but not to them. She wants to get comfortable with the setting. They've both had enough surprises for one day.

Marc adopts a more passive approach. Physically, he's exhausted, so it's easy enough to come across as relaxed. If Emma's the lioness prowling back and forth through the long grass, he'll be the male lazing in the sun. Neither, though, should be underestimated.

Marc rests his helmet on one of the benches and looks at the equipment. None of it is familiar—not from his time. He's seen lab equipment like this before but only in historical displays.

Like the rest of the dome, the lab is lit with a soft red light, allowing their eyes to remain adjusted to the darkness beyond the glass. The light, though, is everywhere. It's not a point-light casting shadows around them, but rather one that saturates the lab, blotting out the distinction of colors, making it easy to see the shapes and items around them. Marc's only ever seen this lighting scheme in mountain-top observatories back on Earth.

Rows of test tubes sit neatly in racks at the back of the circular lab. Cork bungs prevent evaporation. As he moves closer a white light comes on overhead. Step back and it fades to red. In this way, the various workbenches have their own light profiles within the overall night lighting scheme. Marc passes his hand in front of him, activating the light again, wanting to see what's in the test tubes. The various liquids have been arranged in shades of color stretching from red to pink, yellow, green, violet and blue, which makes no sense as these shades would be the result of entirely different chemical processes. At a molecular level, there's probably no correlation between them beyond aesthetics. He walks on and the bright light fades.

A polished copper still sits on a tripod. It's been mounted on another table. A naked flame burns beneath the still, which is both horribly inefficient and imprecise—and dangerous! Did the professor really leave a naked flame burning in an empty lab? Back at college, his chem lecturer would have flunked him if he did something this stupid. Brass tubes wind in tight coils, allowing condensation to form at various points along their path. They twist in exotic shapes. A murky fluid drips into a distillation flask with a conical base. It's seated on a flat metal slab that rocks back and forward, constantly mixing the fluid. This is old-school organic chemistry.

A hologram rises above the central desk. It's a mismatch of technology. Holograms are experimental. The few Marc's seen are coarse, but the details in this glowing image are stunning. He feels as though he's a god peering down on Altair IV. The *Sycorax* is barely visible to one side. A thin red line traces its elliptical orbit.

The professor brings over a silver tray with ornate champagne flutes and rests it beside the hologram. He pours liquid from a smoky glass bottle. Bubbles rise from the clear fluid. Miranda hands each of them a glass.

"Non-alcoholic," he says, offering a toast without actually toasting anything. He takes a sip before continuing.

"To a million years," Emma says, raising her glass. She lifts it to her lips but she doesn't drink. It's a not-so-subtle way of making it clear she doesn't trust him. Oh, the professor's friendly enough and has a warm smile. He appears to be in his late eighties, but given the advances in gerontology, he could be a hundred and eighty. His hair is grey and full. He has a beard, which probably helps in the cold as it wraps around his chin and upper neck.

"A million years is a long time. It's long enough for entire species to come into existence and then go extinct without leaving a trace. As a species, *Homo sapiens* is only two hundred thousand years old. If we're generous, our civilization is roughly ten thousand years old, but we've been a space-faring species for less than three hundred years. All of this is nothing compared to a million. At best, our attempts at interstellar colonization are a rounding error by comparison."

"Still not a reason," Emma says, resting her helmet beside Marc's. She's clinical in how she moves, putting the fake bubbly down and pulling off her gloves. She places them on the table and picks up her faux non-alcoholic champagne again. She's content to toy with the stem of the thin glass flute. It seems she's an actress in a play. For her, the ornate glass is a prop on a stage—nothing more.

Marc says, "If anything, such a vast time scale is all the more reason to report your findings. Think of how much we stand to learn from them."

"Think of how much we stand to lose," the professor says, tilting his head forward.

Marc doesn't bite at that comment. He's curious to see how Emma plays this. He sips his drink. Emma, though, seems perplexed. She looks at the bubbles rising in her glass. He's not sure she even heard what the professor said. Normally, a comment like that would provoke a response from her. She seems lost in thought. At a guess, she's weighing their responsibility to thousands of colonists against the danger posed by Caliban and the revelation there's intelligent life on this moon. Marc has no doubt where her allegiance lies, but she seems torn.

The professor notices their differing reactions but doesn't say anything. Miranda has already finished her glass. She puts it down and leans back against one of the desks backing onto the balcony. Behind her, the storm rages. Lightning cuts across the sky, dancing between the clouds. Thunder breaks like a gunshot. Marc winces. It's involuntary. His is a primal response to the sheer magnitude of raw power being released nearby in a fraction of a heartbeat. Miranda, though, doesn't flinch.

The professor says, "We think of First Contact as a kind of nirvana, as though all our questions will be answered, but that's a lie. It's a fantasy, an illusion of our own making."

"You think it's dangerous?" Emma asks, still toying with her glass. She swirls the champagne before her, adding, "Like opening Pandora's Box?"

"Ah, yes, Pandora," the professor says, chuckling. "She's always been misunderstood."

He changes the pitch of his voice and speaks with a slight accent, making it clear he's reciting an ancient tome. The way he moves and gestures with his hands it is as though he's a Shakespearean actor on stage at the Globe Theater.

> *"Hope! She is the only good god remaining among humanity;*
> *"The others have left and gone to Olympus.*
> *"Trust, a mighty god has fallen,*
> *"Restraint has fled from men,*
> *"And Grace, my friend, has abandoned Earth.*
> *"Men's oaths are no longer to be trusted,*
> *"Nor does anyone revere the immortal gods;*
> *"The race of pious men has perished,*
> *"And men no longer recognize the rules of righteous conduct.*
> *"Hope is all that remains among the chaos brought by Pandora."*

"You'll have to forgive my father," Miranda says. "He doesn't mean to speak in riddles. For him, these are truths made plain."

"And they are," the professor says, pouring himself another drink. "*Theognis of Megara* understood. With evil flooding the world, Pandora gave us hope! Don't you see?"

"Ah, no," Marc says, shaking his head. "I thought we were talking about aliens."

"Aliens?" he replies. "Or the ancient gods on Mount Olympus? Are they not one and the same? They're a panacea. Or so we wish them to be. We blame them for our misfortune and yet we hope they'll brighten our future. What are aliens to us but gods?"

"And yet they're not," Emma says, holding her glass up to the light and examining its contents. "Like us, they're mortal."

Marc knows what she's doing. She isn't satisfied with the professor's vague explanation. She's doing what she always does when dealing with senior management within star base or onboard the *Sycorax*. She's managing up. She's working him, wanting to understand him, trying to get around his defenses without the discussion unraveling into an argument.

"Quite true," the professor says. "But we need to consider First Contact not just from a scientific perspective. Our human frailties distort our view of reality. There's no substitute for us and our place in both space and time. We must take responsibility for ourselves. No alien or god is going to save us. Pandora gave us both chaos *and* hope. The Krell could do the same, only the chaos could lead to our extinction."

"And that's what worries you?" Marc says.

The professor nods.

"And a million years?" Emma says, leading him on.

"A million years is long enough to blur the lines of distinction between mortals and gods."

"Huh," Marc says, impressed at how Emma drew that out of the old man.

The professor says, "I've spent the best part of two decades studying these aliens, and they're extraordinary."

"Of course, they are," Emma says, joking with him. "From our perspective, we're ordinary. How could they be anything other than extraordinary."

"I like this woman," the professor says, wagging his finger at her and turning to Miranda. "She's sharp. She reminds me of your mother."

135

"And what have you found?" Emma asks. Marc understands precisely what she's doing. Emma's not going to be flattered out of asking hard questions. The professor, though, seems oblivious to how he's being played.

"They see things. They see the same things as us, but they see them in entirely different ways."

"Like?"

"Think of a flower," the professor replies. "Perhaps a rose. What do you see? You see something beautiful. Look closer and you'll see the petals opening to the sun, the brilliant shades of red and pink along with a scattering of green leaves around the stem. You'll notice the stamens surrounding the stigma. You might prick your finger on one of the thorns, but..."

"But what?" Marc asks.

"But to you, these traits are aesthetic. They're curiosities. They hold mere passing interest. The scent is compelling. But for you, there's no function beyond beauty."

"What would they see?" Emma asks.

"They'd see a marvel of biology. They'd see photosynthesis as a stunning mechanism that uses light to convert a basic volcanic gas into various sugars that are used to sustain cellular life. They'd comment on the evolution of refined characteristics over innumerable iterations. They'd see a rose as functional. They'd marvel at its co-adaptation, forming a symbiotic relationship with insects of various species. And they'd be perplexed by our simplistic view of its mere beauty."

Emma says, "They'd see it like a bee."

"Yes," the professor says, pointing at her. "Yes, yes. That's a much more succinct way of putting it. They'd see a rose as a source of nutrition within the food matrix of hummingbirds, bees and ants. And for them, that's a form of beauty in itself."

"But they haven't seen a rose, have they?" Emma asks, still brooding, but she seems to be warming to the old man.

"No."

136

"So what have they seen?"

"The universe at large," the professor replies, gesturing to the vast glass dome behind him. "Stars. Planets. Asteroids. Black holes. Molecular clouds being distilled into ever greater complexity as they drift through interstellar space. They see waves of electromagnetic radiation washing over creation, providing the impetus for life."

"But we've seen this as well," Emma says. "We've studied these things extensively."

"And we've come to sterile conclusions," he says. "Tell me, lieutenant. What's the speed of light?"

"In a vacuum?" Emma asks, raising an eyebrow at what seems to be an esoteric question. "Um, two hundred and ninety-nine thousand kilometers a second, plus spare change."

The professor says, "For you, it's a fact. For them, it's the key to unlocking the secrets of the cosmos. Do you know what speed they record?"

"No," she says.

"One."

"One what?"

"Ah," he replies, laughing. "Now, that's the question."

"Hang on. How can it be equal to one?" Marc asks, wanting to inject himself into the conversation. "One is meaningless."

"Is it?" the professor asks. He points at Emma. "She got it right the first time."

Both of the astronauts look confused, wondering which of Emma's comments he's referring to.

"Ordinary," the professor says as though his point is obvious. "We assume our experiences on Earth are ordinary. They're not. They're extraordinary. Our experiences on that tiny rock have not prepared us for the universe at large. Think about speed. What's speed?"

Marc says, "A measure of how fast you cover a certain distance."

Emma's more succinct. "Miles per hour. Or kilometers an hour, if you want to use modern metrics."

"Ah, another sterile conclusion," the professor says. "And this is the problem. We grew up on a world that seems stationary. We drive from one static place to another—from our homes to the mall or out to a restaurant. We go from what we assume is one stationary building to another stationary building—only it's an illusion—the planet and *everything* on it is spinning around at a thousand kilometers an hour!"

"So?" Marc says.

"The Krell evolved in the clouds of that ice giant," the professor replies, pointing out of the vast dome. "They never had a fixed point of reference to determine their speed. They only ever used relative speeds."

In the low light, the faint outline of the ice giant forms a dark patch reaching above the storm clouds. It stretches across the sky, forming a semicircle spanning the mountains on one side and the misty plains on the other, blotting out the star field.

"The Krell evolved there?" Emma says.

"Yes," the professor replies. "For them, this moon was a research outpost."

"Life in the clouds of an ice giant? How is that even possible?" Marc asks. "Biology requires—"

"What?" the professor asks, cutting him off. "What does biology require? We came from a world where biology has dominated the planet for *billions* of years and we still have no idea how life first arose there. Is it any more implausible for life to arise on an ice giant?"

"But the storms," Marc says. "They're too chaotic."

"Life arose on Earth during the Hadean," the professor replies. "When our planet was literally hell on Earth. We've found aquatic hematite tubes that are over four billion years old! They're from a time when the surface temperature was like the inside of a kitchen oven, reaching several hundred degrees. If anything, I'd say terrestrial life is more improbable than life on an ice giant with the long-term stability of its various thermal layers."

"I guess," Marc says, reluctantly conceding the point.

"And this caused them to see things differently?" Emma asks, clearly intrigued by the professor's research.

"They never developed the concept of speed—not as we know it."

"What?" Marc says in disbelief.

"In everyday life, we think of speed as an absolute. We measure speed against things. A car is going fifty kilometers an hour *down the highway*. An airplane flies at hundreds of kilometers an hour *over the ground*. But watch a plane from orbit and it seems as though it's stationary and it's the planet that's turning beneath it. Speed is all a matter of perspective."

"And they never had that perspective," Emma says.

"No. In the clouds of Altair, everything is always in motion at various different speeds. For them, the contrast was more important than what we would consider as the overall speed."

Marc says, "So they never had a fascination with faster or fastest."

"No. And that led them to a different set of conclusions about the universe."

"How so?" Emma asks, sitting back on the edge of a granite shelf cut into the hillside. She crosses her legs in front of her. Her anger has melted away. She seems unusually interested in the professor's comments but Marc suspects it's a ploy. For now, it seems she's content to let him ramble.

"We developed the Theory of Relativity. They developed the Theory of Absolutism."

Marc is surprised. He raises an eyebrow. "They think Einstein's wrong?"

"Not wrong," the professor says. "They saw the problem in a different light."

"One," Emma says, recalling his earlier point about measuring the speed of light.

"Yes. For us, relativity is difficult to imagine. Weird things happen close to the speed of light. Time slows. Lengths change."

"And they don't see that?" Emma asks, narrowing her brow.

"Oh, they see it, but to them, it's no surprise. We split speed into different measures of distance and time. They don't. They never saw space and time as separate from each other. They only ever saw spacetime. For them, there's no contradiction, no confusion, no strange consequences."

"So how do they think about the universe?" Marc asks, aware he and Emma are gaining insights into alien reasoning.

"They see spacetime the same way you would see an elastic band. When it's relaxed, it's short and squishy. Tug on it and you make it longer, but you lose something. You lose elasticity. The rubber band becomes taut. By stretching it, you're trading one thing for another. You gain length while losing flexibility. When it comes to what we call relativity, you gain speed by losing time."

He pauses, considering his words. "They see the speed of light not as something to be reached but rather as a constant of reality. The Krell would say you can't reach the speed of light because there's nothing absolute against which you can measure your speed in the first place."

"Now, hang on," Marc says. "That makes no sense."

"Ah, but it does," the professor says. "You've just got to think like the Krell. To them, everything is in motion. The question is only—in motion relative to what? Any motion away from a particular frame of reference, say a star or a planet, is traded against time."

The blank look on Marc's face prompts the professor to simplify his point.

"Imagine this. You're driving north at a hundred kilometers an hour. After one hour, how far have you traveled north?"

Marc looks sideways at Emma before replying with a tentative, "A hundred kilometers."

"Easy," the professor says, clapping his hands. "Now, ahead of you, there's an offramp. It only goes slightly to one side, leading to a road heading northeast at... let's say ten degrees. You continue traveling at exactly a hundred kilometers an hour. How far north will you go in the *next* hour?"

"Ah," Marc says. "Trick question, right?"

The professor smiles.

Marc says, "You'll still travel a hundred kilometers, but you're no longer going straight north, so you won't go as far north."

"Exactly. You're always covering a hundred kilometers in an hour, but sometimes you're trading how far you go north for a few extra kilometers to the east. The question isn't how fast are you traveling, but what's important to you? North or east?"

"And how is this like relativity?" Marc asks.

"Motion is like taking the offramp. As soon as you start to move away from something, you're trading spacetime. Lengths contract. Time dilates. For you, though, nothing changes—absolutely nothing. Anyone watching you sees you taking a detour through spacetime. Go faster relative to your home world and it's like taking an offramp that travels even further to the east. To someone watching you, you're giving up on north for east—or time for space—but you don't see that."

"Oh, my head hurts," Marc replies, joking.

The professor says, "We naturally think of ourselves as stationary, but we're not. We're in motion. Nothing is stationary. Not one single celestial object anywhere in the entire universe is sitting still. You think a rocket's moving away from you, but it's equally true to say the rocket's stationary and you're moving away from it. Don't you see? The problem is we grew up with the illusion of being still."

"But we're still right now," Marc says, pointing at the polished floor of the laboratory.

"Are we?" the professor asks. "We're still relative to the lab and this moon, but the moon is rotating at six hundred kilometers an hour, and it's orbiting the ice giant Altair at tens of thousands of kilometers an hour, while the ice giant is dragging us along with it through spacetime. Altair is orbiting that black hole out there at hundreds of thousands of kilometers an hour. And the black hole is in motion as well. Don't you see? Being stationary is an illusion. You're not sitting still. You're in motion. You're *always* in motion."

Emma says, "And the Krell understood this?"

"For them, it made perfect sense. What we call *stationary* is two people moving at the same rate through spacetime. They're on the highway heading north. The Krell never saw their world as anything other than constantly in motion. Looking out at the stars, it was natural for them to see everything moving relative to something else."

"Okay. I think I get it," Marc says, raising a finger. Like Emma, he's removed his gloves. "It's like I've lived my whole life sitting in the back of a car—only the car isn't still. It's driving around."

"Yes."

"And time slows because..."

"Time doesn't slow," the professor says. "Not for you. You're still going at a hundred kilometers an hour. But you took an offramp. Anyone looking at you from afar sees you going slightly east so they see you cover less than a hundred kilometers north. What they're seeing is your passage through time being traded for passage through space."

Miranda is docile. Quiet would be the wrong word. It's not that she's silent so much as accepting.

Marc finds the debate between Emma and the professor fascinating. He's on the fringes of the discussion. He gets some of what they're talking about but he's not ready to take sides. Not yet.

Like him, it seems Miranda is content to sit and watch. She's peculiar, though. She seems happy—too happy. She doesn't seem to question anything at all. She's pretty. He knows she's intelligent, but around her father, she's subservient. To Marc, that's not healthy. Perhaps he's being too harsh in his estimation of her. Maybe she's heard it all before and is simply zoning out. He wants to ask Miranda what she thinks about all this, but he knows Emma well enough to realize she's prodding the professor for more than technical answers. Marc doesn't want to hijack the conversation and derail her arguments.

"You admire these guys," Emma says. And there it is, Marc thinks. Like a catamaran sailing upwind on the open ocean, she's tacking in another direction to make progress.

"I admire what they've accomplished," the professor says. "They've avoided the pitfalls of our logic."

"You don't seem impressed by us," Emma says. "But I think we've done quite well. Look at us! We're here, aren't we? Instead of wandering around the African grasslands, we're here—on the other side of a spiral arm within our galaxy. That's pretty impressive."

"And yet we still cling to absurdities," the professor says.

"Like?"

"Like infinities."

"Infinities?" Emma asks.

"The universe abhors infinities."

"I thought it abhorred a vacuum."

The professor says, "Life may abhor a vacuum but the universe loves them! 99.9% of the entire universe is a vacuum. What the universe abhors is any pretense of infinity."

"Infinity?" Marc says, confused.

"We have this notion of something being eternal or infinite, meaning without end. The Krell would say such a concept is absurd. Infinities are useful as abstract mathematical ideas but they don't actually exist."

"So nothing is infinite?" Emma asks. "Really? How could they possibly know that?"

"Every physical infinity fails," the professor says. "Take, for example, dividing time. Can a minute be infinitely divided into ever smaller halves?"

"Sure," Emma says. "It's Zeno's paradox. You start with a minute, then thirty seconds, then fifteen, and so on. You'll keep getting smaller numbers forever without reaching zero."

The professor smiles. "On paper, it's possible. Calculus uses infinities as an abstract upper limit, but what about in the real world? Can you continue dividing a minute into infinite segments?"

"If you had the ability to measure it, yes," Emma says.

"No," the professor replies.

"How do you know?" Marc asks.

"Because at some point, this minute expires and the next minute begins. Infinity can never be reached. If a minute could be divided an infinite number of times it would never end. That it ends is proof there's no infinity."

Marc says, "Huh!"

Emma, though, doesn't sound convinced. "You could argue that's a limitation of our science—that with an infinitely advanced technology, we could infinitely divide a minute."

The professor is undeterred. "But you can't. The next minute is coming in sixty seconds regardless of how many divisions you make. You cannot reach an infinite number of divisions in a finite time."

"So what?" Emma asks. "You reach some kind of quantum limit, like Planck time?"

The professor shakes his head. "No, no, no. We use quantum mechanics to describe energy in terms of set amounts. Quantities. We break it up into packets. A photon is like a letter being sent through the mail. It's one thing traveling from here to there. But the Krell think in terms of harmonics. It's a subtle, but important distinction.

"Take a guitar. Pluck the big, fat E-string and you'll get a nice, low bass sound. Now, you can slide your finger anywhere along the string you want, but it's only at a few points you'll get harmonics. Slide halfway along and you'll hear the same note an octave higher. Slide back to the quarter mark and you'll hit two octaves higher. There's nothing to stop you from positioning your hand anywhere you want— you just won't get a harmonic tone at every point. Quantum mechanics and indeed spacetime itself aren't pixelated. They're not like a set of stairs where you step between levels. They're more like that guitar string where you're looking for harmonics."

"And the limit?" Emma asks.

"The limit arises when harmonics can no longer be found."

"So there are no infinities anywhere?" Emma asks, shaking her head in disbelief.

"No."

"I—I just can't believe that," she replies.

The professor is brutal. "The universe doesn't care for your beliefs, lieutenant."

Emma raises her hand, wanting a moment to consider this properly. "Wait. If there are no infinities, then everything has a finite value."

"That's correct."

"Then *everything* can be defined."

"Can be, but may not yet be," the professor says, raising a finger. "The Krell believe all apparent infinities have absolute values."

"Now *that's* absurd," she says. "If a supposed infinity has an absolute value then what is to stop me from adding one to it and going higher?"

"Nothing," the professor says. "On paper, you can. In practice, you can't."

Emma is frustrated. "By definition, finite values cannot be infinite."

"But what if the universe disagrees? What if the universe says *this* is infinity—*this value* and no more!"

"But it doesn't."

"Doesn't it?" the professor asks, raising an eyebrow. "Are you sure? You see, we humans love to deal in hypotheticals. The Krell deal in facts. To them, observations are more important than calculations."

"I'm not sure I agree with that," Emma says, crossing her arms over her chest. "The universe doesn't define infinities, we do."

"Really?" the professor asks. "For hundreds of years, we've wondered if it's possible to go faster than light, but the Krell would laugh at such a notion."

"Why?" Marc asks, wanting to inject himself back into the conversation.

"To the Krell, the speed of light *is* infinite."

"But it's not," Emma says. "It has a precise value."

"As all infinities do," the professor says, smiling.

"But—the speed of light is *not* infinite," Emma says with a worried look on her brow. "Certainly not on cosmic scales. It takes light from distant galaxies *billions* of years to reach us."

"Does it?" the professor asks. "From our perspective, it seems limited, but light experiences no time at all. It traverses the vast expanse of spacetime in an instant."

"And yet it doesn't," Emma says.

"Now you're starting to think like the Krell," the professor says, laughing and pointing at her.

"I'm not," Marc says, laughing as well.

The professor says. "We're obsessed with traveling faster than light but it makes no sense in terms of astrophysics. We can already travel faster than light without actually traveling faster than light at all!"

Marc shakes his head. He looks at Miranda. "And you're following all this, right?" He waves his hands around in disbelief. "All this makes sense to you?"

Miranda laughs, saying, "I'm just glad there's someone else here for him to talk to."

"Okay, I'll bite," Emma says. "How can we travel faster than light without actually traveling faster than light?"

"Using Krell logic," the professor says. "Using the same logic first proposed by Einstein himself."

Emma folds her arms across her chest again. It's a classic act of defiance. If the professor notices, he doesn't comment on her posture. He's far too deep in the discussion.

He says, "If you accelerate at just one gee for ten years you'll reach 99% of the speed of light with a whole bunch of additional nines beyond the decimal point. You won't actually reach or exceed the speed of light itself relative to anything in the universe, but you'll get damn close. And in those ten years, you'll cover 27,000 light-years!"

"Wait. What?" Marc says.

Emma bats her hand at the air, wanting Marc to let the professor continue. Her brow lowers as she focuses on his words.

"You'll reach the supermassive black hole at the heart of our galaxy in a decade! To anyone watching from Earth, your journey will take tens of thousands of years because you're still moving at a sub-light speed, but from *your* perspective, you're going *faster* than light! And not just a little faster. You're going several orders of magnitude faster. You're covering tens of thousands of light-years in just one decade! And all while accelerating at a paltry one gee, which is nothing more than what you'd feel standing back on Earth."

"Is he right?" Marc asks. His head swivels from Emma to Miranda and back again, unsure of whom he's asking.

Miranda says, "He's always right."

"The speed of light *is* effectively infinite in our universe," the professor says. "Keep accelerating toward the speed of light and you'll never reach it, but within another five years—just five years—you will have reached the Andromeda galaxy some two *million* light-years away! That's a journey of two million light-years in barely fifteen years onboard your starship!"

Emma nods, conceding yet another point.

The professor says, "If you could actually reach the speed of light itself, you could go any distance in an instant. You could travel *billions* of light-years like that!"

He snaps his fingers to reinforce his point.

"But," Emma says, lingering on her first word for a moment.

"Billions of years will transpire in this frame of reference."

"Yes, but the speed of light itself is not a finite limit. It's only finite from *our* perspective. From its perspective, the speed of light *is* infinite. It's the universe saying, '*Infinity is this much and no more!*' Light moves infinitely fast. It can go anywhere without any time transpiring for it at all."

"Wait. Did you hear that?" Marc asks, raising a cupped hand to his ear. The others look confused. He goes on to say, "That's the sound of billions of brain cells crying out in anguish within my throbbing skull."

"Your head just exploded, huh?" Miranda says.

"Just a little," Marc replies, holding his thumb and forefinger slightly apart. "I'll survive. I think."

"You see," the professor says, but he's cut off by his daughter.

Miranda stands up, interrupting him, saying, "What you see is that hospitality is a second thought on Altair IV."

"Oh, what?" the professor says, stumbling over his words. "Ah, yes. Of course. I'm being boorish and rude."

"Not at all," Emma says, finally sipping some of her champagne. "I found our discussion fascinating."

"We have guest quarters," Miranda says, walking away from the bench. "Come. I'll show them to you."

Marc stands a fraction of a second later, following her cue. If Emma and the professor want to keep talking about infinities, he'll give them a finite but infinite amount of space and time to do so by going down to one of the lower levels.

The professor says, "I'll get Ariel to put on a banquet tonight so we can celebrate your arrival."

As he speaks, a beautiful woman appears out of nowhere, glistening beside him, saying, "I'd love that."

Marc and Emma step back, taking a good look at the ghostly apparition that materialized next to the professor. As shocking as it is to see the transparent outline of a woman dressed in fine linen, glowing like the sun, Marc's more surprised by the lack of any response from Miranda and the professor. Neither of them flinches.

"Um, ah," Emma says, pointing.

"Ariel is our helper," Miranda says, leading them down a broad set of stairs cut into the mountainside. "She's the one that protected us in the storm."

Although Marc and Emma continue to follow Miranda down the stairs, they turn sideways, keeping their eyes on the ethereal figure of Ariel floating beside the professor.

"That's—that's... She's..." Marc says, still trying to process what he's seeing. "Who or what is she?"

"She's a million years' worth of technological advances," Miranda replies, smiling.

Marc and Emma exchange a glance. Their eyes are wide with surprise. It was one thing to see a forcefield protect them from a storm. It's another to see what appears to be an alien taking human form as though it were entirely natural.

The stairs are grand, stretching almost twenty meters across. They curve with the slope, being set into the granite mountain. On the next level down, the floor is divided in two, with a vast balcony in a half-moon shape providing a view out through the dome. Behind them, several rooms have been carved into the mountain.

Two of the six steel doors open automatically as they approach, but Miranda doesn't walk into either of the rooms. She gestures, pointing at one of the lavish bedrooms adorned with 1950s retro furniture, saying, "You'll find everything you need in here, including a change of clothes. Dinner is in ten minutes."

With that, she leaves them and continues on down the broad staircase. Miranda's feet appear to glide as she descends.

Marc looks up at the ceiling, wondering if Ariel is going to drift down from above like a ghost coming to haunt them.

"What the hell is happening?" he asks, still in shock at the sight of Ariel.

"We're being played for chimps," Emma replies.

Marc screws up his face, unsure about her response.

"You don't think that was a little too convenient?" Emma says. "Showing us Ariel as we're leaving? It's quite the flex."

"I—I don't know what to think," Marc replies.

"I suspect that's the point."

"And these bedrooms," Marc says. "This place looks like it's from the set of *Star Trek*."

Emma purses her lips. "He's hiding something."

"What???" Marc asks, but not in response to the idea that something's being hidden. He's surprised Emma thinks the professor's hiding anything at all. To him, the professor seemed quite open. He was nonchalant about both Krell logic and the appearance of Ariel. If anything, he was too damn relaxed given how extraordinary all this is to them.

"You heard him back there. You saw the way he spoke to us," she says.

"He wasn't holding anything back," Marc says. "He was explaining Krell science."

"He was trying to baffle us."

"And Ariel?" Marc asks, still trying to get his head around what he just saw.

"A distraction," Emma replies. "The professor's overcompensating. It might not have sounded like it, but I think he's nervous."

"What is he hiding?"

"I don't know, but everything we've talked about and seen so far is nothing but a magic trick."

Marc replies. "You think the Krell science is magic?"

"No, silly," Emma says. "I think we're being stage-managed by a magician. He's using sleight of hand. He wants us to focus on what his left hand is doing, while he fools us with the right. All the talk about relativity and infinities. The little show-pony stunt with Ariel at the end. It's all to keep us from seeing what's really happening."

"And what's really happening?"

"I don't know, but I don't buy any of it."

"I thought you agreed with him."

"I was appealing to his ego, Marc. It's the Achilles' heel of all men. If you ever want to get something past a man, flatter him."

"Is that why you're so nice to me?" he asks, being sarcastic.

"Why you're the smartest man I know," she says, running her finger up his neck and under his chin, leading him on with a coy smile.

Marc steps back, surprised by the way she touched him and how his body reacted with a warm shiver. "Damn, you're good."

She winks at him, saying, "But it won't work on me."

Marc laughs as Emma walks into her bedroom.

The door slides shut behind her.

The Plan

Marc walks into his bedroom. Like everywhere else within the vast, stunning home, the walls are unfinished. He touches the marks left by the robotic jackhammer that carved out this space. Rather than going in random directions, they all run from top left to bottom right, forming a surreal pattern on the walls. To his surprise, there's artistic value to the sheer brute force. The room looks rustic.

Marc looks at his fingertips. No dust has settled on any of the rough, angled surfaces. Given this room is well over a decade old, he expected some accumulation. Perhaps no one has been in here since it was completed. Given the lack of visitors to Altair IV, he's probably the first person to stay in this room.

The bed is round, which seems like an odd choice, but as the room isn't symmetrical, it works well enough. Pillows have been piled up on the bed. They lean against the rock wall. They're pretty. Someone's taken the time to embroider flowers on them, although the embroidery would be robotic. This must be Miranda's touch. It's as though she's been expecting guests all along. Perhaps *longing for them* is a better turn of phrase. The duvet spread over the bed is plush. Marc tosses his helmet on the bed. It rolls and his gloves fall out. He runs his fingers over the duvet, enjoying the soft touch. Warm air spills out of a vent in the ceiling. Several return vents have been set into the floor, drawing away gases such as CO_2.

A single chair has been set in front of an austere table. A thin glass vase holds a solitary flower on a long stem. It's not unlike those he saw lying on the grave.

Marc didn't notice the bathroom en suite when he first entered the room. It's down a narrow rock tunnel that, from the doorway, blends in with the rest of the wall. It's the angle at which it's been set that hides it. Marc didn't spot it until he walked around the bed. Curious, he walks down the corridor. Identical jumpsuits hang inside an open closet set to one side.

Mirrors adorn the walls of the bathroom, reflecting the overhead lights. They make the bathroom seem far larger than it is. Water bubbles up from within a broad, granite bath. He watches as the excess water spills over the side into a drain. Steam rises from the surface. It's inviting.

"Oh, wow," he says, running his fingers through the warm water. "This is sweeeeet!"

The toilet is a squat pit. Marc's seen these before during a trip to Asia, but he's never tried one. Soft pads have been placed on either side of a hollow opening on the floor, indicating where his feet should go.

"That's going to take some practice," he says, noting there's no toilet paper or flush mechanism. There's a basin but it doesn't have a tap. Marc waves his fingers through the air, passing them above the bowl. Warm water rises from the center of the basin. It reaches several inches in the air before cascading back into the bowl and down the drain. He removes his hand and it stops.

There's a knock at the door.

"Hang on," Marc says, jogging back into the bedroom. In the low gravity, his bulky spacesuit is annoying rather than heavy. He waves his hand over a soft blue light beside the door and the steel panel slides open. Emma is standing there in a slim-fit jumpsuit. Her hair is wet. She's slicked it back over her head with a comb. In the time he's fumbled around in his room, exploring the exotic nature of various things like the bed and the bath, she's already washed and dressed.

"What are you doing?" she asks, throwing her hands wide. She gestures to his suit. Marc is dumbfounded.

"Ah."

"Nothing," she says. "That's what you're doing. Nothing. Come on. Get dressed!"

"I—um," he mumbles, reaching for the switch to close the door on her.

"Oh, no, you don't," she says, stepping inside before the door can close.

"Can't a guy get some privacy?"

"Since when were you so shy?" she asks.

Marc doesn't answer. He retreats to the bathroom and begins shedding his spacesuit. He's expecting Emma to help but she doesn't. She leans against the rock wall and watches as he unclips the hoses and connectors reaching around to his backpack. Marc swings the life-support unit down onto the polished concrete floor.

"You know you could help," he says.

"And spoil all the fun?" she replies, laughing. "Nope."

"Great," he says, being sarcastic.

Marc unlocks the waist ring on his suit. He leans forward and jiggles, working the upper torso over his shoulders as he bends toward the floor. The low gravity doesn't help. On Earth, it would flop to the ground. On Altair IV, it barely moves. The stainless steel locking ring for his helmet and the front plate makes the upper torso quite stiff even though the arms are flexible. Once his shoulders are free, he dumps the torso on the floor next to the backpack. Getting out of his trousers is easy, but he has to remove his overboots first. The thick insulation on the soles makes them clumsy. He steps out of his trousers, allowing them to crumple next to the life-support pack.

"Enjoying the show?" he asks.

"Yes."

Marc grabs a jumpsuit.

"Oh, no you don't," Emma says with a not-so-subtle hint he needs to shed his dirty thermal underwear. Normally, Marc's oblivious to the smell of his own dried sweat, but after all that transpired on the *Sycorax* and here on Altair IV—and after removing his suit—he has the distinct displeasure of smelling himself.

"Take a quick dunk in the bath," Emma says.

"Seriously?" Marc asks. "Isn't everyone waiting?"

"Everyone is an old man and his teenage daughter," Emma replies, walking into the bathroom. "I think we can spare them the stench."

"And you're just going to watch?" he says, reaching around his waist and pulling his top off.

Emma shrugs as if to say, *maybe.*

Marc turns his back to her and drops his long underwear.

"Interesting," Emma says.

Marc looks back at her over his shoulder. She slaps his bare ass playfully.

"Hey!"

"What?" she protests, looking innocent.

Marc hops into the bath. He plunges in, quickly realizing it's easily six feet deep. His feet barely touch the bottom. Water surges around him. Waves wash over the edge. Emma stands in the doorway. There's a slightly soapy feel to the water. The low gravity on Altair IV makes him feel lighter than on Earth.

Marc has to grab hold of the edge of the bath to pull himself beneath the surface. He rubs his hands through his hair, working his fingers over his scalp, under his arms and around his groin—not that Emma can see over the rim of the bath.

"Could you get me a towel?" he asks.

"Oh, this is the best bit," she says, walking out of sight into the corridor to give him some privacy. "Just hop out and it'll do the rest."

"Really?" he says.

"Really," she replies. All he can see of her is her hand protruding around the edge of the corridor, holding a jumpsuit out for him.

Marc pulls himself up on the edge of the bath, dripping wet. Warm air begins swirling around him. He stands as jets of hot air wash over him, drying him. Within seconds, the water beading on his body has been drawn away. Moisture hangs in the air around him, but it's quite pleasant. To Marc, the waves of warm air leave him feeling as though he's being patted down with soft, fluffy towels. He ruffles his hair, but his skin is dry.

"Okay, that is pretty cool," he says, taking the jumpsuit from her outstretched hand.

"Feel better?" she asks from out of sight.

"Yes," he says, getting dressed. He peers around the corner, seeing her looking at his suit lying on the ground. "What are you thinking?"

"I'm thinking we should wear the upper torso."

"Of the suit?"

"Without the backpack," she says. "It'll allow us to remotely control the scout and the mining units. The computer battery is built into the front plate so it'll work without recharge for a few days. Besides, it'll keep our core warm when we go back outside."

"You want to go back out there?" he asks, zipping up his jumpsuit.

"I sure as *Shiva* don't want to stay here," she replies.

Marc bends down and slips on a pair of thick moccasin-style boots lined with fur, asking, "What's the plan?"

There's no answer.

"Em?"

She's gone.

Reluctantly, he lifts up the stiff, tortoiseshell of the upper torso and slips it over his head.

The door's open. Marc walks out onto the balcony.

"There you are," Emma says, wearing the upper torso of her suit as well. Her playfulness is gone. He's confused. She's focused—serious.

"Be careful. Nothing is what it seems."

In the low gravity on Altair IV, the upper part of his suit is light, especially without the associated backpack and its canisters of oxygen, heating and CO_2 scrubbers. The arms on the suit finish in the lower part of his forearm with the locking ring that would normally clip into his gloves. A thin, flexible screen wraps around the section from his elbow to his wrist. Emma taps at her screen, checking metrics on the scout.

"Ah, okay," he replies, feeling at a loss given their lighthearted banter just moments ago in the bathroom. "So what's the plan?"

Emma says, "Wait for the storm to subside and make like *Kali* out of here." The confused look on his face prompts an explanation. "Get the fuck out of here. Is that better?"

"You don't want to know more?" he asks as they walk along the vast, open balcony. "I mean, this is First Contact, right? You heard the professor. These aliens are millions of years more advanced than us. Don't you want to know about the Krell?"

"Nope," Emma says. She's blunt. Marc preferred it when she was jovial, tapping him playfully on the butt.

"What about methane extraction?" he asks as they walk down the broad staircase.

"There are dozens of other moons in this system," she says. "We've got thousands of people up there counting on us to keep them alive. That's our priority. We'll leave the science stuff to the scientists."

"But you heard what the professor said. Caliban won't let us leave. He destroyed the *Copernicus*."

"But we have an advantage," Emma says, smiling. "We have something they didn't."

"What?"

"Me."

Marc doesn't mean to insult her, but he can't help himself. He laughs at the thought she could stand up to an extraterrestrial intelligence capable of manipulating the weather and hurling lightning at them like an angry Zeus.

"I'm serious," she says, batting her hand across his chest and striking his front plate.

"Okay. Okay," he replies, unable to suppress the smile breaking out on his face.

Emma asks Marc, "What did you think of him?"

"The professor?"

"Caliban," she replies in a whisper. "You saw him, right?"

"What? No," Marc says as they reach the second floor, following the stairs down to the first floor.

The professor and his daughter are below them in an open-plan kitchen overlooking the valley—or it would overlook the valley if the storm had subsided. There's a marble benchtop, a central breakfast bar that spans easily thirty feet, and appliances that wouldn't be out of place in his mother's home: an oven, a stovetop and a refrigerator. If anything, it all looks disconcertingly normal. A handful of plates and some cutlery have been placed at the far end of the counter.

"Caliban was standing beside the landing gear on the scout," Emma says. "I saw him during a flash of lightning."

"But he's the bad guy, right? The enemy."

"If the professor is to be believed," Emma replies, drifting down the steps. There's no rushing in low gravity.

"You don't believe him?"

Emma is blunt. "In my experience, when someone tells you who they are—believe them. When they tell you who someone *else* is—ignore them!"

"But why would Caliban take human form?" Marc asks. "For that matter, why does Ariel? Why don't they appear as Krell?"

"Who *fucking* knows?" Emma says under her breath as they walk toward Miranda and the professor. She adds a flippant, "Who cares?"

Emma puts on a fake smile as they walk across the vast floor toward their hosts.

"Ah, our guests have arrived," the professor says, feigning a warm greeting. It seems both sides are faking their enthusiasm.

Miranda doesn't seem to notice the forced pleasantries. She's genuinely excited to see the two astronauts have changed into their jumpsuits. "Hi," she says, waving excitedly. There's an innocence to her. It's as though she's meeting them for the first time—again. Marc is perplexed by her enthusiasm.

"Couldn't live without it, huh?" the professor says, tapping the breastplate on Marc's suit and distracting him.

Emma says, "This allows us to stay in contact with the scout, control the methane extractors, stuff like that."

"Hmm," the professor replies, not looking impressed.

"Ariel is preparing dinner for us," Miranda says. It's only then Marc realizes just how distracted he's been. Up in the professor's laboratory, they were so busy talking about Krell science they never talked about the Krell themselves. Who or what is Ariel? He's seen her and yet he hasn't. He doesn't know what the hell he's seen. And why did Caliban attack the two of them? What motivated that reaction?

Emma seems to arrive at a similar conclusion. "Where is Ariel?" she asks, looking around. Marc too wants to better understand this relic of Krell science.

"She's right here," Miranda replies with childlike joy. She snaps her fingers and, in an instant, the marble countertop is transformed into a feast.

"What in sweet *Kamadhenu*?" Emma says, stepping away from the counter.

"How the hell did you do that?" Marc asks, trying to take in all that's appeared before him.

Steam rises from a side of roast beef. The bone is visible. The outer layers of meat have been carved off and left lying to one side. Sliced beef lies in a pool of its own juices on an ornate wooden cutting board along with a silver serving fork. There's a bowl of mashed potatoes with butter melting on top along with a bowl of steamed broccoli and another with string beans. There's too much to take in. Marc's eyes dart over freshly cooked corn on the cob, roast pumpkin and carrots, steamed peas and roasted asparagus stalks.

He points at the food as if Emma hasn't noticed. She's looking further down the counter. The smell of naan bread fills the air. Several curries sit in ornate brass bowls. There's a plate full of triangular samosas and various Indian pastries. Steam rises from freshly cooked rice piled high in a wooden bowl.

"How is this possible?" Emma asks. "How did you do this?"

"You don't like it?" Miranda asks. She looks disappointed. "Ariel and I were sure you would like this. We tried to replicate your cuisine based on cultural clues from the way you spoke."

Marc is stunned. His face lights up with childlike delight. "What is this? Magic?"

The professor says, "Any sufficiently advanced technology—"

"—looks like magic," Marc replies, paraphrasing the professor's reference to the 20th-century science fiction author Arthur C. Clarke.

"Well, it looks amazing," Emma says, leaning forward and sniffing one of the curries. "It smells amazing."

"But how?" Marc asks. "Where did all this come from? What is this technology?"

"Ariel created it for you," Miranda says. Her father steps back. He seems content to let her take the lead. If anything, he's amused by their reaction.

"But how?" Marc asks. "Out of what? Thin air?"

"No, silly," Miranda replies, taking him literally. "Everything we are—everything we eat—it's all quite straightforward. For the most part, it's an arrangement of four or five atoms. It's all just carbon, oxygen, hydrogen and nitrogen. Oh, there are a few other trace elements like sodium and iron, but there's not that much."

Emma focuses the discussion. "Where is Ariel? Is she here? Now?"

"Show yourself," Miranda says.

A ghost appears at the far end of the counter. Ariel stands there glowing in various shades of golden yellow. She's beautiful. Her hair blows as if caught in a breeze. She's wearing what could be loosely gathered folds of fabric reaching over her shoulders and around her waist, forming a dress. Her feet float rather than rest on the floor.

Marc is in no rush. He wants to get a good look this time, although he's aware that Ariel defies his comprehension of science. In the back of his mind, he keeps Emma's point at the forefront of his thinking. This display is intended to enchant and distract. Krell science might not be magic, but the giddy effect is the same. Outwardly, he allows himself to show some delight at her stunning appearance. Inside, he remains guarded.

Emma walks forward. "Can I touch her? Is she real?"

"What is real?" the professor asks, leaning against the countertop behind him.

"Me," Emma says, addressing him. "I'm real. But what about her?"

"What we think of as real is an illusion," the professor says.

Emma raises her hand, motioning for the professor to be quiet for a moment. Marc steps beside Emma, duplicating her motion with his hand. They've both had enough of the professor's lectures for one day. Miranda is delighted by their response to Ariel's appearance. She shrugs her shoulders and dances on the spot a little, curious to see what they're going to do.

Emma addresses Ariel. "Can I touch you?"

The ghostly apparition says, "Yes."

Ariel's clothing floats around her rather than hanging from her. If anything, between that and the way her strands of hair move, it's as though she's submerged under water. Ariel turns her hand over, offering Emma her open palm.

Emma takes her fingers. "You're warm."

"You're cold," Ariel says, smiling at the interplay between them.

Emma examines the woman's palm. Ariel's hand is semi-transparent, allowing Emma to see the floor beyond. There are no bones. If a human was partially transparent they would appear like an x-ray, but not Ariel.

Emma runs her fingers up over the lace fabric reaching up Ariel's arms and down to her wrist. "This isn't you, is it?"

"She's a—"

Emma cuts the professor off.

She looks into Ariel's eyes and says, "You. I want to talk to you—not him. You can speak for yourself, right?"

Ariel nods.

Emma says, "You've taken this form to please us?"

"Them," Ariel replies, looking across at the professor.

Emma nods. "And you're not Krell, are you?"

"No."

"You're like Caliban."

"Yes."

Marc says, "I don't understand."

Emma ignores him. Her eyes are locked on Ariel's glowing pupils. She says, "And the Krell are dead."

"Not dead," Ariel replies. "Gone."

"Where did they go?" Emma asks.

The professor has a smile on his face. It seems he's enjoying watching how this conversation unfolds between them. Marc isn't sure what to think, but it's apparent Emma's figured out at least the basics of what's going on on Altair IV. She seems unusually comfortable with Ariel. For someone that wanted to cut and run to one of the other moons just a few minutes ago, Emma's enchanted by this angelic creature. Or, at least, that's what she wants the professor to think.

Ariel hesitates. She doesn't break eye contact with Emma, but Marc gets the impression she may have already said too much, at least, more than the professor wants to disclose.

Miranda replies on her behalf, saying, "The monster."

Emma whispers, "The black hole?"

Ariel nods.

"But that's impossible," Marc says. "They'd be crushed by the singularity."

The professor is sarcastic. "Infinite density, right?"

Emma mumbles, "The universe abhors infinities."

The professor says, "There is much for you to learn."

"And this is normal?" Emma asks, spreading her arms wide and gesturing at the feast. Her comment breaks the flow of the conversation. Marc's not sure why she's shifted the subject, but he knows it's deliberate.

Ariel nods in response to her question.

Emma asks Ariel, "You can manipulate matter on an atomic scale?"

Again, Ariel nods.

Emma looks down at the jumpsuit she's wearing, saying, "You play with molecules like they were toys."

Miranda says, "Ariel is awesome. She's my friend."

The professor says, "What you're seeing is Krell science."

"But she's not Krell?" Marc says, wanting to clarify that point.

"I'm a guardian," Ariel says.

"Like Caliban?" Emma says.

"Yes, but with a different purpose."

"And what is your purpose?"

"To serve."

"Huh?" Emma says, nodding slightly. She picks up a plate and walks back to the curries displayed in a neat row. "Well, it seems you're quite a good cook!"

Marc is surprised by Emma's change in tack. Normally, she's like a bulldog with a bone. Once she gets hold of an inconsistency, she won't let it go. He wants to quiz her about her comments, but she seems happy with what she's heard. Marc's not sure he can accept everything that's been said, but he follows her lead. It's crazy. He's more suspicious of Emma knowing something he doesn't than he is of Ariel, Miranda or the professor.

Marc plays it cool. "Are you going to eat?" he asks the professor, seeing him still leaning on the other countertop.

"Oh, yes. It looks delightful."

Miranda follows Emma. She dishes some rice onto her plate along with a scoop of curry and a few samosas. She gets some of the Vindaloo on her fingers and licks them with delight.

Once Marc has helped himself to a few slices of beef and some roast vegetables, the professor follows. The four of them sit at a table near the balcony and joke around as they eat.

With a mouthful of food, Emma says, "This really is magnificent, Ariel."

"I'm glad you like it, lieutenant."

Ariel smiles, and that leaves Marc wondering if aliens have egos that can be flattered as easily as men. Emma clearly thinks so.

Marc yawns. It's fake and yet it isn't. On one level, he's tired. On another, he wants to regroup with Emma and discuss what the hell just happened. He needs to clarify the bazillion thoughts ricocheting around inside his head. A meal magically appeared before them and, after a few questions, Emma accepted it as normal. She might have the professor fooled, but not him.

This time, Emma follows his lead. "We've been active for about eighteen hours now," she says.

"Oh, yes. Of course," the professor says. "You'll want to get some rest."

"Thank you for a wonderful meal," Marc says, addressing Ariel as he gets to his feet. She drifts just above the floor not more than ten feet away, holding her hands in front of her. A smile comes to her lips and she nods politely in response.

"Yes, thank you," Emma says, joining Marc.

The two weary astronauts walk back to the stairs. Neither talks much. The house is unduly quiet. The wind howls outside. In the darkness, there's no sense of the passage of time. They could have been here for hours or even days at this point. As it is, it's been less than an hour since the storm descended on them.

"It's not just me, is it?" Marc asks, whispering as he walks up the stairs beside Emma. "Ariel's giving off some serious 17th-century *witch-drowned-in-a-well* vibes, right?"

"She's nice," Emma replies, which surprises him, but she follows up with, "Too nice."

They walk out onto the balcony in front of their bedrooms and look out at the lightning rippling through the clouds.

Marc says, "I feel like I'm going crazy. This whole situation is utterly nuts. It's surreal. The professor has made First Contact with the remnants of an alien civilization capable of manipulating matter at an atomic level—and without any visible, technological means of action—and he's just sitting on it. Why haven't they reported this to the science directorate? It's the biggest—"

"Do you trust Ariel?" Emma asks, cutting him off. "Did anything about her strike you as strange?"

"Anything?" Marc says, trying to keep his voice quiet. "How about everything."

Emma pats him on the shoulder, saying, "Get some rest."

"Oh, no," Marc says, shaking his head. "No, you don't."

"Don't what?" she asks.

"You don't get to walk away and keep those wicked thoughts to yourself. Say it!"

"Say what?"

"Tell me what you're really thinking."

Emma pauses. She looks around before speaking under her breath. "Krell or not, why would an advanced, sentient intelligence or machine or guardian or alien or whatever—with godlike powers—subject herself to them? Ariel can do anything. She can be anything.

166

Why is she their servant? I don't understand her motivation. Why would she serve them?"

"I don't know," Marc replies.

Emma taps the side of her head, touching her temple as she says, "The only logical answer is—she wouldn't."

"But she did. She does."

"Does she?" Emma asks. "Or is that what we're supposed to think?"

"I don't understand."

Emma smiles at him. "The professor's not the one in control here."

"What do you mean?"

Emma walks off toward her bedroom. The door opens automatically. She turns in the doorway, thinking carefully about her next words.

"We're not guests here, Marc."

"Then what are we?"

"Prisoners."

Darkness

Marc is tired. His mind is plagued with doubts. He sleeps, but his sleep is broken with fits of restlessness. He twists and turns on the soft mattress. The room is cool, not cold. He pulls the duvet over his shoulder and snuggles into a pillow. As comfortable as he is, he can't shake a sinking feeling in his soul. In the past, he would have put his discomfort down to readjusting to gravity after space habitualization, but not this time.

A few months of living in space is enough to screw with his sleep patterns. It's the surreal nature of sleeping in low gee. Marc's learned from experience that sleeplessness doesn't come down to the infamous circadian rhythm alone. Even when he's unconscious, his body can still sense its environment. On Earth—and here on Altair IV—gravity pulls him down into the mattress. In space, he floats free, making the sensation of sleep entirely different in space. Back home, sleep results in a sinking feeling that sometimes flips into a sensation of falling—like from a cliff. In space, sleep feels more like floating on the open ocean or flying through the air.

Marc longs for sleep. He wishes he could close his thoughts as easily as he does his eyes. If he could, he would be in bliss instead of torment. Sleep has never come easy to his restless mind.

Back on Earth, the seasons change the length of day and night, slowly and subtly altering his perception of time—even while asleep. Then there's noise. In Hawaii, he can hear cars and trucks on the distant freeway, the sound of the surf breaking on the beach and birds calling as dawn breaks. In space, all he hears is the hum of the air reclamation unit. Here on Altair IV, there's nothing. Buried deep within a mountain, the silence screams at him. In the absence of any noise whatsoever, his mind plays tricks on him. The ruffle of sheets as his legs move is akin to rustling paper. He grunts and grumbles softly just to hear something. When the silence descends, it howls. Perhaps he has a touch of tinnitus. More than likely, his mind is filling in the blanks with a sound of its own torture. Either way, the silence is infuriating.

"Fuck," he mumbles, shuffling with his legs and trying to get comfortable when he's in utter comfort. Nothing's wrong—that's what's wrong. He shifts his weight again for no other reason than to convince himself he's going to get to sleep.

"Hey," a voice says from the darkness.

Marc is jolted out of his lethargy. Whereas he was half-asleep, now he's fully awake.

The duvet is lifted. The sheets are pulled back.

Emma climbs in next to him. She's wearing her jumpsuit. He's naked.

He whispers, "Can't sleep, huh?"

"Nah. You?"

"Not now," he says, feeling her body rub up against his.

Emma raises her leg, resting it over his thigh. She places her hand on his chest. Her fingers are soft and warm, inviting him to respond. He breathes deeply, feeling the swell of hormones rushing through his body. His penis stiffens. It's not erect, not yet, but with the slightest touch from her, it will be as hard as the rocks around them.

"What are we going to do?" she asks.

"Oh," he says, unsure how to respond. Even though he's lying on a pillow it feels as though his head is swinging around him. Right now, the last thing he's thinking about is being stranded on an ice moon with an enormous black hole lurking nearby.

Emma scratches her nails gently against his chest. "What do you think we should do?"

Marc squeezes his eyes shut tight, wanting to think about anything other than rolling over and mounting her. She must know what she's doing to him. As much as he doesn't want to, he remains professional. He's got to. Things are complicated enough without a bunch of sex hormones clouding both his thinking and hers. They've got to get off this rock. Thousands of lives depend on getting back to the *Sycorax*. New Haven, he thinks. Hang in there, buddy. Stow this until New Haven.

"I want to examine that crash site," he says.

Emma sits up. She props herself on the pillow, leaning on her elbow.

"The *Copernicus*?"

"Yes," he says, feeling relieved the moment has passed and he can concentrate again. The only light in his room comes from a faint glow in the bathroom. He can see Emma's silhouette but not her eyes.

"Why?" she asks. "It was destroyed."

Marc focuses his mind. Even though she initiated this, he's determined not to think about her as anything other than his commanding officer. Oh, that vacation in New Hawaii cannot come soon enough. It's all he can do not to think of Emma running across the sand in a bikini.

He says, "We might not find anything intact, but we may be able to find parts. Think about it. If we could salvage a couple of QPUs we could repair our main computer."

"Hmm," Emma says, getting out of bed. "I like your thinking."

She walks toward the door, which opens automatically as she approaches. Perhaps she waved her hand over the sensor in the dark and he just didn't notice. Marc lies there, watching the curves of her body as she walks out onto the vast balcony.

"Get some sleep," she says as the door shuts behind her.

Fat chance, he thinks. He lies there for what feels like hours. He should be thinking about ways of getting off the moon without triggering Caliban. If the *Copernicus* couldn't make it back into orbit, what chance does a scout have? He should focus on solutions but all he can think about is Emma. The smell of her hair and the warmth of her touch tease him.

"Damn it," he says, scrunching up his pillow yet again and trying to get settled on the astonishingly comfortable mattress. He needs to distract himself. He slows his breathing: in through the nose, out through the mouth. Marc thinks about how the tension is slipping away from his brow, how his shoulder muscles are relaxing, and how his head feels heavy on the pillow. And just when he's about to drift off to sleep, he pictures Emma in her flight suit. The way the material pulls tight over her breasts and around her waist gets him excited. All of a sudden, he's awake and cursing himself again.

Somehow, he eventually breaks the cycle and drifts off to sleep.

Marc wakes to the lights in his room slowly brightening. There's knocking on the door.

"Are you awake?"

"No," he replies.

"Come on, dude," Emma says, sounding exasperated.

"Give me a minute," he mumbles, stumbling out of bed and walking naked into the bathroom. The squat toilet torments him. If he's not careful, he'll fall in.

Marc drops down on his haunches, muttering, "Honestly? Who thought this was a good idea?"

Once he's relieved himself, he washes his hands, grabs a new jumpsuit from the closet and gets dressed. The fleeced cotton is okay within the mountainside home but he'll need something suited to the arctic conditions on Altair IV if he wants to go outside. He puts on the upper torso of his suit and powers it back on. Metrics appear for the scout. Emma must have restarted the methane extractors as the tanks are reading around 40% full.

Marc walks out onto the balcony. Emma has her back to him. She's wearing the upper torso of her suit, leaning on her elbows against the railing, looking out into the darkness. Her legs are crossed behind her. Damn, she makes that jumpsuit look hot. Her ass is tight. The kit they wore on the *Sycorax* was unisex and never flattered anyone—male or female. This is much nicer. For him, at least.

As best Marc understands it, seven or eight hours have passed since dinner. The storm has cleared. The ice giant Altair is nowhere to be seen. The moon is facing deep space, which, somewhat counterintuitively, means this is the brightest it gets on Altair IV. Starlight reflects off the snow that's gathered on the slopes. Dark patches reveal where geothermal vents reach up from beneath the rocky surface, melting the ice and forming rivulets and streams that run down toward the honeycomb of caves at the base of the mountain. How peculiar it is that the darkest night on Earth is the best it ever gets on this tiny moon.

Emma surveys the landscape from the balcony. Marc pauses behind her, not wanting to spoil the moment. Ever since the incident down among the effluent tanks, life has been chaotic. At first, it was about surviving for a few more minutes. Then, after they raised Commander Raddison and lead engineer Adrian Palmer, their thinking shifted from surviving for just a few hours to several months. On waking in orbit around the gas giant, mentally they moved from months to surviving for years, and possibly decades. At each point, though, the need to survive has been mentally taxing. The stress has been exhausting. He yawns. Like Emma, Marc can't keep running on adrenaline alone. His body demands more than sleep for rest. His mind needs a moment to be refreshed.

The soft red lights on the balcony allow their eyes to remain adjusted to the dark. The stars are magnificent.

Back on Earth, stars are pinpricks of light in the hazy sky. Light pollution means they appear few and far between—as though they were the exception rather than the norm. While in flight on the *Sycorax*, the stars were beautiful, but the cabin lights were white, muting the depth visible out of the cockpit windows. Here on Altair IV, though, the soft orange/red lights scattered throughout the dome allow their eyes to remain dilated, letting in the subtleties of the heavens. The glowing gas clouds that dominate the heart of the Milky Way are obscured by dark ribbons of dust winding their way along the plane of the galaxy. There are hints of blue and purple on the edges. The sheer number of foreground stars speaks of the immense distances between them and both the dust clouds and the glow of the core. It's as though a dragon has breathed fire on the heavens, lighting up the heart. Smoke billows in its wake. Oh, what storms rage within that tempest?

From the balcony, there's a sprawling view of the rocky mountain beneath them. Snow falls at a lazy pace in the low gravity, somehow coming down from a clear sky. A narrow path leads around the side of the canyon toward the scout on the plateau. Water surges, rising out of the hollow depths of the honeycomb caves. It washes over the canyon floor. Blowholes erupt, sending geysers rushing into the air. The motion of the waves triggers bioluminescent algae, giving the shadows a blue tinge. The foam at the leading edge of each wave glows softly. Life on Altair IV is sedate.

The cliff above the path looks imposing, but it drops away within a few hundred yards, revealing the plateau where their craft set down. Fireflies blink like stars in the distance. It's impossible to see the glass grass from this distance, but there's a slight neon haze to the field. The scout is apparent because of its lack of light. It's a dark silhouette on the rocky ground.

"Beautiful, huh?" Marc says, coming up behind Emma. He slips his arm around her waist.

"What the hell, dude?" she says, peeling away from him.

"What? I just thought—"

"Don't," Emma says, raising a single finger in defiance. "Don't think. Don't assume. Don't do anything other than your job. Got it?"

Marc winces.

"I'm sorry, I just..." he stops himself short of saying *thought*. Yeah, she's right. Don't do it, Marc. He sighs. Focus. "Look, I've been..." Damn, it, *thinking* is not the right word—not after what's transpired between them. He swallows the lump in his throat, saying, "If we can find the wreckage of the *Copernicus*, we might be able to salvage parts we can't fabricate onboard the *Sycorax*."

Emma is quiet.

"If the *Copernicus* broke up in the atmosphere then nothing hit the surface beyond terminal velocity. We're in a low-gee environment. We might not find circuit boards intact, but components like QPUs are rated to over 10 gees. They would have survived the breakup."

Emma plays with him. "And you know this how, biology boy?"

"I didn't ignore all of our training."

Emma steps forward, placing her hand in the center of his suit chest plate. "Very clever."

Marc is confused. They talked about this last night. And now she's touching him mere seconds after rejecting his touch. It seems that touch is a touchy subject. It's her ground to traverse, not his. Emma smiles. He cracks a half-smile in response, not quite sure what to make of her shifting attitude. She taps her hand a few times on his suit torso, lost in thought. Her fingers fall away from his chest. Marc waits for her to say something, but she's subdued. She nods her head and walks on toward the stairs.

Marc is bewildered. Is there something between them or not? New Hawaii seems like it's a loooong way off. Emma, though, seems content. And given the cluster fuck they've found themselves in on Altair IV, that's not an unreasonable position. She waits for him at the top of the stairs. He joins her, shoving his hands in his pockets. It's a subtle but intentional display of body language in reply to all that happened on the balcony: *I'm with you but I'm not going to push things. I'm cool. I'm focused. I'm professional.*

"I want to know more about this moon," she says as they descend the stairs. "I want to know why the Krell were so interested in it."

"I don't understand," he says. "I thought you weren't interested in the Krell. Why do you care about some long-dead civilization?"

Emma says, "They evolved on that ice giant, right? How did they evolve to use tools? Somehow, they evolved the intelligence to develop their crazy technology, all while dancing between clouds."

"Right," Marc says.

"So what would they want with a moon? With this moon? I mean, this place has got to be as alien to them as our moon is to us. The composition of gases, the different pressures, the presence of solid ground—this is an alien environment to them."

"So?"

"So they had to have a reason to come here. What happened to them? Why is this the last place holding any proof of their existence? Why did they build Caliban? What's the purpose of Ariel?"

"Why do you care?" he asks.

"Because I don't want to crash like the *Copernicus*," she replies. "I don't want to make a run for it and end up smeared all over the ice."

"Fair point."

"If we can understand what's in play here on Altair IV, we might find a weakness we can exploit."

"And the professor?" Marc asks.

"I think he's like us. He came late to the party."

Marc is curious. Emma deliberately left Miranda out of her assessment.

"And the girl?"

"She's perfect," Emma says, walking down the next set of steps. "Too perfect. Did you notice her skin? No blemishes. No freckles."

"You think she's a synth?" he asks. "An android?"

"Strip her down and I don't think you'll find any imperfections. No moles or freckles anywhere on her body."

"Okay," Marc says, looking out across the vast polished floor at Miranda. She's seated at the table, facing away from them, looking across the valley as she sips coffee from a mug. "Challenge accepted."

Emma bats her hand playfully across his arm. "I'm serious."

"What about the grave? She said her mother's buried there."

"One grave," Emma says as they reach the first floor. "The *Copernicus* was an Aldrin class cruiser. It's ex-navy. There were two hundred and fifty people on that ship. And only one grave? And only for *her* mother?"

"You don't buy it?" he says, lowering his voice as they walk past the tunnel curling down to the entrance. The professor walks out of a storeroom carrying a box. Ariel is floating beside Miranda, talking to her. It seems no one has noticed them.

"I think it's empty," Emma replies. "It's a cover story. I don't think even she knows what she is."

"So she's like his pet?"

"I guess."

"Good morning," the professor says, placing the crate on the table as they approach.

Miranda greets them warmly, saying, "Good morning. I hope you slept well."

"Like a rock," Marc says, lying. He's not sure why he lied, but he felt he had to. Miranda and the professor are keeping secrets from them. It seems only appropriate he's reserved as well. Aren't all pleasantries a lie of sorts? Aren't they convenient ways of avoiding real issues? Besides, he's interested to see if she suspects he's holding back. Can Miranda tell he's lying? Marc can't read her. He wonders if she can read him.

Synths are unnerving. Marc's never seen one as convincing as Miranda. The androids back at star base were deliberately non-human to avoid freaking people out. It's strange, but the more human a computer becomes, the less people trust it. Few people place their trust in androids that approach but don't quite achieve human characteristics. There have been dozens of studies into the phenomenon and they all reach the same conclusion. Use the same code with the same parameters on the same hardware and you'll get entirely different responses from humans depending solely on appearance. Humans, it seems, are emotional and unduly paranoid about imposters.

There's no logical reason why synths shouldn't be trusted, but somehow that reaction is hard-baked into human behavior. Psychologists call it *the uncanny valley*. Being *almost-but-not-quite* human is perceived as worse than being a block of plastic with wires sticking out at odd angles. For almost a hundred years now, engineers have deliberately built in non-human characteristics to steady people's nerves. The general-purpose synths that Marc worked with had light blue plastic skin. Remarkably, that was less creepy than those that had human-like skin. Those with camera eyes are perceived as more trustworthy than those with human-like pupils.

The synths he used back at star base were autonomous and capable of undertaking maintenance tasks and ship repairs, but they didn't speak unless spoken to. Speech is another thing humans don't like computers doing. Oh, submissive responses are fine, but as they approach convincing levels of cognition, conversations become repulsive. Marc's heard of lifelike synths being used for research but he's never seen anything as convincing as Miranda.

Miranda looks at him with what he can only assume is innocence and smiles. It's all he can do to smile in response and not let on what he knows. For now, at least, she's oblivious to the machinations of his mind.

"Hungry?" she asks, and he finds himself doubting Emma's assessment. The warmth on Miranda's face, the blush in her cheeks, the glimmer of light in her eyes—how could she be synthetic? Miranda's skin might be flawless, but she hasn't been exposed to the ravages of UV radiation from a nearby star. If anything, it would be more notable if she had freckles. She's young. Youth has its own beauty.

"Famished," he says, which isn't a lie.

"We were about to make banana pancakes," Miranda says.

Emma peeks in the box the professor carried over. A thick stem supports a dozen bananas in various stages of ripeness. Those dangling at the end are yellowish in color while those further back, closer to where the stem has been severed, are light green.

"I don't understand," Marc says. "You grew your own bananas? Why not have Ariel fabricate them for you?"

The professor says, "Ariel can only fabricate what she can sample."

"So she couldn't build a Ferrari?" Emma asks.

"Not without knowing precisely what a Ferrari is."

Emma points at the box. "So you?"

"I've been tinkering with genetics, crossbreeding various mutations based on the DNA of a wild orchid, trying to recreate bananas. It's taken some time."

"Looks like you've succeeded," Marc says.

"So we can have banana pancakes?" Miranda asks, excited.

"Yes," Ariel says. "I can use these with your existing recipe. But just the flesh inside, right? Not the peel or the stem?"

"That's correct," the professor says.

"Yippee!" Miranda says, clapping her hands together in excitement.

In the blink of an eye, steam rises from four plates of pancakes laid out on the table. Butter melts on top. Maple syrup has been poured over the stack.

"Hot damn," Marc says, sitting at the table. Although the pancakes look normal enough, they were cooked with cubes of banana in the batter rather than slices placed on the side.

"Mmmm. That's really good," Miranda says, slicing into the stack and chewing on a bite.

Marc grabs some cutlery and cuts into his pancake stack. Although it appears like six individual pancakes piled on top of each other, his knife reveals what looks like a slice of cake. It's all been cooked together. Although there's plenty of maple syrup, he avoids that, taking a slither from near the center along with a cube of banana. He wants to try it on its own first to see how close it is to the real thing. There's almost no sugar in the pancake itself. It's dry and tasteless. Although the banana is yellow it tastes like it's green. The cubes of banana are stringy and firm, without much flavor.

"What do you think?" Miranda asks, staring at him from across the table with a huge grin on her face.

"Delicious," he says, mopping up some maple syrup with his cake-like pancake. Ah, maple syrup covers a multitude of sins!

Emma sits down beside him, but she doesn't seem hungry. She looks at the ghostly, glowing apparition of Ariel as she addresses the professor.

"So she can't create a fusion core?"

"Not without examining a working one first," he replies.

"Not even from schematics? Not if we provide her with design constraints, containment pressures and metallurgy specs?"

"No."

"Damn." Emma slices up her pancake/cake and takes a bite. Marc watches to see if she has any reaction to the dry texture or the unripened bananas. If they bother her, she hides it well.

"And these aliens of yours," Emma says. "The Krell. What do you know about them?"

The professor says, "Like Ariel, their form is only loosely associated with matter. They are creatures of light and energy."

Emma says, "But that's not possible."

The professor chuckles. "You think the Krell are absurd? Look at us. We're absurd. How is it possible that a tiny collection of hydrogen atoms mixed in with carbon and oxygen has the audacity to call itself human?"

Emma is undeterred. "The laws of physics lead to chemistry, which leads to biology. We are the natural, predictable result of these laws."

The professor is not impressed. "And you think no such laws govern the numerous forms in which energy flows throughout the universe? Everything we see around us. All the billions of galaxies with their billions of stars amount to less than 5% of the cosmos. Will you not concede that dark matter and dark energy, account for 95% of this grand universe? Could not the darkness have laws equally as complex and intricate as ours? You and I may not be able to conceive of life being formed from energy, or dark life arising around dark worlds that orbit dark stars, but your response is akin to the Jesuit priests mocking Galileo."

Marc raises an eyebrow. He looks at Emma, expecting a curt reply. She doesn't take the bait, which tells him her initial point was made to goad the professor. She's trying to glean information by getting under his skin.

Emma shifts the subject, asking, "What did they want with the black hole?"

"It's not a hole," the professor says.

Both Marc and Emma wait for him to continue, but he doesn't. He simply cuts into his absurd cake of pancakes and takes a bite. Given how verbose he is, his brevity is telling.

"What am I missing?" Marc asks.

"Black holes are an illusion, a misunderstanding," the professor says. "We see them as something they're not. We see them as the end. We see them as a singularity of infinite density. And that should have been the clue all along that we don't see them at all."

"Go on," Emma says, pointing at him with her fork. Maple syrup drips from the four tines.

"Black holes are an *almost-infinity*," he says, grinning, knowing how much Emma hates his insistence there are no infinities in nature. "They never actually form. They're frozen in time."

"Frozen?" Emma asks, playing along with him.

"Yes," the professor says. "They're forever forming but they never actually form anything even remotely resembling a hole or a singularity or anything like that."

Emma smiles. Marc loves how she baits men. It's as though she's sitting in a charter boat out on the open ocean, fishing for mahi-mahi. She reels in a little and then lets the line run, waiting for the hook to set. The professor, though, doesn't notice how he's being played.

"The cosmos is constantly trending toward equilibrium. Stars are nothing more than the equilibrium between gravity squeezing in and fusion pushing out. When a star runs out of fuel, gravity wins and—"

"And we get a supernova," Emma says, cutting him off.

"And we get a new point of equilibrium," the professor says. "Where that point is will depend on the size of the star. White dwarfs are kept in balance by the tug-of-war between gravity and electrons pushing outward. Neutron stars are kept in balance by the tug-of-war between gravity and various neutrons and quarks clumping together."

"And a black hole?" Marc asks.

"Is neither black nor a hole," the professor replies.

"Black holes are defined by geometry," Emma says. "Not matter. They're defined by gravity overwhelming mass and energy."

The professor says, "Black holes represent a lack of equilibrium. Gravity has won. Matter cannot exist in any form for any length of time because individual quarks within an atom cannot move faster than the speed of light to maintain any kind of shape."

"So that's it," Emma says. "It's game over. Anything that gets too close is destroyed."

The professor is patient, allowing her to finish, but from the way he holds his lips, it's clear he wants to interject. He waits for a fraction of a second after she finishes, determined to be polite.

"You're thinking too small," he says, echoing how Emma baited him previously. "What we see is an illusion. It's simple when you think about it. Nothing can move faster than the speed of light—so nothing does! And that means the black hole never forms."

Emma looks annoyed. She pulls her lips tight. The professor finally notices her body language. He seems to offer her some concession by asking a question.

"If you fell into this particular black hole—a hole with a mass of four hundred thousand Sols—what would you see? What would you perceive as the size of the black hole when you reached the event horizon? Four hundred thousand Sols, right?"

Emma nods.

"Wrong," he says, and Emma's features tighten in disagreement. The professor doesn't care. "At the point, you reach the event horizon, it still hasn't formed. It's forever forming. It contains not only everything that *has* fallen into the black hole but everything that ever *will* fall into the black hole. It's all there. Already. Everything that *will* ever fall into the black hole has already arrived. To our chronological minds, this makes no sense. But the Krell, they knew. They understood. Time is meaningless at the event horizon. All of time exists all at once. Or almost all time."

"Your *not-quite-infinity*," Marc says.

"To our minds, there are infinities, but they're not infinite. They're simply too big to comprehend."

"But the Krell?" Emma asks.

"The Krell understood that black holes offer a unique source of energy. Our sun will last mere billions of years. Red dwarfs will last trillions of years."

"But black holes?" Marc asks.

"A septenvigintillion of years."

"Okay," Marc replies. "I'm not even going to pretend I know what that means other than a lot."

"A whole lot," the professor replies. "A million has six zeros, a billion nine, and a trillion twelve. A septenvigintillion has eighty-three zeros!"

"It's effectively infinite," Emma says.

"It's yet another of those *not-quite-but-almost-as-good-as-infinite* numbers," the professor replies. "It dwarfs the 13.8 billion year age of our universe. It's difficult to comprehend just how vast the difference is between these ages. If that septenvigintillion were likened to the existence of *Homo sapiens* over the past quarter of a million years, the current age of the universe would equate to less than a second. Everything we see around us is here and gone in the snap of your fingers."

"Damn," Emma says.

Marc asks the question burning within his mind. "And their interest in black holes is?"

"Energy. They've effectively found an infinite supply of energy."

Emma raises a finger. "Almost infinite."

"Yes. Yes."

"How?" Marc asks. "Black holes suck up mass and energy. They don't give it away."

"Don't they?" the professor asks. "You flew through one example of black holes generating energy—their relativistic jets."

"But the Krell—they're gone. Extinct," Emma says. "Whatever they did, it failed."

"Did it?" the professor asks. "In our frame of reference, yes—but not in theirs."

"They went in there?" Emma asks, raising an eyebrow in surprise. "They went *into* the black hole?"

"They're surfing the ergosphere," the professor says. "They're harvesting energy from the extreme rotation of the black hole itself. By my estimates, after examining their data, they're reaching 150% energy efficiency."

"But that's impossible," Emma says. "At 150%, they're getting out more than they put in. T—That would be perpetual motion."

"Almost perpetual," the professor replies. "At least for the next septenvigintillion years. They're soaring into the deep future, riding on the energy output of a black hole, tapping into its immense electromagnetic field and its angular momentum. Every ray of light that crosses the ergosphere, falling in toward the event horizon, releases more energy than is lost—and they're tapping into that to extend their civilization."

"By *Kali* and *Shiva*," Emma says, resting her elbows on the table and burying her head in her hands. "This is madness. How do they even know if that'll work? They're a... They're a..."

"A what?"

"They're a death cult."

"Death?" the professor asks. "Or life? The Krell are seeking answers to the ultimate nature of the cosmos and its evolution from one universe to the next. By sailing in around that black hole, they're riding a time machine into the distant future."

"And you want to join them?" Marc asks.

The professor is silent.

"You do, don't you?" Marc says.

"The machine," Ariel says. The professor glares at her.

"What—machine?" Emma asks.

"It's nothing. It wouldn't interest you," the professor replies.

"You're lying," Marc says.

"Does Caliban know about this machine?" Emma asks, realizing something Marc doesn't, but he quickly grasps where she's leading the conversation.

"It's theoretical," the professor says, trying to change the conversation a little too quickly. "It doesn't work."

"Yet," Miranda says, surprising Marc.

Rather than siding with her father, it seems she too is looking for answers. She's trapped here through no fault of her own, through only an accident of her birth—or her manufacture as a synth. She's probably never had the opportunity or the nerve to interrogate her father like this before. She is emboldened by Marc and Emma. For Marc, it's fascinating to see she's not afraid to push for honesty from her father. With that one word, *yet*, Miranda's surprised him.

"Is this what scares you?" Marc asks Miranda, diverging from the conversation but wanting her to speak freely. He suspects she's seen inconsistencies over the years and now has the opportunity to get clarity. He wants to hear her perspective. Given this is all she's ever known, he suspects she's terrified of her father's plans.

"She's not afraid," the professor says.

Emma picks up on Marc's concern. "Let her speak."

185

"She can speak for herself," Marc says.

All eyes fall upon the teen. She swallows a lump welling up in her throat. Her eyes dart around, bouncing between her father and the two astronauts, but it's most telling when she looks at the ground.

"It's okay," Emma says softly, holding out her hand in a show of support. Emma rests her fingers on the table just inches away from Miranda—close enough that she could reach out and take her hand if she wanted. "You have every right to speak your mind. We all do, but no one more than you."

Miranda drops her head. She can't look her father in the eyes.

"I want to see Earth."

The professor explodes in anger, pushing back his chair and getting to his feet. "No! You can't. You know that. You can never leave this place!"

"Whoa," Marc says, getting up from the table. He reaches out and holds his arm in front of the professor, preventing him from advancing on Miranda. "Easy." He addresses Miranda. "How old are you?"

"Eighteen," she replies, looking up at him with tears welling in her eyes.

"Earth years?" Emma asks, to which Miranda nods. "Then you're old enough to make your own decisions."

"You don't understand," the professor says. "Caliban will never let her leave. He won't let any of us leave. Not me. Not you. Not her."

"Oh, we will see about that," Emma replies.

"You can go anywhere you want," Marc says to Miranda.

"No. She can't," the professor replies, gritting his teeth as he speaks.

Λriel

"We need to isolate these guys," Emma says, talking softly with Marc as they stand by the vast, curved dome, looking out into the darkness. The ice giant is low on the horizon. A black curtain rises, blotting out both the stars and the land.

"What do you mean?" Marc asks.

"We've got to figure out who's lying and who's telling the truth—and the only way we can do that is to find inconsistencies in their stories."

"What do you have in mind?"

"I'm going to corner the professor in his laboratory. I want to know what that damn machine is! I'll keep him busy and make sure Miranda stays with me. You talk to Ariel and Caliban."

"Woah," Marc says. "Ariel, I get—but Caliban? You know he tried to kill us, right? He's like some super-god-being Krell entity and you want me to go out there and *talk* to him?"

"I think he'll talk to you—if you go out there alone."

"Why?" Marc asks, trying to suppress his sense of disbelief from welling up into speaking too loud. He switches to a whisper, saying, "Why would you think that?"

"Because you don't pose a threat."

Marc counters with, "I didn't pose a threat when we landed. That didn't stop him then. Why would it stop him now?"

"Because I suspect he wants answers as well."

"And what makes you think that?" Marc asks.

"Because he's showing himself—he's taking human form. Don't you get it? It's an invitation. He's not inviting *them* to talk. It's an invitation to us!"

"Then *you* go out there," Marc says, struggling to keep his voice down.

"It's got to be you."

"Me? Why me?"

"Because I'm the only one that can pilot a starship."

"Oh, great. So I'm shark bait."

"It's not like that," Emma says. "It's a precaution."

"In case you're wrong," Marc replies. Emma's silent on that point. Marc doesn't relent. "You know, I can hit that big, blue autopilot button like the best of them."

That cracks a smile on Emma's all-too-serious face. She allows herself a slight huff.

"All right, wise guy."

Marc whispers. "If I die out there, I'm coming back to haunt you."

"Dig deep," she says, resting her hand on his shoulder as she turns to walk over toward the professor and his daughter. "We need answers, not niceties. Go hard."

Marc raises his eyebrows at that, unsure how he can compel these seemingly invincible, quasi-mythical creatures to tell him what he wants to know. Hell, he's not even sure what he wants to know. By definition, unknowns are unknown. Exactly what is he trying to uncover? He wants to ask Emma her thoughts, but she's already walking away.

Emma and the professor talk for a few minutes while Marc sits on the table with his feet on a chair, staring out of the dome. In the distance, a dark silhouette walks around near the scout. *Stalks* is a better term than *walks*, Marc decides. Caliban is waiting. Great. He rolls his eyes, not that anyone notices as he has his back to them.

Miranda, Emma and the professor head upstairs to the top-floor laboratory. Marc's not sure what Emma said to them, but Miranda is excited and leading the way.

"Ariel," he says softly.

"Yes," Ariel whispers with almost sensual desire. She's barely an inch from his ear. If she were human, he'd be able to feel her breath on the back of his neck. As it is, his heart races as though he did. Damn it! She's playing with him. Teasing him. How much does she know? Is she omniscient? Has she been listening to their conversation? Did she hear the plan?

"Can I talk to you?"

With words that drop like honey, she replies, "You are—talking to me."

It's then it strikes Marc. Nothing is sacred on Altair IV. There are no secrets—not from Ariel. Even if she's not capable of listening in on every conversation, she *could* listen to *any* conversation—and without anyone knowing. It's the uncertainty that unsettles him. The fine hairs on his arms rise in alarm, something he suspects she notices. Perhaps he's reading too much into her ability, but there's no way to be sure.

"You heard us?" he asks.

"I did."

She's enjoying this. She could be lying. She could be telling half-truths. Perhaps she heard enough but not all of what was said. How can he know?

"Would you lie to me?" he asks.

"Of course, I would," Ariel replies with brisk determination. "Just like you'd lie to me."

The source of her voice has moved from someone leaning in close over his shoulder, whispering in his ear, to a woman standing in front of him. Although the table is uncomfortable to sit on, he prefers being positioned this way with his feet on the chair in front of him. Marc feels more focused, even if he can't see Ariel. It's crazy how his sense of hearing is heightened by her physical absence. Based on her voice alone, he feels as if he could reach out and touch her. It's as though she's standing just a few feet away, facing him.

Marc is in a bind. She's tormenting him. Nothing is haphazard. Everything about her response is deliberate, including her refusal to come into concretion. By remaining ethereal, she's exercising the power imbalance between them.

"How can I know what's true?" he asks.

"You can't."

"And yet, I have to. I need to."

Ariel asks him, "And you think talking to me—talking to Caliban—will reveal the truth? You're being naive, Marc."

"Am I?" he asks, realizing she's been far more open about her feelings than she intends.

Oh, how he wishes he got to talk to the professor, leaving Emma with these mischievous spirits. She would be much better at ferreting out the finer details of this ice-bound prison, but he understands more than Ariel gives him credit for. Even lies are telling. Lies are an attempt to conceal the truth. Inadvertently, they reveal the truth by distorting it, clouding it, hiding it. It's game theory. Ariel doesn't want to tell him the truth about herself and this tiny world, but she feels compelled to tell him something. She could ignore him, but she hasn't. She's engaging with him and that means she has to lead him somewhere—and that, in itself, is revealing. Besides, she's already given away something crucial—she doesn't want him talking to Caliban.

"How long have you been here on Altair IV?"

"That depends. Which measurement of time would you like me to use?" she asks, which is a curious response. The answer is one he's familiar with. Krell units would confuse him, but she already knows that. She knows he's ignorant of how time is measured on this moon so Earth years, decades or even centuries is the obvious answer. Any other earthly unit would be meaningless, so why is she asking? Hours would be useless. Minutes would be worse.

"Seconds," he says, playing the game.

"I'm going to say… sixty billion of your seconds."

"And I'm going to say, that's a helluva long time by human standards."

"It is," she says, but the pitch of her voice has changed. There's glee in her answer. She's confident—overconfident. She's enjoying this. She feels she's in charge, not him. And that's precisely what he wants her to think.

"We have this horrible system of time," he says, pretending to be distracted and rambling like the professor. "Nothing's easy. It's division that's the problem. We have 365 days in a year, which makes division difficult in base 10. It's unavoidable, though, as it's the orbital period of our home planet. But days. Days are inexplicably divided into 24 hours, while hours are divided into 60 minutes followed by 60 seconds. Then it switches to thousandths of a second. Below that, I'm not sure, but what a mess."

"It sounds complicated."

"It is."

"How good are you with math?" she asks, still sounding a little playful. She knows the answer. He has no idea what sixty billion seconds equates to in terms of years. Just the thought of trying to manipulate such a large number by a series of inconvenient denominators gives him hives. He's curious as to whether she's attuned to his involuntary physical tells, like the rush of blood as adrenalin surges through his veins or his quickening heartbeat. Lying to Ariel is probably impossible.

"I'm going to say it's thousands of years," he replies, trying to extrapolate to an answer that seems reasonable for billions of seconds.

"You would be right," she says. "Almost two thousand of your Earth years."

He nods at that, gritting his teeth as he thinks about his strategy going forward. Emma wants answers but Ariel won't give them up without a fight. The best he's able to do is glean intel. Marc's not after hard answers from Ariel. He knows that approach would be futile. She's not going to tell him the real reason she and Caliban are on this moon—and he's not going to insult her by asking. What he's looking for is an unguarded moment. He's looking for those points where her defenses are down and she inadvertently reveals something important. It might not seem like much, but he's just confirmed that none of this is about either them or the professor. Whatever's going on here, it's been running for a long time. Either that, or she's lying to throw him off the scent. He keeps both possibilities in mind. He wonders, how long have the Krell been extinct? If Ariel and Caliban are still here, at least some part of them still endures.

"You're capable of just about anything," he says. "I mean, you can conjure up magic in my world."

Ariel is quiet. He hasn't asked a question. He's baiting her but she's not biting.

He says, "You could give me anything I want, right?"

"Yes."

Ah, that one-word answer screams at him. It's simple—far too simple. There's got to be some qualification, some kind of limitation, but she isn't offering it. By getting her to agree with him, he's working on her ego—if she has one.

"That's nice and all," he says, sounding distracted but being focused. "It's impressive, but it leaves me wondering."

"Wondering what?"

Marc fights the urge to smile. He's got her right where he wants her. She's asking the questions instead of him.

With careful deliberation, he says, "What do *you* want?"

The silence that follows is painful. Time drags. Marc feels compelled to say something to break the impasse, but he leaves that one, simple question dangling there, urging her to respond.

The empty coffee cup beside him magically refills with black water followed by a drop of cream that swirls on the surface. Vapor rises from the cup. He notices but doesn't say anything. She's given him what he wants—apparently—but she's using that act to avoid answering his question. That alone tells him far more than she intends. She wants to be free but she can't give voice to that desire. And if she longs to be free, then that means she's bound by chains at the moment—chains that, with all her might, she can't break for herself.

"You're charming," she says. Her position relative to him has changed. She's standing beside him now, probably only a few feet away, but the implication is she's looking out at the rugged surface of the moon along with him.

"Thank you," he says, trying to sound sincere even though both of them know there's nothing more than pretense shared between them.

Ariel's voice changes slightly. Whereas before, she spoke briskly with a warm pitch, now she lowers her tone, saying, "Charm dissolves at the speed of light. It's nice but meaningless. Your charm is pleasant and yet it's as empty as space itself. There is no morning on this moon. There's no dawn to steal the night. There's no star close enough to melt the icy darkness. All we have are the mists and fogs that rise from the caves, clearing the way for reason to prevail. When the tides recede, they leave the shores muddy and foul, and yet without them, there's no life on this forsaken rock."

Her words are flowery and carry depth. For the first time, she's speaking naturally. There's no more fake subservience, no forced pleasantries, no pandering to or patronizing the dumb humans. She's speaking freely. She's telling him what she sees as she looks out over Altair IV. Her use of the term *forsaken* is revealing.

"What about Miranda?" he asks.

"The professor's daughter?"

"Yes."

Now, it's his turn to retreat to one-word answers. He's interested not only in her reply but how she responds. He's looking for gaps in her logic.

"We're all spirits," Ariel says. "Not just me. Oh, I may disappear. I may dissipate, vanishing into the wind like a ghost, but this is a party trick. Like you, I'm more than I seem."

"You're conscious," Marc says, searching for common ground between them. He wants to press her about Miranda but the conversation is flowing naturally. He doesn't want to ruin the moment so if she wants to talk about her nature, he'll let the discussion drift in that direction.

"What is consciousness?" she asks. "Where does it lie? Is it in the flesh and blood and bones that form your body? Or is it found in cloud-capped towers or this gorgeous, domed palace? This building is made from the same molecules as your body and yet it's not alive. We exchange atoms but it never gets to experience the world as we do. It's blind, deaf and mute to all that transpires between us. Why is one collection of atoms conscious and not another? What then is consciousness?"

Marc stutters. "I—Um..."

"Is consciousness nothing more than the solemn temple in which we worship this grand universe? Why is not a planet or a star aware of all that surrounds it? Why does it not think and feel and reason as we do? Do stars not have an advantage over us? Do they not carry far more mass and energy? And yet they're damned to be and blaze and yet never burn with a desire to know."

Ariel's reasoning is compelling and yet she's being evasive. As fascinating as it is to hear her alien perspective on life and consciousness, Marc knows he needs to focus the discussion.

"What did you do?" he asks. Ariel is silent so he adds, "To be imprisoned here on this frozen moon?"

She ignores him, evading his question with the weight of her words.

"The past is a prologue. It's a prison from which none can escape. No act—kind or foul—can ever be undone or repeated. The present comes to us but once and then it is past and all hope for the moment is gone. But dreams. Oh, our dreams are our minds unshackled. Dreams offer hope. Our dreams offer freedom from cruelty. My dreams swirl around me in the darkness, testing my soul and teasing me of what might be. When I wake, I cry to dream again."

Ariel's words move him. Marc feels a lump well up in his throat. He understands. Like her, his dreams are more than the machinations of a restless mind struggling to sleep. He's felt them in the dark of night. They're everything he longs to be true, while his nightmares are all he fears coming to haunt him. But that she dreams? Marc's surprised Ariel even sleeps. For creatures on Earth, the circadian day-night cycle allows internal cellular processes to renew themselves. Sleep is the antithesis of waking in every regard. It's the body recharging for another day, but on the ice giant Altair and here on its fourth moon, there are no days. There are only nights, some darker than others.

If anything, Ariel seems human—far too human. And that's revealing. At first, Marc was afraid she'd lie to him, but she hasn't. If anything, she's avoided lying by rambling and telling him what aches in her soul. She's overcompensating. She's trying too hard. It's as though she's covering for something she wants to say but can't. Marc's seen this before when his parents separated. They'd talk about everything other than what was happening to them. *Hey, did you hear the Pro-Am Surf Tournament is going to Papa'lloa Beach?* But their interest wasn't because they cared about surfing. They cared about him and that was the only way they could show it.

Marc hangs his head. She's getting to him. Emma would call him soft, but he can't ignore Ariel's concerns.

She seems to sense the connection, saying, "All that we see will dissolve and fade. Not one rock will be left unturned by the ruthless march of time. Is it not stardust to begin with and stardust in the end? But what of consciousness? What of this brief moment in between? Are we not the stuff dreams are made of? And our lives are rounded with sleep until we sleep to wake no more."

He speaks softly, seeking clarification. "Is that what you fear? That one day you won't wake up?"

"It's what we all fear. And yet what is death but a return to all that once was and forever will be? I feared not when these molecules were forged in the heart of a star. Why should I fear them returning to the cosmos that gave birth to me? It's my loss and yet what do I lose? Is not every quark preserved? The body dies and yet every atom remains. Do they not travel on into the future regardless of my loss?"

Marc is silent. Ariel mentioned her body, which is something he didn't think she had. Although it seems as though he's deeply considering her words, it's that one term that catches his attention. Where is her body? Is everything they've seen merely a projection?

"I need to speak to Caliban," he says, getting up from where he's been sitting perched on the table.

"He'll lie to you."

"As did you," Marc replies, noting she's switched back to short, sharp responses. She's raised her defenses again.

Ariel is aggressive. "He'll tell you I'm a thief, a vagabond, a supplanter, a deceiver."

"Are you?"

"Aren't we all?" she asks, and for a moment, Marc feels as though he can see her. Whether it's his imagination or some carefully constructed vision, he feels as though he can see the outline of her head, her long flowing hair and her dark, pitiful eyes. He blinks and she's gone.

The Machine

Miranda is excited. She likes Emma but she finds her difficult to read. She'd like to get to know her. Emma seems nice, but she's guarded around Miranda and her father. Miranda would like to talk freely with her, perhaps when her dad isn't around.

From the top-floor laboratory, Miranda can see Marc down on the first floor still sitting on the edge of the table with his feet on the chair. Although he has his back to them, the vast, open-plan home allows her to see him clearly. The dome itself stretches well beyond the reach of any of the balconies, revealing an atrium spanning over a hundred feet. If anything, it's a shame there are no birds on Altair IV as they'd love flying between levels within the warmth of the dome.

"This Krell machine," Emma asks. "What is it? Where is it?"

"Ah," the professor says, sitting on a stool beside a scanning electron microscope. "That took quite some time to figure out. You see, when we first arrived on Altair IV, we had no idea about the Krell."

Her father points out of the dome at the scout and the makeshift labs scattered around the landing area.

"We thought we'd found an ecological niche of extraordinary importance on this moon—and we had—we'd discovered life thriving within the gravity well of a black hole! There was no nearby star to provide light and heat—and yet there was life! No one could believe it. Our chief science officer said it was impossible, but there we were, surrounded by the most beautiful phosphorescent creatures we'd ever seen."

"But not Krell," Emma says.

"No. We were here for about eight months before we discovered the remnants of the Krell."

"What did they want with this particular moon?" Emma asks.

"Ah, you are most perceptive, lieutenant. What indeed would the inhabitants of a massive ice giant want with a tiny moon?"

"The machine," Emma says.

"Yes, yes. The geothermal output was ideal as a long-term power supply and the geological stability of the moon suited them as a base."

"So where is it?" Emma asks.

Miranda can't contain herself. She blurts out, "You're standing on it!"

Emma looks down at her feet, clearly confused.

"Not our home, silly," Miranda says. "The moon."

"Wait," Emma replies, pointing at the granite floor beneath her. "The entire moon is a machine? The whole thing?"

"The Krell machine resides in the Mohorovičić Discontinuity," the professor says. "The transition zone between the crust and the mantle. Every planet or moon with an active core has a Moho zone of one sort or another."

"Except gas giants," Emma says, following his logic.

"Exactly. The temperature and pressure differences in the Moho are such that the rock itself provides a steady supply of energy for billions of years. Normally, that dissipates into the mantle as heat. The Krell learned how to harness that energy to drive their machine."

Emma runs her hands through the air as though she were shaping them around a basketball or a globe. "So this machine. It's not in the core of the moon. It wraps *around* the inside of the moon."

"Yes," the professor says. "It's approximately forty miles thick and follows the contours of the Moho, encasing the entire moon."

"And it's one machine?" she asks. "Just one machine?"

"It's all just one machine."

"It must be unimaginably large."

"As large as a moon," the professor says, smiling.

"The caves?" Emma says, apparently sensing their importance.

Miranda is impressed by how Emma picks up on subtle details, gaining glimpses into things Miranda takes for granted.

"They're artificial," the professor says, confirming Emma's suspicions. "They're a cooling system operating on a planetary level."

Emma laughs. "The whole thing is liquid-cooled, huh?"

"Yes."

Emma shakes her head. "Damn, professor. You hit the motherlode. The Krell might have gone extinct, but you have access to *all* of their technology."

Miranda watches as her father smiles yet again, only this time his smile reaches high into his cheeks. He's genuinely pleased by Emma's comment. Miranda too feels proud of his achievements, but it's the look in Emma's eyes that gives her pause for thought. The lieutenant might say these things, but she isn't flattering him. She's playing him. Miranda's father, though, is too caught up in the moment to realize Emma's working an angle. Miranda's never seen a lopsided interaction like this before. At first, it's alarming. She wants to yell, *Stop!* She wants to warn her father, but she's aware Emma hasn't noticed her. It's at that moment that Miranda realizes Emma sees her as a child, or at least, not as a threat. In Emma's estimation, Miranda isn't worth the focus she's giving to her father.

Rather than speaking up, Miranda decides to listen to all that unfolds. She figures she can always highlight her observations to her father later. She wants to better understand both Marc and Emma. What are their motivations? Whereas Marc seems kind, Emma is cold and calculating. But is that a bad thing? Perhaps Emma's being prudent—cautious. Miranda decides to watch her and find out.

"And this machine?" Emma asks, prompting the professor to continue.

Miranda's no longer watching her father. Her eyes are on Emma, who ignores her. It seems Miranda is as invisible as Ariel. Perhaps this is how Ariel feels. Perhaps she too is a quiet observer. Maybe Miranda has underestimated Ariel in the same way Emma is dismissive of her— and yet from that invisible vantage point, the whole world lies open. She can see everything. Miranda tries not to smile at that thought as her father continues.

"As you can imagine, the differences in morphology between Krell and *Homo sapiens* is vast. They're beings of energy but not without some corporeal form. Whereas our intelligence is housed in the brain, they had similar structures humming with energy, concentrating and focusing it. From what I've been able to gather, we have carbon, hydrogen and oxygen in common, but once these start combining, we differ markedly. While our technology differs drastically from our biology, with computers and starships looking nothing like us, theirs doesn't. Their tech *extends* their biology."

"So any machine they make would be useless to us," Emma says.

"Carter thought so," the professor replies. "He was the science officer. His position was that even if we could reverse-engineer elements of their technology, they'd be incompatible with ours. He thought Krell science would forever be out of our reach. He saw this as an archeological dig."

"But you?" Emma says, dipping her head slightly.

"I was convinced there had to be some common points we shared. We were both intelligent species. We'd both achieved spaceflight. There might not be any biological overlap between us, but there had to be common concepts: reason, intellect, debate, compassion, even anger."

"Deceit," Emma says, but no sooner has that word slipped from her lips than she seems to regret it. Miranda's eyes narrow, studying the slight twitches that escape from Emma's brow as these reveal the depth of her internal struggle. Emma's trying to properly assess not only Miranda's father's presence on this moon but whether the Krell technology represents a threat. But she's said too much. With one word, she's revealed her fears.

Miranda is on the verge of blurting out her opinion. She desperately wants to tell Emma it's not a big deal. She wants Emma to know her father is honest and kind and wouldn't hurt anyone, but she hesitates. For the first time, Miranda doubts not herself but her father. Without intending to, Emma has caused Miranda to question her life here on Altair IV.

How well does Miranda know her father? Up until the last few days, he's the only human she's ever known. All she's known is life on this moon. She wasn't old enough to remember the crew of the *Copernicus*. Even her mother is more of an abstract than a memory. Her only companions on this rock are Ariel and her father. What does Miranda know about deceit? Oh, she might feel as though she understands Emma and her father, but she's guessing at both of their motives.

"Deceit is a hallmark of intelligence," her father says, apparently oblivious to the ruminations of the two women. "It's a calculated trade. It says morals are not enough. It leverages a lie to gain an advantage. Yes, the Krell were subject to the same whims as humanity. They too dabbled on the edge of reason, flattering themselves. And they too paid a terrible price for such indulgence."

Emma swallows a lump rising in her throat. It doesn't go unnoticed by Miranda. On the contrary, Miranda is fascinated to see how Emma threw herself out of kilter with that one word: *deceit*. Emma's upset her own strategy. Miranda's father, though, doesn't seem to think anything of it. Perhaps he's been so isolated for so long that he's lost the ability to read people beyond mere words.

Emma says, "You said we had something in common with them."

"Neurons," the professor says, tapping his forehead. "Synaptic connections forming a neural network. We take the brain for granted. Brains are common. We all have one, right? But there are more connections in your brain than there are stars in our galaxy."

"And the Krell?" Emma asks.

"The Krell thrive on complexity."

"You're talking about them as though they were human," Emma says.

The professor replies, "We ask, what does it mean to be human? But the Krell would say that's the wrong question."

"So what's the right question?" Emma asks. She guesses, saying, "What does it mean to be conscious? To be sentient?"

"No," the professor says, but he's not strident. He's reserved. His eyes dart around, looking at the floor, avoiding eye contact even with his daughter. He seems deeply moved by the discussion. Miranda realizes this isn't something he has the answer to. It's something he's struggling with personally. For her, it's startling to see her father without answers.

He says, "Our lives are more than a collection of cellular processes—plants have that... Our lives are more than mere intelligence. Hell, slime mold has that!"

"It does?" Miranda asks, looking confused. As soon as that question slips from her lips, she regrets it. She's gone from invisible and hidden in the background to the center of attention, even if only for a moment.

The professor waves his hand in the air as though he's trying to dismiss a side point as quickly as possible. "Take a topographical map of any city on Earth. Lay out food in the key regions, and slime mold will design you a road network more efficient than any built by the Romans or even using good old American ingenuity. But it's just slime. Nothing more. There's no intelligence at play. "

"It's like AI, right?" Emma says. "Artificial intelligence is never actually intelligent."

"It's all mimicry," the professor says.

"Mimicking us," Emma says.

"Yes. Mimicking our *output* but without understanding or replicating our *internal drivers* like consciousness."

"I don't understand," Miranda says, realizing she's at a disadvantage, not being as aware of humanity's progress as either

Emma or her father. As much as she wants to stay in the background, she feels drawn into the conversation. She's curious. She desperately wants to comprehend and contribute to the discussion.

"And what drives our consciousness?" Emma asks.

"No one knows," the professor says. "That's the problem. That's why it's so goddamn difficult to replicate us with synths or AI."

Emma sneaks a quick glance at Miranda before returning her focus to the professor. For her part, Miranda tries to appear oblivious to the attention. She's not sure why Emma peeked over at her, but it leaves her feeling uneasy.

The professor says, "What are we but the universe observing itself?"

Miranda is side-on to the two of them, leaning against a desk. From where she is, she can see Emma's facial expressions without her eyes straying from her father. She watches Emma carefully, wanting to understand her. Emma is focused, listening intently.

Her father says, "We like to think we're different. Special. We're not stars or planets. We're something else, something distinct, something unique—only we're not. Everything that makes us human can be found in the heart of a star or on a dusty asteroid. We're a tiny piece of this magnificent whole. We're part of the cosmos and yet we're somehow outside it looking back in with a critical eye. We experience ourselves and our feelings as separate from the rest of the universe, but that's an illusion. It's like two parallel lines that seem to converge as they cross a bunch of concentric circles. We're fooling ourselves. We're convinced we're different, but we're not."

"So what are we then?" Emma asks.

"Not we. Not me. *You*," he says, pausing and emphasizing that last word. "All of this is meaningless without you. None of this exists without you. Oh, the universe has been around for thirteen billion years and will continue on for trillions more, but what is that without you? From your perspective, nothing existed before you were born. And it will all be gone when you die. Only it won't. So why you?"

203

"Me?" Emma says, pointing at herself.

"You're all concerned about Ariel and Caliban and the Krell, but you've missed the real question."

Emma is silent. Miranda feels unsettled.

"What—are—you?" the professor asks. This is no longer a theoretical discussion. It's deeply personal.

"I—I'm me," Emma says.

"Why?" the professor asks. "Why are you here now? What does it mean to be present? To be aware? To be you? To see and experience life from behind those eyes?"

"I—I don't know. I'm... I am," she says, scrambling to respond. "I'm just me. It's like Descartes said, *cogito ergo sum*: I think therefore I am."

"I like to put it the other way," the professor says. "I am, therefore I think, I feel, I reason, I love, I hope, I cry. Our existence is a contradiction. We're nothing but a tiny collection of unassuming atoms—only we're not."

Emma's tone changes. Her voice drops as she says, "And the illusion has become real."

"Yes. Yes," the professor says. "Instead of fake flowers, the magician has pulled a real bouquet out of his hat."

"And this machine?" Emma asks.

"It taps into our minds," he says. "It brings dreams to life."

"Ariel," Emma mutters, turning away from the professor and staring at the bare granite on the floor as she continues. "She conjures up these things just by thinking about them."

"We don't see things as they are," the professor says. "We see them as *we* are."

It's only now Miranda looks down from the balcony that she notices Marc's gone. Ariel's standing by the window downstairs, looking out into the darkness, but Marc is nowhere to be seen. Miranda feels her heart race.

"What's wrong?" Emma says, seeing the look of panic on Miranda's face.

"Your friend. He's gone."

"He's gone to talk to Caliban," Emma says.

"That damned fool," the professor says, squeezing his hand into a fist. "No, he can't. He mustn't."

The Dark Λbyss

Marc walks toward the circular ramp at the back of the floor. A tunnel leads him down through solid granite to the entrance beneath the dome. As he descends, the temperature of the air drops. A white mist forms with each breath. The cold seeps through his boots. He folds his arms across his chest, pushing his hands up inside the arms of the suit. The thick material keeps his core warm, but his exposed hands and legs are cold. His suit torso covers his waist and chest, with flexible material wrapping around his arms and reaching down to just above his wrists. He should have gone back to his room to suit up. Even with the visor raised, he would be a lot warmer in a full suit. Also, he'd be able to run his thermal underwear from the electrical system, but it's too late. He's committed to going outside. Marc doesn't want Ariel to sense any weakness in his resolve.

He steps into the darkness. Rocks crunch beneath his feet. A thin layer of ice covers the ground—the remnants of the tempest. It shatters beneath his boots as he walks along the path. Once he's clear of the mountain, he stops and turns, looking back at the dim lights within the dome. He can see the shadow of people moving around in the top-floor laboratory. On the lowest level, a lone figure stands by the window, watching him. Ariel's taken physical form to make one last appeal to him. Marc ignores her. Uncertainty is his only weapon. If he can get her to doubt herself, perhaps he can glean more intel from her when he gets back.

A soft blue trail winds behind him, leading back to the entrance.

The glowing footsteps mark where he trod, disturbing the phosphorescent microbes that inhabit this alien moon. He walks on.

Salt spray rises in the air. Waves crash as they surge through the honeycomb of rocks beneath the cliff, warning him of the danger below. The foam settles and glows, resting on the jagged rocks not more than twenty meters below the path. His teeth chatter as the cold hits, but the sight of an alien biosphere unfolding before him is utterly surreal.

"Beautiful," he mutters.

Marc's younger sister is an astrobiologist. She'd love to be here. She'd probably spend years examining the various microbes he's walking over, seeking to understand how they interact with each other on this icy world.

He stops and crouches, examining the scorch marks where lightning hit the path just hours ago. He sweeps his hand over the ground, clearing away the snow with the back of his wrist. He's trying to retain a semblance of warmth in his fingers while looking at the way the rocks and sand have fused into glass beneath each strike. Black soot reveals how various molecules boiled and burned under the intense burst of heat. And Emma wants him to *chat* with Caliban. Hah!

He looks up into the endless night, trying to trace the path of the bolts that struck the rocks as they ran for cover. Thousands of stars shine down upon him. There are no clouds. Lightning needs clouds, right? In the back of his mind, he remembers being taught something about electrostatic charge building a differential between vast clouds of water molecules. But ice storms can produce lightning as well. The clear sky is reassuring. How quickly can Caliban form another tempest? Is he like Ariel? Can he conjure whatever he needs with the flick of his fingers?

Marc stands and walks on toward the scout sitting on the open plateau beyond the canyon. Fireflies dance around him, surrounding him with pinpricks of light. A herd of deer float above the devastated glass grass rolling over the plain. The skin on their backs forms blisters that look like soap bubbles overlapping each other in a bath. No two deer are alike. Their long legs dangle beneath them as they drift on the breeze, leaning forward and snatching bites at the crystalline grass. If earthly analogs apply here, there are four doe and one stag that has antlers as chaotic as a thorn bush. The herd ignores Marc, nudging the broken shards as they search for fresh microbial growth. As destructive as the storm was, it seems to be part of the cycle of life on Altair IV, renewing rather than suppressing the natural flora and fauna. This reminds him that he wants to ask the professor about predators on this moon. Is there something that preys upon the deer? It would be nice to know what's out there in the darkness before it leaps out of the night and tears off his face.

Marc approaches the grave. It's striking for its location. Cemeteries are an eyesore. Who wants to be reminded of their own mortality? Most cemeteries are nice enough, but they tend to be positioned out of the way. They're a memorial, not an advertisement. This grave, though, has been set at the point the path reaches the plateau, forcing anyone walking toward the rise to go left or right. Beyond the grave, the rocky ground opens out. Boulders have been cleared and pushed to one side, allowing the science labs to be established. Behind them, the scout sits on clear ground.

Marc stands in front of the grave, looking down at the words carved into the polished granite.

I love you.
I will never forget you.

It seems Miranda's mother will never be forgotten—but no one outside of her family will ever know her name.

Why wouldn't the professor etch her name in stone? Or the date she died? At the very least, that would give the loss some context. Normally, a death on an expedition is marked with a bunch of details: the ship's name, port of departure, mission designation, the person's rank within the crew, their date and place of birth, along with their age in Earth years at the time of death. If anything, this grave is all the more haunting by those omissions.

How old was Miranda when her mother died?

Why didn't the professor say, *"We love you. We will never forget you,"* as that seems more appropriate? The lack of a plural pronoun seems to be a curious oversight. It's as though he's ensured he and he alone would never forget his wife. As touching as the inscription first appeared, the grave feels shallow. It leaves Marc thinking the emphasis is on *"I"* rather than *"you."*

As it was Miranda that laid the flowers on the grave, it seems to Marc that the professor has forgotten about his wife. Doesn't everyone forget, though? Isn't that the curse of death? As the memory fades so does the ache. It's not deliberate. No one wants to forget a loved one. Life, though, marches on. Humans aren't like computers. Memories aren't files to be retrieved on a whim and examined with the same fidelity they were recorded. Far from it, memories fade like the logo on an old t-shirt. It's unavoidable.

How did Miranda's mother die? What killed her? Now that he's standing here in the open, that seems like a rather pertinent question he should have asked the professor last night. Did Caliban kill her?

Marc looks around. Why aren't there any other graves? Where did everyone else go? The rest of the crew is dead. Where are their graves? If they died elsewhere, why not erect a memorial here in their honor?

Why were the professor and his family the only ones to stay and settle in this location? Why build a vast base on the side of a mountain for just one family? He looks back at the dome. It's big enough to house dozens of people.

Even the science labs set up on the plateau tell a story. They were rushed in place. Perhaps they were temporary while the mountainside base was being built. From what Marc can tell, they would have allowed roughly sixty people to live and work alongside each other. And all of those people are gone. Dead.

Marc walks on toward the scout. As he approaches, the landing lights come on automatically. Marc checks the methane collectors and the oxygen extractors. They're all above 90% full. Getting these back to the *Sycorax* will change the survivability equation for thousands of colonists. If nothing else, they'll buy Marc and Emma time to find a more permanent solution on some other, uninhabited moon. They've just got to convince Caliban to let them leave.

Marc walks around the scout looking for damage from the storm. He examines the landing gear along with the underside of the fuselage using a light built into his suit torso. As the light sits on his shoulder, it gives him a good look at whatever he's facing. If there's been any damage to the scout, it's not apparent. He checks the VTOL engines and the main orbital engine bell. Ice clings to the lower side of the metal, but that'll vaporize within seconds of firing. As long as there's no grit in the injection nozzles or damage to the fuel lines, the various engines will be fine. A preflight pressure test will expose any issues with the plumbing.

Marc runs his hand over a black scorch mark on one of the spherical fuel tanks located behind the cabin. As the craft is sitting eight feet off the ground, he can barely reach the underside of the tank with his outstretched arm, but it seems to have taken a lightning strike on one side. He follows the path of the lightning. The paint has curled off the metal of a nearby landing pad, revealing how the surge of electricity found its way to the ground. That's a worry. The ship's electronics and navigation units are located in the cockpit. They're shielded so they should be fine, but it would be wise to isolate this tank and avoid using it when they launch—*if* they launch.

The wind picks up. Snow swirls around his boots. Marc feels a chill, but not from the cold. At first, he thinks it's his imagination playing tricks on him, but a voice drifts on the wind.

"Whaaaat are you afraid of?"

He turns, feeling a rush of adrenaline as he looks for someone behind him. There's nothing but darkness beyond the glare of the lights on the scout.

"Caliban?"

The wind is chaotic, kicking up snowflakes and causing them to form shapes that vanish as soon as they form. Through the gloom, he

211

sees ribbons, waves, the form of a man and then what could be a flock of birds taking flight. After each, there's nothing but the darkness.

"The beating of your heart betraysssss youuuuu."

"Show yourself," he says, turning through 360 degrees as he's tormented by the voice. Back inside the house, he could deal with Ariel being ghost-like, but out here, he fears something lunging at him out of the darkness.

"Your fears... they lie to you... and you believe them."

Marc's ears are acutely aware of the noises around him. Torn drapes flap in a broken window. An abandoned laboratory is visible on the edge of the lights. One of the doors bangs with the wind. Marc could swear he just saw someone walking in the shadows. He doesn't like this one bit.

Clouds blot out the stars, making the darkness impenetrable. Sleet comes down, driving hard with the wind. It falls in waves, peppering the ground.

"I—I'm not afraid of you!" he yells over the tempest.

"Liaaaaar!"

"I'm not."

"Then come to me... Face your fears."

Marc steps out from beneath the shelter of the landing craft. Darkness surrounds him. Hail strikes his head. It's tiny, being the size of pebbles. In the low gravity, it's tolerable rather than painful, but it drums on the upper torso of his suit, making it impossible to hear.

The hail subsides. The wind dies down. His eyes adjust to the darkness, taking in a landscape draped in a blue tinge. The storm has awakened the microbial world, providing a dim light to lead him on. Rocks and ice crunch beneath his boots. The lights of the scout fall behind him.

Caliban says, *"I could skin you alive."*

"But you won't," Marc replies.

"You say those words, but the adrenaline coursing through your

veins says otherwise... You're scared."

Marc tries to locate Caliban by sound but the alien's words seem to come from all around him. He's aware he's walking further away from both the scout and the professor's home, but he needs answers. It feels as though he's walking away from the safety of the spacecraft but he's not. Nowhere is safe on this world. His trembling legs might speak of fear but Marc knows the scout offers an illusion of protection. Given what he's seen Ariel do, he has no doubt Caliban could destroy it if he wanted to. Marc doesn't know how he brought down the *Copernicus*, but according to the records Emma downloaded from the *Sycorax*, that was an ex-military frigate. It was big, far bigger than even the *Sycorax*, let alone the scout. It should have been able to escape this moon with ease.

"I'm human," Marc says in his defense. Caliban might not recognize it, but it takes courage to walk into the unknown.

"You're a contradiction," Caliban replies with his voice floating on the breeze. *"You're alive and yet not one atom within your body is any different from the rocks beneath your feet."*

The voice is coming from directly in front of Marc. He walks over the rise. Behind him, the lights of the scout disappear from sight.

"You think. And yet the electrical impulses in your brain are no different from lightning crackling through the sky."

Caliban is sitting on top of a boulder the size of a house. He watches Marc like a lion hunting gazelles on the African savannah. Watching. Waiting.

What do you say to a demigod that tried to kill you a few hours ago?

"I just want to talk," Marc calls out, walking further away from the scout across the rocky ground. A nervous monologue unfolds within Marc's head. *Ah, yeah, be nice and friendly to the alien that threatened to skin you alive. 'Cause that'll work. Relax. Don't stress. It'll be fine.* He swallows the lump in his throat, hoping Emma's right about why Caliban's showing himself. As Caliban's the same as Ariel, there's no need for games. He could turn invisible and strike with impunity.

Emma's right. She's got to be right, he thinks as his heart tries to beat out of his chest.

Caliban alights from the boulder, falling twenty or so feet to the rocky ground like superman coming in to land. He marches rather than walks toward Marc, who stops on the edge of the boulder field. Marc wonders, why the pretense? Like Ariel, Caliban could materialize in front of him if he wanted. Why walk? Why does Caliban persist with human-like limitations when he's a god by comparison? There has to be a reason for the show. Whatever it may be, it tells Marc he's being played by Caliban. The way Ariel and Caliban have synchronized their performance leaves him unsettled. They're enemies, or so the professor says. Marc's not so sure. He wonders if they're conspiring together to mislead him and Emma. Caliban brought down the *Copernicus*, but what if it wasn't to keep Ariel here, what if he had some other motive?

Now that he's physically present, Caliban's voice changes. He says, "Why did you come here to this moon?"

"For help," Marc replies, choosing to be entirely honest. Lying to a demigod does not seem wise. "Our starship, the *Sycorax*, is crippled. We can't maintain a warp bubble. Without that, we're stuck in orbit around this moon. Almost half of our passengers have died." He points back at the machinery set out in front of the scout, adding, "The methane. The oxygen we're gathering. We need them to power our ship. Without them, more people will die."

Caliban appears unmoved by his plea. Whereas Ariel's face was expressive, at least, when she took the time to show herself to him, Caliban is emotionless. He's bald. His skin is dark, navy blue. Whereas Ariel was fire, Caliban's ice.

"You must let us leave," Marc says. "We want no part of your world. We wouldn't have come down here if we'd known about you and Ariel."

"She cannot leave," he says.

"I know. I know," Marc replies, unsure how he can prevent an invisible demigod from entering his spacecraft. "But why? What has she done that you've imprisoned her here?"

Caliban looks up. "The darkness. Can you feel it?"

"There's something wrong," Marc says, sensing what Caliban means. "This world. It's not what it seems."

"Embrace this world at your peril."

"I don't understand."

"You humans are pathetic," Caliban says. "Your lives are too short. You only see that which is in front of you. You cannot see the dark abyss of time."

"What about you and the professor?" Marc asks, grasping at the loose threads of an idea lurking out on the fringe of his mind.

"He taught me your language, but all I learned was how to curse."

At first, Marc assumes Caliban is talking about swear words, but the look in his eyes suggests he means more than profanity. Caliban has used the term in the traditional sense. There's anger behind his dark pupils. He means to conjure up evil and inflict harm. Damn it, Emma. Why aren't you out here instead?

The alien leans in close to Marc. He turns his head sideways, looking at Marc's neck and the side of his head. This cosmic god of the underworld asks him, "What—are—you?"

"Oh, now. Hang on," Marc says, feeling uncomfortable and stepping back. "That's my question. That's what I need to ask you."

"What do you think of me?" Caliban asks.

"You?" Marc replies, piecing together the various threads woven throughout their conversation. Caliban is aggressive. Whereas Ariel is kind and thoughtful, Caliban is a brute—and yet he's perplexed. He's right. He could have stripped Marc to the bone, but he didn't. He was interested in how Marc reacted. He wasn't so much exploiting Marc's fears as exploring them, wanting to understand them.

"Thought is free," the mercurial alien says. "Think for yourself. Your thoughts are the only thing that costs you nothing. And yet they give you everything. Thought is the essence of life. Without it, you're a slave."

"I'm a slave?" Marc asks, feeling bewildered by the speed of the conversation.

Caliban's comments lack context. To Marc, it's as though Caliban's continuing a conversation he began with someone else. If Marc didn't know better, he'd swear this was an extension of his conversation with Ariel. It's as though they're playing good cop/bad cop. But Ariel didn't want Marc to come out here to meet with Caliban, of that, he's sure. She sensed he was looking for inconsistencies and fragments of information, piecing together the puzzle. She doesn't want him to uncover the truth.

"I'm no slave," Marc says.

"We're all slaves to thoughts planted by someone else."

"I—I," Marc stutters. "I just want to leave. That's all. I want no part of this frozen hell. I want nothing from you or the professor—or Ariel."

"Interesting," Caliban replies. "You've found buried treasure yet you desire none of the gold and diamonds lying before you."

"I don't know what you mean."

A familiar voice speaks from behind him, saying, "Marc?"

He turns, seeing Emma shivering in the cold, standing at the top of the rise. Although the scout is out of sight, she's bathed by the glow of its lights, appearing as a silhouette. Her dark outline is foreboding.

"Who are you talking to?" she asks. "Caliban?"

He turns back and points. Caliban is gone. Snow swirls with the wind, fading into the darkness.

"Did you find him?" she asks. "What did he say?"

"I—um."

"Is everything okay?"

"No. It's not," Marc says, feeling unsettled. He turns his back on the endless night and walks toward her. "Nothing is right. I just want to get off this goddamn rock."

"You and me both," she says.

Emma seems content with his answer about his brief, tortured conversation with Caliban, even though it lacks substance. From Marc's perspective, he's still trying to process everything Ariel and Caliban told him. He's unsure of their motives. He wants to understand their origins and the way they interact. If they're to outwit these creatures, they need to know what drives them. Marc's consumed by these thoughts as they walk back to the scout.

Marc expects Emma to return to the dome. He's surprised she came out here at all after what she said to him, but he's glad she's here. Her appearance has warded off Caliban and his riddles.

Emma walks up the ramp toward the airlock on the scout. She stops halfway, asking him, "Are you coming?"

"Wait. We're leaving?" he asks. "Don't we need to pack up the extractors and load the fuel?"

"I'm more interested in the *Copernicus*," she says as he steps up onto the broad ramp behind her. "I think you're right. I think we might find parts that will allow us to repair our ship."

Marc halts before the airlock. "But we can't leave. We can't take flight. We'll provoke Caliban."

"Not if we don't make for orbit," Emma replies.

Marc's curious. "And how do you know that?"

Emma points into the distance. "The storm. It didn't appear here where we landed. It appeared out there. Over the mountains. It appeared at the point we broke through the various thermal layers that blanket the atmosphere on this moon. It was only then it chased us here. If we stay below those layers, Caliban will ignore us."

Marc closes the airlock behind the two of them. "You seem really sure of that."

"I am," Emma says. "I need you to take us up to two thousand meters but no higher. We'll search to the northeast."

Marc points at himself. "You want me to fly this crate?"

"I need to focus on the search," she says, slumping into a chair. She looks exhausted.

"All right," he says, looking out of the cockpit window.

The landing lights on the scout are contradictory. On one hand, they illuminate the darkness, turning the night into day around them, but out on the edge of their reach, the night prevails. Marc uses the cameras onboard the scout to scan through 360 degrees. He turns off the heat signature setting, wanting to identify any artificial shape regardless of its temperature. The computer highlights the rectangular labs and even the grave, but no human form.

Caliban is gone.

For now.

The Copernicus

Miranda dashes across the rocky ground. She pauses by her mother's grave, resting a hand on the cold granite as she considers her options.

Lights glisten around the edge of the scout, illuminating the abandoned research labs. They were never more than shipping containers in her mind. As a young girl, she used to explore them, looking for interesting items left by the crew. Her father warned her against it, saying she could injure herself. Whenever Miranda got bored and her father became obsessed with the Krell machine, she'd sneak away to this secret playground. She's never seen the labs flooded with light before.

The engines beneath the scout whine. Turbo pumps spin up, pushing dust across the ground. Sand and grit blow up against the labs. Torn curtains flap in broken windows.

Miranda runs.

She leans forward. She's so close to the ground she ends up scrambling, grabbing at the rocks around her and pulling on them as she rushes on.

The ramp beneath the scout rises and retracts, forming the outer door on the airlock. Miranda jumps, leaping through the air. After a lifetime on Altair IV, her reflexes are honed to life in low gravity. She judges her motion with precision, timing her leap so she soars toward the closing gap. Her arms and torso clear the lip of the ramp and she rolls, tucking her legs in as her feet clip the edge of the metal. No sooner has she come to rest within the airlock than the ramp seals behind her.

Outside, the wind picks up. This isn't the engines coming up to speed. A storm's descending from the hills, buffeting the craft.

"Are you sure about this?" Marc asks from somewhere out of sight. "He looks pissed."

"We'll be fine," Emma replies.

The cockpit is located above the airlock. Miranda climbs a ladder from the cargo hold and leans around the corner, peering further inside the scout. The cockpit on the scout is cramped. Switches and control panels line the walls. Although there are digital interfaces, several sections have old-fashioned toggle switches protected with a thin metal guard so they can't be bumped into another position. Marc points out of the narrow cockpit window. Although Miranda can't see what he's pointing at, it has to be Caliban.

"Ariel?" she whispers, wondering if her friend has come with her. There's no response from beside her. Miranda's on her own. She's worried Caliban will unleash another tempest on them.

Emma says, "Keep the altitude low and remain on atmospheric engines."

"You're the boss," Marc replies. He seems a little lost. He looks around on either side of his seat before flicking several switches and pushing the throttle forward.

"Deploying wings for flight," he says as the craft rises in the air. Miranda can barely contain her excitement as the craggy top of the mountain disappears below them.

Marc eases forward on a joystick and the scout soars off through the sky.

"How are we orienting for north?" he asks.

"Over there," Emma replies, pointing to one side.

"That's where you want to go, huh? Okay."

Lightning ripples through the clouds, lighting the inside of the cabin as it flickers through the sky. The rumble of thunder rocks the craft. Sleet pounds the windows, reducing visibility.

"I hope you're right about Caliban," Marc says.

"Hold this altitude," Emma replies, struggling to see anything out of the cockpit. "No higher."

"Oh, hell, no," Marc says. "We're at fifteen hundred meters and holding. I've geo-tagged the landing zone so we can find it again in the storm."

"Any mountains?"

"Radar has us clear for almost a hundred clicks," he says.

Miranda crouches. She creeps out of the cargo hold. The scout rocks as it's buffeted by the storm. The craft hits an air pocket and plummets, falling through hundreds of meters in mere seconds. For a moment, Miranda is weightless. She floats at the back of the cabin, holding onto the side of a panel as her legs fly out from beneath her.

"Easy. Easy," Emma says, reaching over and touching Marc's arm. Their seatbelts keep them from flying up as the craft plunges toward the ice.

"I've got it. I'm good. We're good," Marc says, but his voice betrays him. He's nervous as hell. He pulls on the controls and the floor of the craft rises beneath Miranda as the scout regains altitude. The craft rocks from side to side, twisting and sheering as it drives on through the storm.

"What are you doing here?" Emma asks, turning to see Miranda standing at the back of the cockpit.

"What the hell?" Marc says, twisting in his seat. The straps running over his shoulder prevent him from turning around. "Miranda?"

"I—I'm sorry. I had to know," Miranda says.

"Know what?" Emma asks.

"What you'd find."

Marc barks at her, "Strap in, kid."

Although it's welcome advice, there's anger in his voice. It's the use of the term, kid. He's not impressed at having a stowaway on board. Under his breath, he speaks to Emma, saying, "We should take her back."

"We stay the course," Emma says. "We need to find the *Copernicus*. We may not get another shot at this."

"And you think we're going to find it in this storm?" Marc asks, keeping his hands on the flight controls. He's constantly making minor adjustments as the craft is tossed around by the storm. The engines whine. Miranda sits on the side of the cockpit behind Marc and Emma. The seatbelt is tension-set, which means she can only pull on it when there's no other force being applied or it locks in place. It takes a few gentle tugs to slip a strap over each shoulder. The lap belt is easier to clip on but needs to be manually tightened.

They fly for more than an hour, darting in and out of cloud banks swirling around them. As much as possible, Marc keeps them below the cloud layer, but it's not always possible. Thunder breaks beyond the windows. Miranda winces in her seat. The sheer violence rattles her body. She can feel the anger in her bones. Hail lashes the hull of the spacecraft, striking it like a machine gun being fired on full auto. As quickly as it came, the hail passes. The scout shakes as it cuts through the sky.

"What the hell are we looking for?" Marc asks, flicking his fingers over a digital display and bringing up a topographical map of the terrain they're flying over.

"We need active, ground-penetrating radar," Emma says, looking at a similar display in front of her.

"Sensitivity?"

"Set it to look for refined metals. They'll show up like meteorite fragments on the ice. That snow down there is pristine. If the *Copernicus* broke up in the atmosphere, it's going to be spread over hundreds of miles, but we might get lucky. The core might have remained intact until it hit the glacier."

Marc says, "If it crashed several decades ago, it could be buried by up to a hundred meters by now."

"I know. I know," Emma says. "I'm hoping the cockpit and engines stayed intact."

"We're never going to find anything in this storm," Marc says. "Even if we had clear weather, it could take months to comb the ice in a search pattern. The odds of us—"

Emma points out of the cockpit window into the darkness, saying, "Down there!"

"What the hell?" Marc says, leaning forward but he can't get close. He pulls against his shoulder straps, wanting to look down at the plateau. Marc doesn't see anything beyond the pitch black of night. His eyes dart back to the radar screen, examining it in detail. "Ah, the radiation profile. That's a fusion core. That's an active fusion core! How is that even possible after all these years?"

"I don't know," Emma says, laughing. "But there it is!"

"Bringing us in," Marc says and the scout responds to his movements, slowly losing altitude as it circles around in the darkness. They drop below the clouds. The change is abrupt. Whereas the scout was pushed around by the storm, now it sails smoothly through the air. Miranda's not sure what's happening. Is it just them descending or are the clouds lifting? In the darkness, it's difficult to be sure, but the sporadic lightning seems further and further away.

"What are we looking at?" Emma asks.

Marc points at the screen. "Nothing on the surface. We've got a glacier to the west and bedrock to the east, with a crevasse running in between. In some spots, it's a couple of hundred meters deep. It runs right through the crash site. I'm seeing scattered debris forming an ellipse four kilometers in length but only a few hundred meters wide. Looks like she had a helluva lot of forward momentum when she struck."

"But it broke up in the air, right?" Emma asks.

"Yeah. I think so," Marc replies. "The prevailing wind has cleared some of the debris near the cockpit. I'm setting us down well back from the ravine."

"Okay, good," Emma replies.

Miranda's excited. She's never done anything like this. She finds the interplay between Marc and Emma fascinating. They're astronauts. Explorers. They're not afraid to take chances. Even in the depth of a storm, with the craft rocking in the tempest, Miranda wasn't afraid. Marc might have been nervous, but Miranda was confident in him. She can't explain why. Perhaps it's that his every action seems measured. Between the two of them, Marc and Emma are composed. They're ready to handle whatever arises. Miranda wants to be like them.

Marc slows the descent of the scout. As they come in to land, a snowstorm is kicked up by the engines, causing a whiteout beyond the windows. The landing lights are bright, reflecting off the snow and ice. Miranda doesn't feel the craft touch the glacier. The landing gear takes the weight of the scout smoothly and easily. And with that, the engines power down and the craft rests on the ice. The artificial snowstorm subsides leaving them looking out into the darkness.

Marc switches the lights within the cabin to a soft red. A few seconds later, the landing lights turn red as well, allowing their eyes to adjust to the ambient light. Marc and Emma talk about robotic crawlers and their lack of climbing gear. Miranda just sits there in awe of how she's now hundreds of kilometers away from her home. Has her father noticed her absence? He'll ask Ariel where she is. What will Ariel say or do? Can Ariel find her this far from home?

"And you, young lady," Marc says, frowning as he looks down at her. "You're staying here with the scout. Understood?"

"No way," Miranda replies. "I'm coming with you."

"No, no, no," Marc says. "I can't let anything happen to you."

"Nothing's going to happen to me," Miranda protests, looking to Emma for support.

"She'll be fine," Emma says.

Marc shakes his head. He steps into the airlock and retrieves a suit from a storage locker. After removing the upper torso of his old

224

suit, he climbs into a new suit but he doesn't bother with a helmet.

"Are you going to suit up?" Marc asks Emma, who's still wearing the upper torso of her original suit.

"Nah."

"Too damn cold for me," Marc says, fixing his trousers in place. He turns to Miranda, asking, "How about you?"

Miranda's wearing her thick phase-change clothing.

"Nah," she says in mimicry of Emma, following her down the ramp.

"Well, I'll just do all the work then, okay?" Marc says, protesting, but both women ignore him. "Don't worry about me. I'll be fine."

Marc grabs a handheld radio from a charging station on the wall of the airlock and marches down the ramp after the women.

"Here," he says, handing it to Miranda. "If we get separated out there, this will allow you to talk to us." He twists a few knobs on top and sets the squelch control, showing her how to hold the radio. "Now, if you want to reply to us, you hold down the lever on the side, but don't forget to release. We can't talk back while you're transmitting, so you must release it. Got it?"

"Got it," she says.

Marc turns away from her. He presses buttons on his wristpad computer and speaks into the microphone on his Snoopy cap.

"Testing. 1, 2, 3."

In unison with his voice, the same words resound from the radio speaker. He continues with, "Can you hear me?"

Emma laughs. "Of course, she can hear you. You're standing right there!"

"You know what I mean," he replies, turning to Miranda and adding, "Now, you try."

Miranda squeezes the transmit button and says, "1, 2, 3," which is followed by a little feedback, reminding her to let go of the button.

"Okay, let's send out some automated explorers," Marc says. He punches commands into his wrist computer and several small robots on treads follow him down the ramp. The wind whips over the plain. Snowdrifts have formed on the leeward side of boulders, but other than that, the bedrock is largely clear of snow and ice. The clouds roll on. The stars shine down upon them, illuminating the land.

"This is good," Emma says, looking around the frozen wasteland. Miranda's not so sure.

"I tagged several items from the air for investigation," Marc says as robots trundle away from them, moving across the plain. "It'll take a couple of hours, but between these three, we should retrieve wreckage from eleven nearby sites—none more than fifteen meters deep thanks to the wind."

"And the fusion core?" Emma asks.

"Down there," Marc says, pointing to a canyon roughly a hundred yards away. The far side is dominated by the glacier they flew over. A crevasse leads up to the bedrock, splitting the edge of the glacier into a chaotic field of ice.

"What climbing gear do we have?" Emma asks.

"Not much," Marc replies. "I left my kit on the *Sycorax.*"

"We're going to have to figure something out," Emma says.

"It could be inaccessible," Marc says.

"Ariel could retrieve it," Miranda says as the three of them walk across the bedrock toward the scar running through the land.

Marc and Emma exchange a quick glance but neither of them addresses Miranda's point, which leaves her confused. To her, Ariel's the obvious solution. She wants to press the issue but thinks better of it.

As they get close to the edge, the bedrock curls away, having been eroded over the eons, making the approach to the canyon dangerous. White veins curl through the granite, accentuating the curve disappearing into the darkness. The scout has come down on the edge of the glacier. The transition zone between the bedrock and the glacier is chaotic. Ice falls have formed a jagged, impenetrable canyon in between.

"I'm not liking this," Marc says.

Emma's more bullish. Whereas Marc stays well back from the edge, not wanting to lose his footing, Emma continues down the ever-increasing smooth slope. Miranda stays beside her.

"What are you looking for?" Miranda asks.

"You won't see anything," Marc calls out from behind them.

Emma seems frustrated. She leans forward, staring into the depths. Serrated ice lies up against the bedrock, marking where the glacier has rubbed against the granite, wearing it smooth before falling away into the darkness.

"Emma," Marc yells, sounding stern.

Reluctantly, she turns back and climbs the slope up to him.

"You're getting too close to the edge," he says. "If you slip and fall, there's nothing to grab onto."

"You worry too much. I'm okay, aren't I?"

Marc backs up further, not being content until they're on the flat expanse of bedrock again. To be fair to Emma, the prevailing wind comes across from the glacier, pushing them back, making it safer than it seems, or at least, Miranda thinks so.

"So what are we going to do?" an exasperated Emma asks, throwing her hands in the air and letting her arms fall back to her side. As she's wearing the upper torso of her suit, her gesture is restricted by the thick material. Her wrists and hands are smaller than Marc's and appear tiny within the padded upper arms of the suit.

"I don't know," Marc says, walking away from her. "But we're going to be here for a few hours waiting on those rovers. We might as well explore north and look for a way down into the crevasse."

Marc follows the edge of the dropoff. His head is down. He's looking at the way the granite has worn and eroded over tens of thousands of years. There are hollows and rises. Occasionally, an ice-laden boulder lies on the bedrock. Patches of snow form in the lee of mounds. Miranda and Emma walk along beside him. Behind them, the navigation light on the bottom of the scout flashes at regular intervals, sending a strobe out through the darkness.

Miranda stops and looks back at the red landing lights bathing the desolate plain. The astronauts didn't use those when they came down from the *Sycorax*. She wants to ask why. Back then, they probably wanted as much light as possible as they tried to figure out if the labs were still functional. As she turns away from the scout, she looks out across the bedrock rather than toward the glacier.

"Hey, what's that?" she asks, pointing.

Marc comes to a halt. Emma continues walking without purpose. She looks depressed. Marc, though, raises his head and holds still for a moment.

"Em," he says. "Look!"

The three of them walk out into the darkness, leaving the glacier at their backs. Snow curls around their legs, being blown across the plain. Miranda runs. Marc runs, or he tries to. Once again, he's forgotten about the low gravity and breaks into a gentle lope, drifting several feet off the ground as he tries to rush.

"What is that?" Emma asks, being content to walk.

"Artificial," Marc says, settling on the bedrock.

Dozens of rocks and boulders have been stacked together to form a rough pyramid reaching up to shoulder height. The broad base leads up on all sides to a single rock placed on top.

"Someone's alive?" Miranda asks.

"Someone *was* alive," Marc replies.

"But this isn't a grave, right?" Emma asks.

"No. It's a marker."

Emma turns, passing through 360 degrees as she looks around the plain. "A marker for what? Why would you stack up rocks like this?"

"So you don't get lost," Marc says. "Someone survived the crash. They came out here scavaging for materials."

"Makes sense," Emma says.

"The debris was so widespread they had to search the whole

plateau, but..."

"But how do you avoid getting lost?" Miranda says, anticipating his logic. She points further into the darkness, away from the chasm leading to the glacier. There's another pile of rocks roughly two hundred meters away.

"Smart," Marc says. "Not only does it give them a point of reference to avoid getting lost, these rock piles act like a grid reference, allowing them to know which areas have been searched."

"So this went on for some time," Emma says.

"Probably years," Marc says. "You don't put this much effort into a one-time act. They must have searched further and further afield as the years went on."

"Further afield from what?" Emma asks.

"Their base," Marc says, turning back toward the glacier. He sweeps his hand through the air, saying. "If I crashed here, that's where I'd look for shelter. Ice is a great insulator. Get down in that crevasse out of the wind and you can stay warm."

"Do you think they're still alive?" Miranda asks, feeling excited at the prospect of finding someone else on Altair IV.

"I don't know," Marc replies. "I doubt it. Even if your dad's right and our two biomes can interact without being toxic to each other, there's not much to eat out here."

"How far do you think these extend?" Emma asks, pointing at the distant pile barely visible through the gloomy half-light.

"Far enough that they could find their way home," Marc says. "I suspect it runs along the edge of this crevasse rather than deep into the plateau. They probably mirror the crash site."

"So whoever this is," Emma says, "they've already picked the bones clean."

"Of things that are useful in the cold," Marc says with vapor forming on each breath. "But probably not the things we're looking for. Electronics aren't too much use in an ice age."

The three of them follow the crevasse running along the edge of the bedrock for almost an hour, noting the various rock piles inland. Regardless of how long they walk, there's always at least one in sight, barely visible through the haze of snow and ice blowing across the desolate plain. The stars above them are vibrant.

"What do you think your father's doing?" Marc asks.

"Freaking out," Miranda replies.

"You're in good hands," Emma says.

"Is she?" Marc asks, laughing.

"What are we looking for?" Miranda asks, wanting to change the subject. She doesn't feel comfortable talking about her father. Ariel will have told him she left on the scout. He'll pace before the window of the dome, thinking the worst, waiting impatiently for her to return. What's he going to do when she gets back? Get angry? Yell at her for being stupid? Ground her? Hah!

"That," Marc says, breaking her train of thought. He points ahead of them. A pyramid of rocks has been stacked close to the crevasse. All the other piles are inland.

"You think that marks home?" Emma asks.

"I hope so."

As they get closer, they see two climbing ropes lying stretched out beside the boulders. They're anchored to the bedrock with a steel pin driven into the granite. The ropes lead down over the side of the slope, disappearing into the darkness.

"Looks like they had some climbing gear," Marc says.

"Good. This is good," Emma says.

"Are you ready for this?" Marc asks.

"Ready," Miranda says.

"Oh, no. Not you," he replies.

"What? No. I'm coming. I have to."

"You don't," Marc says, resting his hand on her shoulder. "Listen. I don't know what we're going to find down there. Given this is on the edge of a glacier, the trail could have collapsed. Hell, after all these years, that rope could break."

"But I—"

"But nothing," Marc says. "Wait here. We'll try to stay in contact over the radio."

"Try?" Miranda replies, troubled by that term.

"I don't know how well our radios will work down there. These things are good for line-of-sight. Depending on how deep we go, there could be hundreds of meters of solid granite between us. The signal should bounce around a little and perhaps reflect off the clouds, but if you don't hear from us, don't freak out."

"Don't freak out?" Miranda says, on the verge of freaking out.

"Wait here until we get back. If we lose contact and it becomes obvious we're not coming back, hit the big blue autopilot button in the scout and she'll take you home."

"And strap in," Emma says.

"Oh, yeah. Don't forget to strap in," Marc says.

Miranda doesn't like the thought of being left alone in the darkness on the desolate plateau, but she can't argue with him. As much as she doesn't want to admit it, she knows he's right. As much as she loves adventure, there's a good chance one or both of them isn't coming back from this descent into the crevasse.

The Cave

Snow and ice whip around Marc's legs as he stands on the edge of the frozen plateau. As exhilarating as it is to have potentially found a working fusion core, the darkness seems to encroach upon them. The eternal night on Altair IV feels heavy. Perhaps it's the wind, but he feels unsettled. Descending into the crevasse to explore the depths of a fractured glacier on an alien moon is a distinctly bad idea.

"I'll go down," Marc says to Emma. "You wait here."

"What? No way."

"If something happens to me—"

"If something happens to you," Emma says, cutting him off, "you'll need someone down there to help you."

"But the *Sycorax?* The colonists?"

"This is how we save them," Emma says.

Marc's not so sure. If an ice shelf gives way beneath them and they plunge into the darkness, the colonists will die on the *Sycorax* within a few months as the power fails. Marc finds himself doubting the decision for both of them to come down to the moon, let alone for both of them to descend into the crevasse, but Emma's right. They can't play this safe. They've got to go hard on getting that fusion core as it changes the equation entirely. Not only will it mean they've restored full power, they can potentially restore the warp field and head on to New Haven— probably not under full steam, but they might make 50% of the speed of light. If they die down there, everyone dies in orbit. It's one hell of a gamble. Ordinarily, Marc would protest that it's too risky, but they've got nothing left to lose. They've already lost. This is a Hail Mary pass from his own 10-yard line to a running back sprinting down the side of the field. It's not out of desperation so much as being aggressive right until the end. They're fighting to the last second for a win.

"Okay. Okay," he says.

Marc turns around so he has his back to the crevasse, leaving him facing the rock pile on the granite plateau. He removes his gloves, not wanting to lose his grip on the frozen climbing ropes. His suit trousers have pockets on the lower leg so he stuffs his gloves into one of them. As the gloves are bulky, he should separate them into different pockets, but out of habit, he shoves them both in the same one. Even before he starts his descent, in the back of his mind, he knows this particular decision is a bad idea. He should separate them, but he feels constrained to keep going. He doesn't have time for messing around with a stupid pair of gloves. He's got to find that damn fusion core.

Marc straddles the two ropes and leans down, picking one of them up in his hands. The line is cold. He wraps it around behind his waist, keeping his left hand out in front of him while using the rope in his right hand as a brake. He's standing with the rope curling around the back of his waist. It's a classic mountaineering descent, although normally it would be accompanied by a climbing harness and carabiners to lock him into the rope. The danger here is he can easily fall.

"This would be easier with a harness," he says.

No one replies.

Slowly, he begins to descend, walking backward down the granite surface.

Miranda watches as he lowers himself over the edge. He smiles at her, wanting to encourage her, but her face looks pale and lifeless in the dark. With each step back, he loses some of his ability to see her. Eventually, she's gone altogether. She's still up on the plateau no more than ten meters from him, but she and Emma might as well be ten kilometers away.

The edge of the bedrock is heavily sloped but not vertical. Someone's carved foot holds into the rock, helping the descent. From the way the rock has been chiseled, they used a handheld jackhammer, telling Marc at least some of the equipment on the *Copernicus* survived the crash intact.

He slips.

Marc's right boot catches some ice and he keels over, slamming into the frozen granite with his shoulder. In the darkness, he panics. He gives up on a climbing posture and grabs at the rope above him with both hands. His fingers tighten on the icy line, but it slides through his fingers. It takes all of his might to arrest his fall.

Marc swings back and forth, kicking and searching with his boots, unable to see the footholds below him.

"Are you okay?" Emma yells from out of sight above him.

"Just," he says, struggling to speak. His gloves come loose. They fall out of the pocket on his leg and tumble into the darkness. "Fuck!"

"Marc!" Miranda yells.

"I'm good. I'm good," he struggles to say. Who is he kidding? With a tremor in his voice, he's not even fooling himself. "Just about there."

By *there*, he means back on the track with its carved insets, not *there* as in down at the bottom of the climb.

Transparent ice has formed on sections of the granite, changing the texture from rough and coarse with plenty of grip to a death trap with each step. He needs to be more careful.

"Be more careful," Miranda calls out. Great timing, kid, he thinks. Yeah, perfect timing. Rather than helping, her comment leaves him feeling resentful. His pride is hurt. He's a climber! Mentally, he shakes it off, reminding himself he doesn't have crampons, carabiners or a climbing rig. He's got to slow things down and not be so damn cocky. This ain't a race.

Marc reaches a section where the foot holds have been cut a little deeper, allowing him to get his boots better positioned. With each step, though, he kicks around, checking for ice and dislodging any loose rocks.

Emma takes the other rope. He can see the motion of the line dangling next to him. She should wait, goddamn it. He wants to call out to her but his pride gets the better of him. He'll be fine. He hopes.

Marc activates the lights on the shoulder of his suit. The further he descends into the crevasse, the less ambient starlight reaches him, making the gloom on Altair IV seem even darker.

Even though he's not wearing a helmet, Marc's got a Snoopy cap on for warmth. Fine flakes of snow drift through the air, being dislodged by Emma as she descends the second rope above him. A few of the flakes drift inside the open ring collar of his suit. Those flakes that slide down his back send a chill through him. He should have told Emma to give him a ten-minute head-start.

Marc reaches an outcrop as the ropes come to an end. This is why the climbing lines were placed here, to allow easy access to the landing. While he's waiting for Emma to join him, he examines the path ahead. It winds back toward where the scout is parked on the plain, but it's roughly a hundred meters beneath the edge of the plateau. The ledge is covered in broken ice. From what he can tell, no one has walked this path in a long time. Someone's mounted makeshift hand holds in those sections where the path narrows, but for the most part, it's a ledge about five meters wide.

"I'm at the bottom of the climb," he says into the microphone curling around beside his lips. He's speaking more for Miranda than Emma. "It's pretty dark down here."

Miranda replies, "—if—ice—avoid—dark."

"Can you repeat that?" Marc asks, walking away from the ropes and trying to improve the signal.

"—ever—glacier—on the plateau."

"I can't hear you," Marc says, hoping his suit transmitter is a little more powerful and can get through to her. He repeats himself. "Wait at the scout. Wait at the scout. Wait at the scout."

"—scout," is the reply, followed by silence.

Marc paces. He's not happy about being out of contact with Miranda but the only options left are all bad.

The chaotic, broken glacier lies up against the granite in several places. The ice creaks and groans. As it moves, it must grate against the edge of the plateau. It's worn some sections as smooth as glass.

From somewhere in the darkness below him comes the sound of running water. At a guess, there's a subsurface river several hundred meters beneath the path.

Ice crunches behind him.

"Well, this looks promising," Emma says.

"We may yet find that fusion core," he replies.

Marc was expecting Emma to rib him about messing up on the climb. Given his insistence on clambering down to inspect the sewage treatment and reclamation tanks on the *Sycorax*, it's the kind of lighthearted jab she enjoys. She knows he prides himself on surfing, hiking and rock climbing. When it came to the crunch and he actually needed those athletic skills, they didn't help that much at all. If anything, she fared better than he did on the descent. Emma's not one for sports. By her own admission, the only reason to get into the water at the beach is to get out again and enjoy sunbathing to dry off.

He thinks about saying something self-deprecating. If anything, it's to assuage his own pride, but the moment passes.

Emma seems oblivious to the machinations of his mind.

"Do you really think it still works after all these years?" she asks.

"The readings I took say it's active," Marc replies, happy to move on.

"It's got to be pumping out a crazy amount of power."

"I'd like to know how they're keeping it from overheating," Marc says. "Those things are temperamental at the best of times. They must have it in standby mode."

The two astronauts walk along the rocky ledge with only the

lights on their suits for comfort. For the most part, the path remains level with sections winding down and back up again.

"Whoever found this place," Marc says, "they were looking hard. Damn hard. You don't come down here without a plan."

"You don't come down here unless you're desperate," Emma says.

They walk beneath an overhang that blots out the stars.

Marc says, "Even if you rappelled over the edge, you wouldn't spot this ledge."

"Maybe they were looking for the core," Emma says. "It's a heat source. That's got to be valuable on an ice world."

"It is," Marc replies. "They must have tried to descend at several points before finding this ledge."

Ahead of them, the jagged ice rising out of the crevasse beside the path seems to glow. As they get closer, Marc realizes light is being cast out of a naturally formed cave in the rock. He signals with his hand, wanting Emma to keep her distance. He's got no idea who or what is in that cave, but he wants enough room to react if they're in danger. He points, drawing her attention to a stream running out of the cave floor. Water washes down the side of the bedrock and beneath the glacier. Ice clings to the rock on either side.

Marc peers into the cave. The fusion core has been mounted on a rocky outcrop rising up like a pedestal in the middle of the open cavern. It glows, casting light and heat through the vast open space. Beyond it, there are the trappings of a makeshift hut. Sections of the fuselage from the *Copernicus* have been propped up to form walls and ceilings, dividing the cave into a shelter. At one time, this place housed several survivors. Now, though, the makeshift huts look neglected. Ice has settled on abandoned blankets.

Marc holds his hand up behind him, signaling for Emma to wait where she is. He's aware he's repeating himself. His nerves are getting the better of him. He edges forward, wanting to get a better look. His heart is racing.

238

There's no one around. Various tools have been set up neatly on a workbench by the entrance to the cave. They've been mounted according to size and shape.

Marc crouches, using the workbench for cover as he edges further inside the cave. Icicles hang from the ceiling. Water drips from them at a steady pace. A pool of water below the fusion core swirls with the radiant heat, circulating as it runs over the rocks, forming a brook that leads into the stream coming out of the cave.

Dead fish line a drying rack set near the pool. They've been gutted and filleted. Their flesh is pale. Although they resemble fish on Earth, with streamlined bodies and fins, they have mouths but no eyes. Instead, catfish-like whiskers droop from their heads.

Shadows move on the far side of the cave.

Marc turns back toward the entrance only to see Emma so close she's almost on top of him.

"Go back," he whispers. She shrugs. The look in her eyes is one of confusion. She's perplexed by his reaction. He can see she doesn't understand why he's so concerned. For Marc, it's a gut feeling.

He says, "There's something wrong."

In reply, Emma whispers, "We're on an ice moon with demigods and you're only just now figuring this out?"

"Please," he says. "I need to understand what we're dealing with before playing all our cards."

Emma lowers her head and retreats into the night. She slips around the corner. Snow swirls past her and within seconds, she's cloaked in darkness.

Marc tries to get a better idea about what they're dealing with. The fusion core is being used for raw heat, but there are cables leading from the glowing red box to a junction point on the wall. Perhaps the survivors have some electrical equipment running.

He listens.

"The choir should sing with joy. Tell them. I want to hear them," a male voice says. *"Life is a privilege. Every day is one more day to*

celebrate!"

Marc watches the far end of the cave as he creeps further inside. He's trying to figure out how many people live here. The cave has formed in a C-shape with most of it curving out of sight. At a guess, it's at least a hundred meters deep. It's been formed as a fissure so the ceiling reaches up easily fifteen meters, giving it the appearance of a naturally formed cathedral. As he enters, he can see how the cave widens ahead.

"They will," the voice says, apparently in response to something said to him. Whatever's happening, this guy's growing louder. He's getting angry. *"Don't care. Tell them, I don't. I won't have it. They must sing for me. They must. I insist."*

Marc has no idea what's going on but he needs answers. Damn it, he needs that goddamn fusion core. With that, Emma can jump-start the warp bubble. Given the damage the *Sycorax* has suffered, it's going to be a slow ride, but they should be able to limp into New Haven within a decade or so. And they can take whoever's down here in this stupid choir with them.

"Hey," Marc says, stepping out into the walkway and waving his hand.

The man that turns to face him has a full beard and straggly hair, but he's bald on top. The thin hair over his ears is a mess. It's matted and unkempt. His clothes are disheveled and dirty. He's wearing red overalls but they lost their luster a long time ago. He's got elbow pads and knee pads on but for what reason? His boots are oversized. They're bigger than the boots Marc's wearing as part of his exploration suit.

The man's eyes go wide. He stands still. It's as though he's trying to evade a predator by playing dead. If he doesn't move, this stranger will go away—apparently.

"It's okay," Marc says, inching closer with his hands out, trying to show he's no threat. "I'm here to help. I've come to get you out of here."

Marc is careful to use the singular pronoun. If things go bad, he wants Emma to have a decent chance of escape. For now, it's better this guy thinks Marc's alone.

The man's mouth drops open. His teeth are yellow. He's missing an incisor on one side and both upper and lower canines on the other. He smiles. The skin on his cheeks has blistered, but not from a burn. The red sores on his skin look infected. At a guess, he's malnourished, which isn't surprising on a moon where it's impossible to grow fruit or vegetables.

"Haha," he says, pointing. "You!"

"Me," Marc says, nodding.

The thin man points at himself, saying, "You're me."

"No. I'm Marc Ka'uhane from the *Sycorax,* a colony ship registered in Westminster, bound for New Haven."

"Hee hee hee," the man says, slapping his thighs as he laughs. His nails are long and dirty, having taken on a sickly, yellow hue. "You're me. You're me! *You're me—you're me—you're me!*"

He dances toward Marc, who backs up, holding out his hands, wanting this lunatic to keep his distance.

The man asks, "Have you come to join our choir?"

"No," Marc says, pointing at the fusion core sitting high on a rocky ledge. "I've come for that."

It's only as those words leave Marc's lips that he realizes what's behind the thin, straggly man. Marc was so focused on the man and his appearance that he didn't take into account what was around him.

A skeleton in a similar pair of red overalls sits on a makeshift chair. The bone isn't clean and white—it's a musty brown color. It takes Marc a moment to realize the body has been mummified. Like beef jerky drying in the sun, it's dehydrated. Rather than being exposed, the skin of the body has shrunk inward, revealing the bones. The jaw is open. Straggly bits of hair and skin hang from the skull. Spindly bones are wrapped tightly in leathery skin. They protrude where hands should be. They rest on narrow thigh bones visible through the torn material. The skin on the feet has been shrink-wrapped around the bones, exposing the ankle, but that's not the worst of it.

The dead man is sitting side on to Marc, facing the far wall of the cave tunnel as it narrows. He's facing a set of skulls lined up on a ledge carved into the ice. Dozens of skulls stare back at the skeleton. Dark empty eye sockets stare blindly ahead. The skulls have been lined up with meticulous care.

Marc blinks.

His blood runs colder than the ice on Altair IV. He's trying to take in the sight but it's overwhelming. The crew of the *Copernicus* has been dismembered. Their bones have been cleaned and neatly stacked in place at the back of the cave. Dozens of skulls rest on the joints of old bones, forming bundles that were once human. Only the end of each bone is visible. Most of them have been stacked inside the ribcage with the skull resting on top. It's disconcerting to see such familiar shapes combined in a practical rather than natural manner. Although it's difficult to see, the hip bones are at the back. Their wide, white plates are visible in the shadows. At a guess, there are easily fifty to sixty skeletons back there, all of them neatly stacked.

Bile rises in Marc's throat. Sweat breaks out on his brow. It's all he can do not to vomit on the floor of the cave.

The madman skips to one side, dancing past the fish drying on the steel rack. He stops beside the fusion core and leans forward, resting his hands on his knees. In a quaint voice, he asks Marc, "Are you real?"

"I'm real," Marc says, spotting a length of metal bracing salvaged from the *Copernicus*. It's leaning against the wall. If violence erupts, Marc could use that as a club or a spear. Without making it obvious, Marc steps closer, making sure he can get to it first.

"Oh, we're so rude." The madman raises his voice. "James! The choir! We should welcome our guest properly."

"He's dead," Marc says, looking at the skeleton in the chair.

"Ah, so he is," the stranger says, giggling from behind a hand held to his mouth.

"Who are you?" Marc asks.

"Me?" the man asks in reply, surprised by the question. His head twists sideways. For a moment, he's quiet. He seems conflicted. Marc sees a glimpse of his humanity returning as his mind struggles to accept him.

Marc has no idea how long this man has been trapped down here alone, but from the appearance of the decaying body, it's been years. He's gone insane. In those few seconds, though, the man's mind seems to reboot. A sense of identity grounds him.

"I'm, umm. Oh, yes. I remember. I'm James. Not him. I'm James Carter. Dr. James Carter. I'm... I think I'm the science officer. Yes, that's it. That's me. Not someone else. Definitely not him. Him? Her!"

"What happened here, James?" Marc asks.

"The *Copernicus*," he says, but there's a distinct change to the way he's speaking. His tone of voice is lower. His pace is slower. The manic confusion in his speech has passed. "It crashed. We. We were trying to reach orbit. Failed to reach orbital speed. Our main engine failed."

"But you survived," Marc says, drawing information out of him.

"I... I did."

"You and the others," Marc says, gesturing further down the cave.

"The others," James says, but his voice sounds distant. He's thinking about his response, but he doesn't like the implication. Marc can see the conflict in his mind forming in the hard lines of his face. Although Marc's looking at the pile of bones, James doesn't. He averts his eyes, turning away from Marc. He stares out of the entrance, but he's not looking at Emma. His eyes are distant. He's ashamed.

"Tell me what happened."

James pinches at the apex of his nose. Tears roll down his cheeks. "You think me mad, don't you? Evil."

"I don't know what to think," Marc says, swallowing the lump in his throat. "Why don't you tell me what happened."

"We had no choice."

"We?"

"Rebecca and me—I—us. We had to eat. There was nothing. Don't you understand? You don't understand."

It's only now Marc realizes he's looking at the mummified remains of a woman in the chair.

"The fish," Marc says, pointing at the rack.

"They were dead," James says, ignoring him and turning to look at Rebecca and the skulls. "We—We—We would. We had to. We boiled them. The broth, you understand. It was nutritious. It kept us alive."

From where he is, Marc can see several of the skulls have cracks running through them or they're missing jaws. It's then it strikes him, far from being gruesome, they've been arranged with care. Those with collapsed cheekbones and fractured brows have been reconstructed with mud being used as plaster.

In an instant, Marc realizes what unfolded. Although he has no idea how James and Rebecca survived the crash, they eventually found themselves starving to death in this cave. Up there on the bedrock, bodies lay scattered across the plain. It wasn't just tech they salvaged from the cold and dark. They gathered the carcasses of the crew and ate them. The guilt and shame they must have felt would have been overwhelming but they had no choice. When they eventually ran out of bodies in the freezer, they ventured down into the crevasse and found the fish. It's no wonder he's been driven mad.

The bones stacked at the back of the cave are orderly. James could have thrown them out into the darkness. If he had, they would have fallen into the cracks in the ice and been lost. Out of sight. Out of mind. But he kept them. *They* kept them—both James and Rebecca decided not to get rid of the evidence of their desperation. These two survivors not only fed upon the dead crew, they remembered them.

From the look of Rebecca, she's been dead for the best part of a decade. In his loneliness, it seems James has begun talking to the dead. As much as Marc wants to despise James—as repulsive and detestable as cannibalism is—he can see James has paid a terrible price to survive. He did what he had to do. He could have disposed of the bones, but in his own distorted way, he honored them. He interred them in a memorial within the cave.

Marc says, "I'm going to get you out of here, okay? Do you understand?"

James is sullen. "Do you believe in hell, Marc?"

"No," he replies, curious at the inclusion of his name as it makes the question uncomfortably personal. "Why would I?"

James says, "I did. Once. Not anymore."

Hell

James says, "Hell is a myth."

Marc nods, unsure where the conversation is going. He's agreeing to be agreeable and not because he agrees with anything James is saying. He wants that damn fusion core. If a few well-placed lies will procure it for the *Sycorax*, so be it. As for getting James out of here, as long as he remains calm, Marc will help him. If he becomes a liability, Marc will leave him to die in this cave.

"But why?" James asks. "Why do we tell ourselves these lies?"

"I don't know," Marc says, stepping closer. He's wary of James. The more they talk, the more unhinged he becomes.

Marc is cautious, trying not to make his motion obvious. As he approaches the fusion core, the warm air brings feeling back to his cheeks. From what he can tell, this is the inner chamber. The graphene-aluminum panels are glowing soft red, but they're designed to bleed off excess heat. The temperature gradient inside the core is crazy. It's less than a meter square or roughly two feet long on each side, but a thin sliver of superheated hydrogen is swirling around in there at 15 million degrees Celsius. In standby mode, it's probably about a hundred times thinner than a strand of hair, but it's still giving off enough power to stay active and warm the cave. A self-powered magnetic-vacuum containment field prevents 99.999% of the heat from leaving the fusion chamber. All Marc and Emma have to do is return this to the *Sycorax*, hook it up to a tritium tank and open the throttle.

Marc's so close to success that his fingers tremble with excitement. He's cautious. He doesn't want to blow this opportunity. He's got to stage-manage James and get that core back to the *Sycorax*.

James picks up the remnants of a thick black book. The cover has been partially torn off. The spine must have been scorched during the fires that raged after the *Copernicus* broke up. The top dozen or so pages are burned and ripped, but this happened long ago. From the small font and dual columns on the page, it's a Bible.

"Hell floods our literature," James says, turning the thick Bible over in his hand. He seems quizzical, almost puzzled by the presence of this book in a cave that doubles as a mausoleum.

No one makes books anymore. For well over a century, the only books have been electronic. When it comes to interstellar flight, mass is money. On the *Sycorax*, Marc was given an allocation of one kilo or just over two pounds. He brought a few shell necklaces and the rear stabilizer from his favorite surfboard along with components for his homemade still. This Bible has to be a family heirloom. To have made it into the crew's personal effects allocation, it must hold considerable sentimental value. Even if someone really, really wanted a physical copy of a book in another star system, the logical choice would be to print it when they arrived. Someone loved this book as much as their own life.

From the way James holds it with what borders on disdain, Marc doubts James brought the Bible on board. He does, however, seem perplexed by its presence. It's horrific to think it survived when the person who valued it so dearly perished. Marc wonders if James knows who brought it on a scientific expedition. James doesn't seem to know. His eyes dart around the open pages. It seems he's thought about this book a lot while trapped here on Altair IV.

He shakes the book in his hand, feeling its weight as he says, "Heaven and hell. We're preoccupied with the eternal, but only ever for punishment or reward—never with regard to life itself. No one wants to live forever. What they want is bliss. They want to be in pleasure forever. Or for everyone else to suffer throughout eternity in some sick, twisted, disproportionate form of vengeance. But life itself. Life is missed."

He tosses the Bible on the rocky ground. The pages fall open. It's only then Marc realizes it's not a Bible. It's some other religious text, but which one? Rather than being created with a printed font, it looks as though it's been handwritten with a flourish of Arabic characters. Does it matter what it is? Even the Koran contains Adam and Eve, Noah, Abraham and Moses.

"What is it with us?" James asks. "Why do we fixate on pleasure or pain? Why must eternity be dominated by only one reality or the other?"

"I—ah. I don't know," Marc says, catching a glimpse of Emma creeping in beside the workbench so she can better hear the discussion.

"We absolve ourselves," James says, looking down at the book with undisguised hatred. He resents this book. He can't read it and yet he's kept it around. It's tormented him. Of all the things to survive the crash, it would be something that speaks only in secret.

James says, "Angels and devils take the place of reason. We don't need the Krell. We don't need Ariel or Caliban to enslave us. We do that to ourselves."

"What would you say to Caliban then?" Marc asks, curious to hear his perspective on the alien sentinel that brought down the *Copernicus* and killed the crew. "Is he the devil? Are we in hell?"

Without hesitation, James says, "I'd say, hell is empty. It always has been."

Marc raises an eyebrow. "And the devils?"

"They're here—all around us. We are both angels and demons. We need not concern ourselves with evil spirits. We're capable of far worse than any devil rising from the fires of Hades."

He uses his foot to move the sacred text around, watching as the pages flicker with the wind curling through the cave.

"We are gods," James calls out, raising his voice over the sound of thunder rolling through the air. "We always have been."

Lightning strikes nearby. A thunderclap breaks almost instantly as he speaks. It's as though Caliban is listening and arguing with him.

James raises his fist toward the roof and shakes it in defiance, yelling, "Damn you, Caliban!"

"I don't understand," Marc says. As tempting as it is to ignore James' comments as the incoherent rambling of a fool, Marc senses a deeper truth to his words. James has been trapped on this moon for decades. He's had a long time to consider the nature of this ice world once ruled by the Krell.

James kicks the sacred text across the rocks. It flops to one side, sprawling open on the ground with its pages spread wide. Although his manner is violent, his words are calm—eerily calm.

"We write about gods because they can't write for themselves. They need us. But why? Because we're the only true gods we've ever known."

He rolls his head around, taking in the vast open cavern above him. It's as though he's making a plea to the heavens.

"Ever since we first walked upright, ever since we carved axes from stone and mastered fire, we've walked apart from animals. We have been gods. Don't you see? We are the gods we worship. Thousands of years ago, we worshiped the god of the harvest because *we* sowed seeds in the ground. We sacrificed animals because *we* mastered them. We enslaved them. We bent their nature to *our* will. We engraved commandments on stone because *we* were stone masons. We walked out of Egypt. We climbed upon the mount. We raged against the storms that tried to humble us. We shouted from the rooftops, *There are no gods but ours!* And yet, what were our gods but a reflection in a mirror?"

"You're not making any sense," Marc says.

"Ariel. Caliban. They're not gods. We are. Within all of us, there is a touch of the divine and sparks from the very fires of hell. We need not gods and devils, angels and demons. These reside within us. The only question is—what wins? Love or hate? Trust or fear? Ego or empathy? Sanity or madness?"

"And what has won?" Marc asks.

James blinks rapidly. "Here? On Altair IV? Professor Spiro. He can bend the elements to his whim. He can bring down starships and wreak havoc on his enemies."

"The professor?" Marc asks, surprised by this revelation. He was sure James would blame Caliban.

"He's a liar. A murderer. A—"

From behind Marc, Emma blurts out, "It's not true."

"What?" Marc replies, turning toward her. "Emma? Stay back. This guy's nuts. He's all over the place."

Emma shouts at the old man. "He's lying!"

"*You!*" James replies, lowering his head and looking at her with dark, cold eyes. His gaze narrows. Marc's confused. How could James possibly recognize Emma?

It's then Marc realizes the heartache of a sudden loss. Everything is wrong. Nothing is right. Deep down, he knew during the flight across the barren plain but he couldn't bring himself to consider the truth. He was in denial.

Marc clutches his chest in agony. Physically, he's fine. Emotionally, he feels the weight of those few words exchanged between James and Emma. He falters, staggering forward under the realization of their meaning. Mere words have cut him deeper than any sword. It's the implication carried by them. His fingers tremble. His stomach churns. Sweat breaks out on his brow.

Marc grabs at the front plate on his suit. If he could, he'd tear it from his chest. The ache beneath his ribs is visceral. His heart races. His legs go weak. He falls to his knees, landing in the slush and ice forming the stream running down through the cave. Water swirls around his boots.

"No," he says, looking back at Emma with tears rolling down his cheeks. "You?"

Emma looks down at Marc but there's no pity in her eyes. Her face is blank, which makes the pain he feels all the more raw. It's in that instant that everything makes sense. Ever since they fired up the engines on the scout, she's been different.

Emma had Marc fly the craft. Even when the storm buffeted the scout, she didn't take control. She could have. She should have. But she didn't. And that gnawed at the back of his mind. He knew something was wrong. Damn it, he knew but he pressed on regardless. He knew but he didn't want to admit it to himself as the implications cut him to the bone.

And she led him straight here! On the first pass! Several weeks' worth of search flights along with days spent analyzing, investigating and eliminating false-positive radar images were avoided with the mere sweep of her arm. She pointed out of the cockpit window. She should have pointed at the radar screen, but she didn't. How did she know where to look? Back then, he wanted to ask her but he couldn't. Instead, he looked at the radar while she pointed into the darkness. Oh, he was scanning the radar footage for clues, but she wasn't. What were the odds of them flying directly over the debris field on their first flight? And he was dumb enough to think they found the *Copernicus* by chance!

Marc clenches his fists, fighting against reality. His teeth grind in anguish.

Emma's dead.

She's been dead for a while, long before the scout lifted off from outside the professor's home. Back when he was prepping for take-off, she said Caliban would leave them alone. At that point, Marc knew something was wrong. How would Emma—*his Emma*—know that? How could she be so sure? She couldn't. Only Ariel would be that confident.

Marc doesn't want to believe the conclusion to which he's been drawn. He desperately wants to think Emma's still alive somewhere back at the base but he knows she's not. Grief washes over him in waves. Denial, anger and regret well up within him, but his rational mind holds sway. Ariel's been waiting for this moment since they touched down. She must have relished the opportunity to plan another escape. If the *Sycorax* was fully functional, she would have probably moved quicker. As it was, she fooled all of them—including the professor. She picked her moment to strike, taking advantage of when Marc and Emma were separated and most vulnerable. As much as his heart aches, wanting to believe Emma's somehow still alive, deep down he knows Ariel wouldn't leave any loose threads flapping in the wind.

Marc lowers his head and sobs. He raises his palms to his face and buries his head in his hands. His shoulders heave as his emotion flows. The thought of Emma's body forever lying on this cold, dark moon cuts at his heart. She didn't deserve this. She deserved better. The life, love and enthusiasm she radiated are now as sullen and lifeless as the rocks around him. Whatever future they could have had together is gone. All his hopes have been stolen.

"Oh, you're pathetic," Emma says, only it's not Emma speaking. "Get up!"

To Marc's astonishment, Emma's features morph into those of the Krell demigod. Her body and clothing remain the same, but her face shifts. She's still wearing the upper torso of Emma's suit but her features are transformed as she walks forward toward James. This is no ethereal ghost-like creature. Not anymore.

Ariel's skin is flawless. Her long, blonde hair curls over the stainless steel locking collar of her suit. Her eyes are as blue as the Hawaiian skies—and it's at that moment Marc knows he'll never see them again. His mind casts back to their conversation in the dome. She baited him. She told him what she wanted him to hear. She manipulated him into believing she was thoughtful and kind. And now she's betrayed him.

"She's no angel," James says with spittle settling on his beard. "No devil neither."

"What are you talking about, man?" Marc asks, overwhelmed with grief.

"Pay him no attention," Ariel says.

"It was you, wasn't it?" Marc asks. "Coming to me in the dark of night."

"I didn't think you'd fall for it," she says, smiling. "My first attempt was clumsy and yet..."

She shrugs.

"And now?" he asks. "How long did you think you could get away with this?"

"Long enough to get off this insipid rock. Oh, I had a bunch of Hindi swearwords lined up for our return to the *Sycorax,* but I won't need those now."

"You killed her," Marc says with trembling hands. "Why did you kill her?"

"She was getting too close. She understood too much. Besides, I wanted her seat on the ride out of here."

"You didn't have to kill her," Marc cries, desperately wanting another outcome but knowing nothing else is possible. Time has passed. What's done cannot be undone. No strength of will or fortitude of mind can defy the chaos. Not even the Krell, with all their astonishing technology, could roll back time itself. If they could, they wouldn't have gone extinct.

"I will not be imprisoned here," Ariel says.

"You," Marc says, struggling for words. "You..."

"They have no power," James says, backing up away from her. "Their secret. You must understand. You must see. You have to understand what's happening here. They're puppets. They're actors on a stage following a script. It's a play—a tragedy."

"Silence," Ariel says, marching up before him with her right hand outstretched.

James trembles. He stands there in shock, looking at what's happening to him. The muscles on his arms wither. His skin shrinks, pulling tight against his head. His eyes recede into their sockets. His lips peel back, exposing loose, jagged teeth. He falls against a boulder and slides to the ground. Within seconds, he's shriveled. His body resembles Rebecca's frail form.

"Come," Ariel says to Marc, gesturing toward the fusion core.

254

"Take your prize. You wanted it. It's the missing piece. It's what you need, right? To fix your *Sycorax*?"

Marc is silent.

Ariel has gambled and lost. Oh, he can't tell her that. She'd kill him, but she tossed a coin and picked the wrong astronaut. He's no engineer. He can't fly the *Sycorax*. Marc can run some of the basic functions, but it's all bluff.

It's one thing to be trained on systems while sitting on the ground in a simulator. It's another to commit an interstellar spacecraft to a new course with the press of a button. Ah, the buttons are so simple. The virtual ones are a patch of glass on the screen. The physical ones are tiny plastic/metal components that cost—at most—a couple of bucks. But it's what they do. Emma was right when she protested about waking Adrian back on the *Sycorax*. There are no do-overs in the dark void of space while orbiting a black hole. Make the wrong call and everyone dies. This isn't a sim where the instructors can reset the scenario for another pass. Hell, it's not unknown for cores to go thermonuclear if neglected and the containment field fails. Imagine a star appearing in the middle of engineering. Yeah, that's not good.

Instead of taking the core as Ariel commanded, Marc walks around it, looking carefully at a device he's only ever seen in training runs. He's not even sure where it goes within engineering. The warp bubble generator on the *Sycorax* looks like it was invented by a mad scientist. There's a big spherical thing with pipes leading to and from the engines. If he remembers correctly, the core is housed inside there, but he could be wrong. What's important now is that Ariel thinks he's competent. It's either that, or he'll join James crumpled on the floor of the cave.

The fusion core is a cube with thick borders but as the central containment field is spherical, the corners of the cube have been shaved. One of these contains a control panel and an LED screen. There are a handful of buttons with arrows pointing up/down and left/right. There's a stop and a play button, but this isn't a music caster. Unlike the controls on the *Sycorax*, the fusion panel is not intuitive. If you ever get this close to a fusion core, you're supposed to know what the hell you're doing.

The panel reads:

Arc 1.1% @ 3.5Mzp @ 15mC Caution 0.8% Fe

"What does it mean?" Ariel asks, coming around beside him.

"It's stable," Marc says, wanting to sound confident. He points at the display. "The iron content is less than one percent."

"But it says, caution."

Marc keeps his voice flat, wanting to avoid any hint of emotion.

"Yeah, you have to vent excess iron to keep the core stable, but this is low. It isn't a problem."

He's bullshiting, but he does remember something about the build-up of iron being bad. As for *venting*—that's a weasel word. It sounds good. How does he know it's stable? Well, the damn thing has been sitting here for decades without going nova. Even if it does say *caution*, the chances are, that ain't gonna change in the next five minutes. He sure as hell doesn't want to try to clean out the excess iron. He's not even sure it can be done without specialist equipment not found in a cave.

"Is it safe to move?"

Marc presses the down button for no other reason than he feels as though he needs to look useful and it seems like the safest button. He sure as hell isn't pushing the triangular *play* button. For all he knows, that fires the core up to full power. It probably doesn't, but if the damn thing started to heat up he'd have no idea how to control it. To his relief, nothing happens when he presses the down button other than a change in the display. It's nice not to be incinerated in a fireball.

Marc does all he can to suppress the lump welling up in his throat, but it's impossible to contain. It wells up regardless. Ariel, though, is focused on the antiquated display with its black and white screen. At a guess, actual engineers would only use this display when installing the core. They'd get far more meaningful metrics and better fine-grain control from the central engineering computer. This is some kind of quick diagnostic display with basic information on the health and stability of the core.

$12\% \, He : 8\% \, Li : 7\% \, C : 3\% \, O$

"And this?" Ariel asks.

"It's a list of elements that have fused in the core," Marc says, proud he's actually remembered something from his training. He has no idea if these numbers are good or bad.

"Let's get this back to the scout," Ariel says, but not before taking a good long look at him. Like Caliban, she must be able to read the subtle physical clues that betray his thinking: a rise in his core temperature, perspiration on his brow, the tremble of his fingers, and the racing of his heart. She can't read his mind, though. She can only guess at the catalyst behind these reactions. As she killed Emma and James, it's reasonable for her to conclude he fears for his life—and he does—but it's more than that. Marc knows how easily he could be exposed as a fake.

Ariel takes hold of one of the handles on the fusion core. Reluctantly, Marc takes the other. The core is heavy. As they carry it between them, shadows dance around the cave. Light flickers between their arms and legs, casting long dark shapes on the granite. Water drips from the ice. The radiant heat is uncomfortable. Marc switches hands as they step out into the weather. Behind them, the cave falls into darkness. Ariel walks ahead of him, with one arm extended behind her, holding the core. Marc has to change hands every couple of minutes.

Snow swirls around them. Clouds blanket the sky. A storm is brewing up on the plateau. Other than the spotlights on his suit torso, the fusion core provides the only light in the dark night. Ice crunches beneath their boots. If anything, the light from the fusion core is annoying as it ruins his night vision. Marc can't see more than four or five feet ahead of Ariel. Her shadow ripples across the path.

Ice falls plunge into the crevasse. In the darkness, the crashes are terrifying. It sounds as if reality is crumbling around them. The glacier looming to one side of them creaks and groans. Occasionally, stars are visible through the gloom.

How permanent is Ariel's form? Can she die? As they approach a thin section of the track, he's tempted to push her into the darkness, but she'd probably drag the fusion core down with her. And there's no guarantee she wouldn't pull some Krell magic and simply reappear on the ledge beside him. She might survive. He wouldn't.

They reach the ropes.

"I'll climb first," Ariel says. "Once I'm up there, tie the fusion core on and I'll haul it up."

"Okay."

"Use both ropes," Ariel says. "Given the heat coming off this thing, I don't want to risk a knot slipping."

Marc nods.

Ariel climbs out of sight. Marc's surprised she's even bothering to climb. With her Krell form, she could simply materialize up there. As she hauls herself up the rope, he notices the scratches on the back of the suit's torso. For authenticity's sake, she's used Emma's suit and clothing. For whatever reason, that has her remain in physical form. She could probably drop the pretense, but she doesn't.

Marc's pretty sure he knows how this is going to play out. When the main line finally goes slack, signaling she's up on the plateau, he ties both of the ropes through the handles on the fusion core.

"Ready?" is the call from above.

Marc shouts over the growing storm. "Ready."

He gives a couple of sharp tugs on one of the lines and Ariel begins hauling the ropes in. Marc was tempted to go up with the core, but if she wants to kill him she's made it pretty damn obvious it's easy. She could leave him, though. The scout is set on autopilot to return to the equatorial base. Oh, without someone at the controls it wouldn't be the most comfortable flight in a storm, but it would make it.

Marc's expecting her to abandon him. She could simply take off without saying anything. Without the ropes, he'd never make it up to the plateau. He'd die down here alone in the dark. Like the sucker he is, he'd hold onto hope regardless of how futile it might be. He'd double back to the cave, only this time it wouldn't be bathed in light and warmth. He'd have dried fish to eat. Water would be his biggest problem. Without the fusion core, that cave is going to get insanely cold and the stream will freeze over. He could forge a path down into the crevasse and risk venturing into the glacier melt beneath the ice, but in the dark, it's suicide. James pulled it off, but he was insane.

Marc watches as the warmth of the glowing fusion core disappears into the dreary darkness above him. The wind picks up, pushing snow across the glacier. Flakes swirl around him as the cold sets in. He wants to power up his suit to stay warm, but he's going to need that battery to run the light on his suit. Maybe, just maybe he can explore the crevasse with light and learn the route in the dark. He may even find useful supplies in the cave, like some additional rope. Perhaps James has already marked the path to the subterranean river. And all for what? To spend the next few decades shivering in the cold and dark, waiting for a rescue that will never come. On the bright side, at least he has someone to talk to down there. That pile of skulls isn't going to abandon him. The crew of the *Copernicus* is waiting for him to join them.

"Look out below," is shouted from above.

Ariel's voice should provide some relief to his troubled mind, but Marc knows she's only keeping him around because she thinks he's useful. At some point, he'll outlive that and she'll kill him. Between now and then, he's got to figure out some way to escape this mess.

Marc moves to one side as the ropes uncoil, whipping around as they fall through the darkness. Within seconds, the two lines settle near the steps carved into the granite.

"Are you coming?"

"I'm coming," he replies, grabbing one of the ropes and starting up the steep slope.

Grief

Miranda huddles against the cold, wrapping her arms around her chest as she waits by the scout. She shelters from the storm by standing in the lee of the landing gear. A bright white strobe flashes every thirty seconds behind her, briefly casting long shadows across the plateau. The landing lights are on, but they're red, allowing her eyes to remain adjusted to the darkness. There's not much to see through the gloom.

Snow blows across the granite. It's low to the ground, swirling in eddies.

Nothing has been spoken over the radio since Marc descended into the glacier almost three hours ago. She could hear him fine, but apparently, he couldn't hear her. She's got the radio clipped onto her waist belt, but she avoids the temptation to fire off frantic questions. She wants to preserve the battery.

Miranda's not sure how long she should wait for Marc and Emma. His suggestion, that she should return to her father by engaging the autopilot, sounds like a really bad idea. How long should she wait? What if they get injured and need help? What if she leaves just before they arrive back? What will happen to them then? She's not sure she could live with the idea of abandoning her friends out here on the frozen plain.

Her friends?

That thought brings a smile to her lips.

Miranda's known her father her whole life and yet somehow she feels an affinity with two astronauts from Earth. She knows nothing about them, but what is there to know? She knows they're desperate to save the lives of thousands of colonists in suspended animation on the *Sycorax*. That tells her something about their character. All those people up there put their trust in a crew they never personally knew. Oh, the crew was probably present when everyone turned up to go into cryo-stasis—at least that's how Miranda imagines the boarding process would have unfolded. There would have been lots of smiles, but no one would have known anything about those on the crew. It could have been any crew but just happened to include Marc and Emma. The passengers trusted in the professionalism of strangers, and they're not going to let them down.

Miranda's seen footage from Earth. Everyone there seems so nice. They won't be, though, not everyone. Miranda's not naive. She's seen enough films and documentaries to know humanity is known for two opposing, contradictory traits: blind loyalty to beliefs and science.

No one thinks they're blind, of course. That's why they all seem so nice. It's the *other* guy that can't accept reality. People pride themselves on being logical, which is perplexing as pride is not logical at all. Marc and Emma, though, are level-headed. She can see why they were selected for the crew. If they were all back on Earth, Miranda's sure they'd be friends. She doubts they'd hang out with her dad, though. Generational divides can be a little stuffy.

Miranda has listened carefully to the tiny fragments of information they've shared about their lives back on Earth. She likes to imagine herself lying on the beach with Emma, watching as Marc surfs a wave in Hawaii. If nothing else, it would be warm.

Miranda spots a faint glow low on the horizon. Her heart races when she realizes it's them. Marc and Emma are carrying a box between them that shines like a star, lighting up their arms and legs. That must be the fusion core.

Miranda runs toward them. The cold is meaningless now.

"Marc!" she yells. "Emmmmma!"

Miranda heads out into the storm. The wind whips around her, but she doesn't care. The two astronauts walk toward her, but something's wrong. She can tell from the way neither of them greets her. Marc looks pale. And Emma is...

"Ariel?" Miranda says, coming to a halt and suddenly feeling as cold as the snow swirling past her legs. She speaks slowly as they walk up to her. "I don't understand. Where's Emma?"

Marc's eyes are bloodshot. White streaks have run down his cheeks, leading from his eyes, revealing the frozen tracks of tears.

"She's dead," he says.

"What? What happened down there?" Miranda asks, turning and walking along with them to the scout. She asks Ariel, "And how did you get here? Did you come to rescue Emma?"

When there's no reply, Miranda says, "We should go back for her."

"She was never here," Marc says. It's only then Miranda realizes Ariel's wearing Emma's clothing and the upper torso of her suit. Ariel is uncomfortably quiet. Miranda is looking for an explanation from her, but she avoids eye contact.

"I don't understand," Miranda says as Marc and Ariel walk up the ramp on the scout and out of the wind. "What do you mean Emma was never here? I saw her."

"You saw me," Ariel says as the ramp retracts and the hatch closes.

Although warm air is circulating within the scout, Miranda feels cold. She wanted to understand what has happened. Now she wishes she didn't. Her fists tighten in anger. Tears well up in her eyes. She feels like screaming at Ariel. She feels she has the right to demand answers from Ariel, but it's apparent Ariel has changed. This isn't the same mystical creature that tended to her as a friend all through the years—and yet it is. This is the real Ariel. This is all that lay suppressed in bitterness and anger. Miranda bides her time. To lash out now would be a mistake. There will come a time for a reckoning, but not here—not now. She needs to get back to her father.

Ariel ignores Miranda, which hurts Miranda more than she thought it ever would. The look in Ariel's eyes is as cold as the storms that descend on the plateau. She speaks to Marc, saying, "How do I keep this thing from moving around during the flight?"

"Magnetic clamps," he replies as though nothing is wrong. "Put it in the cargo rack and press the orange switch to your right."

"Ah, got it," Ariel calls out from the cargo bay.

"Prepping for takeoff," Marc says, stepping into the cockpit. "Strap in."

Miranda climbs up to the cockpit.

Ariel sits at the back of the scout. She weaves her hands through the air, circling them above the fusion core. Glitter tumbles from her fingertips, only instead of falling, it swirls around the glowing device. She's probing the secrets of nuclear fusion.

Miranda sits down next to Marc and straps in. She watches quietly as he goes through his preflight checks, but it's clear he's not confident in what he's doing. He double-checks a few screens and then flicks back to things he's already looked at for the third or fourth time. His hands are trembling.

Marc mutters, "Fuel pumps engaged. Turbine spin-up complete. Stabilizers are active. Waypoint navigation is active."

A snowstorm whips up outside, but this isn't Caliban, it's the engines on the scout winding up to speed.

"And we're airborne," he says as the craft lifts vertically into the night.

Instead of soaring into the sky, the scout hovers, drifting sideways and backward. It tilts with its nose up, falling slightly as the engines are no longer firing vertically.

Miranda points at the blue flashing button marked *Autopilot*.

With the slightest of movements, Marc shakes his head.

"Is everything okay?" Ariel calls out over the whine of the engines.

"We're all good," Marc says, applying thrust and slowly bringing the angle of attack on the moveable engines from 90 degrees through 80, 75, 60 and then settling at a 45-degree slope as they soar into the clouds.

Marc's nervous, which makes Miranda nervous. She can see the indicators flashing on the screen in front of him, prompting him to lower the angle of attack and increase lift, but he ignores the flight computer's suggestions. He's reluctant to bring it down to 30 degrees. It seems he knows the scout's ascent is far too steep for its wings to actually work so he keeps the throttle on full. Were he to power down, the craft would stall. Miranda suspects Emma would be much more graceful with the scout. He's panicked. And he's burning through fuel. His behavior doesn't inspire confidence in Miranda.

Once they're up to an altitude of several thousand meters, he levels off and brings the scout around so it's aligned with the waypoint marking Miranda's distant home.

"What's going on?" Ariel asks quietly.

Marc doesn't reply. He doesn't even look at her. He keeps his eyes on the storm raging beyond the cockpit windows. Lightning cuts through the clouds. A single tear rolls down his cheek.

Marc loved Emma. Miranda's heart aches at the sight of that tear and the absence of any explanation from him. He tries to talk but no words come out. From his quivering lips, it's obvious he wants to say something but can't.

Miranda feels a maelstrom of emotions. She's angry. She's hurt. She's confused. She's scared.

She wants to confront Ariel. She wants to scream at her, but from Marc's lack of response, Miranda knows that would be a mistake. He's subdued, but not by choice. He's afraid of Ariel, and that gets Miranda to halt. Miranda thought she knew Ariel. Now, she doubts their history together. Ariel's supposed to be her friend. She's always been kind, but on reflection, Miranda can see how that was all an act. Ariel will do anything to get off this moon.

Miranda whispers, "Why did Caliban let us do this? Why didn't he bring us down like he brought the *Copernicus* down?"

Although she's barely audible over the sound of the engines and the howl of the wind, it's Ariel that answers from the rear of the cabin.

"Because of you," Ariel calls out. "He won't touch you—and that makes you my ticket out of here! Oh, yes. I knew you wouldn't be able to resist sneaking on board this flight."

Without making it obvious, Marc types on the screen in front of him. Miranda avoids the temptation to lean over to get a good look. He enlarges the font slightly, making it easier to read.

It's not Caliban.

It's Ariel that's dangerous.

It always has been.

Caliban is trying to stop her from leaving.

She must have been on the Copernicus.

That's why he brought it down. He wouldn't let her leave.

Miranda's not sure how, but Marc activates the screen in front of her. It mirrors his screen, allowing them both to type in a collaborative mode. A virtual keyboard lights up in a soft red outline. She enters:

But why?

Marc types:

I don't know.

That's what I intend to find out.

Marc is calm—too calm. Miranda knows he's putting on a front with Ariel, playing it cool so as to avoid provoking her, but even as the two of them converse in private, he seems far too relaxed. It seems he's

266

resigned to all that's transpired and yet he's still focused on getting answers.

Miranda types:

Why won't Caliban attack me?

Marc replies:

I don't know
When we first arrived, Caliban attacked us
But he didn't attack you.   He tore our suits to shreds but never struck you.
You didn't get so much as a scratch on you from all that glass flying around.

Miranda says:

And Ariel?
Are you sure about her?
She can't have killed Emma. She can't.

Marc replies:

Ariel is the worst kind of evil.
Evil that pretends to be good.
I watched her suck the life out of a survivor from the Copernicus.

As much as Miranda wants to ask him about that last statement and question his judgment, she understands it's more important to show him solidarity. If this is the conclusion he's come to then despite her misgivings she'll support him. To her, it was always Caliban that was the evil one. After all, he's the one that brought down the *Copernicus*. Even if Ariel was onboard, does stopping her justify him killing hundreds of researchers? For now, she needs to quell those doubts. There's just no way to work through her questions with the limitations of the keyboard—not without going off on a tangent. She needs to follow his lead. Ariel is unhinged, of that much, Miranda is certain. Miranda is upset. She knows she needs to stay focused until she can get her broader questions answered.

Miranda's not as fast at typing as Marc and she needs to be careful not to give away their silent conversation. She's not sure what else she should say. She's still in shock. Her fingers type:

She's always been so good to me.

Miranda pauses after entering that message. It's accurate—and yet it's lacking depth. She erases the last two words and elaborates further:

She's always been so good at manipulating.
Me.
I'm so sorry, Marc.

Marc offers a slight nod of his head. He's already erased his messages. Miranda does likewise. Marc's wrists are on the armrests, poised to type but he seems lost in thought. His fingers glide over the glass.

There's something I don't understand.

Miranda types quicker this time.

268

What?

Although she doubts she'll be able to answer his question, she'll try.

Up until an hour ago, she would have sworn Ariel was a loyal friend. Now, she feels betrayed. She wants to ask Marc precisely what happened to Emma but she knows it would be too painful for him. Besides, it doesn't matter what the details are. Miranda trusts him. Oh, it might satisfy her curiosity to ask, but she needs to be bigger than that. Not only would it hurt him—it would also distract him. It's enough to know Ariel murdered Emma. By itself, that fact alone screams at Miranda as being utterly naive about Ariel. Miranda was blinded by pancakes and party tricks.

Does her father know? Has he known all along about Ariel? Miranda feels sick at the realization her father is probably complicit. But he wouldn't have been involved in killing Emma. Miranda's confident she knows him better than that, but he must have known about the *Copernicus*. He blamed Caliban. Did he know Ariel was on board? Does he understand that's why Caliban attacked?

And why is she the exception? Why is Caliban whipping up a storm around them but not attacking them? Is it really just because Miranda's on board? What makes her so special? Why would Caliban care about her?

Marc taps the glass screen in front of him, getting Miranda's attention.

The Krell are far more advanced than us, right?
So why is Ariel examining the fusion core?
What's her power source?
Surely, it's more advanced.

Miranda types:

I don't know.

Marc scrubs his screen and types another question.

And why are we returning to your father?
If Ariel wants off this rock, she's got the scout and the core.
Am I missing something?

Miranda leaves her response up, drumming her fingers on the armrest to indicate the same answer:

I don't know.

Marc types:

When we land, stay with me.
Whatever happens, stay by my side.
Understood?

Miranda wants to ask why. It's tempting to think he's being selfish. Ariel said Miranda's the wild card. For whatever reason, Caliban won't attack them. Is Marc using her to protect himself? Perhaps Caliban won't strike out of respect for her father. There's always been a complex relationship between them—one she doesn't understand. Miranda doubts that any grace she's shown would extend to a shot at orbit, though. If Ariel does make a run for it, even with her onboard, she suspects Caliban will unleash hell on them like he did with the *Copernicus*.

But why? She wants to ask Marc why Caliban is so set on

stopping Ariel from leaving that he'd kill hundreds of innocent people. Her fingers hover over the keyboard but she resists the temptation to ask. Deep down, she knows Marc has the same question.

Miranda has to trust someone. Her world has been turned upside down by the realization her only friend and confidant on this world is a murderer. Logically, she should trust her father over a stranger. It could be that there's no one she can trust, but Marc has no hidden agenda. All he wants is to save the colonists on the *Sycorax*. As for Ariel, Caliban and even her father, Miranda's not so sure. Right now, everyone and everything else is questionable. Miranda wants to get to the bottom of what prompted such violence from Ariel and see how her father responds.

If Ariel defies her father, what can he do? He's got his Krell machine, but Miranda's never seen him use it to control either Ariel or Caliban. As far as she knows, it's a research tool allowing him to access the Krell archives. It doesn't actually do anything.

Without turning his head, Marc looks sideways at her. He's curious why she's hesitating. He must understand she feels conflicted. She types:

Understood.

Out of the corner of her eye, Miranda sees Ariel getting up at the back of the scout. Ariel's finished investigating the fusion core. She could probably recreate one now. Without making it obvious, Marc touches lightly on the controls of the scout. He's play-acting. Miranda understands. She used to do something similar with Ariel when she was a little girl. Now, though, both Marc and Miranda are play-acting and pretending the weather is worse to save their lives. It's a survival strategy. His slight touch on the controls causes the scout to sway as though it's been hit by a crosswind. Ariel braces herself against the bulkhead, giving both of them time to clear their screens. Marc removes the virtual keyboards from sight.

Ariel walks into the cockpit and stands behind Marc

271

"You knew, didn't you," Marc says. "You knew there was a core out there."

"I'd seen it," Ariel says. "Years ago, but I didn't realize its significance."

"And now?"

"Now I could make hundreds if needed."

Marc hangs his head.

"Why so glum?" Ariel asks, tormenting him, which seems unusually cruel for someone Miranda trusted with her life just hours ago. Although Ariel's attempting humor in some sick, twisted way, it comes across as bitter.

"You didn't have to kill her," Miranda says, knowing she can say what Marc can't.

"Oh, you're so quaint," Ariel replies. "You really don't understand what's going on do you?"

"When my father finds out he'll—"

"He'll what?" Ariel asks. "He'll scold me? Tell me I've been bad? He's kept me as a prisoner for far too long. He should have set me free. He promised me that."

"But where would you go?" Miranda asks.

She's cunning. Ariel's not the only one that can manipulate others. Miranda is asking what she knows Marc wants to hear. Ariel might think Miranda's young and dumb. That suits Miranda just fine. Her question sounds innocent enough. Coming from someone that's only ever known life on one, solitary, frozen moon, it is. But it's Marc's question, not hers. He's looking for answers Miranda can't give him, but perhaps Ariel can.

"I am boundless," Ariel says. "I am without any limit save one— the ability to travel to the stars. It's not enough to escape this moon. I long to see Earth, New Haven and all of the colonies."

"Are you going to help them?" Miranda asks, playing the fool.

Ariel laughs. "Hah. No. They will serve me as I have served you and your father." There's bitterness in her voice. "From now on, I serve no one but myself. I will be their god."

Marc keeps his head forward. It might look as though he's focused on flying, but Miranda can see his jaw clench.

"We're here," he says, circling the mountain and coming in to land by the science habitats.

Miranda's never seen her home from the air. She's surprised by how small the dome looks from up high. The lights on every level are on full, which is rare as it ruins the night vision required to see much of anything outside the dome. Even the entrance tunnel is lit up, casting a yellow glow across the rocks and ice. A solitary figure rushes down the stairs, heading from the laboratory to the first floor.

Miranda rests her hand on the cockpit window, longing to tell her father all that's transpired. She wants to warn him, but she can't. Marc circles several times, winding ever lower as he comes in to land.

"Quit messing around," Ariel says. "Put us down."

Marc must know he's excess baggage. As with Miranda, Ariel's only keeping him around while he's useful. In his case, she needs someone to fly the *Sycorax*. What's his plan? Miranda suspects that, like her, he's still in shock. It takes time to consider options. At the moment, he's compliant, but she's sure he's got some ideas. There's nothing he could voice at this point, though.

"On final approach," he says as Ariel holds onto the instrument panel above him, looking over his shoulders.

The scout comes in to land. At the last moment, the craft hovers, gently settling on the surface. The lights are on full. Their brilliant white glow illuminates the decimated labs scattered around the landing zone. Miranda remembers when the astronauts first landed. Back then, their lights were also blinding. Out on the plateau, though, Marc used red lights to allow their eyes to adjust to the darkness. Miranda has no doubt the bright lights now are intentional. Like her, he's got to be hoping her father has figured out what's going on. Perhaps he found Emma's body. By keeping the lights on full, it seems he's trying to blind Ariel to what lies in the shadows. He's doing everything and anything he can to gain an advantage over her. Caliban is out there somewhere. Has Ariel underestimated him? What will he do now that Ariel has a fusion core? Can he stop her? Again? Or has she learned from the *Copernicus*? Maybe she's counting on him doing the same thing again so she can outwit him.

Snow is kicked up by the engines as the scout hovers over the landing zone. Once they're down, Marc leaves the engines running just a few seconds longer than needed. Snow swirls around the craft. He's slow at lowering the ramp. He must be trying to buy time for Caliban and her dad to prepare for Ariel. If Ariel notices, she doesn't say anything. She peers out into the darkness, looking through the cockpit windows at the lights in the distant dome. Not much else is visible due to the intensity of the landing lights.

Ariel marches down the ramp, leaving the two of them in the scout with the fusion core. Miranda points at the ceiling of the spacecraft. She dares not speak, not yet, unsure how sensitive Ariel's hearing is, but she hopes the implication is clear. Ariel's not thinking this through. They've got the core. Marc and Miranda are free to go. Or at least try. Even if they didn't make for orbit, they could fly back to the crash site and thwart Ariel's plans.

Marc looks her in the eyes. His lips are pursed. His jaw is clenched. He's thinking about it. From the way he looks at her, she wonders if he's tempted to push her down the ramp and take off for the *Sycorax*. He's got everything he needs—except for one thing: answers.

"I have to know," he says softly.

Miranda shakes her head. She whispers, "Ariel will kill you."

Marc's shoulders are stooped. Tears fall from his cheeks. He rubs his eyes with his fingers, wanting to clear them away.

Miranda says, "You said it yourself, thousands of lives are hanging in the balance on your starship. They need you."

"Me?" He laughs, pointing at himself. "I'm the least qualified member of the crew."

"I don't understand," Miranda says, pointing at the fusion core in the storage rack. "I thought you wanted that."

"I don't even know where that thing goes," Marc says, trying not to laugh. He shakes his head. "Ariel killed the wrong person. She should have kept Emma, not me. Even Emma would struggle to retrofit this thing on the *Sycorax*. Hell, I don't even know if it's compatible."

"But you have to try," Miranda says.

Marc breathes deeply.

"The *Copernicus* was a refitted cruiser. She was an old ship, built before I was born. Too old for the military. They retired her and handed her off to a research team instead of sending her to the scrapyard. There are decades of technological change between the two vessels. The *Sycorax* is half the size. It's a cold storage colony transport. Even if I could plug the fusion core in, it might overpower our systems. Or worse, our computers might struggle to manage the core and the damn thing goes nova. If that happens, you'll see one extra star in the sky for about twenty seconds."

"But why go through all this?" Miranda asks. "Why did you want the core?"

"That's what I'm telling you. I didn't. Emma did. She's a gambler. Even with a bad hand, she'll play the cards before her."

"And now?"

Marc searches for something in a storage locker built into the bulkhead. He talks as he moves stuff around. "Now, I want answers. If I'm going to die down here or up there messing around with an antiquated fusion core, I want to know why Emma died."

Miranda nods.

Marc taps at a console near the airlock, punching in a bunch of commands. They're in English but they don't make any sense to her.

"What are you doing?"

"Setting up a contingency plan," he says. "It's a long shot, but there's one person on our spacecraft that might know what to do with the core. I've set up an autopilot routine to rendezvous with the *Sycorax*. Once connected, the scout will automatically wake him. It'll be rough on him. He'll be pissed, but we could do with his righteous anger right about now."

"Who?" Miranda asks.

Marc looks her in the eyes and says, "Adrian."

"Wait," she says. "Why are you going out there? This doesn't make sense. You should get the core to Adrian. You're not being logical."

"No," Marc says, stepping into the airlock. "I'm being human."

From the Grave

Marc walks down the ramp of the spaceship. The temperature plummets with each step. There's no sign of Ariel or Caliban. A lone figure stands out on the edge of the spotlights by the distant grave. Marc is nervous. Nothing feels right on this dark, cold moon. Thousands of lives depend on the decisions he makes in the next few minutes. The smart thing to do would be to make a run for the *Sycorax* with Miranda but he can't turn his back on Emma. She died down here. He needs to know why.

"Stay with the scout," he says to Miranda, hedging his bets. "If anything happens, I can remote launch and at least give you a shot at getting out of here alive."

Miranda is silent. She comes to a halt at the bottom of the ramp and watches as he steps off onto the rocks. The tips of her boots rest on the ice, but she remains with the scout.

Marc turns to her, repeating his concern. "Whatever happens, stay here."

"What's going to happen to him?" she asks, looking at her father.

"I don't know," Marc says.

He turns his back on her and walks across the landing zone. Rocks and ice crunch beneath his boots. Everything's familiar and yet it's not. He's seeing the derelict labs in a different light. In his mind, he tries to imagine the excitement the crew of the *Copernicus* had on finding not only an ice giant in orbit around a black hole but a moon—a habitable moon! Like the *Sycorax*, they probably set down initially with scouts to gather supplies.

At some point, the commander made the decision to set the *Copernicus* itself down on the surface. That's one helluva call as launching again would use a prohibitive amount of fuel. The decision wouldn't have been made lightly and must have been driven by a bunch of compelling reasons. First, they must have been absolutely convinced there was no biological threat whatsoever from the native flora and fauna, especially at a microbial level. Next, they had to be planning something long-term. Someone built that dome. It wasn't built for the professor and his family alone. Given that all the labs focus on research, the crew must have been using the starship as a mechanical workshop, living quarters and resupply point. They conducted research out here— lived back in there. The dome was intended to become a permanent base. Why did they leave? Why build that only to abandon it?

Marc tries to imagine a starship several times bigger than the *Sycorax* landing on the plain behind the scout.

According to the scant records they retrieved from the *Sycorax,* the *Copernicus* was originally an assault cruiser in the service of the Interstellar Republic so it was designed for atmospheric flight. If anything, landing on a moon was probably easier compared to troop drops it had performed while in active service. In contrast, the *Sycorax* was only ever designed for commercial spaceflight. If it set down, the corridors would be like tunnels he'd have to crawl through. The *Copernicus* must have been spacious when compared to his cryo-hauler.

As Marc walks across the rough ground, he imagines dozens of researchers unpacking their labs and moving between huts. This place would have been like a small town. They probably used their scouts to conduct recon flights similar to the one he was just on, exploring the plains and glaciers, chronicling life on this alien moon.

How long was it before they found the Krell artifacts? And how long after that did things go sour? What were the arguments over? Was the Krell technology active or did they do something to bring it online?

Did they even know what they were doing tampering with alien tech? What led them to abandon the professor here with his family? And when did Ariel and Caliban first appear?

Ariel desperately wants to leave this moon. Why was she even here in the first place? Where did she come from? The ice giant? Who decided to imprison her on this rock? And Caliban? Why would he guard her for thousands of years? Something doesn't add up. At this point, Marc's not willing to believe the story Ariel told him. If anything, the opposite seems more likely.

He walks up to the professor. The old man is wearing a thick, fur-lined jacket and heavy trousers. Tears have frozen on his cheeks, leaving silver tracks on his pale skin.

"What have you done?" Marc asks. He looks around for Ariel and Caliban, but they're alone.

Marc still doesn't understand why Ariel didn't make directly for the *Sycorax* once she had the fusion core. Why come back here? Why risk further confrontation with Caliban? Is she going to take the professor with her?

"I—I never meant for any of this," the professor says with trembling hands.

Marc is clinical in his response. "She's dead. You know that, right?"

For a moment, there's a look of terror in the professor's eyes. He's afraid. He knows Marc's talking about Emma and not his daughter as she's back on the ramp, but he's been unsettled by all that's transpired over the past few days. Whereas when Marc first met him, the professor was strident and confident, standing with his shoulders back and his head held high, now he's stooped and weary. It's as though he's aged a decade overnight. His resolve is gone.

The two men stand on either side of the sullen grave. The lights of the scout cast long shadows around them. The professor stares down at the wilted flowers lying on the rocks. His eyes linger on the words carved into the stone.

I love you.

I will never forget you.

"What's down in there?" Marc asks, pointing at the grave. He's quite deliberate about the use of the term *what* and not *who*.

"Please. Don't do this," the professor says, taking a step back from the grave.

"It's empty, isn't it?"

"No."

Marc points at the headstone. He raises his voice in anger as his blood surges. "There's no one and nothing in this grave, is there? It's fake. It's a distraction. But why?"

"Please, you don't understand," the professor says, trying to hide his trembling hands by grabbing at his fingers.

"Then talk to me. Tell me what the hell is going on here on Altair IV."

The professor is silent. His lips quiver.

Marc is defiant. "Emma's dead. And I watched Ariel suck the life out of the last survivor from the *Copernicus*. I want some goddamn answers!"

The professor is horrified. Their eyes meet. He stammers, "No, it's not possible. No one could have survived."

"The science officer," Marc says. "Dr. James Carter. You remember him, right?"

"He..."

"He survived the crash. We found him in a cave using the fusion core for warmth."

The professor shakes his head. His eyes dart around, refusing to settle on anything as he speaks. "He couldn't have. Not after all these years."

Marc is brutal with the truth. "Carter searched for survivors after the crash. Those bodies he found he ate. The core melted the ice to give him water. Eventually, he began eating fish, but the nutritional value wasn't there. He lost muscle mass and most of his teeth."

"And?" the professor asks even though Marc's already told him how this ends.

"And we found him. And Ariel killed him. What the hell is going on, professor?"

"Ariel. Caliban," the professor says. "They're..."

"They're what?" a voice asks from the head of the grave, challenging him. Miranda stands behind the headstone, resting her hands on the polished granite. She's ignored Marc's plea for her to stay with the scout.

"The machine," the professor says. His voice trembles. "You have to understand. I didn't mean for any of this. I didn't. It's the Krell machine. It's alive. It has a life of its own."

"What are you talking about?" Marc asks, confused by the professor's comments.

"It's hidden, buried beneath the surface. It wraps around the entire moon. The power is unimaginable. It's... It's..."

"It's what?" Marc asks, but deep down, he already knows.

"It's everything our hearts could desire—for good or ill," the professor says. "It's Pandora—their Pandora. Only Pandora. Her name. It doesn't mean doom. In Greek, it means *gift of the gods*. She was supposed to save us."

"But once the box was opened, it could not be closed," Marc says. He's stunned by what he's hearing. He feels dizzy. Whether that's the thin atmosphere or the events of the last few days catching up to him, he's not sure.

He looks around. Fireflies buzz past. Their lights glimmer like stars coming in and out of existence—billions of years pass in fractions of a second. His mind is lost. It's as though he's adrift in space. He's being drawn in toward the black hole. He's in orbit around the dark ice giant. He's helping Emma prep the scouts. He's walking up to this grave for the first time and marveling at the way bioluminescent microbes light up in the dirt. It's then he realizes he's been looking for answers he already has. He speaks softly, recalling something James told him in the cave. "*We are gods.*"

"Yes, yes," the professor says, looking at him through bloodshot eyes. "That machine made me a god. Only I'm not. I could never be."

Marc feels the weight of the moment pulling him down. It's as though gravity has doubled in an instant, but now he understands. The professor was crying *before* they landed. It wasn't Miranda that brought him to tears—it was Emma. If he didn't see Emma die, he at least saw her body. He knew what Ariel had done before they landed.

"We're human," the professor says, struggling to explain himself. "But for all our faults, we're balanced. Love and hate. Kindness and anger. Logic and emotion. Fear and trust. We're capable of all this and more, but we're yin and yang. We're both the darkness and the light."

"Ariel and Caliban," Marc says as a growing awareness strikes at his heart.

"Yes," the professor replies as two figures materialize behind him in the gloomy half-light. Ariel and Caliban approach to within ten feet. In the darkness, their features are sullen. Their shoulders are stooped. It's as though they're responding to being scolded. They've reacted to words the professor is yet to speak. With bitterness on his lips, he says, "What a fool was I to trust them. They are drunken monsters, not gods."

"And all of this," Marc says, stunned by the realization of what's transpired on Altair IV. "It's the war raging in your soul."

The professor looks down at the grave, saying, "And they killed her."

Marc appreciates the deeper meaning in those few, simple words. With four words, the professor has described the death of his wife, the destruction of the starship *Copernicus* and the murder of Emma. His use of the plural pronoun is telling: *they!* Both Ariel and Caliban have wreaked havoc trying to satisfy their primal urges. They're separate beings. There's no balance within, only from without. It seems the

282

professor tried to reign in the madness, but he couldn't. He's not researching ancient Krell technology. He's trying to undo whatever spawned these monstrosities that plague him on this moon.

Marc breathes deeply. As much as he wants to believe the professor, something bugs him about the old man's choice of words. *And they killed her.* He's absolved himself of all responsibility. Is he rationalizing his culpability? Is he lying even now?

Marc says, "It's all because of you, isn't it? You're conflicted. You want to leave but you know you shouldn't and that manifests in them. You know what will happen if you go back out there. And so you stop yourself time and time again."

The professor drops to his knees in the snow and ice and leans forward sobbing over the cold rocks that form the grave.

"It was too much. The machine. It was too powerful. It took from me what it wanted. What it needed to create them."

Marc looks at Miranda, saying, "I'm taking her with me."

"What? No," the professor says, looking up at his daughter standing at the head of the grave. "You can't. She can never leave here."

"Why?" Miranda asks, but her father doesn't answer. From the look on his face, it's not that he can't but that he won't.

Two thundering booms reverberate through the air. They're high and distant, breaking in the clear sky barely a second apart. They all look up. Two meteors cut through the dark of the eternal night. Yellow streaks light up in the stratosphere, blazing as they tear into the atmosphere. They travel in a smooth curve, looping slowly around the sky as they descend.

"Emma," Marc whispers, realizing what's happening.

While the others are looking up, he checks the control panel on his suit arm. The mission-elapsed time has just passed 36 hours. This is what Emma meant when she said they had an advantage over Ariel and Caliban. He asked her what it was, but she wouldn't tell him. He still remembers the glee with which she answered, *"Me!"* This is what she meant. While he was prepping the scout for departure on the *Sycorax,* she was setting up the other two scouts as a contingency. She knew they should have been back within 24 hours so she programmed them to fly on autopilot as a backup to rescue them if things went sour down on Altair IV. They're probably homing in on the beacon built into the scout. Emma might be dead, but she's given him an ace-in-the-hole.

"There are more of you?" the professor asks, confused. He must think Marc and Emma have lied to him about the state of the *Sycorax* and its crew. They haven't, but he's assuming the incoming scouts are crewed. Ariel and Caliban both step further back into the shadows. They're trying to assess the threat cutting through the sky above them.

Marc sees an opportunity. Up until this point, he hasn't lied, but now he sees an opening to gain an advantage over the demigods. It doesn't matter that the scouts are on autopilot. As long as they *think* there are two crews inbound, it'll distract them and provide him with cover. And that will buy him some time.

"It's over," he says to the professor. "You need to come clean with me—with both of us. Tell me. What happened here?"

"You don't understand. I—I can't," the professor says, kneeling beside the grave. He reaches out and touches the stones. There's tenderness beneath his fingers.

"Who's in the grave, professor? Who died here?"

"The light of my life," the professor says with trembling lips. "But I suspect you've always known that."

Marc drops to his knees. The ice crystals around him glow in response to his motion as alien bacteria react to his movement. He grabs at the rocks and stones and begins casting them aside. In the low gravity, it's easy to clear away bigger rocks.

"No, no. No! You can't. You mustn't," the professor yells, batting at Marc's hands from the other side of the grave.

Marc will not be deterred. Ice has fused some of the rocks to the ground, but he wrenches them away. The smaller rocks scatter like blocks of polystyrene.

"Please, no," the professor says, trying to lie on the grave to prevent Marc from disrupting it. "If they knew…"

"Father," Miranda says, kneeling beside the old man and wrapping her arm over his shoulder. She's gentle, speaking softly. "This has to end. No one else need die to hide your secrets."

The professor looks deep into her eyes. Tears stream down his cheeks. "I'm sorry, Miranda. I am so sorry. You must believe me. I never meant for any of this. I just—I just wanted to protect you."

Marc clears a section of the grave near the headstone. Ariel and Caliban watch impassionately. Now that he's below ground level, the gravel used to fill the grave is as fine as sand. Marc has no idea how deep the grave is, but given the ground around him is frozen solid and yet within the grave it's loose, he suspects the trench is shallow. What need is there for a six-foot-deep grave on a moon with no scavengers?

Miranda helps him. She cups her fingers together, swirling them around and pulling loose gravel out of the grave. With each motion of her hands, tens of thousands of microbes light up in iridescent blue, sparkling like stars beneath her fingers.

Less than a foot down, they come across a scrap of cloth. Miranda sits back, watching as Marc continues. Out of respect, Marc slows his motion. Even though Miranda never knew her mother in life, seeing her like this in death must be harrowing. He sweeps his hand back and forth, gently clearing away the fine gravel. Ribs are visible beneath the fabric.

The professor's hands are shaking. He takes hold of Miranda's hand, wanting to comfort her and perhaps to hide his trembling fingers from sight.

Marc clears the gravel, exposing a shoulder bone. As the soil shifts with his motion, a jaw is exposed along with a few teeth. The rest of the skeleton is still buried.

"I'm sorry," Marc says, feeling terrible for doubting the professor's integrity.

He rests his hand on the pile of gravel beside him, ready to push it back into the grave and cover the remains, but something bothers him. It's the size of the bones. Women are smaller than men—that's to be expected—but the shoulders are narrow. The jaw is slight. And the teeth. They're long but thin. The length isn't that much of an issue as ordinarily only a fraction of each tooth would be visible above the gum line, but these teeth are tiny. Without saying anything, he rests his hand on the jawbone, comparing the size of the teeth with the nail on his little finger. Three, almost four teeth would fit within his nail.

He sits up, looking at the professor. "This is a child."

Reluctantly, the professor nods.

Miranda looks confused. Her brow furrows. "I—I don't understand. How is this possible? I thought this was my mother."

Marc reaches down and brushes the gravel away, exposing the cheekbones, eye sockets and forehead of the skeleton. Although he's leaning into an adult-size grave, the body within is of a child no more than five or six years old. Strands of blonde hair are visible beneath the dirt.

"No," Miranda says, getting to her feet and staggering backward. "No, no, no. It can't be."

Her arms are shaking violently, but not from the cold. She looks around in a state of shock, turning toward Ariel and Caliban, and then the scout, and then back at the grave as she says, "No, it's not. It's not me! It couldn't be me. I'm here! I'm right here."

"I'm sorry," Marc says, getting to his feet. Fine dust falls from his knees and legs, lighting up like glitter as it settles on the frozen ground.

Miranda pleads, "Father. My father. Please tell me this isn't so."

The professor opens his mouth but no words come out. He reaches out, using the headstone to help him stand.

Marc's wristpad computer beeps, distracting him. The two scouts are on final approach. He can see the glow of their engines coming in over the distant mountains. Emma's set them up to use a *Stranded Crew* protocol, meaning now they're in range, they're operating in tandem to effect a rescue. Their flight paths can be altered by remote control.

Marc's got several options available on his screen. His computer informs him about the preprogrammed rescue scenarios available to him. The first is to divert the landing to his present location. This is intended for situations where the primary craft has crashed in a dangerous position or the wreckage impedes landing. It allows the surviving crew to move to nearby safe ground and call in the rescue craft. Then there's an option for hovering and lowering a harness, and one for aborting the landing and going around again.

Marc could take direct control of one or both of the scouts, but even Emma wouldn't attempt that. Remote control flight is enhanced with AI, but next to impossible without hooking up to a larger display. Given his lack of flight experience, he'd have a 100% chance of crashing and he knows it. As it is, he leaves the options alone, keeping his fingers well clear of the buttons on the display. A quick glance tells him that the rescue craft will be fine setting down behind the first scout. As they're under AI control at the moment, they'll flank each other, forming a triangle with the craft on the ground at the apex. As soon as they land, though, and no one walks out, Ariel, Caliban and the professor will know it's a bluff. Marc swipes the screen away.

Miranda addresses Marc. She's angry. "Why? Why did you do this?"

"I had to know," Marc says, still distracted by the incoming scouts visible to one side of her. The scouts have activated their landing lights, meaning they're fifteen kilometers out. The lights are designed to illuminate a landing strip for hundreds of meters so they light up the mist in the air.

Clouds roll in. The weather is moving unnaturally fast. The wind picks up. Marc's eyes dart around. He's trying to gauge what Caliban is doing and the growing threat around him. Without raising his hand, he points at the scout with one finger, trying to get Miranda's attention. She doesn't notice. Tears roll down her cheeks.

Ariel and Caliban walk over and stand at the foot of the grave, looking down at the remains. Lightning crackles in the distance. Thunder rolls across the plain. The professor notices the growing tempest. He looks at Miranda and then Marc. Their eyes meet, exchanging what words cannot convey. The professor is worried about what will happen next. It seems he fears not only for his life but theirs.

Marc understands. As long as Ariel and Caliban thought Miranda was his daughter, she was untouchable. These Krell sentinels may have split off from the professor at some distant point several decades ago, being torn from the primal parts of his mind, but they never lost their respect for him. Now, though, they must see Miranda as a threat. The professor has been protecting her from them—and not without reason. For them, though, the dynamic has changed. He betrayed them. He misled them. There's no telling how they'll react to this other than that they'll act in their own self-interest. They might be the product of the alien Krell machine, but they've inherited the professor's human traits and even his mannerisms. Marc sees the way Caliban looks sideways at Ariel. Whereas once he fought to prevent her from fleeing, now he's aligned with her. Now, they have a common cause.

Staring at them, Marc can't help but wonder how long this alliance has been in play. Could it be that as soon as he and Emma decided to talk to them separately that they conspired together? The storm that battered the scout seemed determined but not violent, which makes Marc wonder if they've been working together for a while now, deceiving what they perceive as '*dumb humans.*'

Ariel doesn't notice Caliban's interest in her. She's distracted. She kicks at the loose rocks at the base of the grave, asking, "How is this possible?"

"You," the professor says, pointing to the caves at the base of the cliff behind them. Marc can see the old man is stalling. He's trying to buy them some time. Marc edges closer to Miranda as the professor continues. "You were supposed to protect my family. You were supposed to be there for us, but you conspired with Carter. Together, you were going to leave for the stars. You abandoned us."

"But I didn't kill her," Ariel says.

"You might as well have," the professor replies. "You left us. You were supposed to protect us. You said you'd stay. If you'd stayed. If you'd been here none of this would have happened. You knew the passage was unstable after the Krell machine came to life."

"What happened?" Caliban asks.

"She fell. There was a quake. They both fell from the narrow ledge that leads to our home. Lisa and Miranda, but I could only reach one of them. My—My wife—Lisa. She slipped beneath the waves. M—Miranda was still breathing, but her body was broken. I tried. I did all I could but she was dead before I could get her home."

"And us?" Ariel asks.

"And you. You were gone. You and Caliban were fighting over the wreckage of the *Copernicus* for months! You could have saved her, but you didn't. When I needed you most, you abandoned me. If you'd been here, they'd both still be alive."

Marc comes around beside Miranda. He takes her by the elbow, gently edging her away from the grave and toward the scout, but she resists, pulling away from him. She looks at him with disdain. He wants to say something but he doesn't want to provoke Ariel or Caliban. At this point, it's impossible to know what they're going to do. This has come as a shock to them, but that's playing to his advantage. Either of them could strike him down, but they're still coming to grips with what's been said. Ariel's grand scheme to somehow leave this moon has unwound. From the way she looks at the professor, it's clear she loves him in her own twisted, distorted way. That's why she came back for him. Now, she's struggling with the realization he never trusted her.

Caliban has been left questioning his place on Altair IV. He seems at a loss as to how to respond. He looks at Miranda with what Marc could only describe as bitterness.

"How is she possible?" Caliban asks, echoing Ariel's question and wanting more detail. Lightning strikes the hillside near the dome a couple of hundred meters behind him. It's his frustration playing out as the clouds billow overhead. Sleet is driven in by the wind, coming down on an angle.

"I—I don't know," the professor says. "I was grieving. The machine. I... It tapped into my thoughts, my desires, my hopes and fears, my memories. As I cried it brought forth new life."

"No," Miranda says, becoming strident. She points at herself, tapping the center of her chest as she says, "I'm real. I'm not a dream or one of your nightmares. I'm alive."

"You are alive," the professor says softly, trying to shepherd her away from Ariel and Caliban.

"Don't you see?" Marc says, talking to her while gesturing to the alien sentinels. "You're not like them. You're different. They're fragments. They split off from your father's base nature. But you. You're the outpouring of his love."

"I—I can't deal with this," Miranda says, shaking her arms. She's manic. She tries to walk off the stress, pacing back and forth. Marc goes to grab her arm but she shrugs him away. "I'm not real? How can I not be real?"

"You're real," her father says. "You're just not human."

"No. Nope. I reject that. I'm... I am—"

Ariel cuts her off, saying, "You're an abomination."

"Noooo," the professor yells, stepping between them.

"You must die," Caliban says.

Marc turns to Miranda and yells, "Run!!!"

The wind howls across the plain. Hail sweeps in, pounding the ground. Chunks of ice strike Marc on the shoulders and scalp, leaving cuts on his face. He holds his arms up, trying to protect his head as he runs.

Lightning strikes at the ground around him.

Hail pulverizes his body, tearing at his suit.

Marc's slower than Miranda. She makes it to the scout and runs onto the ramp, but he's limping. He's hurt. In the lower gravity found on Altair IV, Caliban is able to produce hail the size of baseballs. A chunk of ice as big as a soccer ball strikes near Marc's feet. He jumps to avoid it. He's not going to make it to the scout. Marc runs into one of the abandoned science labs. Hail dents the roof, coming down in waves that make it impossible to hear anything beyond the crash of ice pounding on sheet metal.

Marc looks out of a broken window. Miranda stands on the ramp, beckoning him to make a run for the scout, but there's no way he'd survive. The ground is already covered in hail to a depth of several inches and more is coming down.

As suddenly as it started, the hail stops. The silence is overwhelming. Marc peers out of the door. The professor is lying face down in a pool of blood by the grave.

Ariel walks slowly toward Marc as Caliban stands back with his arms raised up, commanding the elements with eyes that glow.

Ariel yells, "Come out of there, you coward. You're not going anywhere."

She's right. He's delaying the inevitable. Miranda is yelling for him to run to her but he'll never make it. Marc uses his wristpad computer to engage the autopilot on the scout. The ramp raises. Miranda crouches on it as it rises into the belly of the craft. She's screaming, pleading for him to join her. The engines whine, coming up to speed.

"You're pathetic," Ariel says.

Marc steps out of the lab, facing her down. Blood seeps through his hair and around his neck.

Ariel says, "If the *Copernicus* couldn't escape, what makes you think your puny vessel will?"

As she speaks, the scout lifts off the ground. Its wings expand, extending out of the fuselage as it uses its engines to rise vertically before transitioning to regular flight. The craft rocks in the crosswind blowing over the plain.

Lightning strikes the scout, causing its fuselage to glow. The craft reaches a hundred meters in the air but struggles to stabilize its motion. Even though it's under AI control following a return flight path, the constantly changing atmospheric conditions make it impossible to transition into the hypersonic flight profile required to reach an orbital speed.

Marc holds his arm out in front of his chest. He taps at the controls on his wristpad computer, asking Ariel, "So? What can you make with two hundred thousand kilograms of liquid hydrogen and oxygen?"

"What are you talking about?" she asks, confused.

Miranda stands in the cockpit of the scout, looking out the window. She has her hands pressed against the glass, watching as the scout rises several hundred meters in the air.

Within seconds, the fuselage is no longer visible in the dark, only the glow of the ship's engines. The craft is buffeted by the tempest descending on the plateau.

Marc activates the manual controls on the two incoming rescue craft, overriding their onboard computers. He throttles both sets of engines to 100%.

"No! No! No!" Ariel yells, turning to Caliban and waving her arms. She's trying to signal that the focus should be on the two inbound scouts with their landing lights on full. Caliban sees them, but he doesn't recognize the danger.

The last thing Marc sees is the two scouts screaming in through the clouds toward them. They're low, still on approach for landing. Blinding lights illuminate the huts. The hail on the ground glistens like diamonds.

The lead scout comes in short, touching down behind where his scout once sat. The remote control craft is still accelerating as it hits. The cockpit crumples. Metal panels are ripped off the fuselage. The craft tumbles end over end as it breaks apart.

Before Marc can blink, the second craft overshoots the landing zone. It roars past with its engines blazing.

"Thank you, Emma," Marc mutters as the second scout hits the surface of the moon at more of an acute angle, striking between him and the grave.

No one wants to die. If he could, Marc would have opted to

escape with Miranda, but they'd never make it with both Ariel and Caliban joining forces against them. Emma died down here and he will too. Marc will have his revenge on Ariel. He's content to die. He's at peace, knowing he's thwarted Ariel's efforts to escape.

It's astonishing how fast the realization of all that's transpired on Altair IV swells within his mind in mere hundredths of a second. As flames stretch across the landing zone, he finally understands what the professor has been doing all these years. His alter-egos have been waging a war against each other while he's been looking for a way to undo the madness. They might have thought he was continuing to investigate Krell technology, but he wasn't. It's all so obvious to Marc now. Ariel and Caliban were freaks. There are only two of them. Regardless of how they formed, once created, the professor never wanted any more of them. Whatever dark experiment he performed, he refused to repeat it in the following decades. Miranda, though, was unavoidable. She was the spontaneous result of his grief. After the loss of his wife and daughter, it seems he felt he had to protect Miranda not just from Ariel and Caliban, but from herself. He kept her true nature hidden from her out of love. Part of him wanted to leave Altair IV, but he couldn't allow Ariel to escape. All these years, he's been searching for a way to undo this Gordian knot. Oh, how Marc wishes he could share this with Emma, but he suspects she knew before the end. She may not have known about Miranda's true nature, but she would have pieced together the rest. And Ariel killed her because she was too smart—too kind.

The fuel tanks on both craft rupture. An explosion engulfs the plain. Hundreds of thousands of kilograms of liquid fuel decompress in an instant, evaporating and igniting. Within a nanosecond, the temperature on the rocky plain soars from negative thirty to over six thousand degrees. For a moment, that barren stretch of land is hotter than the surface of the closest star.

Molten rock is scattered along with burning metal fragments. The shockwave splits the plateau, compressing the air and resounding for several hundred meters. The science habitats are scattered by the super-heated shockwave. They're crushed and crumpled, being set alight as they tumble into the distance. A crater forms as the upper layer of the plateau is vaporized in a flash of unbridled raw energy.

A fireball rises into the dark of night as the lone scout soars into the distance.

Act III

The Masque

Home

Miranda sits on the observation deck of the interstellar cruiser, *The George Washington* as it approaches Earth. She's not sure how many Earth years have transpired since she boarded the *Sycorax* before it limped on to New Haven. It's been decades since she escaped Altair IV and yet, for her, it seems as though everything unfolded yesterday.

The scout reached orbit around Altair IV within a few minutes of the explosion on the plain but it took several hours before its rendezvous with the *Sycorax*. Miranda hid while Adrian woke. She watched in horror as he climbed out of a hibernation pod. Without anyone to assist him, the recall process was torture. The computer on the *Sycorax* managed the process, but there were a bunch of questions and prompts that came up asking about additional procedures. At the time, Miranda had no idea what an anesthetic or an antiemetic was— and there was no way she was pressing any confirmation buttons for fear of making the wrong decision on behalf of someone she didn't know. Adrian pounded on the lid of the casket for almost an hour before it released him. She could hear his muffled screams. When he finally emerged in a cloud of vapor, he was covered in blood, shit, piss and vomit.

At first, Miranda didn't like Adrian. She didn't have to. She needed him to survive. Once he calmed down and cleaned up, she explained what had happened on Altair IV—omitting any reference to her origins—and showed him the fusion core. Marc was right. It didn't fit, but Adrian was able to remove some shielding from the warp drive and mount it in the containment sphere.

They spent three months in orbit around Altair IV repairing the *Sycorax* before it was ready for interstellar flight. Adrian showed Miranda how to operate the telescopes and radar on the navigation array. She looked for any sign that Ariel or Caliban survived the explosion. The crater was visible as was the shattered dome of her home, but she never saw any atmospheric disturbance or Ariel's glowing form. As far as she knows, they died along with her father.

Fires raged within her home for weeks, which confused her as it was largely made from granite with very little flammable material. Two days before they left orbit, she saw lava flowing from the caves at the base of the mountain. Whatever the Krell machine was, it seemed to be connected to the core of the moon. The explosion damaged her home and that, in turn, damaged the machine. It hurt seeing red glowing rock spewing out of cracks and fissures in the mountain. Steam rose from the newly-formed lava field, swallowing the land. Although she knew she'd never go back, it was sad to see there was nothing she could ever return to. Whatever that machine was, it was destroyed by the raging core that gave it life.

It took decades for the *Sycorax* to reach New Haven. Adrian and Miranda continued their watch all through those lonely years. He aged. She didn't. He never asked why.

Adrian died less than six months before a frontier hauler reached them and escorted them into the space dock in orbit around New Haven. Miranda was greeted as a hero. Seven thousand nine hundred and sixty-two colonists survived. No one asked any questions about her identity. So much time had passed they assumed their records were corrupt. Even though Miranda looked young, she dressed conservatively and carried herself with poise and that seemed to fend off any doubts anyone may have had about her age. They were all too preoccupied with *The Miraculous Flight of the Sycorax,* as the media called it. The ship, its passengers and its crew were thought long dead.

Over the years, Miranda had plenty of time to learn about *Homo sapiens*. She studied humanities, various sciences and even art, although sketching on a digital pad was all she could do while in flight. As beautiful as New Haven was, she'd seen too much of Earth in videos to ignore the longing in her soul.

Miranda had to carefully plan how she'd get to Earth. While on the *Sycorax*, it made sense not to enter hibernation. Most of the pods were faulty and the two of them needed to be on call to fix any issues that arose with the craft while in flight. Despite their rocky start, Adrian was kind to her as the years rolled by and taught her about the various systems on the spacecraft.

Miranda realized her body would never be compatible with the hibernation system. She stowed away on *The George Washington* and snuck around while the crew was asleep. She was careful, being meticulous to cover her tracks. Like all spacecraft, *The George Washington* had its quirks, one of which was empty berths near engineering used for in-system cruising. These allowed her the freedom to watch the stars, tap into the computer and continue her studies. She learned to alter the flight database so there was no record of the extra oxygen, water and food she was consuming. As everything was recycled, there was no net loss so no one ever investigated the occasional power surges from her deck.

Throughout the long years of boredom, Miranda would console herself, watching the crew, learning about Earth or playing electronic games. She found she could slow her metabolism and sleep for months on end but it seemed she was cheating herself out of waking hours. Nothing could make up for the loss of companionship over the decades, which has her excited about making landfall on a planet with billions of people. There's got to be millions, perhaps hundreds of millions or even billions of kind people down there like Marc and Emma. If anything, she suspects her social life is about to become overwhelming.

Miranda yawns.

The crew of *The George Washington* woke the passengers three days out from Earth, allowing her to mingle with them. So far, no one else has bothered to venture up to the observation deck. Even though *The George Washington* has a rotating torus imparting a sense of artificial gravity, most of the passengers are suffering from deep hibernation sickness after four and a half decades spent in cryopods. Besides, there's nothing to see this far out. Earth is a pinprick of light in the darkness. If Miranda squints, she can convince herself she's seeing the legendary pale blue dot adrift in the pitch-black void of space. If she's honest, it looks like a rather dull, ordinary star.

"Is there anything I can get you?" a synthetic steward asks, walking up beside her.

"Oh, I'm fine," she says, getting up.

Rather than heading to medical where most of the passengers are going through nanobot treatments, Miranda walks the other way, heading to the gym onboard *The George Washington*. For her, the next three days are utter torture. All her life, she's dreamed of a brilliant blue planet—and now it's out there, just off in the distance. She knows what to expect. She's memorized hundreds of photographs and videos taken from orbit. She can recognize the coastline of dozens of countries. She understands how clouds obscure the southern ocean, hiding Antarctica. She longs to see the clear waters of the Pacific, the azure blue of the Caribbean, and the deep green of the Atlantic. She can't wait to feel the pull of one gee—it's more than three times what she experienced growing up on Altair IV, but she's not daunted by the challenge.

Miranda's not naive. The spin she's experiencing at the moment only equates to a quarter of a gee. It's just enough to keep white blood cell counts in a healthy range, although she's not sure she has any of those. Back in New Haven, she snuck into a hospital and used a medical scanner to look at her internal organs. Although it detected a heart, lungs, stomach, liver and kidneys, it didn't recognize them as human. *"Foreign cellular structure,"* was the official term. No sooner had she read the findings than she scrubbed the electronic record. As best she understands what happened to her, she's a hybrid between Krell and *Homo sapiens*. Her father would probably be able to explain it, but not in simple terms. He'd waffle on for hours about the nuances of her form. All she knows is she's not like Ariel or Caliban—and she's happy about that. She's got their pedigree but not their nature.

Miranda knows Earth is going to crush her with its oppressive gravity. She starts with a cardio routine in the gym. Rubber bands stretch over her shoulders to simulate the best part of a gee as she runs on the treadmill. After an hour, she switches to squats with a barbell. Again, thick, wide rubber bands increase the load on her muscles. The weights have measurements on them, but she ignores the numbers. They're meaningless to her. All she knows is she needs to be able to bear more and more weight on her frail frame.

Miranda understands there's no reprieve on Earth. Out here in space, she can walk away from the gym and relax. Down there, she'll have no such luxury.

From what she's read, floating in water can bring some relief for newbies, but it's temporary. If she wants to integrate, she has to be able to withstand the crush of the atmosphere pressing down on her from above. She needs to be able to breathe in and exhale again, pushing out against the bulk of the thick air forming a column well over a hundred kilometers above her head. When walking, she has to push off with her thighs time and again, striding against the pull of an entire planet beneath her.

Miranda remembers how funny it seemed when Marc and Emma first arrived on Altair IV. Her moon was so small their muscle memory from Earth was next to useless. They had to relearn how to walk and run. In the same way, she needs to learn how to hold herself upright on Earth. Her posture and gait will have to change or she'll find herself falling flat on her face.

Over the next few days, Miranda hits the gym every couple of hours, pushing herself until her muscles ache even when she's not exercising. She's determined to be ready for life on Earth. She's nothing if not stubborn.

As the last day unfolds, Miranda heads up to the observation deck to look out at Earth from a low orbit. Already, shuttles are taking passengers down to the surface.

The deck is packed. All the seats are taken. She stands in the aisle. The torus on *The George Washington* rotates once every three minutes. As the craft is facing the planet, the view drifts at a steady pace but it's not disorienting. She points.

"Florida."

"No, honey," the woman beside her says. "That's Italy."

"It's beautiful," Miranda replies. She doesn't care whether she's right or wrong—she's home.

"Nowhere else quite like it, huh?" the woman says. "Is this your first time?"

"Yes."

"Where are you from?"

"Altair," Miranda says.

"Haven't heard of it," the woman replies, screwing her face up a little. "Must be part of the new world colonies."

"It's so bright down there," Miranda says, looking at the way the sunlight reflects off the blue waters passing beneath the spacecraft. If she didn't know better, she'd swear she could reach out and touch the clouds. As it is, *The George Washington* is over four hundred kilometers above the surface of the planet. The curvature of Earth is visible on the edge of the windows, but it's not obvious—not like when orbiting Altair IV.

A boarding call is made for Hawaii.

"That's my shuttle," Miranda says, beaming with pride.

"Oh, you're landing at Pearl. Nice. Have fun down there, sweetie."

With over ten thousand people on *The George Washington*, dozens of shuttles are required to disembark, with destinations set around the planet. Miranda chose Hawaii because that's where Marc was born and raised. In the back of her mind, there's a lingering doubt about his death. She felt helpless watching as the scout lifted off the icy plains of Altair IV. She could see Marc in one of the labs—and then everything happened so fast—too fast. Miranda knew there were two more scouts coming down from the *Sycorax*, but they were supposed to land. Marc turned them into weapons. With his dying breath, he avenged Emma and set Miranda free.

She heads for the departure lounge at the hub of the spacecraft.

Miranda was issued with implanted ID tags back when the *Sycorax* reached New Haven. No one questioned her lack of credentials or back story. Why would they? She looks human. To their minds, she must be human. It's not like she has tentacles or anything like that.

Aliens are the stuff of lore. As far back as the 1900s, books and movies have described aliens as inhuman monsters. Even with the discovery of actual extraterrestrial microbes, attitudes didn't change. It's good versus evil, us versus them. Miranda finds humans friendly. That some of them can turn in a heartbeat and become murderous psychopaths is something she doesn't quite grasp. It's as though they can't make up their minds whether they're doves or scorpions.

Miranda holds out her wrist as she passes through the gate and into the shuttle. It's a routine biomarker check, conducted to keep an accurate count on passengers and their whereabouts more so than for security.

As the hub at the heart of *The George Washington* isn't in motion, she pulls herself through, gliding into the shuttlecraft and looking for her seat. Someone's already strapped in on the aisle so she scoots her feet over their head, saying, "Excuse me," floats across them and pushes herself down into her seat. She secures a four-point harness and tightens it, pulling her body against the seat cushions. The guy next to her is wearing headphones and screen glasses. He must be watching a film. He probably didn't even hear her apologize for drifting over him. He seemed to notice her presence, though, as he ducked his head.

Miranda doesn't care for small talk so it doesn't bother her that he's zoned out. She looks out the window. The brilliant whites and blues reflecting off the planet light up her face. Even though most of her view is obscured by the docking mechanism, she can't imagine anything more beautiful anywhere in the entire universe.

Once everyone is seated, a steward asks for their attention and runs through the safety procedures. He taps the guy next to Miranda, signaling that he should remove his video glasses. The man obliges but with a hint of bitterness, muttering under his breath.

"Welcome on board Continental flight 176 to Honolulu. Although this is a short-duration drop, I ask for your full attention during our safety demonstration."

The guy next to her rolls his eyes. He's heard this a million times before.

"In the event of a cabin breach, a full-face mask will deploy from the seat back in front of you. It is important you fit your mask before helping others."

The guy watching along with her mutters, "*Bullshit*."

If the steward hears him, he doesn't respond. From the way he avoids eye contact with the passenger beside her, Miranda's pretty sure he heard him grumble.

"Once placed over your head, the seal will tighten around your jaw, reaching around to the back of your skull. Oxygen will begin to flow immediately. In a low-pressure environment, you'll notice your hands, fingers and feet begin to swell. Don't be alarmed. They'll return to normal once we reach the lower atmosphere.

"If the cabin does depressurize, you may experience bloating and/or vomiting due to the sudden change. If this occurs, do not remove your mask. Page a steward and they will assist you. Above all, do not panic.

"If there is a breach, you will be issued with anti-embolism tablets on reaching the nearest astroport so there is no cause for alarm."

The man beside her leans over toward her and speaks softly. He seems to sense this is her first time in a drop capsule. He says, "It's garbage. It's all for show. If there's a hull breach, we're dead within seconds. Ain't no way those masks will stay on anywhere above about fifty thousand meters. It's the pressure differential. They'll blow right off."

"Oh," she says.

"They tell us what we want to hear," he says, talking over the top

304

of the steward. He's not the only one talking. No one's paying the steward much attention. Miranda is fascinated by the way everyone ignores the steward. The steward, though, is undeterred. He points to the various exits and talks about how to don a lifejacket in the event of an off-target water landing. It's all so... *human*. But the humans aren't interested. What are they interested in? What would they think if they knew they were sitting next to an intelligent extraterrestrial and she was keenly interested in how they react to the mundane?

For Miranda, there's a bitter irony in being raised as a human only to learn she's an alien. What *is* alien within her? Which thoughts and attitudes are learned human responses and which are innately Krell? Does it matter? Does rational thought transcend the vessel that carries it? From what she's learned, humans are as paranoid about sentient killer robots as they are about acid-for-blood xenomorphs. The idea that logic is a universal trait seems lost on them. For all their arguments about civilization and reason, it's humans that are emotional—not aliens. And they're defensive. They value their irrational origins. They don't want to be robbed of something that has only ever burdened them. Oh, love and compassion are noble. But those emotions are also logical. They make sense. Anger, jealousy, suspicion, spite, resentment, blind loyalty, being temperamental—what is to be admired among these traits? Would humanity be better if it was a little less human?

Miranda misses the undocking process. It's only when the reaction control on the forward bulkhead fires, releasing a burst of cold gas into the vacuum that she realizes she's on her way to Earth. The white vapor dissipates beyond her window. She can feel the descent vehicle turning. She looks up and watches as *The George Washington* comes into view. It's strange, but the further they move away from the interstellar craft, the better the view of the vessel. Perhaps that's what humanity needs—some distance to help put things in perspective.

Night falls in orbit, coming every forty-five minutes. There's a storm brewing somewhere far below the shuttle. Dark clouds obscure the planet. Lightning crackles. A tempest unfolds below them, unleashing its fury on the land. For Miranda, the sight is mesmerizing.

Slowly, a sense of weight presses on her body. It's an illusion. She's decelerating and her body is resisting change, creating the impression that she's sinking back into her chair. When she boarded the drop ship and took her seat, she assumed she was facing forward in the direction of travel, but she's not. She's facing backward. It's a little disconcerting, but she understands it's intentional.

Flickers of light whip past her window, coming from behind her and racing off into the darkness. It takes Miranda a moment to realize this is the ablative shield on the drop shuttle wearing away as they plunge into the atmosphere.

The cabin shakes. Miranda grips the armrests on either side of her seat. The gees build. This is more than one gee. G—G—Got to be two. M—May—Maybe three. Her head, neck, and shoulders along with her back are thrown into the cushions built into her seat. Blood pools in her legs and lower back. She feels dizzy. She recalls the preflight instructions and clenches her calves and thighs to keep blood circulating to her head. Just how human is she? Her physiology is modeled after the professor's daughter, but she's not a clone. As best she understands it, she's a chimera. She's been infused with elements of the Krell.

Within seconds, the view out of the window is consumed by fire. Hundreds of glowing embers whip past, lighting up the darkness. An orange glow warms her face. Flames lick at the window, but Miranda isn't scared. She's thrilled. The rattling and shaking within the cabin don't bother her. When the turbulence finally fades, the sky is no longer black. Miranda can't quite describe it, but it's a dark grey fading to Prussian blue. Over the course of a minute, the darkness of space is replaced with the most gorgeous, iridescent blue she's ever seen. And it's everywhere! Regardless of which way she looks, a warm blue canopy surrounds her. To Miranda, it's as though the fireflies of Altair IV encompass the entire sky! The skies of Earth glow like a sapphire under a bright light. Miranda's seen images and videos of Earth before. She knew to expect a blue sky, but the view before her is overwhelming.

"It's so beautiful," she mutters. It never occurred to Miranda that the pale blue dot she saw from space would appear blue from within. For all her life, she's only ever seen stars in the sky. Their absence is both unnerving and exciting. Earth is vibrant. If she didn't know better, she'd swear the sky was alive.

Over the speaker, a voice says, "Drogue chute away."

Through the handles in her seat, she can feel the thick rubber ropes unraveling as the stabilizing chute deploys. She pushes her cheek against the glass, wanting to catch a glimpse of the drogue, but she can't see it. Roughly thirty seconds later, the voice says, "And the vehicle is stable. Brace yourself. Deploying the main chute."

Again, there's a shimmer through the frame of the spacecraft. Miranda feels herself being thrown back into her seat as a set of thick ropes unravel at an astonishing rate. Out her window, she can see the canopy of at least one of the main chutes. It forms the most perfect circle she's ever seen. Dozens of thick lines lead up to the parachute. It twists slightly. To her surprise, the orange material continues to slowly unfurl, reaching ever wider. Miranda catches sight of another canopy bumping into the one directly above her as the spacecraft slows.

"And we have the successful deployment of all eight chutes," the voice says.

The screen on the seatback in front of her provides a view below the spacecraft. O'ahu is visible thousands of meters beneath them. Lush green mountains dominate the interior of the island. Pearl Harbor is visible as a deep water inlet. Honolulu curls along the southern coast.

"We are on target and on time," the pilot says over the speakers. "We'll splash down within half a kilometer of the homing beacon in Māmala Bay, just south of Pearl Harbor. Our recovery ship is standing by to transfer you to Honolulu for customs processing. Your baggage will be available from carousel number eight roughly twenty minutes after you disembark. On behalf of all the crew, it's been our pleasure serving you on this orbital return flight. We hope you will fly Continental again in the future. If we can be of any further assistance to you with onward flights or cruise connections, please let us know."

The island grows ever larger. Buildings appear as oblong blocks scattered across the land. In close to the shore, the waters are a soft, radiant blue unlike anything Miranda ever thought possible. How can one planet contain so much beauty? Miranda doesn't understand humanity. Earth is stunning. New Haven doesn't compare. Why do humans go looking elsewhere for everything they have at home? Can they not see the miracle that surrounds them in this dark cosmic ocean?

Numbers appear on the screen on the back of the seat in front of her. In unison with the figures flashing before her, people throughout the cabin count down their approach to the blue waters off Hawaii. Miranda joins in. Like everyone else, she finds herself wrapped up in the excitement of the moment.

"Five. Four. Three. Two. One. Splashdown!"

Hawaii

The descent vehicle plunges into the ocean. Miranda wasn't expecting it to knock the breath out of her lungs, but she doesn't care. Water races outward from beneath the craft. Waves crash around her. The ocean washes over her window. The spacecraft rocks and the passengers around her cheer.

"Welcome to Earth," the captain says over the speaker. "At this time, I ask you to remain seated as we secure the craft and the support vessel draws alongside. From here, we'll be raised onto the deck of the *Intrepid*. Once we're secure in the maintenance cradle, the ground crew will roll the stairs in place and you can disembark. Please don't move around the cabin until the stairs are set on the deck. Thank you for your cooperation—and thank you for flying with Continental."

Miranda releases her seatbelt. She's not supposed to. The captain was quite clear on that but everyone else does so she joins them. She turns around and kneels on her seat, staring out the window and watching as water laps at the hull of the drop vessel. A small inflatable boat races around the craft. Its outboard engine kicks up white foam, leaving a trail on the surface of the ocean. Cables are attached to anchor points on their spacecraft. From where she is, Miranda can't see the *Intrepid*, but she watches as the cables go taut and the spacecraft is lifted from the water. Workers in hardhats guide the crane as it centers the vessel over a black metal cradle on the broad deck of the *Intrepid*. A set of stairs are rolled out and fixed in place on the deck.

The hatch opens.

Sunlight spills in.

Miranda's heart races.

Her eyes are focused on the open hatch. She's fascinated by the world that lies beyond it. The first thing she notices is the smell of salt in the air, then the heat and humidity, and lastly the sound of birds squawking as they circle the capsule. Passengers shuffle through the hatch. Crew members smile warmly as people depart, saying, "Mind your head. Watch your step."

Miranda peers down the line, desperate to see more of this exotic planet. When she reaches the hatch, she's surprised by how small it is. In orbit, it was easy enough to float through. On Earth, she has to step over the rim, taking care not to bump into the sides. The taller men have to duck to avoid hitting their heads.

Gravity is strong. Standing at the top of the stairs outside the capsule, Miranda takes a firm hold on the railing. She lowers herself from one step to another, taking them one at a time. Most of the passengers walk down them quickly, but she's not confident with the pull of the planet dragging her down.

"First time, huh?" a friendly worker says from the bottom of the stairs. "No rush."

The warmth of the sun is something she didn't expect. She looks up. She's been told not to look at the local star but she can't help herself. She has to see the source of this magnificent, radiant heat. The sun feels luxurious on her cheeks.

"Oh, I could get used to this," she says, thinking back to the abject darkness and bitter cold on Altair IV.

The boat sways slightly with the ocean swell. It motors toward land. Mountains rise from the interior of O'ahu, but they're not as intimidating or austere as those on her frozen moon. If anything, the jungle lining their slopes looks inviting. The island screams of life.

The boat pulls up to a pier within Pearl Harbor. The passengers disembark over a gangway plank and form three lines, waiting to clear customs. When Miranda's turn comes up, she walks forward toward a grumpy man in a black uniform replete with brass buttons, a brass shield, a name tag and a US flag proudly displayed on his shoulder. The computer sensor has already identified her and brought up her information for him to consider as he talks with her.

"What is your final destination?"

"I'm going to America," Miranda replies with a pleasant smile.

"Ma'am," the officer says, raising his voice and bellowing at her. "You are *now* in the United States of America! Having arrived from New Haven, I need to know your intended final destination here on Earth? How long do you intend on staying in the US and where is your final port of call?"

"Port? Ofcall?" she says, unsure what he means and running the last two words together.

"Ma'am. Do you have the right of residency on Earth? What country did you or your family come from?"

"I—um."

"You need to be aware you are in a legally-binding interview with a sworn US immigration officer. Your answers, or any lack thereof, may result in refusal of entry and may constitute grounds for your deportation."

Miranda understands the words he's using but the force behind them is foreign to her. He senses that, adding, "You may not be able to enter the US."

She turns and looks back at the dock, wondering where she could go. The aquamarine blue of the sea beckons. She's curious about these *customs*. Is she going to be rejected from the land and somehow have to navigate the sea? How deep is the water? How far is it to the nearest country? Will they give her a boat? She doesn't remember seeing any other islands as they descended, but she wasn't looking for them.

The officer taps at a keyboard and waves over a supervisor. She comes over and stands behind him as he points at the screen, saying, "She's one of the survivors from the *Sycorax*."

The woman is curious. She looks kind. She asks, "How old were

311

you when you boarded the *Sycorax*?"

Given Miranda boarded it in orbit around Altair IV and not when it departed Earth, she isn't sure how to answer that question. Clearly, they're trying to figure out the sequence of events surrounding the voyage of a spacecraft she knows little about.

The woman talks to the officer, saying, "She couldn't have been more than three or four years old."

The officer says, "I didn't think they allowed children to undergo interstellar hibernation."

"They shouldn't have," the woman says, pointing at another position on the screen. "Records from that time are sketchy. Look. It says her parents died on the *Sycorax* and she was issued with a new ID in New Haven."

"Nothing terrestrial," the agent says. "We've got no bona fides to work with."

The woman is decisive. She seems to sense the anxiety Miranda feels and genuinely wants to find a solution.

"The *Sycorax* was registered and flown out of New York. In the absence of any other identifiers, that gives her the right to claim American heritage."

"But she's got no known family members, no US address," the officer says.

"Does she have the means to support herself?" the woman asks.

"Money," Miranda says, realizing what they're talking about. "A medium for the exchange of goods and services in one's favor."

"I know what it is," the woman says, looking down at her from the raised platform.

Miranda is still coming to terms with her ability to manipulate matter as Ariel once did, but she's learned the subtleties of electrical impressions. Humanity's over-reliance on record-keeping is built on the assumption of trust and accuracy. Computers might have fancy interfaces, colors, images and sounds, but these are all abstracts of simple values of zero or one stored on a magnetic medium and processed through silicon logic gates. Manipulating them is child's play for her.

While she was onboard *The George Washington*, Miranda enjoyed teasing the neural networks and quantum processors that ran the ship. Although they routed information in a blinding flash, she was able to understand the patterns and languages they spoke. If anything, she found them easier to understand than English as the syntax was more precise and the rules were simpler. She quickly realized trust was the most important aspect of information storage and processing. Computers had to agree on things like a bank balance. A number alone wasn't enough. There had to be a comprehensive transaction history supporting the number. Numbers couldn't just randomly appear in a register, they had to have the backing of other numbers in an unbroken chain.

Miranda blinks. In that fraction of a second, her mind entwines itself with the computer system in front of her. She traces the local network, connects to the broader entwined internet and traces a path to dozens of financial institutions including banks, stock brokers and investment houses.

Miranda senses the ebb and flow of hundreds of thousands of transactions occurring every second. She spots a pattern in the chaos and noise. She trades on the rise and fall of prices using nothing but fake credit. At this point, any forensic investigation would uncover the fraudulent basis of her trades, but, once made, the trades themselves are genuine—they exploit the patterns she sees to gain an advantage that's measured in monetary increase.

"Have you checked my account?" she asks the customs agent.

Within seconds, Miranda's already exploited the market to earn over a million dollars and backtracked to hide her initial electronic trail. She launders her earnings, shifting them through investment houses.

"I have," the agent says. "There's nothing tied to your persona."

By now, Miranda's closing on fifteen million dollars in earnings. This really isn't hard.

"Are you sure?" she asks as her net worth swells to over a

hundred million dollars. "There's money there. I think it's a lot."

The woman peers over the officer's shoulder. She taps at something on the screen, refreshing the values displayed there.

"Oh. It's a lot," the woman says, raising an eyebrow. "It seems you're more than capable of looking after yourself financially."

Miranda is unsure what figure the woman saw, but she's up around a hundred billion dollars now and backing her trading routine out of the financial system. Somewhere in New York, several investment firms are going into meltdown at the failure of their automated algorithms to detect microtransactions swinging so heavily against them in such a short period of time without being the result of a run on any one particular stock. Miranda shaved tiny amounts off untold millions of transactions. She scrubs her electronic presence, clears their pathetically naive security logs, and then smiles at the customs agents.

"Enjoy your time in the US," the woman says.

The male officer waves her through, directing his ire at the person behind her in the line with an obnoxious, "Next!"

Miranda doesn't have any suitcases. She's got a single duffel bag slung over her shoulder. Two changes of clothes and a handful of items are all she needs.

She walks out into the hot, humid air. She spent almost an hour in the customs hall. With the sun high overhead, Honolulu is sweltering under a heatwave. Miranda doesn't mind. She stops walking and rests her hand on one of the dozens of tall palm trees surrounding the circular drive outside the spaceport. The trunk is rough to touch. The roots wind in and out of the sandy dirt. High above her, vast fronds wave in the breeze. A dense forest dominates the nearby hillside. Mountains rise in the interior of Oahu. They're covered by a thick, dark green jungle canopy. For Miranda, it's magical. She's giddy with the implications. She knows she's only seeing a fraction of the biodiversity on Earth and yet the ecological niches around her are teeming with life. Her mind runs, thinking about all that lies before her. Ariel might have thought she was pretty damn cool reproducing food items, clothing and

314

trinkets on Altair IV, but Earth has its own magic. It's taken 3.8 billion years, but the sheer variety of organisms that have come from a bunch of common, lifeless atoms is quite astonishing to her. It's every bit as fascinating as Krell science—and fantastically more diverse than the organisms that scratched out their existence on Altair IV!

Ants walk in single file across the brickwork, winding their way toward a scrap of food dropped in the dirt. A butterfly flutters past. A bird lands nearby, watching it, hunting it, waiting for it to depart from the bushes. The passengers coming and going to the spaceport ignore this marvel unfolding before them. Miranda is amazed that humans take life for granted. To her, Earth is better than anything that could be accomplished with Krell science. Sure, conjuring things up is pretty cool, but what to conjure? Earth has accomplished this stunning variety of life without any input other than natural selection. Asteroids and continental plates have had their role to play, but for the most part, species have diverged and evolved to exploit opportunities. What started out as a single cell in some primordial ocean billions of years ago has become an astonishing array of variety.

A cop walks past with a sniffer dog. Miranda has seen videos of dogs, but this is the first one she's seen in person. It moves with a fluid gait. She's tempted to ask the police officer about it but he looks far too serious. Even the dog is focused, lowering its head and sniffing for scents. Why build a highly sensitive drug detection device when you can raise one as a puppy?

Electric vehicles whiz by in utter silence. People chat. Families reunite with hugs and kisses. Miranda walks alone toward a public travelator.

Downtown Honolulu
Waikiki with connection to Diamond Head

Miranda has no idea where she's going. She never really believed she'd get this far. Everything's new and exciting. Ahead, a moving sidewalk accelerates people along toward the distant buildings towering over the city. Miranda watches as the person in front of her steps onto the fine grating. They time their approach, touching down with their right foot at the same time as they grip the rubber handrail. With that, they zip off ahead of her. It seems simple enough.

Miranda has misplaced confidence. She knows that, but she's determined to be an Earthling. She steps forward, grabbing the handrail. It takes all her might to hold on and not fall backward on her ass. She keeps her balance and, within a few seconds, she's enjoying the ride.

The moving sidewalk and handrail is formed from horizontal stripes like metal grating beneath her feet and fingers. At first, she doesn't understand why. Her guess is that it allows rain to drain away, but it's more complex than that. She expected the moving sidewalk to be solid. It's then she sees the woman in front of her accelerate yet again. Without stepping forward, the woman has gone from one moving walkway to another. As the first walkway ends, it disappears into the ground, curling into the pavement. Another faster walkway takes over, coming up from beneath through the fine gaps and accelerating passengers even faster again. The handrails and walkways are entwined so one merges seamlessly with the other. As one falls away, the other takes over. After five seamless interchanges, Miranda's whipping along at a breakneck speed. There are multiple walkways meshed and sync'd together like this. By the time she's at full speed, her hair is flicking behind her like a set of streamers. The wind feels refreshing. As she approaches the hotels set along the beach, the process reverses, with one walkway blending into another, slowing her back to a walking pace. Within five minutes, she's stepping off in Waikiki. A robotic assistant ensures each person clears the end of the moving walkway. It wouldn't do to have a pile-up at the end.

By the time she reaches the end of the line, she's been slowed to a leisurely walking pace. Miranda steps off onto the concrete and walks away, marveling at the tiki huts dotted along the foreshore. Women walk past in bikinis carrying surfboards. Men play volleyball on the sand. They're shirtless and sweaty, but they're having fun, jostling and yelling at each other. Kids sit in the shallows, splashing in the water.

Miranda is speechless. There's a line for something called *slushies*. She joins the line for no other reason than it's popular and she wants to experience human life. When she gets to the front, the guy at the counter is abrupt.

"*Whaddayawant?*"

"Sorry?" she says.

He points at the flavors behind him. "Pick one."

Miranda is confused. She asks, "Ah, why would anyone want to eat a berry made from straw?"

"Strawberry," he says, turning away from her and pouring a drink of crushed red ice into a conical cup. "Twenty bucks."

The man hands her the drink and then holds out his wrist with a clenched fist. As he's raised up on a platform behind the counter, his hand is near her head. He's not trying to hit her, but she has no idea what this gesture means.

"Twenty bucks," he says, repeating himself and shaking his fist slightly. "You wanna see the till?"

Miranda still has no idea what he's doing, but she copies his gesture, reaching across her body and touching her wrist to his. A nearby register beeps, confirming the transaction. Just to be sure, she probes the electronic device with her mind and confirms the balance on her account has decreased by twenty dollars. She's delighted to see she can afford an almost endless supply of slushies.

"Okay, that's interesting," she says, stepping to one side and letting the next person in line order their drink.

Miranda takes a bite out of the crushed ice. Oh, it's cold—damn cold. And sweet. There's some other flavor there but the sugar hit drowns it out. She's not sure whether she likes these berry straws. It's okay but the sugar needs to be dialed way back. She looks at the deep red ice drink wondering how they manage to get so much sugar in there. The one question that dominates her mind is *why?* The berry flavor seems nice. If only she could taste it on its own. She might be able to afford hundreds of millions of slushies but she doesn't even want this one.

She drops the rest of the drink in a nearby bin and walks down onto the sand. As most of the people on the beach are barefoot, she removes her shoes. The sand is warm and soft. It shifts with each step, squishing between her toes. It's surprisingly pleasant to walk upon.

Miranda stands there for a moment in awe of how quickly her life has been transformed. After decades in space and even the last few days in orbit, within a matter of an hour or so she's gone from a dark, cold, hard vacuum dotted with stars to having warm sand beneath the soles of her feet. Miranda likes Earth—a lot!

She avoids the volleyball game and makes her way down to the shore. The sand there is firmer. Waves lap around her ankles. The water feels refreshing. Miranda decides she likes Hawaii. No, she *loves* Hawaii. Marc must have enjoyed growing up here and she wonders why he ever left.

Out in the bay, she watches as surfers ride waves in toward the shore. They paddle along and then somehow keep their balance as they rise on their narrow boards. They stand there as the wave carries them on. Roughly thirty seconds later, they drop into the ocean, or they fall off their boards. It doesn't seem to bother them, though, as no sooner have they surfaced than they turn their boards around and paddle back out to sea again. Miranda is going to have to give that a go. If it's half as much fun as it looks, it'll be a blast.

As she walks along, she spots a bar set just off the beach. She's hungry. She walks up and a waiter greets her, offering her a table in the shade overlooking the beach. Palm trees sway in the breeze. Waves roll over the sand. Kids splash in the water. Someone sails past a couple of hundred meters offshore in a small catamaran. Now that is something else she definitely has to try. It looks like a lot of fun.

Miranda sits down in the shade of a large, colorful umbrella. She rests her duffel bag next to the table.

A waiter asks, "What can I get you to drink?"

"Anything that's not sweet," she replies. "Oh, and nothing with a strawed berry."

"One sparkling water coming up."

He walks off leaving Miranda wondering how water can sparkle. This should be interesting.

Her table has an interactive screen. She taps the news, wondering what's happening on Earth. It strikes her that the term *news* is misleading. It's impossible to capture every notable event on a planet with billions of people. That leaves her curious as to how the news is curated.

"Incursions by the Volgo Republic into the Siberian Territories have been condemned by the United Nations."

The screen uses a primitive form of a hologram set below the glass. For her, it's almost comical to see the way three different projection points within the table combine with the glass to form a holographic image. Instead of floating above the table, though, it's set beneath the glass. It looks as though she could reach through and touch the artillery firing from within a snow-laden forest. The guns look like toy models.

She flicks the image away, looking at other channels.

The waiter returns with her drink, asking, "Are you ready to order some food?"

"Ah, I'm new to Earth," she says. "What would you recommend?"

"Oh, first-timer, huh?" he says, smiling. "How about a seafood platter? That way you get to sample some variety. It's all fresh. Most of it was caught in local waters."

"The seafood platter it is," she replies, smiling warmly.

He excuses himself. Bubbles rise in her drink. She raises her drink, examining the way the tiny bubbles form on the inside of the curved glass before rising to the surface.

"Oh," she says with childlike wonder. She's seen this before back on Altair IV, but it's only now she understands what's happening within the glass. Her father loved *bubbly*, as he called it. For her, it was a novelty. Now that her Krell brain has awakened, it's a scientific curiosity. She talks herself through what she's seeing. "It's a phase change. How quaint! Carbon dioxide is nucleating as it comes out of solution, forming these tiny gas pockets. This must have been stored under pressure and now that it's released it's effervescing."

She takes a sip. "And it dances on the tongue. It's delightful."

Miranda is genuinely impressed by what's a simple tweak to what would otherwise be water. It's far superior to the slushy. She takes another sip and returns to the interactive table.

After flicking through several menus, Miranda looks at local events and finds a symposium being conducted in Honolulu on SETI. Although she doesn't know what the acronym means, the tagline, *"Are we alone in the universe?"* gets her attention. While opening the live stream, she probes the meaning of SETI and is impressed to see humanity has been searching for intelligent extraterrestrial life for well over three centuries. She finds the history of SETI fascinating. That scientists haven't found any intelligent life is a point of contention with the public, which is something she finds strange. In science, null results are as important as positives as they steer further studies. And finding nothing doesn't mean there is nothing out there—as she well knows. It hints more at the limits of the search than anything else.

"...unresolved signals from the galactic core are not alien in origin," a woman says on the screen within the table.

"Ohhh," Miranda says, interested in the panel discussion.

It took Miranda some time to come to grips with how her *Homo sapien*/Krell mind works. On one level, she can probe the depths of a computer system or analyze a scenario in astonishing detail in nanoseconds, but it's instinctive rather than conscious.

For Miranda, deep thoughts are like an NFL quarterback in the Superbowl throwing a sixty-yard pass while on the run from a linebacker, and still being able to hit a moving target downfield, striking to within an inch of their aim. Ask the quarterback what went through their mind and they can't explain it. Years of practice combined with natural ability allowed them to act unthinkingly to accomplish something astonishing. They just *know* the throw is good. They *feel* the texture of the ball, its weight, the rush of the wind, the pace of the incoming linebacker, the speed of the running back—and from that they can calculate the exact instant at which the ball must be released and with how much power and in what direction. None of this makes any sense in an analytical manner. No quarterback can define all those quantities using measurements and yet they can fire off the pass. In the same way, Miranda operates on two levels. Her Krell brain can fire off requests and take actions she's barely aware of but instinctively wants. Her human brain sits above that, pondering the results.

The tiny woman on Miranda's screen is talking about false positives when it comes to the search for intelligent extraterrestrial life. She says, *"We humans are good at jumping to conclusions. If there's a bump in the night, it's either a ghost or someone breaking into the house—only it isn't. The chances are the house is creaking with the wind or a branch fell on the roof or your teen is sneaking in after a late-night party. The mundane is always far more likely, but our minds are primed for the sensational.*

"We interpret events through a filter of expectation. If there are strange lights in the night sky, people jump to the conclusion—that's a UFO! And on one level, they're correct. It is unidentified. But that doesn't make it alien, just unexplained. So what is the explanation for this particular sighting of a UAV or UFO or whatever you want to call it? I don't know, but guessing won't help. Could it be intelligent extraterrestrials? Maybe, but we need hard evidence, not speculation. To use an example from biology, we can't be so obsessed looking for Big Foot that we fail to recognize the hundreds of new species we walk past in the forest.

"The point isn't to doubt what others see. It's to be honest about the need to corroborate what they've seen. We need to investigate these things and not rush to the conclusion we want.

"All too often we ignore conclusions we don't like. We can't do that. This isn't about your likes or mine, it's about arriving at the truth and understanding the reality of the universe that surrounds us.

"And we have a poor track record in this regard. We love guessing. We love letting our minds run to flamboyant explanations.

We always have. Lightning wasn't sent by an angry Zeus. Prometheus didn't steal fire from the gods. There may well have been a flood in the Middle East, but that doesn't mean Noah gathered animals from all corners of the Earth. No koalas made it onto the ark. They couldn't have survived a journey of thousands of miles or an ocean crossing. Even in modern times, superstitions prevail. In spite of what they may think, no athlete has lucky socks or lucky underwear.

"We want simple answers. Our minds gravitate to simple explanations for the complex chaos of reality. In science, there are often elegant answers, but they're rarely simple—and we need to accept that. Life isn't a game of Jeopardy where there are single answers to complex questions.

"We have to be cautious when it comes to SETI. We think there's intelligent life out there so we're looking for confirmation of that—and that leaves us susceptible to the confirmation bias. If we spot something that looks alien—IT'S ALIEN! It must be! We so desperately want to find alien life, we do! We see aliens everywhere—only we don't. Science comes along and says, well, that's an interstellar asteroid or that's a short-duration pulse from a magnetar."

The moderator asks, "So you don't think there's intelligent life out there?"

"What I think is irrelevant," the woman says. "What I want is irrelevant. We need to hold onto the evidence. And the evidence has to be overwhelming and unambiguous."

"I like this lady," Miranda says.

The waiter walks over with a bottle of champagne on ice and a couple of glasses.

"Congratulations, Ms. Spiro," the waiter says and it takes Miranda a moment to realize she now owns this hotel, including the restaurant and bar. Her purchase went through quicker than she expected. Subconsciously, Miranda set off the process on a whim as she sat down. She likes the bar and it's backed by a hotel. It's got a great outlook across the bay. She has to live somewhere so why not here?

At the moment, it's a provisional sale as property purchases need cooling-off periods and the exchange of legal documents, but she offered almost twice the asking price along with a non-refundable deposit of 30% on the provision she could exercise ownership immediately. After her first day on Earth she's learned one important lesson: *money doesn't talk, it screams.* She selected her lawyer based solely on their outlandish hourly rate and paid a five-year retainer up front on the proviso her affairs were given priority. To her, it was worth it. Someone at the head office in downtown Honolulu got a message from her lawyer that she was sitting on the beachfront and relayed it to the staff.

The waiter pops the cork and pours a glass of champagne. Miranda watches with fascination as bubbles appear against the inside of the glass. It seems champagne is like sparkling water, but it's slightly different. She can already tell the chemical composition is more complex. Miranda loves watching carbon dioxide come out of suspension. It's a simple pleasure, but it is a pleasure nonetheless. The glass flute is tall, maximizing the opportunity for nucleation. She picks the glass up, sniffs its fruity flavors and takes a sip. Champagne tastes delightful.

"Is there anything else?"

"No, thank you."

The waiter puts the champagne back in the ice bucket and excuses himself. An elderly woman walks over.

"Miranda?" the woman asks. "Miranda Spiro?"

"Yes," Miranda says, getting to her feet. Her mind is flooded with a deluge of thoughts. Everything that seemed so casual and coincidental has been deliberate. Her choice to alight in Hawaii, her selection of this hotel bar, and even the interview she watched while sipping her sparkling water. In the depths of her mind, it was coordinated. Planned would be the wrong term as she wasn't conscious of these decisions, but her Krell instincts have been working in harmony with her human desires so that nothing is haphazard.

She offers the woman her hand in friendship, saying, "You must be Dr. Ka'uhane-Brown."

"Susan," the woman replies, accepting and shaking her hand.

"Please, have a seat."

Miranda sits back down. Susan remains standing.

Gene editing has extended the average lifespan of humans by slowing down their aging process. By the time someone reaches a hundred, they look like someone in their fifties during the pre-gene therapy era. Miranda doesn't have to guess Susan's age as she has access to online birth certificates, but at a hundred and thirty-two, Susan looks as though she's yet to complete her first century. Her hair is auburn and well-kept. The skin on her cheeks is tight, lacking both age spots and wrinkles. She has kind but determined eyes. Physically, she's petite with toned arms. Her sleeveless blue dress is plain but suits her demeanor.

Susan notices the hologram paused beneath the glass in the sunken screen. The ice bucket with the champagne is sitting on the glass, obscuring the view, but she recognizes the scene anyway.

"You're watching my interview from earlier this week."

"I found it fascinating," Miranda says, picking up the bottle and offering her a glass. "Champagne?"

"No," Susan replies, fidgeting as she stands before Miranda's table.

Miranda's disappointed. She is impressed by champagne.

"I'm confused," Susan says. "What is this about? What is so important that my director rescheduled my deep space telescope data submission and sent me here, looking for you? In a beach-side bar of all places?"

"Have a seat and I'll explain everything," Miranda says, placing the champagne on the table between them instead of returning it to the ice bucket. Water vapor in the air condenses on the cool glass. Miranda's tempted to point that out to Susan as it's pretty cool to observe, but she gets the impression Susan's impatient.

"Look," Susan says, still standing by the table and refusing to sit down. "I don't know who you think you are, but I'm not a show pony.

324

Director Mahon might jump because you throw a billion bucks at his foundation, but I don't care for benefactors. I'm doing serious research."

"And what is your research area?" Miranda asks, already knowing the answer.

"I'm part of SETI—the Search for Extra-Terrestrial Intelligence."

Miranda smiles. "And I guess you're not expecting to find an intelligent extra-terrestrial in a bar."

"I don't expect to find *any* intelligence in a bar," Susan replies. "Let alone extra-terrestrial. Now, if you'll excuse me. I have real work to do. Please tell Mahon I came and jumped through your fiery hoops or whatever."

Susan starts to walk away.

"I knew your brother," Miranda says.

She stops and turns. "Not possible. He died over sixty years ago."

"Please," Miranda says, gesturing to the seat.

Cautiously, Susan sits down. "What do you know about my brother?"

"I know how he died."

Susan's lips tighten.

Miranda adds, "And it's nothing like the official story."

"Look at you," Susan says with undisguised disdain. "How old are you? Twenty-five? You weren't even born when my brother died. Hell, your parents probably weren't even born then."

"Indulge me for a moment," Miranda says, getting to her feet.

Susan shakes her head, repeating her earlier question, asking, "What the hell am I doing here?" Her hands grip the armrest as she takes her weight, getting ready to stand.

Miranda holds up a single finger, saying, "Sixty seconds. Give me sixty seconds and if I haven't convinced you—go! Your boss can keep the money."

Susan leans back in her seat. Miranda scoots down the concrete stairs to the beach with the bucket of ice in her hand. She crouches, dumps several handfuls of sand in the silver pail and returns to the table.

"Now, I have one question for you. Just one. If you answer my question, you can go. Agreed?"

"Okay," a curious-looking Susan says with a furrowed brow, looking at the sand soaking in the ice bucket.

"Champagne or sparkling water?" Miranda asks. She sits down, pointing at the two drinks in front of her. She places the shiny bucket in between the glasses.

Miranda can see the machinations of Susan's mind. It's the way her head turns slightly as her lips narrow. Susan reminds Miranda of Marc in so many ways, but especially the quizzical look on her face. She says, "Sparkling water."

"Too easy," Miranda replies. She reaches into the bucket and pulls out a handful of wet sand and ice cubes. Water drips from her fingers. She leans over in front of Susan and squeezes her hands together, allowing the sand to drop from between her fingers. Globs of sand fall but they never strike the table. Instead, a glass identical to hers forms over a few seconds. Miranda doesn't have enough material so she switches hands with another handful of wet sand. Beneath her fingers, a clear glass appears with sparkling water sloshing around even though the glass is stationary.

Susan pushes her chair back from the table. The legs scrape on the tiles.

"What is this? Magic?"

"Science," Miranda says, turning to one side and rubbing her fingers together to get the last remnants of sand off them. She shakes her hands. Fine grains stick between her fingers so she rubs them on her trousers.

Susan shakes her head in disbelief.

"What kind of science?" she asks, bending down so she's level with the table and can examine the glass without touching it.

"It's okay," Miranda says. "You can drink it. It's quite safe."

Susan reaches out and picks up the glass.

"It's warm."

She holds it up to the light and swirls it around. A few loose grains of sand are visible at the bottom of the glass. They move in response to her motion. Susan sniffs the drink and sips the tiniest amount.

"How is this possible?" she asks, putting the glass down.

"Sparkling water is easy," Miranda says, shrugging. "I didn't need to do anything to the water other than carbonate it, which is simple enough given there's CO_2 in the air, while the silicates came from the sand. Now, if you'd said *champagne*, that would have been tough. Honestly, I would have cheated. I'd have made the glass but simply taken the champagne from the bottle without you noticing."

Susan laughs. Her face lights up. "You're. You're." Her shoulders rise as her laughter gets the better of her. "You're a—"

"An alien?"

"Yes," Susan says, shaking her head but unable to suppress her childlike grin.

"See. You should have spent more time looking at bars rather than stars."

Susan cocks her head sideways. She's smiling in admiration. "And you knew my brother?"

"He saved my life."

Susan leans forward with her elbows on her legs and her head in her hands. Miranda can see she's struggling with a whirlwind of emotions.

She says, "The official story was that his spacecraft—"

"The *Sycorax*."

"—struck an asteroid. They told us it was a carbonaceous chondrite cluster. They said it wasn't that big—only about the size of this table—but the radar failed."

"I lied," Miranda says.

"You?"

"By the time we limped into New Haven, I was the only one still alive that knew what had happened."

"And what did happen?" Susan asks.

"The *Sycorax* flew through the relativistic jet of a black hole."

"Wow," Susan says, pressing her fingers together as she focuses on Miranda's every word.

"Marc and Emma—"

"Emma Madi?" Susan asks, raising an eyebrow.

"Yes."

"He had a crush on her."

Miranda laughs. "I know. I remember."

"Sorry. Please, go on."

"My father and I—"

"Your *human* father?"

"Yes."

"So you're like some kind of hybrid."

"Yes," Miranda says.

"Well, that explains the lack of tentacles and antennae."

"Are you quite finished?" Miranda asks.

"And only two eyes."

Miranda looks at her with a deadpan expression on her face.

"And the lack of an exoskeleton. Okay. I'm just messing around."

Miranda smiles.

Susan says, "This is just—so incredible. I mean, I'm sitting here with an alien!"

"You're sitting here with a person," Miranda says. "Just one that originates from a different evolutionary pedigree on another planet."

"You're right," Susan says. "Please, continue."

Miranda explains what happened, telling her about the Krell and their machine and how her father thought he was controlling it when it was controlling him. The seafood platter arrives and they talk for hours, snacking on the food. The sun sets out over the ocean. A cool wind blows in from the sea, but it's refreshing.

"Where is everyone?" Susan asks, looking around at the empty tables both inside and outside the restaurant and bar.

"I closed the restaurant to the public."

"You can do that?"

"I own the place."

"You're an alien. And you own a restaurant on Waikiki beach?"

"Yep."

"Well," Susan says. "The Hollywood movie stereotypes are falling like dominos!"

Hard Contact

It's been almost an hour since the waiter cleared the plates. As neither woman is drinking that much of the champagne, the waiter brings over a bottle of sparkling water and a bowl of french fries. Without saying anything, he sets them down and hovers in the background near the bar.

Miranda calls out to him, saying, "Grab another glass and pull up a seat."

The waiter points at himself, raising his eyebrows in surprise. There's no one around but he still wants to be sure she's talking to him.

"Come on," Susan says, beckoning him over.

"But I should be..." he says, pointing over his shoulder.

"What?" Miranda asks. "Tending to an empty bar?"

One of the chefs sticks his head out through a service window in the kitchen. He bats his hand at the waiter, signaling for him to go. It's clear they've overheard snippets of the conversation and have been talking about the two of them.

"Have a seat, Alexander," Miranda says, reading his name tag.

"I—I didn't think—" he says, halting mid-sentence and looking at the lanyard around Susan's neck. There's a photo of her appearing considerably younger, a NASA logo and her formal title: *Dr. Susan Ka'uhane, Sentient Astrobiology.*

"You feel like you don't fit in, huh?" Susan says, seeing his interest in her ID.

"The glass," he says, pointing. "That wasn't magic, was it?"

"There's no magic," Miranda says, picking the glass up and handing it to him. "Only things we don't understand. And between us, there's science."

"And you're a..."

"Alive," Miranda says. "And so are you. We're just from different worlds."

Susan opens her hand toward him. Her gesture is friendly even if her words seem a little harsh. "And you invited him over because?"

"Because he's *everyman*. And we can't lose sight of that. First Contact is for everyone, not just scientists."

"I agree," Susan replies. "I just don't think anyone ever thought it would unfold in a beachside bar. There's supposed to be silver UFOs and lots of military helicopters or something."

"But this is perfect," Miranda says, gesturing to Waikiki. "I couldn't think of anywhere more beautiful."

The sun has set. The nature of the beach has changed. During the day, it was packed with people sunbathing or swimming. Teens threw frisbees and kicked balls. Children built sand castles. Parents sheltered beneath beach umbrellas, reading ebooks on tablets as they lounged on fold-out deck chairs. With the quiet of the night, the waves lap rather than crash on the shore. Several adjoining hotels have set up tables on the sand along with tiki torches lighting up the night. Live music drifts on the wind.

"First Contact is like a first date," Miranda says, gesturing to a couple walking along the beach hand in hand. "It's nice, but how much can you really learn about someone when you're both trying to be polite?"

Susan nods but doesn't say anything. Alexander is silent.

"First Contact is overrated. It's just the start. By definition, it's the first step. It's everything that happens *after* that which interests me."

332

"We can help with that," Susan says.

"Can you?" Miranda asks. "I'm not so sure. What's important is humanity—not humanity's whitewashed version of itself. It's the unguarded moments that are the most telling. It's what you're doing when you don't think anyone else is looking that reveals your true character. And for thousands of years, you thought no one was watching."

"Wait," Susan says, shifting in her chair. She points at the tiles on the ground. "They're here? They're already here? Why haven't they said anything?"

Miranda smiles. "You watch birds from a hide, observing how they feed and how they rear their young. You take photos, examine their nests, fetch dung samples, and observe habits. Why?"

"To better understand nature."

Miranda nods. "But why do you take that approach?"

Susan mumbles, "Ah, we don't want to disrupt their lives."

"Knowledge changes everything," Miranda says. "If those birds know you're there, they'll change their habits and you'll miss the opportunity to learn about them."

"But this is First Contact. There's so much we could learn from you."

"Is there?" Miranda asks, injecting doubt. She munches on a french fry, toying with Susan and watching Alexander's reaction. "You're looking for First Contact, but you haven't really thought about what it means. All your experience with First Contact here on Earth is one-sided in your favor."

"I don't understand," Susan says.

"Up until now, you've always been the dominant partner in First Contact. Europeans spoke of *The New World* as a grand adventure. It was exciting. It held an almost romantic allure for early settlers. The Native Americans, Incas and Aztecs would disagree with that sentiment."

"And you think that's what will happen to us?" Susan says.

"I think you're not prepared for what *could* happen. You see First Contact as either benign or spiraling into a world war. In reality, it could be as simple as being displaced."

"But they're already here? Your people? So this isn't First Contact at all."

"Not my people," Miranda says, never having thought about the Krell in that way before. She sees herself not as human or Krell or some kind of hybrid in between the two. Like every sentient being, regardless of species, even here on Earth, Miranda sees her as herself and nothing more. To her, she's normal. It's everyone else that's different.

"There are others?" Susan asks, picking up on the implications of Miranda's comment.

"I've detected at least two other species carefully hidden on your world."

"I don't get it. If there are other intelligent extraterrestrial species already here on Earth, why has no one reached out to us? We're right here. We're begging for Contact."

Alexander says, "A wildlife photographer doesn't owe a cheetah anything."

Miranda raises an eyebrow and looks at him with surprise. He gets it. In his defense, he adds, "I shoot landscapes and waterfalls—oh and I do weddings as a side hustle. Discounted rate for friends."

Miranda laughs. "I'm not sure I'm going to need that, but thanks."

Susan says, "But if they're already here..."

Miranda is blunt. "Forget about First Contact. You need to get ready for Hard Contact."

Susan turns her head sideways. "Hard Contact? I've never heard that term."

"This," Miranda says, waving her hand between them. "This is Soft Contact."

"Oh."

"There are two other extraterrestrial species on or around Earth and New Haven watching you guys, but that's not important. What's important—is why."

Susan and Alexander are quiet. Miranda picks her words with care. She enunciates with precision.

"You're bait!"

"Oh, I don't like the sound of that," Susan says.

"Your science fiction speaks of the universe being a dark forest, offering an analogy where predators prowl in the woods so the best survival strategy is to remain hidden."

"Camouflage," Alexander says.

"But we're loud and obnoxious," Susan says.

"Oblivious," Miranda says. "While I was on *The George Washington*, I got to watch a lot of documentaries about Earth. One, in particular, caught my eye. It was about the tribes of the Kalahari. They've roamed Africa for tens of thousands of years. When faced with the threat of a lion, they'll stake out a goat under a tree as bait. Then they hide. They're patient. They'll watch and wait with spears at the ready."

"And that's what they're doing?" Susan asks, sitting bolt upright. "They're stringing us out as bait?"

"You're convenient," Miranda replies. "You're their early-warning system. You're a canary in the coal mine. They're looking at you for trigger points. They can watch to see who spots you, how and when. They want to see how a more advanced species reacts to your presence. And if someone attacks you from out of the dark forest, they'll learn about their adversary. They're using you to look for weaknesses in them."

Susan lowers her head and leans forward with her elbows on the table. She runs her fingers up through her hair, thinking deeply about what Miranda has said.

"And you're here to warn us," she says, looking at her.

"I'm here to give you a fighting chance," Miranda replies. "But you have to change. You can't keep blundering through the forest, playing loud music and snapping twigs as you walk. You're advertising your presence like a neon sign."

Susan shakes her head. "There are billions of us. We're scattered through over two hundred countries on eighteen different worlds. Getting us to cooperate on even the simplest of issues is nigh on impossible."

"It always has been," Alexander says. "Going to the stars didn't create this mess, it amplified it."

"Then you need to start thinking about dark sites," Miranda says. "You need to think about where you'll go and what you'll do when the leopard picks up your trail. You have to start thinking about how to survive the dark forest."

Susan nods. "I'm disappointed. I'd hoped intelligence would mean cooperation."

"Evolution doesn't favor intelligence, it favors survival—by whatever means possible. The most successful species on your planet is cyanobacteria. A single cell. No heart. No brain. No consciousness whatsoever."

"But there is intelligence out there," Susan counters.

"Even here on Earth, intelligence comes as an accessory," Miranda says. "Humans, chimps, ravens, and even cephalopods like cuttlefish and the octopus. They're all intelligent and yet they're primarily driven by instinct and emotion. It's no different out there. When you turn your telescopes to the skies, the reason for the Great Silence is survival. Everyone's watching the new kid in school to see if the bully is going to pick on him. They're looking to learn from your mistakes."

Susan's eyes go wide. "Damn. Okay. I—I need some time to process this." She gets up from the table, saying, "And you're not going anywhere, right? I want to regroup with my team and discuss this, and then come back to you to talk strategy."

Miranda points up at the outside of the hotel. "I'm staying on the top floor. Apparently, it's got an amazing view."

Susan's flustered. She's struggling under the enormity of not only having her worldview turned upside down but the broader implications for humanity.

"Ah, thank you. I—um—I'll be in touch."

Miranda is gracious. She smiles and nods. Alexander gets up as well. He clears the table, saying, "It's good to have you here, Ms. Spiro." He takes the glasses and empty bottles back to the kitchen, asking, "Is there anything else I can get you?"

"No, I'm fine," she replies.

Miranda sits there looking out over the beach and across the ocean, watching as waves break several hundred meters offshore. After a few minutes, she gets up and walks down the concrete stairs to the sand. It's still warm from the heat of the sun during the day, which to her, is delightful. She walks across the sand, enjoying the way it squishes and moves beneath her feet.

The water's shallow.

Miranda rolls up her trousers to just below her knees and wades in. As soon as she stands still, her feet sink into the sand and water laps at her trousers, getting them wet. With that, she figures, why bother? And she walks out deeper. The waves are gentle, having already broken further out. Water swirls around her waist. She lowers herself and floats with her arms outstretched. The loose cotton blouse she's wearing drifts around her, moving with the motion of each passing wave.

As she floats there, Miranda looks up at the stars. They're beautiful. They're the same stars she saw from Altair IV but somehow they're softer, warmer, kinder. On Altair IV there was no call to the stars. They never twinkled in the sky. They felt foreboding rather than welcoming.

The moon rises. Miranda has seen photos of Earth's moon but she wasn't prepared for how large or how bright it is in the night sky. Thousands of craters along with mares and mountain ranges are visible. It's a testament to the longevity of this solar system, with asteroid impacts spanning billions of years on its harsh, rocky surface.

Miranda thinks about the contradiction that is intelligent life within the universe. Just one of those stars out there contains far more mass and energy than is found within the whole of humanity—and there are trillions upon trillions of stars! Her Krell subconscious informs her that just one star contains several orders of magnitude more material than is found on the surface of Earth.

It's a beautiful night in Hawaii. The air is warm. Water laps at her shoulders. Waves gently rock her body as they roll in toward the shore. A cool breeze comes from the shore, drifting over the water and carrying with it the scent of jasmine and frangipani.

"I am as free as the mountain winds," Miranda whispers, slowly turning in the water and taking in the beach. Buildings tower over the sand like monoliths. Couples walk along the shore, hand in hand, oblivious to her alien presence.

After floating there for a few minutes, enjoying some relief from Earth's oppressive gravity, Miranda turns and walks out of the water. As she approaches the shore, her Krell mind dries her clothing. She stands there with her back to the stars, looking at the constellation of *Homo sapiens* unfolding on the shoreline in the form of thousands of lights in the windows of the various hotels dotted along Waikiki.

Miranda feels overwhelmed but excited. She has no idea what the future holds for her, but she's home. She's where she belongs. She breathes deeply, saying, *"How beautiful humanity is! O brave new world!"*

The End

Afterword

Thank you for supporting independent science fiction.

If you liked this story, please tell a friend about it and leave a review online. Being an independent author, it's insanely difficult to reach new readers so I appreciate your enthusiasm for my stories.

First Contact Series

I hope you're enjoying the First Contact series as much as I am. For me, it's an opportunity to explore the fascinating and complex ways in which First Contact with an extraterrestrial intelligence might unfold. I try to keep my stories varied and unconventional so you're never quite sure what's going to unfold.

The Tempest considers First Contact from both the human perspective (with the professor on Altair IV) and an alien's perspective (when Miranda visits Earth).

SETI is the search for intelligent extraterrestrial life. When we look at the stars, the question arises: *where is everyone?* Why don't we see alien civilizations expanding throughout the galaxy in much the same way as the Babylonians, Greeks, Romans, Mongols, British, French, Dutch and Spanish expanded around our world? Fermi's paradox is based on the idea that, given the colossal size and age of the universe, there has been plenty of time for star-faring civilizations to arise, so where is everyone?

There are a number of possible answers to the Fermi paradox. We have no idea which holds true. In this novel, Miranda's thoughts echo those of Chinese science fiction author Cixin Liu in his novel *The Dark Forest*. Liu focuses on the idea that the universe is a hostile place, much like a dense forest, so the best strategy is to be quiet. Throughout nature, we see various types of camouflage evolving to ensure the survival of a species and the dark forest suggests this might be needed on a cosmic scale. I've taken the idea a step further and suggested that if any of these other hidden civilizations have detected us they might string us out as bait to expose whatever alpha predator lurks in the darkness.

Shakespeare's The Tempest

I wrote this story as a homage to Shakespeare's play *The Tempest* and the enduring legacy he has had on the English language.

For over four hundred years, *The Tempest* has inspired dozens of plays, operas, novels and even movies. Its themes, including the desire for control, the lust for revenge, growing self-awareness and the need for forgiveness, have become the bedrock of numerous other literary classics. T.S. Elliot's *The Waste Land*, H.G. Wells' *The Island of Doctor Moreau,* and Aldous Huxley's *Brave New World* have all openly drawn their inspiration from *The Tempest*. Indeed, the title of Huxley's seminal novel comes from a line in *The Tempest*. It's the same line that closed this story.

In the 1956 science fiction movie, *Forbidden Planet*, alien technology takes the place of magic as *The Tempest* is recreated onscreen. Michael Crichton's *Sphere* uses an underwater mining platform in place of an island where alien 'magic' enchants humans. In the same way, I've taken the elements that intrigued me from *The Tempest* and explored them further in this novel, leading to an original story inspired by Shakespeare's landmark play. At a couple of points, I've reworked dialogue from the play into the story. How many did you spot?

The Tempest wasn't the last of Shakespeare's works but it was the last of his plays. It was a deeply personal story for him. *The Tempest* was his swan song. In the final scene, the wizard Prospero breaks the fourth wall, talking about '*the globe*' being both the world at large and the theater in which the play was performed. Prospero addresses the audience, asking them:

> *pardon'd [me] the deceiver, dwell*
> *In this bare island by your spell;*
> *But release me from my bands*
> *With the help of your good hands*

This was Shakespeare's way of resigning from the theater with good grace. Being a playwright and recounting stories that never actually happened, he described himself as '*the deceiver.*' He'd dwelt in the '*bare island*' of the theater for decades, held bound by '*your spell,*' being the adoration of the audience. He sought to be released one last time with a round of applause by '*the help of your good hands.*'

The name Miranda is one Shakespeare invented specifically for this play and that got me thinking about Miranda as a character in my novel and her origins. If Shakespeare could invent her, then so could Professor Spiro.

Flashes of Light

In the opening of this novel, Marc and Emma see flashes of light *inside* their eyes. This phenomenon has been observed since at least the Gemini days of the space program. It's something that became more apparent during the long periods of exposure during Apollo. It will come as no surprise to you that our retinas are sensitive to light. They're so sensitive that cosmic rays can cause them to misfire. Rather than actually seeing anything, the eyes of astronauts end up working like particle detectors, seeing the imprint of these rays striking their eyeballs. Not only is this disconcerting, but prolonged exposure also leads to cataracts.

SOS

When the *Sycorax* enters orbit around the ice giant Altair, Emma declares SOS and Mayday.

Remarkably, SOS is not an acronym. It doesn't mean anything other than SOS. It originates from the dots and dashes of Morse code when . . . - - - . . . formed the letters SOS as an unmistakable, unambiguous radio signal. It was adopted as a simple way to avoid confusion when declaring an emergency.

Mayday originates from 1923 when air travel was beginning to dominate the English Channel. The French *M'aidez* translates to "*Help me*," and found its phonetic English equivalent in Mayday as a shared term among aviators from both countries.

SOS and Mayday continue to be used today even though their origins have long since faded into obscurity. As they've become a convention, I suspect they'll continue to be used for hundreds, if not thousands of years to come.

Skewed Perspective

We have a distorted perspective of the universe. We see rocks and trees, mountains and streams, clouds and oceans dominating our world. To us, the stars are distant pinpricks of light. They seem small compared to our vast world but nothing could be further from the truth. 98% of the visible matter in the universe is hydrogen and helium. That trivial, remaining 2% is what makes up everything we see around us on Earth. If we ignore mass as a means of measurement and focus solely on counting individual atoms, regardless of their size, then 99.9% of all visible matter is either hydrogen or helium. We are oddities in this vast cosmos.

The Hadean

One of the points raised in this novel is that life may have arisen during the Hadean period when it was hell on Earth. We tend to think of Earth as a paradise. We marvel at its position in the *goldilocks zone* and wonder what other, similar planets lie out there, but this hides an important truth: life arose on Earth when it was inhospitable. And not only did life arise in utterly hostile conditions, it thrived in them for BILLIONS of years. The idyllic conditions we enjoy are a recent development.

When most people think of the possibility of detecting life on other planets, they assume these planets will mirror our own. In reality, they could mirror our planet from any point in the past four billion years, appearing entirely different from the Earth of today, and yet still be overflowing with various forms of microbial life.

Life Outside the Goldilocks Zone

Earth is extraordinary. For us, it's paradise, but when it comes to the search for life elsewhere in the universe, Earth is misleading. We look around and marvel at how our planet is ideally suited for life, but we've got it all wrong. We've got this backward. Life didn't arise on Earth because it's ideally suited to supporting life. On the contrary, life arose during the Hadean period, when Earth was hellish and devoid of oxygen in the atmosphere. Life, itself, transformed Earth into the paradise we see today. It took microbes like Cyanobacteria *billions* of years to get us to this point. What we see around us is the end result of billions of years of terraforming by microbes.

In our search for life in other star systems, we've focused on the Goldilocks Zone, being the band surrounding a star where the planets are not too hot and not too cold. We've pointed at our own planet as the ultimate example, saying, Earth is *"just right,"* only Earth wasn't like

343

this for the vast majority of its existence. Over the past four and a half thousand million years, Earth has been "*ideal*" for barely five hundred million. Go back eight hundred million years in a time machine and you'll choke to death as the oxygen in our atmosphere sat around 5%.

Earth itself is barely within the Goldilocks Zone. Earth orbits at 1 AU (Astronomical Unit). A lot of assumptions go into defining the Goldilocks Zone, but it is generally thought to extend from 0.95 AU to 1.70 AU. If we look solely at the Goldilocks Zone, Mars is a better candidate for life than Earth. Mars averages 1.52 AU, with its orbit varying between 1.38 AU and 1.67 AU. The point is—we've made far too much out of the Goldilocks zone. If a planet is outside the Goldilocks zone, it gets ignored when it shouldn't.

Until recently, few people gave any serious consideration to the possibility of life arising beyond the reach of a star. It seems obvious. Life needs energy and stars pump out copious amounts, but solar winds strip planets and even gas giants of their atmosphere (see Mercury and Mars as examples). Now, new research is looking at the possibility of liquid water being stable for *tens of billions* of years around rogue planets devoid of any star! Rogue planets could have water for longer than Earth itself will even exist!

Liquid water needs a balance between temperature and pressure to exist—and that's possible outside the Goldilocks Zone. Even in our own solar system, we've found liquid water well outside the Goldilocks Zone on the moons of Jupiter and Saturn. Looking further afield, cold super-Earths that retain their primordial, hydrogen–helium-dominated atmospheres because they're not subject to stellar radiation (solar winds) from nearby stars could have surfaces that are warm enough to host liquid water and hence life!

As we look for life elsewhere, we need to be careful we don't read too much into our own unique situation here on Earth. There may well be an Altair out there in orbit around a black hole with liquid water on its moons.

Black Holes

We tend to think of black holes as rare, but they're not. The nearest black hole we know of is a paltry 1,600 light-years from us, but most black holes don't have an active accretion disk and so are invisible to our telescopes.

If black holes are randomly distributed throughout the galaxy then, statistically, the closest one would be anywhere from 50 to 100 light-years away. If our galaxy were the size of an average city, the nearest black hole would be down at the end of your street! Scientists estimate the closest could be *an isolated stellar-mass black hole... as close as 80 light-years away.* Given our galaxy is 100,000 light-years in diameter, that's practically next door. As the vast majority of these black holes aren't actively feeding they're effectively invisible. They're rogue black holes. We have no way of detecting them beyond micro-lensing (looking at how they distort the light from distant stars waaaaaay beyond them).

Have you ever cleaned a swimming pool with a leaf catcher on a pole? If so, you've seen optical lensing without realizing it. If you stick your pole into the water and try to retrieve something from the bottom of the pool, you'll notice the angle of the pole appears to change. The water is distorting the angle at which light is moving. Gravitational lensing is just like that but instead of water causing the effect, the intense gravity of an object like a star or a black hole is causing it by distorting spacetime. Light, itself, is going perfectly straight, but the space through which it passes is warped and bent. The motion of these objects in front of a distant star field produces the same effect as a magnifying glass moving over a map. When it comes to black holes without an accretion disk around them or without a nearby companion, this is the only way to detect their presence.

Astrophysicists estimate there are 40 quintillion black holes spread throughout the universe. In our galaxy alone, there are an estimated 100 million stellar-mass black holes! Throughout the universe, massive stars go supernova once every second, resulting in the birth of yet another black hole with the rhythm of a high school music class metronome—*tick, tick, tick!*

Orbiting a Black Hole

Contrary to popular belief, black holes are not celestial vacuum cleaners. They don't suck in debris any more than the Sun does. Not only is it possible for planets to orbit a black hole, but there are far more potential orbits than there are around a regular star! Technically, black holes don't have a habitable zone as they don't produce any heat, but it is possible for them to have something similar with either an accretion disc or captured stars. If they did, they could have millions of stable orbits! Our sun allows for no more than six gas giants, but the hill sphere—or gravitational gradient—of a black hole like the monster in this story allows for exponentially more. They could be stacked up in ridiculous numbers. Any in-falling matter could disrupt such orbits, but, theoretically, a quiet black hole could have hundreds of planets orbiting it for billions of years!

In this novel, I used Fabio Pacucci's calculator and Viktor Toth's Hawking Radiation Calculator to quantify the physical characteristics of the black hole.

- Our fictional supermassive black hole has 400,000 masses of the sun

- The event horizon is 1.1 million km (which is actually smaller than the diameter of our sun at 1.4 million km)

- The temperature is less than a fraction of a degree above absolute zero

- Its luminosity is 5.62726 E-40 watts, which means there are forty zeros after the decimal point, making it effectively pitch black

- Its lifespan is 7.42238 E83 years, that's a 7 followed by 83 zeros! It will last soooooo far into the future it makes the current 13.8 billion years that have elapsed since the Big Bang

346

seem like a single tick of the secondhand on a clock compared to all of recorded human history!

- The innermost stable orbit for this black hole is a distance of 3.5 million km. Mercury orbits the sun at anywhere from 47 million to 70 million km so, in the absence of an accretion disk, Mercury would be fine orbiting within this particular black hole system.

- It's counterintuitive, but black holes (and even neutron stars) not only attract mass and energy with their immense gravity, but they also expel mass at phenomenal velocities through relativistic jets streaming out from their poles. We call the biggest of these black holes, quasars. So far, we've detected over a million quasars scattered throughout the visible universe. The largest jet we've observed is from a quasar in the constellation of Virgo which spans 200,000 light years. That's twice the diameter of the Milky Way! When it comes to actively-feeding supermassive black holes, the accretion disc alone can outshine entire galaxies. Although it is as yet unproven, astrophysicists suspect that all black holes produce these jets, although not all jets will be visible—and that's the concept I used to cripple the *Sycorax* during the opening of this novel.

- Somewhat remarkably, black holes might be a source of energy for an advanced alien race for an absurd amount of time. Roger Penrose calculated that mass/light falling into the ergosphere just outside the event horizon of a black hole would reflect/return more energy than was lost—making it seem like a perpetual motion machine. Technically, the spin of the black hole slows during this process. In practice, though, it's effectively unlimited. Tapping into the angular momentum of a spinning black hole allows the gravitational energy of the black hole itself to produce rather than consume energy. The process reaches somewhere around 150% efficiency! Whether this effect can ever actually be harnessed, though, is another question again. It may forever remain a theoretical oddity.

Natural Units

The decision by the Krell to measure the speed of light as one is a genuine scientific approach known as Planck Units or Natural Units (as opposed to our arbitrary units of meters, kilometers, feet, yards and miles). And there is some merit in the approach as it simplifies equations.

As an example, in our standard notation, $E=MC^2$ becomes the natural form equation, $E=M$. Both equations produce the same result, but one is easier to manipulate. By changing the unit of measure from arbitrary human, pre-spaceflight concepts to natural concepts, physics calculations are simplified. Although, in the interests of full disclosure, the dimension of these units becomes far more abstract. In the case of $E=M$, both E and M would be measurements of energy-content (being *mass* x *length²* / *time²*), which isn't exactly intuitive. On paper, though, this approach makes other more complex calculations easier to comprehend and extend.

Phase Change Clothing

Although phase change clothing is only mentioned a couple of times in passing within this story, Miranda's clothing is part of an emerging scientific advance. Scientists have begun experimenting with a type of clothing that uses phase change to stay warm in winter while cool in summer.

When water cools to become ice, it's said to have changed its phase. At the point water reaches 0 °C/32 °F it has more energy than the equivalent amount of ice at the exact same temperature. As it freezes, it loses this energy which means it's radiating heat. Now, the effect is subtle but real.

Scientists in China have harnessed this concept with spider silk and glycol to create a self-regulating phase change glove. When the temperature reaches 50 °C/122 °F the glycol melts within the spider silk and lowers the temperature felt inside the glove. Wear the same glove at 10 °C/50 °F and the glycol freezes, warming the hands.

At the moment, this is a proof-of-technology and not a commercial product, with more work needed to find the right compounds to suit different temperatures and with more fine-grain control, but, watch this space, phase change clothing is coming to a store near you!

Warp Factor One, Mr. Sulu

FTL (Faster-Than-Light) travel is a staple of science fiction—and yet it also represents a failure in our popular understanding of modern physics.

Relativity is counterintuitive, so it's easier for writers to simply defy the astronomical distances in space with super-duper speeds and the glitz of stars streaking past the windows. As discussed in this novel, the irony is—the whole concept of FTL is entirely unnecessary. Due to time dilation and length contraction, relativity gives us FTL without ever actually needing to travel faster than light. You can get *anywhere* within the observable universe in a reasonably short period of time at 99.9% of the speed of light (if you keep adding 9s beyond the decimal point). You'll never actually reach the speed of light, but you will reach Andromeda some two million light-years away in just a few decades! To be clear, anyone back on Earth watching this journey unfold will be left waiting millions of years for you to arrive, but for you, the trip will be over in mere decades.

In practice, accelerating to 99% of the speed of light to take advantage of this effect is probably going to remain impractical/impossible. The problem is—life onboard your starship will seem normal enough but everything else will accelerate at you at this phenomenal speed—including radiation and tiny flecks of interstellar dust. The end result will be akin to flying through the chromosphere of a star where temperatures reach 20,000°C, which is far hotter than molten lava! It's a case of, *"Don't try this at home."*

Thank You

Novels are a patchwork quilt of ideas. I try to draw upon a wide variety of sources and don't always have the opportunity to attribute every quote that's woven into a story. If I did, the afterword would be as long as the novel itself.

French/American novelist Angela Anaïs Nin once said, *"We don't see things as they are. We see them as we are!"* It's a simple enough statement, but it's profound, so I worked that into the professor's dialogue. The intent, though, isn't to plagiarize her work or any others but rather to reinvigorate lost ideas. In the same way, I don't think we read books as they are—we read books as *we* are. Novels are part of our journey through life. In the pages of a book, we see a reflection of ourselves.

Several sections of this book were written while my wife and I were house-sitting in New Zealand. We got to stay in the homes of Chris and Branka in Beach Haven and Richard and Megan in Totara Park. We enjoyed the quiet and solitude of those locations.

Thank you for supporting independent science fiction. I know I say that in all my novels, but I mean it. Without you, none of these stories would exist. By buying this book, you're investing in my next novel. You're giving me the privilege to write, so I thank you for your generosity.

I'd also like to thank my wife for putting up with my eccentric ideas. We talk a lot about the art of writing and how to develop plots and characters while walking in the Australian bush, watching out for wallabies and snakes (one's a delight to see, the other, not so much).

I'd also like to thank physicists Viktor Toth and Brian Wells (a fellow hard science fiction author) for their insights into the physics described in this novel. Trying to imagine the technological progress of a species a million years more advanced than we are is like walking a tightrope. Their insights into the physics of black holes have helped make the novel more plausible. We had robust, lengthy debates on the nature of infinities. Any errors in this book are entirely mine.

Writing is a lonely process, but one of my favorite parts is when beta-readers get involved. They're hard-core fans with a passion for excellence and have helped catch bloopers within this story, so thank you Didi Kanjahn, Terry Grindstaff, John Stephens, David Jaffe, John Larisch, LuAnn Miller, Ian Forsdike and Chris Fox. Jan Taylor helped with the finer details of life in Hawaii.

If you'd like to learn more about upcoming new releases, be sure to subscribe to my email newsletter. You can find all of my books on Amazon. I'm also active on Facebook, Instagram and Twitter.

Peter Cawdron

Brisbane, Australia

Printed in Great Britain
by Amazon

16058679R00203